D1927880

RAPTURE ALLEY

WINTER GIRL

STRICTLY FOR THE BOYS

HARRY WHITTINGTON

STARK HOUSE

Stark House Press • Eureka California

RAPTURE ALLEY / WINTER GIRL / STRICTLY FOR THE BOYS

Published by Stark House Press
4720 Herron Road
Eureka, CA 95503, USA
griffinskye3@sbcglobal.net
www.starkhousepress.com

RAPTURE ALLEY
Originally published and copyright © 1953 by Carnival Books, as by Whit Harrison. Copyright © renewed February 2, 1981 by Harry Whittington.

WINTER GIRL
Originally published and copyright © 1966 by Corinth Publications, Inc., as *A Taste of Desire* by Curt Colman. Edited by David Laurence Wilson. Copyright © renewed 2012 by the Kathryn L. Whittington Trust and David Laurence Wilson.

STRICTLY FOR THE BOYS
Originally published and copyright © 1959 by Stanley Library, Inc. Copyright © 2012 by the Katheryn L. Whittington Trust.

Permission to reprint granted by the Kathryn L. Whittington Trust. All rights reserved under International and Pan-American Copyright Conventions.

"Restoration of Harry" copyright © 2012 by David Laurence Wilson

ISBN: 978-1-933586-36-6

Text design by Mark Shepard, shepgraphics.com
Cover design by Jeff Vorzimmer, ¡caliente!design, Austin, Texas
Cover art by Ernest Chiriaka
Proofreading by Rick Ollerman and David L. Wilson

PUBLISHER'S NOTE:
This is a work of fiction. Names, characters, places and incidents are either the products of the author's imagination or used fictionally, and any resemblance to actual persons, living or dead, events or locales, is entirely coincidental.
Without limiting the rights under copyright reserved above, no part of this publication may be reproduced, stored, or introduced into a retrieval system or transmitted in any form or by any means (electronic, mechanical, photocopying, recording or otherwise) without the prior written permission of both the copyright owner and the above publisher of the book.

First Stark House Press Edition: January 2012

RAPTURE ALLEY

No one needs Lora. Ken claims to love her, but he is married to Lora's wheelchair-ridden sister, Chris, and he doesn't really *need* her. And all Lora wants is to be needed. Lora feels alone, defeated by herself. Then Arty comes along. He helps her fill this hole in her heart with something better than love—escape. Through him she meets Boyd, the nightclub singer, with his own brand of addicting salvation. Soon drugs become Lora's cushion against a hurtful world. They allow her to float above her problems. But they can't keep the pain away forever. And when Lora's own needs cause her world to come crashing down around her, all the drugs in the world can't save her.

WINTER GIRL

"An hour after I met Lu Ann again that winter, I knew I was headed for deep, serious trouble. Only I had no idea how deep, how serious..." When Calder Fenton first saw Lu Ann that day at her rich daddy's hunting field, he couldn't take his eyes off her. He'd seen her every year growing up, but she'd never looked like this before. Soon, he's sitting in her jeep, being taunted by her, trying to figure her out. Lu Ann is only looking for thrills, and doesn't care that Calder has problems of his own—like being dirt poor, like having a pa who drinks and whores around town. But Calder likes what he sees, and he wants more. Pretty soon, he's got so much Lu Ann he doesn't know what to do with himself. And that is just the beginning of his troubles.

STRICTLY FOR THE BOYS

Amy can't help the way the boys look at her. It isn't her fault. But Burt doesn't see it that way. He is convinced that Amy is cheating on him and as her husband, he has a right to knock some sense into her. Burt doesn't mean to hurt her, he just can't control himself. So when Amy runs back to her mother and divorces Burt, she expects a little sympathy. But Stella's got problems of her own and no time for Amy's change of heart. She lets her move back home but does everything she can to get Amy and Burt back together. Amy takes a new job, and still Burt follows her around, trying to find out who the new man in her life must be. And this time he's right—this time there's Terry, and a new chance at love. But for Burt, Amy belongs to him and him alone, and he will kill any man that gets in his way.

THE RESTORATION OF HARRY

by David Laurence Wilson

"When her husband asked me to go along on a fishing trip with him and his wife, how could I know that among the beer, tackle and sun lotions, there was nothing to use for bait–except me!"

–from Harry Whittington's file of story ideas

The "King of the Paperbacks" was not served well by the industries in his kingdom, a gaudy and sensational sideshow of American life. If you don't think this "King" had to pay the proper dues, take a look at the publishers he worked for, most of them long gone. Harry Whittington wrote for the high and the low, for the Serie noire and the Gold Medal line of paperbacks and for the publishers of digest novels, the dog paddlers in the low end of the literary pool. A King indeed! Harry was really a commoner, a nine to five laborer in a factory he had to maintain himself. He wrote and published over 170 paperback novels and scores of short stories and serials, as many as a dozen in a year. He was working until the end, superstitious about dying with an unfinished manuscript.

Fewer than half of Whittington's novels appeared under his own name, a ratio that continues to play out in this collection. *Strictly for the Boys* (1959) was written by "Harry Whittington" but *Rapture Alley* (1953) was written by "Whit Harrison." *Winter Girl* was written by Whittington in the early sixties but not published until it was revised and printed in 1966 as *The Taste of Desire*, by "Curt Colman." For decades this was one of Harry's lost novels, "The Unknowns."

For the first time in fifty years and two or three generations of readers, this Stark House collection is reprinting Whittington novels without explicit murders, without a lot of gun play, or poisonings or even lethal pushes down stairs.

These are the seldom reads–Harry Whittington novels nearly without handguns. That doesn't mean these are stories without anger or violence but seldom has this violence been so carefully measured out. Whittington's manipulations have never been more powerful.

These lesser-known Whittington novels feature conflict and pain but no murders. The term "domestic noir" comes to mind but it sounds too nice, like a "cozy" mystery story with shadows. "Social noir" might be a better term. At any rate, it exists. Does it matter what you call it?

□ □ □

Whatever the privations of Whittington's early years in Ocala, Florida, there were cameras around to document his growing up. In the photographs of the young Harry Whittington we do not see the poverty and pain of the rural south, the social and economic changes made more acute by a worldwide depression. Here there were injustices that left Harry feeling smaller, more vulnerable and shamed than he should have been. He described Ocala as "a little town sharply divided: some people had money; the others had none."

In the photographs, Harry appears to be a happy boy, with a steady look and an easy smile. There are also later photographs of Harry as a postman in St. Petersburg, before the war: on a bike, beside a car, holding a baby. He is thin and wiry, a physique he would lose during World War II, when for the first time he could eat as large a meal as he wished. This is the Whittington who had also worked at a movie theater, who dreamed about making his own motion pictures and then actually made them, light silent comedies in eight millimeter, with Harry as the star.

Whittington loved everything about the movie business but his own lack of success. His favorites weren't the stories of gangsters and criminality. He preferred musicals and grand scenes of feasts–ballrooms and chandeliers. It was something to think about when he, himself, was hungry. Story telling, reading and film–it was all escapism. Harry was a poor boy who grew up to become an ordinary man. Writing was his only chance to become great.

It is tempting to reach out to that young Whittington, to lay out the scope of his future accomplishments, and ask him if he believed that path to be worth the price, the uncertainty, insecurity and depression of his career–even the sheer volume of work that it took to make a living as a pulp fiction writer. Did he have to write? Could he have ever had a complete life without seeing his name in print, over and over again, on hundreds of stories?

Whittington didn't start out to write crime fiction. He preferred rags to riches stories of love and light comedy with a pinch of Damon Runyon. This was the same path Whittington wished to emulate himself. He edited and wrote nonfiction stories for the *St. Petersburg Advocate*. His first fiction sales were in 1943, short love stories distributed by the United Features Service: "Night Lifer," "Weary Angel," "Mother's Girl," "Female of the Species" and others.

In 1948 he was working as a mail deliverer and had saved enough money to paint his house when he was persuaded to spend the money on a writer's conference in Chicago. Among the programs was a series given by the Midwest Chapter of the Mystery Writers of America. The writer W. T. Brannon urged him to write a mystery and then Brannon himself sold it to the publisher of Handi-Books. In 1950 Harry gave up his mail job and by 1951 he was selling twelve novels a year, to Gold Medal, Graphic, Avon, Handi-Books and others.

Like a speaker or a musician who is uncomfortable with a pause, the younger Whittington had a tendency to rely upon plotting, to throw as many twists and tricks as he could into a book. His plotting was like a car chase. Surprises gave him security. He jumped right in with action.

□ □ □

So what do you know about Harry Whittington? Do you know that the early years were tough, with patched-up hand-me-downs and three year old shoes. Would you have guessed that his meals were iffy, often provided through the charity of a neighbor. There was no money for lunch, for a yearbook or tickets to his school's sporting events. A date was unthinkable. When Harry wrote about the poor, back country Florida, it was a subject that he knew better than anyone. Later, he wrote at least fifteen novels about the rural South, stories filled with fish camps and small town corruption.

Despite his grand, prolific efforts, those 170 or so paperbacks written during a 36 year career, the breadth of Harry's talents are little known today. Few paperback writers came close to achieving Harry's variety.

What was once a wide range of subjects has been diminished. Wikipedia, that common technological denominator, describes Whittington as an American mystery writer. He is recognized as a major figure in American crime fiction. Since 1960 every new edition has been a crime novel.

Despite this, Whittington's crime stories represent less than half of his production. The characters in these novels feature the same tense obsessive passions that inhabit Harry's crime fictions. They are not unfamiliar, nor should we expect an absence of threat and violence. These characters simply avoid the capital crimes. There are no robberies or murders, only a smattering of detectives.

These novels offer a range of male and female relationships. They include what have been known as "victimless crimes," a euphemism that usually means the victim is a woman.

You can call it noir but what Harry really wrote were the blues. Even in his grandest moments he kept a toehold–a proprietary interest–in pain. His novels were dark, mysterious things, a mix of experience, fear and trauma. They had the gritty sensibility of a movie directed by Sam Fuller or Phil Karlson.

Defining noir is just as contentious as describing the blues. Noir is another category of emotional pain, more of a feeling than the color that defines it. Once you became a noir writer, you were defined by a point of view, whatever the location, whatever the goals of the characters or their professions.

Harry listened to show tunes as he wrote, but he wrote with blues and minor keys, the notes dropping out of his chords. Even at his most triumphant, with success, loss, and then late, unexpected success, Whittington's characters kept their homes on the lost sides of towns. They never forgot their roots in hardship.

Those of you who have read the introductions to Stark House's earlier collections will know of the highs and lows of Whittington's career, how the title "King of the Paperbacks" did not necessarily result in personal gain. He had one big trip to Hollywood, when for twelve weeks he worked under a studio contract, reveling in paychecks from Warner Brothers.

Harry had the characteristics of a man who had grown accustomed to living without money. When he had it, he spent it. During his golden years, his period of high production, he could stay ahead of his enthusiasms, his generosity and impulse buys. It was very difficult for Whittington to take a break. His biggest reward was the opportunity for more work. His life was inextricably linked with the printed word.

Whittington invested heavily, economically and emotionally, into producing and directing his own feature film, *Face of the Phantom*, a goal he had had for over 30 years. He made the film and nothing went right–and the film wasn't right either. It was a failure that left Harry in debt. Like the novel *Winter Girl*, *Face of the Phantom* was never released in its original form.

Harry returned to his life-long companion, his typewriter. It was a burden and a pleasure, his fingers moving fast on the typewriter keys. The more he could write, the faster he could type, the more he could sell. And it all sold, for many years.

It was a sweet deal. Once upon a time there was a great audience of readers for those who wrote to entertain. Like jazz and comic strips, the original paperback novel was an American creation. In their day the paperbacks were the best deal, the cheapest forms of entertainment you could find.

The fit-in-your-pants-pocket books were the inheritors of a great run of literature that lasted for centuries. Dime novels begat pulps (and the slicks, too) and finally the paperback originals. In retrospect, those paperbacks were a bittersweet coda.

Like most sweet deals, it fell apart. It burst. The vultures started circling when the first cathode ray flickered on and they were circling by the time television began broadcasting signals in color. Television was a compact means of entertainment, a theater that had become portable. It was an ubiquitous form of chatter that could be sipped in hour or half-hour increments. Episodic television grabbed the paperback audience. It was survival of the fittest and TV was more efficient. The loser was popular fiction.

The paperbacks began to lose their audience, the slicks began to lose their advertisers. For Harry, the manuscripts stopped selling. Some of the writers of pulp and popular fiction joined forces with the enemy, and moved into television, just as they had moved from one pulp magazine to another, and to slicks and digests.

In 1960 Harry sold ten novels. In 1963 he sold only five, though they included two powerful, mature works, the crime novel *Cora is a Nympho*, reprinted by Stark House in 2009, and *Don't Speak to Strange Girls*, a character-based Hollywood story which he had written in 1958.

Whittington wrote *Winter Girl* in 1963. It was submitted to Gold Medal books and rejected. When it didn't sell it went back in Harry's files.

At this point it might be interesting to consider how Harry's career might have been different if this novel had been printed in 1963 and he had made just a few more sales during a time of desperation. *Winter Girl* is simple, direct and true. It is one of Whittington's most personal stories, a reflection on his boyhood home in Ocala, Florida, the largest city and county seat of Marion County.

Would this depiction of character, desire and melancholy have given

Whittington a new audience or another shot at film sales? Who knows? At any rate, *Winter Girl* is among Whittington's greatest accomplishments. It may not be Whittington's best novel but he didn't write a better one, either. It comes down to time, place and mood. Will anyone notice that same novel today?

The freeze-out, the difficulty in the paperback market, this economic dislocation and frustration came when Harry was at the height of his ability to write complex, meaningful stories. Instead he was writing true confessions, true crime, exploitation novels and novelizations of films. Few of these were even published under his own name. It was getting harder and harder for Harry to stay ahead of his economic needs. It seemed like he couldn't sell his stories anymore, not even a western or a story about nurses.

Whittington still had an option, a means for the "King" to keep a paycheck coming in. Harry was a big producer and boy oh boy, did the Scott Meredith Agency have a market for the big producers. By the end of 1963, with a nudge from his agent, Harry turned to the crafting of what we could discretely call sex novels, books that would no longer be reviewed in the *New York Times*. These novels offered no royalties and no hope for film sales.

"Sex books" is an inexact–and sometimes an inaccurate–description....

For the younger writers, including Donald Westlake and Lawrence Block, Corinth Publications was a chance to get into print, for writers to publish their first books and learn the craft of putting words on paper. They learned how to hook a skeptical reader and keep him engaged between sex scenes, to create intriguing characters. They also learned to write fast, to turn the pages over and send them out. These were all volume guys. The process helped to give them a breezy, conversational style.

For an older, working class writer like Harry, this was like digging ditches after a shot at management. He felt like he had been at the top of his profession. Now, as he approached the age of fifty, Whittington had to admit that the best days of his life were probably over. A mid-life crisis indeed. Harry was defensive. Now his books were distributed in liquor stores and the back rows of newsstands. The covers of his novels were adorned with naked ladies on bright orange, yellow and blue, with titles including: *Lust Farm* (1964), *Sharing Sharon* (1965) and *Blood Lust Orgy* (1966).

By 1963 Corinth had left its home in Chicago and was operating on Mission Gorge Road, in the canyons of Eastern San Diego. Harry never returned to Hollywood, but every month for three years, he sent a novel to Corinth in San Diego. He wrote as Curt Colman, John Dexter and J. X. Williams. There were no book signings for "Curt Colman."

After three years at this labor Harry was depleted, creatively, physically and emotionally. The work had been another trap. The anonymous novels were doing nothing for him professionally. Nor had he been able to make economic progress. In a moment of exhaustion and depression, he burned his unsold manuscripts, his works in progress, thirty years of labor. He sold his home and left the life of a pulp novelist.

After a seven year period of personal and economic recuperation in Washington, D.C., where he worked for the Rural Electrification Administration, Whittington returned to Florida, to Indian Rocks Beach, where he had once camped, picnicked and rented homes; hideaways where he could work on his novels in private. Harry designed this new home, just a block from the Gulf of Mexico. He enjoyed his walks along the beach.

At Indian Rocks Whittington would write as Ashley Carter and social security would kick in, from his early and late years of government work. Finally he had a steady income. He began planning his dream home, a mansion on the water, a big white mansion with chandeliers, a winding staircase and a private dock.

After 1979 there would be no more "Harry Whittington" novels. Harry spent the last ten years of his career writing as Ashley Carter, Tabor Evans and Blaine Stevens. The name that Harry's bride, the former Kathryn Odom, had once found so attractive, the author "Harry Whittington," the younger, harder version of the man, had vanished from the shelves.

□ □ □

Despite the ignominy of this work, this is a moment for the reader to thank Corinth, the anonymous sausage factory that was the publisher of the sex novels. Corinth was the handmaiden of posterity, as well as grief, and the caretaker, in a way, of the novel *Winter Girl*.

When the going got tough one month, Harry turned to his files, to expand short stories to novel length, and to take another look at books that he had written but not yet sold. *Like Mink Like Murder* had been published in France but not in the U.S., so it was rewritten as *Passion Hangover* for Corinth. The sexual scenes in *Winter Girl* were expanded and a new ending was written. The novel was released as *The Taste of Desire*, in 1966. For this Stark House edition the manuscript has been returned, as much as possible, to Harry's original vision.

The Taste of Desire lends credence to Harry's occasional assertions that the emphasis on sex was added later, perhaps by other hands. There is a tone and language in *The Taste of Desire* that clashes with the language and story of *Winter Girl.* It may have been added, at least in part, by the Corinth editorial staff.

Another Southern writer, William Faulkner, ruthlessly proposed that the "Ode on a Grecian Urn" is worth any number of old ladies. "If a writer has to rob his mother, he will not hesitate," he counseled. *Winter Girl* is another argument for the transcendence of art. This is the flower in the asphalt garden. It took the pain of many people, including writers who were interrogated by the F.B.I., and Earl Kemp, an editor who recognized the merit of *Winter Girl* but went to prison for publishing books like it, to allow you to read this book today. This is the book that makes it all worthwhile, the search, the violation of Harry's privacy, the humiliations of its packaging and distribution.

In *Winter Girl*, Lu Ann, the troubled Winter Girl herself, advises Harry's young, frustrated hero: "You're one of those helpless, proud people who think the world ought to be better than it is. Well, it's never going to be. So relax and enjoy it, the way it is."

Harry was not unaware of the inequities of systems and hierarchies–the conflict between the haves and the have-nots–it was more like he was hyper-sensitive. The economic issues are obvious, right up front in this coming-of-age novel. There is the Northeastern millionaire, Frank Berlinger, the kind of guy who is cool and tough enough to use the system to beat up his opponents. A snow bird, he spends his winters with his daughter in this unnamed Southern state that could be Marion County, in Central Florida. Berlinger is hunting with his friends on a private, well-stocked reserve managed by Lutz Fenton, our hero's abusive, alcoholic father. The younger Fenton, Calder, wants Berlinger's daughter. Berlinger wants Calder's dog, a fantastic, one of a kind setter named Fanny.

Lutz tells his son: "You figure I owe you something. All right. So I'm going to tell you–and this is what I owe you–to tell you the facts of life.

"Not life like your ma wants to think it should be, or the way they talk in church, or school, or anywhere else that they make a dime by lying to you about what life is like, or what it ought to be....

"A man is born hungry, Calder, and that is all he's born. Some men it don't take much to satisfy. Some men get spoon-fed all their lives and never know what it is to get hungrier and hungrier every day of his life.

"Some men are born with everything, and some take it from other people, and some can't ever get it. Men like me, Calder, go through life like a scavenger, taking the leavings of other men. Maybe you won't be like me, Calder. I pray that you won't.... Why, I'll get right down on my knees with you right now, and we'll both pray that you won't ever in this world be hungry like I am."

Winter Girl becomes many things, including a back-country story of Romeo and Juliet. This is love not within but between social and economic classes, a hazardous theme that Harry had expanded upon many times.

This also has the elements of a classic dog story. When Harry wrote this novel he had no time for pets. He still spoke movingly, however, about a tan and lemon-colored bird dog named Fanny, a dog that was truly more ally and family member than pet.

According to Harry's son, Howard: "My father and his younger brother Charles, and sister Rosa Lee, two years older, would hunt with Harry Sr. during the depression. They had guns but no bullets, no shells for the shotguns. Harry swore that Fanny knew it too, and as weak from hunger as they were, that dog would run down a rabbit until the rest of them could catch up and club it to death–then Rosa Lee would skin it and prepare it for their next meal.

"It wasn't until I was much older before I knew that hush puppies were made of corn meal and not a piece of bread with gravy. When I was young and all the food was gone Harry would put gravy on bread and call it "hush puppy" and then tell the story of Fanny sitting and crying 'cause she was worried she wasn't going to get anything but the bones of the ole rabbit, or whatever she had run down. So they would give her the gravy bread and say 'hush puppy.'

"I don't think there's any doubt that my father wrote this novel."

□ □ □

The two remaining novels in this collection also buck the trend in Whittington reprints. Although Whittington often featured woman characters, *Rapture Alley* and *Strictly for the Boys* are rare reprints of such stories. Whittington's 1951 novel *Fires That Destroy* was reprinted in 1988 but that one also included murder–albeit from a woman's point of view.

Harry is no Joan of Arc, but there is a lot of variety in his depictions of women. They aren't all pieces of fluff. Usually they are the survivors of trauma and abuse. *Cracker Girl* (1953), according to Harry, was a "Florida back county" story, where a woman's "husband believes a wife his property–to keep, to beat, to use." Usually Harry's women are saved by the intervention of a third party, a flawed but moral man.

Sex is a familiar element in exploitation storytelling–drugs and addiction are a much rarer element, at least in Whittington's fiction. *Rapture Alley* is Harry's drug novel, and one of his most melodramatic exhibitions of storytelling.

Lora Cassel is a small town girl who has moved to California hoping to become an actress. It's like there's a plot against her, and of course there is–Harry's plot. Lora lives with her sister, who is wheelchair bound and in perilous health. She works as a model while she tries to keep hope alive but her biggest problem may be an abusive, manipulative brother-in-law.

Rapture Alley is not only suspenseful, it's scary. Harry's reportage is not necessarily trustworthy, but it is relatively matter of fact. The dated, inexact implication is that everything–booze, marijuana or prescription medications–is a step on the way to heroin, despair and death. Harry writes: "She felt depressed and physically exhausted. Whatever the effect of that marijuana cigarette had been, it was gone. Had there even been any effect?

"Well, she had ten more in her purse. They would save her. The sticks were all that stood between her and the shakes. They would save her. Either they would save her, or they would blow her straight to hell."

Harry piles it on in his description of another character: "He looked as old as the street he lived on. Paralysis had struck his left side, leaving it pulled down. His shoulder sagged, and his left eye was closed, although he kept trying to open it. His mouth pulled downward on the left corner.... Klausmiller's voice was hard. It was without sympathy. 'You won't die. Death is too easy.... I know.'"

Rapture Alley contains more of the character names that make Whittington's stories read like one long, serialized piece of work, one big extended family. Lora Cassel joins the many Loras, Noras and Coras who populate Whittington's novels, all of them a tribute to "Dora," the faraway platonic love of Harry's high school years.

In 1947 Harry wrote about Dora for a correspondence school assignment: "I used to sit in class and wish I could ask her to a movie with me. Once while I was waiting for a school bus, she rode by in Homer's car and she was laughing up at something he was saying, and I stood there, feeling lonely in the afternoon, and looking after her and wondered how nice it would be to have her laughing up at me like that."

□ □ □

For Harry Whittington, past is not necessarily prologue. Twenty-two years after his death, the measurement of his career is still a work in progress.

His monument is there along Florida's Gulf Coast, a tribute on a gravestone: "The King of the Paperbacks." Welcome to the glorious sideshow, a testament to the power of a Gentlemanly Southern outsider and his singular literary voice.

Downieville, CA
September 2011

RAPTURE ALLEY

by Harry Whittington

Chapter 1

Carrying her hat box, Lora went through the side entrance of the shabby building in the garment district. The elevator boy ogled her with wide eyes and round mouth. She got off on the fifth floor. A small, fat woman, standing outside an unmarked door, beckoned Lora with her head.

Lora went into the large room. There were a dozen other girls there, standing in line before a man at a cutter's table. Lora knew a couple of the other girls. She smiled, and they nodded at her.

Lora stood in line. She felt a moment of panic. The job paid twenty dollars an hour. She hoped there was no chance of a refusal. She'd had a lot of luck lately, all of it bad.

The girls ahead answered questions and went through another unmarked door. A few more girls, each with her hat box, filled out the line behind Lora. So far nobody had been rejected. *He's waiting to get to me*, Lora thought. *What happens to no one else happens to me.*

The man was writing on a pile of ledger paper with a mechanical pencil. His tie was at half-mast, collar open, shirt sleeves rolled up. He was wearing no coat. The pockets of his vest looked like catchalls. He glanced up at Lora, squinting his left eye against the smoke from the cigar in the corner of his mouth.

"Name?"

"Lora Cassel."

"Real name or professional?"

"Real."

"You got a professional name you'd rather use?"

"No. That's all right."

"How old are you?"

"Twenty."

"You got your slip from your agency?"

"Yes. Here it is."

She fumbled it out of her purse. He took it with his left hand, still writing with his right, and dropped it on the pile of other slips. She sighed. It looked as though she was in.

He squinted at her again. "They told you what we needed?"

"Yes. Model underthings."

"That's right. We might want some pictures. That okay?"

"Yes. As long as I'm paid for pictures."

He nodded. "Okay. Go right through that door there."

She opened the door and went into the next room. It was the sewing room for wholesale garment makers. The machines were vacated, and the place was being used as a dressing room. The early arrivals were already undressed and were being fitted in sheer nylon bras and panties.

Lora found an empty machine and dropped her hat box on it.

The girl next to her smiled. "You're to wear your shoes, honey, but no stockings."

The girl beyond her laughed. "Looks like they could heat the joint. What are we doing, modeling gooseflesh?"

The first girl laughed. "You won't need a bra for the gooseflesh you're modeling, dearie."

"Die, bag. Least I can walk by a market without the calf liver mooing at me."

Lora unzipped her dress and pulled it over her head. Another small woman came to her with a carton of underthings. She ran a tape measure around Lora's bust and hips. She selected a peach-colored bra without supports or padding.

"This is our toughest number to push, honey. The kind that don't support or build 'em up. Now, for God's sake, make it look good, will you?"

Lora nodded. "All right."

The woman handed her a matching set of panties. She smiled at Lora. "Remember, honey. Just keep those shoulders back."

Lora could hear the whisper of the peach-colored nylon against her flesh as she slipped into the garments the woman had given her. Lora smiled. She knew what it was whispering. Twenty dollars an hour.

She stepped into her shoes again and looked in a narrow mirror. Her face colored slightly. The matching set was almost flesh-colored. It looked very lovely.

A door up at the front of the sewing room opened. Through it came the rustle of a hundred voices, male voices. Lora frowned. The girl next to her twisted around, puzzled.

Lora shrugged. "All I know is, the agency sent me."

The gooseflesh girl whispered. "Sounds like a stag party to me."

Lora tried to smile. "It's on the level. It's got to be. My agency wouldn't have sent me." But something inside her asked a nagging question. *Or would they? How long has it been since you got a call?*

"Sure it is. These underthings are really something special," the girl beside her said.

"All right, girls!" The man who had come through the door was waving his arms back and forth before his head. "Quiet, ladies. If you please, would you shut up a minute?" He looked like the man who had been writing in the back room, except that he was wearing a coat and was smoking a king-size cigarette.

He waited. The noise simmered down, sliding away from him to the rear of the room where the latest arrivals were still undressing.

"You all look very lovely," the man said. "You ought to. The underthings you're wearing will retail from ten to thirty bucks a copy. It's a new line with us. We've spent a lot of money and a lot of research on it. This isn't something we've just thrown together, and we don't want the kind of show out there that's going to look like something we've just thrown together. Remember, Sleeping Beauty underthings make any woman look like a lady. Now, the format is simple. You ladies will come out on the dais at a signal from the m.c. I won't try to tell you how to walk or pose. That's why we hired you girls. You know that."

Gooseflesh whispered, "Why didn't he order a rehearsal?"

"At twenty bills an hour? Are you kidding?" a voluptuous redhead answered.

The man waved his arms again. "After that part of the show is over, you'll all then walk between the tables. Take your time. We're selling this merchandise now–today. Every set you're wearing has a number. The buyers must have time to find out from us what order number you have. Then you can move on."

The man went with the three women close behind him through the room. He would give each girl a number. One of the women marked her model, name and number on a pad.

Lora was number three. When the man came to her, he looked her over slowly, his left brow tilting slightly. "I'm real proud of this number," he said. "One of my own designs."

"Not every woman can wear a bra like that," the woman beside him said.

He smiled. "No. But you gotta admit it looks good on them that can." He patted Lora's shoulder and moved on.

Lora tried to tell herself she was proud that at least here she stood out. Her natural assets moved her right to the front in this group.

The man slapped his hands together and told them to line up in the order he had numbered them. There was the same shoving and confusion there must have been in a slaughter pen as the girls lined up before a curtained arch.

Music started in the display room. It came from a gypsy ensemble of two violins and accordion. The music swelled, then slowed and was muted. The m.c. began to talk. The first girl got her signal, and the show was on the road.

He moved fast then. When Lora's turn came, she stepped through the curtains, and the whispers and toneless whistles struck her in the face.

Her eyes stung. The m.c. kept her in the center of the stage for an eternity. He was talking shop, quality, design, texture, but his voice was the breath of passion.

Flash bulbs exploded. She heard the click of cameras and the excited rush of male voices as the m.c. stopped talking. She pirouetted slowly once and walked off the other side of the dais.

Lora realized the motive behind the hiring of so many girls, one model for each style or color of undergarment. After a while the superfluity of beauty would pall on the audience. They could get their minds back to such matters as price, gross lots and back orders.

When the show ended, the music rose again, and the girls were herded out between the tables.

Lora moved slowly. She tried to keep her eyes above the browlines of the buyers. She attempted concentrating on furrowed brows, sweated foreheads, slick bald spots.

She was not successful. The aisles were narrow, almost too narrow to navigate. When they stopped her and asked her for her number, she answered as impersonally as she could, but it was difficult to remain impersonal.

It was amazing how quickly she could learn, though. She found that after the buyers had the order number, there was really no longer any need for her to remain at that table. The rest, the price and any other related matters, was between buyer and sales representative.

She began giving her number, along with a fixed, professional smile, and then she would move on.

It was odd how quickly the buyers learned, too. They delayed asking her number, keeping her at a table until every buyer had examined her closely. It was never going to end.

Lora began to forget her nakedness. It no longer mattered. All she could see were the faces, the eager eyes, the sweated foreheads, the ruby-burning cigar tips swirling around her head, around and around. There was no longer even a breath of air in the room. There was nothing but the smog of cigar smoke, the distant, insinuating whisper of violins.

Am I a model? she asked herself behind her unflinching smile. *Or am*

I a pony at some thinly-disguised stag show?

She walked off the floor and through the arch to the sewing room when she got a signal. The manager came back in. He was smoking a fresh king-size cigarette. He was beaming, expansive.

"Don't take those things off, girls. Keep 'em. Wear 'em home. Thrill your boyfriends. Tell 'em they're really Sleeping Beauty designs. It was a wonderful show, ladies, and when you get your envelopes you're going to find a real bonus inside. Compliments of me and my partners for a swell job."

He smiled at all of them, and heeled around, almost drunk with success, to get back to the orders piling up on the only empty table out front.

Lora's mouth twisted. Whatever it was she had to have to get to the top in this racket, she just did not have it.

She glared at herself in the mirror. She felt her eyes burn again, stinging. There were no baby spotlights to blame now. There was nothing to blame, except the feeling of insecurity, hollowing a pit in her stomach. Her hands made a claw, and she ripped off the peach-colored bra. All she wanted was to get dressed in her own clothes and get out of there.

Once outside, Lora went straight to the nearest bar and ordered whiskey straight. It did not help any. Something was wrong. They were not even putting whiskey in their whiskey any more.

Chapter 2

Lora got the telephone call about three days later from Arty Elliot.

"Miss Cassel?"

"Yes."

"This is Arthur Elliot. Maybe you don't remember me?"

Sure, she remembered him. He was an engineer with Taylor-Webson Productions, television. They made films for advertising agencies and produced live shows for the networks. She remembered anybody who might help her get a job in television.

"Of course. I remember you, Arty. How are you?"

"Oh, fine. Say, they got an opening up here at Taylor-Webson. It's just a couple hours, but I thought you might like it."

"I'd love it."

Arty laughed. "Don't you even want to know what it is?"

She matched his laughter. "It's work, isn't it?"

"I mentioned you to Mr. Taylor. He remembered you, and he said you could have the place if you could get up here in an hour. I don't know, Lora. It's way uptown."

"If they got subways up there, I'll make it."

"Sure. Take an E train, honey–as quick as you can. We're shooting." He gave her the address. "You won't be able to miss it. It's a converted garage."

She thought Arty was kidding, but when she got there, Lora found that he had not been. There was still grease on the floors that had not been converted into compact sound stages. There were cables and trucks and lights everywhere, and Lora threaded her way through it.

Arty was watching for her and saw her come through the outer door. He wriggled out of the crowd and came hurrying toward her.

He was about twenty-six. His hair was dry and unruly over his forehead. His head was narrow and rather long. There was something odd and glassy about his eyes. His smile was a continual part of his face, but it showed good teeth and was not too offensive.

"Glad you made it, honey," Arty said. "They hired a girl from the agency, but she called in sick. I told them I could save time by getting you up here. That's what they always want to do, save time. But as a matter of fact, Mr. Taylor remembered you, and he said you'd do fine."

Arty took her arm and led her between the spotlights. Up ahead, she could see the smeared faces of the actors. In the middle of them, Ron Taylor was prowling. He was in his shirt sleeves, and he was chewing a cigar.

He was no older than Arty, but to the oldest man on the set he was Mr. Taylor. He was not snobbish. He was familiar and overly affectionate with everybody, male and female alike, but he was young, painfully young, and painfully aware of his age. He never let anybody forget that he was Mr. Taylor.

The director probably hated the taste of that cigar, but it was a prop, as necessary to his ego as the pointed deference he received from his associates. He could have grown a mustache, but he was a natural blonde. A mustache would have been a long, hard process.

"My adventure stories have zip," Taylor was saying. "They got pace. They got to have it. We got to have a sense of movement, even in the restricted space of a living room. Now, Barryfield, when you walk, I want you to stride. Look like you're going somewhere. What the hell, if you smash your nose, you're out of camera range when you hit the wall. I'll buy you a new nose."

Everybody laughed politely, even John Barryfield, the young actor.

"Arty!" Taylor yelled. "Is that girl here? Oh, there you are, sweet darling."

"Miss Cassel is here," Arty said, reminding Taylor of her name without doing it bluntly.

"All right, Miss Cassel. You have just one scene. Come over here."

Lora felt Arty pat her arm reassuringly, but she had already forgotten him. Taylor half-shoved her into a chair. A make-up woman started to work automatically on Lora's face.

"Is this dress all right, Mr. Taylor?" Lora said through the woman's busy hands.

Taylor glanced at his script. "Yeah. *Sureamente*. Any dress is all right darling. That looks sweet. You look sweet. Now we're going to shoot your scene right now."

Taylor started shouting orders. The stage was cleared. The cameras were moved in close.

The make-up woman stepped away from Lora. Lora got up and slithered between the cameras and the spotlight to the set which was very simple, almost bare. A couple of potted plants represented flora: A grass carpet was spread between the plants, and that was the earth. The pots would not show in the completed film.

Taylor followed her out on the set. "Now in this scene, angel, you're dead. You're a corpse. You've been raped. We're keeping it clean, of course. What Barryfield says when he finds you is that you've been assaulted. The audience will know what we mean. Now, lie down will you? That's it. Just fall–right there on the grass between the plants so the leaves will show."

Lora sank to her knees, and then slid down on her side. She rolled on her back and looked up at Taylor. "Remember, beautiful, you've been raped–assaulted west of Broadway–and your face must show it. Of course, you're dead, and actually your face wouldn't show anything except death, but the hell with that. Suppose you turn your body so you're twisted. Okay. Your legs one way and your face rolled over towards the camera. With the grimace now. Remember, the audience has got to see what happened to you–in your face!"

He stepped back, behind the cameras, behind the lights and the microphones. He got down on his knees. He whispered to her, "Stare, angel. Stare. Look right at me, but don't see me. That's it. Now then, grimace. Pull your mouth down. That's lovely, sweetheart. You look assaulted as hell."

He stood up. "Just hold that. Oh, for God's sake, wait a minute. In the name of Heaven, somebody get her dress up above her knees.

The make-up woman crawled out on the grass. She moved the hem of Lora's skirt. Taylor screamed. "No! You trying to get us thrown off the air?

Pull that thing down across her knees. It's got to cover them. Just don't let it look like it's covering 'em. You got it. Fine. Let's shoot it!"

Silence spread over the small stage. The cameras rolled. Lora's face began to ache. She wondered how long Taylor expected her to stare and grimace. She heard movement behind her, but she remembered to keep grimacing, keep staring.

She knew that the cameras and the lights were panning away from her, moving upward to show a close-up of the beautiful Barryfield, registering horror and a desire for revenge.

The cameras stopped. Arty came out on the carpet and helped Lora to her feet. He led her offstage, and the make-up woman pinned a towel around her face and removed the make-up.

"You were fine," Arty said. "You looked good."

She smiled. "Yeah. Good and assaulted."

"That doesn't matter. Taylor appreciates good work. He'll remember you himself, next time."

"Thanks, Arty. Thanks for everything."

The chief engineer yelled for Arty. He blinked his odd eyes at her. "See you," he said. He hurried away.

She started toward the exit. She turned around and approached the director. "Mr. Taylor?"

He heeled around, chewing his cigar. He looked at her blankly a moment, then grinned. "You were fine, sugar. Fine sugar. How do you like that? I'll have to use that in a script. Thanks a lot. Your check will go out from the agency."

"Oh, that's all right, Mr. Taylor. I was just wondering–if there were any more parts–anything else, if you'd have Arty call me."

He frowned, chewing his cigar. "You were the corpse. I can't use you any more in this script."

"I know. But I mean if anything later–"

"Oh? Later. Well, I don't know." He waved his hand. "Get in touch with the agency, doll. Just keep in touch."

He chewed his cigar and stared right through her for a moment. Then he turned around, and she was alone again.

Sure, he would remember her. Good work. He had forgotten her already. He never even knew her name.

Lora had never had any idea that it was not tough, but somewhere she had gotten the belief that if she had beauty and talent, she could at least get a job. She was finding out what a laugh that was. She had beauty. She had won the American Legion Beauty contest back home in Council

Falls. Then she had won the state contest, and that had earned her a movie test. Nothing ever came of the test, but at least she knew she had beauty. Those contests were so often framed, and yet she had won. She had not been the only one who was amazed.

She had talent, a pleasant voice. Maybe it was not sensational. She supposed it was not, but it was better than this. She was being lost in the shuffle. Twenty dollars here, fifty dollars sometimes. A corpse in a TV show. Loneliness and insecurity and worry and doubt. That was what they had for her.

Lora went home. There was no use drinking. There was no kick in whiskey any more. She got nothing from it, not even forgetfulness.

Chapter 3

It always hurt Lora to see Chris in the wheelchair. The pain was like a sudden blow in the diaphragm. Her older sister was blonde and delicate. For the past two years Chris had been confined to bed or chair by a coronary condition and the ills that followed in its wake.

It hurt almost as bad to see Chris smile. If Chris could smile, what in the hell was there for Lora to feel badly about?

Lora shook her head. She knew there were other kinds of ills. A girl walked along the avenues, with her hat box, and her head high, and there were a hundred hurts inside her.

"Hello, baby," Chris said. "Was it a good job?"

Lora made a face and kissed her sister's cheek. I was a corpse. I made a face–like this–for about ten minutes. I'll come over like Ava Gardner."

Chris's chilled fingers stroked her cheek. "You would, too–if you just got a chance."

Lora blinked back tears of anger. "A chance. It takes more than that. I don't know exactly what, but whatever it is, I haven't got it."

"Honey, don't say that. You've got all the life and the beauty in the world. I don't see why every man who sees you isn't insane about you."

Lora forced herself to smile. "I don't know what my poor ego would do without you to build it up."

A frown of worry flitted across Chris's pale blue eyes. "You've got to learn to believe in yourself, Lora. You've got to stand on your own two feet. When somebody slugs you, you've got to slug right back."

"I'm kind of tired of fighting."

"Lora, you can't give up. You've wanted to be what you are ever since

I can remember. Why, honey, I can close my eyes and see you doing Bette Davis before that old mirror in the attic."

"That old mirror appreciated me."

Chris shook her head. She pressed her knuckles against her left breast. Tension, anxiety. Lora knew what they did to Chris, and yet she brought all her woes in this bedroom in a basket of self-pity.

"Chris! I'm all right. Forget it!"

Chris shook her head. "I don't want to forget it, baby. You see I worry about you–and about Ken."

At the mention of Ken's name, Lora felt the chemical change take place in her body, felt the guilt slide upward into her eyes. She was sure Chris could see it, too.

"Don't worry about me. I can take care of myself. And Ken–Ken doesn't have to take care of himself. Ken's–got you."

"You both have me, darling. But what about–when you don't?"

"Chris! Stop talking like that. I won't stay in here and listen."

"That's it, Lora. You've said what I've been trying to say to you. You run away from things. When you don't want to listen, when you don't want to see, when you might get hurt, you run."

Lora patted her sister's hand. "Doesn't everybody?"

"Yes. I suppose so. To a degree. But not the way you do. Honey, there's only one thing going to keep you from–as you said–coming over like Gardner."

"Yes?"

"You."

"Me? How could I try any harder?"

"Just by not being afraid. Admit that things are going to be tough, but you're going to be tougher. Don't run away, Lora. You've got everything–but self-confidence." Chris laughed. "The other day I read that beautiful women are awful suckers because of all the people in the world, they lack self-confidence. I thought about you, baby. I sat there with the magazine in my hands, and through my mind ran everything I'd ever known about you, and I knew it was true."

Lora prowled the room. She picked up a brush from the dresser. She realized it was Ken's. She opened her hand, dropping the brush as though it was hot.

"You've got to fight back, honey," Chris said.

Lora leaned against the dresser. "When you get used for a punching bag long enough, that's what you begin to feel like, a punching bag."

"Who's punching, bag?" Ken called as he came through the bedroom door. He pulled off his hat and sailed it across the room. It landed on Chris's bed. She opened her mouth to protest about bad luck. Ken winked at Lora and bending over Chris's chair, he kissed his wife before she could say anything.

Watching him, Lora felt her heart race and then slow, until she could feel a bar of pain pinned across her ribs. She could feel his kiss against Chris's bloodless lips, or she could feel the loss of it. She felt the loss of all Ken's kisses. Even knowing that he bestowed his kisses like pollen in the wind, she was still jealous of his lips. She had loved him for so long. Such a foolish, helpless love. Just something else to snarl up her insides and keep her ill.

It was not that she had not tried to keep him out of her heart and thoughts–and blood. She had tried.

In her work, she met men by the hundreds. She met writers, and directors and actors, newspapermen, publicity experts, advertising executives. There were always photographers in her life. There were the engineers who kept the shows rolling when she was lucky enough to get a show, but it did not seem to matter. They were cardboard figures, without substance or any excitement for her.

"And how's the stellar attraction this evening?" Ken said to Lora. He looked directly at her, across the top of Chris's blonde head.

In his eyes, Lora could see the need for her. For the long space of a breath, it was as though his eyes opened the way to his insides.

"Lovely." Lora made her voice light to cover the way her heart was pounding. "I was a corpse today. I'll bet I made fourteen dollars after taxes."

"You're rich, kid. So rich, so lovely."

"That's what I tell her, Ken," Chris said. She reached upward, taking Ken's hand. "She has everything, but she's so discouraged. Cheer her up, Ken. Please try."

Ken's voice was dull. "Cheer her up. It's an order. Ken, say something funny. You heard the one about the traveling salesman and the owner of the dog kennels–"

"Such jokes never cheered anybody," Chris said, but her voice was indulgent.

"I'm not a master of ceremonies, baby," Ken said. "I'm just a salesman, a kind of a flop of a salesman. I come home tired evenings. When you want entertainment from me, you'll have to take what you can get. A joke that's been good enough for my customers all day has got to be good enough for you."

Chris laughed, "Just your voice, darling, is good enough for me." The adoration in her voice cut across Lora's heart.

Lora clenched her fists at her sides. She could feel her long nails digging into her palms. When Ken turned his head to look down at Chris, Lora saw the faint smear of lipstick under the squared left jaw. It seemed to mock her.

Lora did not say anything. What was there to say? It was nothing new. Chris had been like this for over two years. Who but a narrow bigot would ask a man like Ken to die just because his wife was dead? But that did not alleviate the empty ache inside of her. It was no comfort.

"I'll get supper," Lora said. "That I can do."

"Thanks, darling," Chris said. She stopped Lora at the door. "There were four calls for you this afternoon."

Lora looked back over her shoulder. She saw the anger flare in Ken's eyes, the jealousy.

"What were they?" Ken's voice was ragged. "Employers or lovers?"

Lora's eyes blazed, but she said nothing.

Chris laughed. "I didn't ask. I left the numbers on a pad. I'll get it."

"Oh, no. Let me." Ken strode over to the bed table where the telephone extension was. He ripped off the top sheet, glanced at it. He brought it to Lora, held it out.

She took it. Their hands touched, their icy hands. Involuntarily their eyes met, and then leaped away like thieves guilty in the night. Lora wanted to rush into his arms. She wanted to soothe him, reassure him, but she stood still.

"I'll get supper," Lora said again, emptily.

She walked toward the small kitchenette. She could hear Chris and Ken talking. Their tones were low. She was shut out from whatever they had to say to each other. That was right, perfectly normal and correct. She did not expect it to be any other way, but it added fuel to the despair and depth of her loneliness that she had been living with for the past few weeks, the failure weeks.

Here was something else. Lora did not belong here. She had no right to be in this apartment. Even if she was not crazy about Ken, she had no place in their lives. She had to get away, but how could she? Sure, she could get a job as a waitress, and support herself in her own apartment or room.

She shook her head. She and Chris had been through that dozens of times. Around the same circle. No, she had to get a good job, one that paid her enough money to make her independent. Then Chris would want her to go, and only then.

Lora was almost at the kitchen door. She glanced down at the pad.

There were only four exchange numbers. At the top, Chris had written: "Call Back."

Lora looked at the numbers a moment, recognizing none of them. She glanced in at the kitchen, and then went into the front room to the telephone.

Four calls. Each time she dialed a new number, Lora felt that old expectancy in her breast. Hope springing eternal. Four different calls. Each time she could hear the wail of the bell in some vacated office, some empty room somewhere in the town.

She pushed the slip of paper under the telephone. She got up thinking that in the morning at least there would be some calls to make. A chance. A chance at what? A new right cross to the jaw?

She found the package of ground lean beef she had brought home from the store. She tossed it on the drain board and found an apron. She slipped it over her neck, tied it at her waist. From beneath the sink, she got Irish potatoes and onions. She pulled a stool to the sink and got to work. The onions made her cry, but she decided she was in the mood for it.

She set the small table for two while the hamburgers were frying. She put a lot of energy into mashing the potatoes. She had a tray prepared for Chris when Ken came into the kitchen.

He looked at her, tilting his left brow. She knew her hair was awry, her forehead was damp, and her eyes were rimmed from crying.

He grinned. "Lovely," he said. "This is what you were made for, baby. Not chasing after contracts."

"How do you know what I was made for?"

His grin widened. "I know, baby. I know."

She flushed. Her mouth trembled. "Stop. Just because it happened once, it's not going to happen again. Not ever. Let me alone, Ken. Please let me alone."

His smile died. "What's the matter. Did one of those calls come from some guy who wants to take you out? I can go to hell when you can get a date. It's just when–"

"Shut up!" She shoved the tray at him. "Take that in to Chris. Your supper is ready whenever you want to come back and eat it."

He took the tray. His voice was dead. "Maybe I don't want to eat." His eyes flashed angrily.

"Suit yourself."

She sat down at the table. She bumped one of the legs so hard the iced water sloshed in the glasses. He grinned at her, an impish grin. "Don't go 'way, baby. I'll be back."

She did not answer. He took the tray and left the kitchenette. She put food on her plate, telling herself she was not waiting for him, but she was sitting there, toying with her food when he came back and sat in the chair around the table from her.

He moved the service she had set for him from across the small table from her. "Too far away," he said, taking three hamburgers. "I'd freeze to death that far from you."

"It wouldn't hurt you any to cool off some."

He ignored that. "Are you going out tonight?"

"I don't think that's any of your business."

His voice was tense. He leaned toward her. "Don't argue. You know Chris will hear if you do. And you know damned well it's my business."

"I don't have to account to you for anything!" she snapped.

She could feel the hardness of his leg against hers under the table. The touch of him left her empty and without will.

It was all so wrong. She sat there, longing to press her hand in his, wanting to tell him how much she loved him, yet knowing how wrong it was, and that she could never tell him.

It was not new. Five years ago, Lora had gone to their wedding, Ken's and Chris's. She had been fifteen, and a bridesmaid, and the tears had choked in her throat, burning and aching her.

Lora had listened to the minister. She had looked at Ken. All she could see was his straight, rugged profile, with the chin jutting. There was a cleft in his chin, she knew, but she could not see it from where she stood. How she longed to kiss the cleft in his chin.

Her mother had known. Her mother had held her, crying in her arms. "You'll get over him, baby. You'll know dozens of men before you're as old as Chris is right now. Surely, Chris got a fine man, and surely you love him. You'll get over it, baby."

Her mother had been wise. She had been able to stop Lora's tears. But her mother had been wrong. Lora never got over it.

Now she sat there, trying to eat, trying to pay attention to the things Ken was saying. The trivial, little things that had happened during the day. He was talking for Chris. He was talking easily so Chris, lying in her bed now, would be reassured and contented.

All Chris wanted was for Ken and Lora to get along together, to be happy, and never to fight. Lora's hand trembled. They had to fight, to keep from flinging themselves at each other.

Lora was not really aware of his words, nor of the food she was eating. All the sensations in her body seemed concentrated in the place where their legs pressed together hard beneath the table.

The doorbell jangled, startling her. She jumped up.

Ken looked up at her, his mouth twisting. "So you are going out tonight?"

"I didn't say I wasn't."

"You didn't say you were."

"Damn you!"

She sighed, dropped her napkin on the table beside her plate. She started out of the kitchen, hesitated, and for a second pressed the backs of her fingers lightly against Ken's cheek.

She opened the front door. It was Arty Elliot. He was wearing a different suit, but the smile on his face was unchanging. His eyes still did not quite focus.

"Hello, Arty. Come on in."

He widened his smile slightly. "Thanks." She closed the front door behind him. "I tried to call you, Lora," he said. "But your sister said you weren't in. I left my number."

She smiled. "I tried to call back, but I guess that you were already gone."

"Yeah." He nodded, twisting his hat in his nervous fingers. "That's the way it is."

"Yes," she said. "Sit down, Arty."

"Oh, well, look. I just wondered if you'd like to go out somewhere tonight. I know a swell Spanish restaurant down on Fourteenth. You ever been there? You walk upstairs–"

"I've just eaten, Arty."

"Fine. I'm not hungry, anyway. We'll hit a club. I know a couple of nice spots. They have music that sends."

Music. She nodded. "I'd like to, Arty–"

Ken stood in the kitchen doorway. He was holding his napkin in his hands. His smile was guileless. "Who is it, sis?"

Sis! Lora glared at Ken. "Mr. Elliot, this is my brother-in-law, Mr. Hunter. Ken, this is Arty. Arty is an engineer with a television company."

"Say! That's fine!" Ken was giving Arty the expansive treatment, but he was looking him over with covert contempt in his face.

Lora was angry. Ken could be so cruel when he wanted to be. The way he looked down at the slender Arty was insulting. Still, Lora found herself wishing that Arty would not smile all the time.

"Glad to know you, Mr. Hunter."

"Why, call me Ken, Arty. And I'm glad to know you. Want to know the kind of men Sis goes out with. Guess you know, a man can't be too careful in a town like this, eh?"

Arty's smile faded. "No sir. I guess he can't."

"Arty and I are going to listen to a band, Ken." Lora's voice was chilled.

"Going out, eh?" Ken's voice remained warm, but his eyes on Lora's face were cold. "Well you go right ahead. Don't you worry, I'll do up the dishes, and clean up the kitchen. I say that when a girl gets a chance to have a date, everybody ought to help her. Don't you think so, Mr. Elliot? Arty?"

Lora looked herself over in the mirror. Her face was flushed with exasperation. She knew she ought to change her dress, freshen up, but she knew better than to leave poor little Arty alone with Ken. She patted at her hair, and found her coat and purse.

"Good night," she said to Ken.

"You won't be late now, will you?" he said.

"I don't know," she answered. She took the napkin from him, scrubbed the lipstick from his jaw, and handed the napkin to him so only he could see the telltale red smear. "If I am, this will give you something to think about until I get back."

"You'll see she gets back at a reasonable hour, Mr. Arty. Won't you?" Ken said. "We worry when she's out late. So many automobile accidents in New York, you know."

Lora slammed the door shut behind them.

Chapter 4

The club to which Arty took Lora was on the fringe of Greenwich Village. It was in a basement, and might have once been a speakeasy, or maybe a day nursery. Regardless, the management had spent as little as possible to decorate it.

The place was crowded. Nobody seemed in the least to mind the shabby walls, the bare tables or the unpainted booths. The bar was less than eight feet long. Behind it was a keg, turned on its side in front of a foggy mirror. Bottles were lined up on both sides of the keg.

The customers were two-deep at the bar, odd-looking people, either talking directly to their companions, or staring moodily at the foggy mirror, but totally unaware of the crowds around them.

At the end of the room was a crowded dais. On this was a spinet-sized piano, drums and instruments standing like soldiers in a row.

When Lora and Arty came in, there was nobody on the bandstand. The room was fifty disjointed conversations, each one trying to be heard above the others.

"Arty, we'll never get in here," Lora said. She did not care much if they didn't.

"Sure we will." Arty spoke to the bartender. A waiter pushed between the tables. "Two." Arty said to the waiter."

"Yes, Mr. Elliot."

Lora could feel Arty swell at the deference shown him by the waiter. Poor Arty. He was yelled at or yelled for all day at the studio. No wonder he liked to go where he was Mr. Elliot at night. Wasn't that what everybody wanted? A little attention? A feeling that he was somebody worthwhile?

The waiter squeezed through the crowded tables, and they followed him, turning and twisting between the people who did not even look up or stop talking to let them pass.

The waiter wiped off a small table for two against a wall. Arty thanked him, and Lora saw the folded bill that Arty gave as a tip. Arty, too, was willing to pay for what he got.

They squeezed into the chairs. Arty said, "What do you want to drink, Lora?"

She shook her head. "I don't care."

"Whiskey?"

Again she shrugged. "Okay by me, Arty."

Arty ordered two whiskeys with water. The waiter went away. "You don't like to drink, Lora?" he asked her.

"It's all right. But what's the use? There's nothing in it–not for me." She told him about the day she had gone to a bar looking for a kick, a lift. "I felt lower than ever after I had three drinks straight."

She felt Arty's odd eyes on her, moving over her face. It was as though he was making up his mind about something. She met his gaze. She was puzzled but she could read nothing there. His continual smile was like a mask, and she could not force his eyes to meet hers directly.

She felt unexplained cold at the nape of her neck.

"What do you want, Lora? What are you looking for? What do you want out of life?"

"Same as anybody, I guess. I want to be somebody. I want to be a success."

He leaned forward. "Well, you can. That's sure. You got everything."

"Sure, I come over like Gardner."

"Sometimes it takes time."

"Yeah. Well, I haven't got time. I am what I am right now, but what am I going to be in a few years after everybody in New York uses me for a punching bag?"

"Don't get discouraged."

"I don't. I stay discouraged.... I want to thank you, Arty, for what you did for me."

"Oh, that's all right. But maybe I didn't do you any favor. You know, I can get you bits like that, pretty regular, eating money."

"What's wrong with eating money?"

"Nothing. But it can get you in a rut. Sometimes when you're hard to get to, they want you more."

She laughed. "No. I tried that. I left my telephone off its hook for fifteen whole minutes one day."

He laughed. "You're just down, kid. What you need is a lift, a real lift."

She did not answer. A blast of music from the dais behind them made further conversation impossible. She watched the three musicians start a session that set every person in the room on the edge of their seat.

The music screamed and wailed and beat at her. Arty sat smiling across the table. His eyes closed a little, and then he stopped smiling. Arty forgot her. She thought casually that Arty looked much better when he was not smiling all the time.

The music began to get at her then. She supposed it meant something different to every person in the room. For her it was all her confusion and futility and insecurity, spinning around her head. All her hopes, and all her failures fled through her mind on the notes of the music.

She found all of her problems in it. Ken, the way she loved him, the hopeless way. Chris, without a chance of living, and no hope of dying, an invalid with a whole life of empty days and nights ahead of her. Modeling, trying harder and slipping lower. The clarinet sobbed at her. The piano was the patter of her tears, falling faster and faster. The trumpet was her crying.

As suddenly as it had begun, the music stopped. Maybe it had lasted for hours, maybe minutes, maybe only seconds, as it seemed to Lora. Whatever it was, it left her empty and shaken, with all her hopelessness like something real in her hands. Only there was no answer. The music just gave her trouble. It did not find an answer for her. Maybe there was no answer.

For the space of a caught breath, the silence was thick in the room. Then everybody applauded. It was as though they were coming out of a spell.

Lora looked around. The faces were sweated. The eyes were haunted, far away. The mouths were pulled down. The music was like some terrible poison to them. It made them more lonely than ever, more miserable than ever, but they could not stay away from it.

She knew why. That music expressed their thoughts for them. Just as it had expressed hers. The loneliness, the hopelessness, the futility.

She pushed back in her chair. "Come on, Arty. Let's go."

He got up. He was worried, but he smiled. "What's the matter, Lora? You didn't like it?"

"It was wonderful–but I've got to get up early, Arty."

The street before Lora's apartment was almost deserted. Arty walked beside her, his hands at his sides. "Lora, I'm going to a party tomorrow night. I didn't think about asking you before. Well–I wasn't sure you'd like it–but I don't like to see you so low. If you'll go, you might have a good time. It'll be different. I promise you that."

Lora looked up at the third floor apartment. It was dark. She thought about Ken. She had to stay away from Ken, and maybe Arty could help her find some way out of the blues.

"Tonight was different, Arty."

"Yeah. But tonight was nothing. This party is real gone."

She looked at him in the light from a dingy window. He was smiling at her.

"I'd like to go, Arty."

"Good. I'll call for you about eight. That be all right?"

"Yes. And Arty, thanks for the job today. If there are any more, I'll take them. We'll let the star parts go for a while."

Lora unlocked the front door. She knew Ken was in the darkened front room, although she could not see him.

"Ken," she whispered.

He turned on a small table lamp. Most of the room remained dark.

He was wearing an old bathrobe over his pajamas. She could see the piles of cigarette stubs in the ashtray under the lamp. His voice was miserable. "Did you have a good time?"

"All right."

He got up from the chair and came toward her. She looked around, wanting to run, and knowing there was nowhere to run.

"I suppose you gave him a good time," he said dully.

Her voice hissed at him. "Stop, Ken! You want Chris to hear your nasty talking?"

"Chris is asleep. You know that. I gave her pills."

"Then I don't want to hear you talk like that."

She laid her purse in a chair and tossed her coat over it.

"Don't you?" he demanded. "Then why do you do it?"

"Ken, you've got to stop it. You're just torturing both of us."

"I'm not torturing us. You are."

"Ken, you're married to Chris. No matter what I think or want, that remains true."

"What do you want me to do? Walk out on her?"

"I don't want you to do anything I'm not criticizing you, no matter what you do. But I've got my own life to live."

"Your own life is mine, and you know it. It has been for years. It's been since two months ago. You begged me then. You said you were mine, and you said you couldn't help it."

"I was crazy then, Ken. I had fought against it as long as I could. I don't pretend to be strong, but I've gone even crazier since then, worrying about it. I'd leave, Ken–"

"You're not going to leave me!" He snarled it at her and grabbed her arms.

She tried to twist away. "Let me alone! You're driving me crazy!"

Ken's breath was hot against her face. "Maybe you think you're not driving me crazy. I sit around here, sit around thinking about you out somewhere, some hotel room somewhere with that smiling jerk."

"It isn't true! It isn't. There's nobody but you. There never has been." Her voice broke. "God help me, there never will be, Ken. I barely know Arty. He's a nice boy. He helped me get a job today."

"Sure. And tonight you had to pay him for it. Is that it?"

"No, Ken. No."

"Oh, God, baby. I can't stand this. All the women in the world, and I can't get you out of my mind. All the drinking, and I still want you. I can't help it."

He was so miserable. Her hands slipped upward, caressing his face. "Poor Ken. Poor Ken."

He sobbed, dragging her against him. She had not meant for him to kiss her. She did not mean to thrust her arms around him. Not there in Chris's front room. Once she could not help it, but not again, not standing with the faint lamp on them, straining towards each other.

It looked as though what she believed, or thought, or intended doing did not matter. It was what she wanted. That was all that mattered.

She wanted Ken. His kiss thrilled her, and his arms crushed her, smashing her flat against him. Her arms slipped around his shoulders, hands caressing the nape of his neck, lips searching for his, because they could not help it.

Chapter 5

Arty had said it was going to be a party. He did not talk much on the way. He seemed to be nervous and excited. When they knocked on the door and it was opened, Lora expected to hear the sounds of laughter. She was shocked, and a little puzzled by the silence that greeted her.

The man at the door was gray-haired, with a tired, handsome face. He did not speak. He just beckoned them in with a movement of his large head.

They stepped past him into a nicely-furnished living room. Only there was something wrong, something very wrong. There was just one other girl there. She did not even look up when Arty and Lora came in.

The Venetian blinds were drawn tightly at the double windows across the front of the living room. There was a rushing hum, and after a moment Lora realized it came from an air conditioning unit.

She felt odd, and a little frightened. She stayed close to Arty. "I thought you said this was a party," she whispered.

He was still smiling, but he looked worried. Lora saw that he was worried about her. He was afraid she was not going to like it, and he had not wanted to tell her all about it before they got up here. Or maybe he felt that he could not.

"It is a party. You'll like it, Lora. It's real gone."

"No music? No dancing? What kind of party?"

He smiled a little wider and pressed her hand. "You'll love it, Lora. Come on over and sit down."

He led her over to a divan. They sat down together.

The gray-haired man came over to them. He sat down in a chair facing them.

"Lora, this is Pete," Arty said. "Pete–Lora."

"Charmed," Pete said.

She noticed in his eyes that same odd look that she had seen sometimes in Arty's. Pete did not really look at her. He seemed drowsy and listless. He was smiling, but it was a loose smile. It was as though he could not really control the muscles around his mouth. His sleepy gaze traveled over her, and then Pete looked at Arty. "A pretty child."

It could have been a compliment, except that it was a question.

"Like a baby," Arty answered, his tone knowing.

This seemed to please Pete. "Hope you'll enjoy yourself, Lora. Glad to have you up here. Any time."

"Thanks," Lora said.

She thought of a dozen excuses for leaving, but she could see that Arty's face was showing his inner anticipation. She looked at the four other men in the room. They were as young as Arty, but they were dreamy, talking languidly, their talk aimless and sprinkled with jive jargon.

Pete brought a small cardboard pack from a locked case across the room. Lora was watching everybody. Two of the men sighed and lay back in their chairs, watching Pete.

Pete went from one to the other. Each of them took a cigarette from the pack, and thanked Pete in an exaggerated, mocking manner.

Pete stopped before the girl. She was on a small loveseat with a shaggy-haired man. Her hair was black and severely straight. She wore a Dutch bob, a man's shirt with a string tie and a long black skirt that clung to her slender legs.

She turned from talking to her shaggy-haired companion, looked up at Pete and laughed. "How many joints does a gal need, Peter, my love? I'm floating now. I'm positively floating." She made a gesture of a bird flying with her long, white hand.

But when Pete bowed and started to move on, she reached quickly in the box.

Pete stopped in front of Lora and Arty on the divan. Arty dampened his lips with the tip of his tongue. He did not wait to offer Lora a cigarette first. He reached at the box like a greedy child after candy. His hand was trembling!

Lora stared at him. This was not like Arty at all.

Pete slid the box over so that it was in front of Lora's face. She looked at the small brown cylinders. She had never seen marijuana before, but she knew what they were.

She shook her head.

Pete's voice was soft. "Why else are you here, my dear?"

"Go on," Arty whispered, looking around. He was afraid some of the others might notice and might laugh. Arty hated to be laughed at. Only squares got themselves laughed at.

"All your troubles, like birds, like feathers," Arty whispered. "Come on, Lora. You'll go out of this world."

The box was before her. Lora looked at it again. She lifted her hand slowly. Her fingers touched the loosely-packed cigarette. She removed it from the box. She held it between her fingers. Now her hands were trembling.

Arty was smiling at her again. He fumbled in his coat pocket and produced his lighter. "Fire?" he said. His eyes glittered now, and there was really some life in his habitual smile.

Lora placed the cigarette in her mouth. He flicked the lighter. It sparked and flamed. She moved forward, seeing the reflection of the flame in Arty's eyes.

She did not think anything. She did not think about Ken, or the jobs she had missed, or the loneliness. She wondered if there was really any kick in such a harmless-looking little weed.

Lora took a couple of drags, and she began to feel dizzy. It did not taste good, and she did not want it. She wanted to say no. She wanted to grind the thing out on an ashtray and walk out.

She looked at Arty. His cigarette was nothing, a small brown stub between his fingers. Startled, she looked at her own cigarette. It was longer, but it was burning down. Had that much time passed between her decision to leave and her actually turning her head to look at Arty?

Arty waved Pete over. Arty was not smiling now. There was something imperious about the wave of his hand. The joint he had blown had made him master of the place, king of the universe.

Pete came over.

"Sticks," Arty said to him. "For both of us."

Pete smiled dreamily. "Sure, Arty. But don't you think you ought to make with the bills, first? You know how you get, Arty."

Arty laughed. "No, how do I get, Pete?" But he reached into his inner coat pocket and took out two bills that he had ready. "This is for us, Peter. Now, stop asking questions."

Pete returned one of the bills. "No, Arty, you know Lora's are on me–all evening. She's my guest tonight. You know that."

Arty took the bill and shoved it into his coat pocket. He shrugged and laughed. He was already firing up his second stick.

Lora stared at the box Pete held in front of her. It looked as full as it had the first time he had passed it around. She shook her head when he offered her a stick, but even as she did, she was reaching out, taking it. That struck Lora as the silliest thing she had ever done, and she laughed.

The laughter started deep inside her and rolled out. It sounded silly in her own ears, but she was pleased. It was the first time she had found anything to laugh about in months, in years. It was the first time she had ever really laughed in all her life.

Arty turned his head on the divan, staring at her sleepily. "See, Lora?" he said. "See?"

Her laughter attracted the other people in the room, too. A moody, dark-faced man had been watching her from across the room. As though her laughter was a signal, he got up and started toward her.

She had to laugh at that. She supposed he was starting toward her, but he was not walking at all. He was floating, and it took an eternity for him to reach the divan. Something deep in her brain whispered that what was really happening was that time had lost all meaning for her. She laughed again at that idea. That was all right with her. In fact, it was fine.

The dark-faced man reached the divan at last. He toppled and fell beside her, bumping her roughly. She turned her head to protest, but laughed instead.

He laughed, too. When he laughed, he was not bad looking. His ears were like the wings on a monoplane, and he had an outsized nose. You forgot that, though, when he smiled.

"Name's Boyd," he said. "Boyd Collins. What's yours?"

"Lora," Lora said. Lora. Such a funny, silly name. Why hadn't she ever noticed before how laughable a name like that could be? "This is Arty," she added, and waved her arm toward Arty.

Boyd's mouth twisted in a slow-motion expression of contempt. "I know Arty," he told her. "Hell with Arty. Forget Arty."

Lora laughed. "I came with him."

"Hell with that. Forget him. He forgot you."

She laughed. That was an absurd idea. To prove it, she turned and clutched Arty's coat sleeve in her hand. She shook him, but he just mumbled. He was staring at the ceiling and pettishly brushed her hand down.

"See, Lora?" Boyd said. "See? The boy dreams. Low resistance. It sends him. If he ever got on H, it would kill him, but Arty don't need it. Arty can get Ward Eight just blowing a joint."

Lora frowned, wondering what Boyd was talking about. "Say it in English now," she said and giggled.

"You're green, kid," Boyd said. "I can see that. Let me put it in English for you. A joint is a marijuana cigarette, and blowing a joint means smoking one, and Ward Eight is violence. Arty could become violent from smoking a marijuana... get it?"

The idea of Arty's becoming violent amused Lora, but it was no longer easy to laugh. Besides, she did not need to laugh. She could suddenly express her inner delight and relaxation with the merest quirk of her lips. She could tilt them upward, and actually she was roaring with laughter on the inside.

She turned her head, looking at Boyd Collins through the fog of her own smoke. "Boyd," she said. She roared inside with laughter, but it felt so good just to express it in a sleepy smile. "Boyd. What a silly name. Who are you, Boyd?"

"Told you. I'm Boyd Collins. I'm a singer–a real singer. I'm looking for a break. I been with some big bands. Been all over the country. Ask 'em. Ask any of 'em. They'll tell you about Boyd Collins." He closed his eyes and began to hum a bluesy song. "Can't you tell?" he asked.

"Singer." She whispered the word. "Who you sing with, Boyd?"

He shook his head. "Right now, Boyd Collins is at liberty. 'Tween engagements."

"What do you do?"

"What do you mean, what I do?"

She gestured. "To live, how do you get along–? How do you afford–?"

"A stick? Honey, I'd starve right down to a nub before I'd go without a stick. You square. Ain't you square? That's what's the matter. I knew it, minute I saw you. A square."

"No." Suddenly it was important that he not believe that. Lora motioned Pete and got another stick. Boyd lighted it for her.

"Maybe you're not square," he said, "but you act square. 'Less you been at this, you're overdoing it. You're going to be sick like nobody ever was sick."

Lora shook her head. "I don't want to be sick. I feel wonderful. Won't more help? I want to stay like this."

"Then stop right where you are. Just hold what you've got." Boyd reached over and took her cigarette. He started smoking it himself. "Don't overdo it on your first trip, sister."

Pete started toward them, angered, but Boyd laughed and waved him away.

"What you do, Lora?" Boyd purred, drawing closer.

"Model, act, sing."

"If you can sing and act, you got it made. You got everything you need."

"Sure–except a job."

"A beautiful girl like you, can sing and act, too. You're in."

"In everything but a job," she said.

"Funny about jobs, Lora. You want one, you can't get it. Got one, you can get twenty. I know. I was on the road once, and I got calls from the Copa and the Chez. You don't know what to do. Now I'm starving, and you know what? No offers. I sit all day and watch the pigeons."

"Watch the pigeons?"

"Sure. On the ledges across from my room. You never saw the pigeons? Honey, you been in New York very long, you got to see the pigeons."

"What do you watch 'em for?"

"What do you think I watch 'em for. I watch 'em for fun. That's what I watch 'em for." He laughed wanly. "I've decided that at the rate they get together on the ledge across from my room, it won't be long before there aren't any people left in New York. Just pigeons."

She laughed at him.

"Let's coo like the pigeons," he said.

She could not help laughing, but she tried to shove him. "What are you talking about?"

"Pigeons. Let's be pigeons. You and me."

"You're crazy! Anyway, the room is full of people."

"Hell with 'em. Do pigeons care? Town's full of people, but the pigeons don't care. Me and you, we're pigeons. We don't care either." Boyd drew closer.

His arms went around her. She tried to thrust him away, and she could not. She felt his face coming closer and closer. He pressed his face against her cheeks. She could hear him cooing! The guy was nuts. He really thought he was a pigeon. She tried to twist away from him.

"Go away, fella," she warned.

"C'mon, square," Boyd said. "Don't be an all-around square. You're too cute-looking for that, pigeon."

She looked around the room frantically, but nobody was paying the slightest attention to her. Arty's eyes were open. He was staring at her, but he did not move.

"Pigeons," Boyd whispered in her ear. "We're pigeons."

It was too much effort to fight Boyd. What difference did it make, anyhow? Nothing mattered. There was nothing on earth that mattered.

She relaxed against the divan, and he leaned over and kissed her. It did not mean anything to her. Her mind stood apart, like a disembodied person, watching her and Boyd Collins.

Suddenly, she saw Boyd move away from her. He lay beside her and cooed once or twice. He grinned at her, but he did not kiss her again. He had just forgotten all about what he started out to do.

He sighed and expired against her shoulder. She pushed him away. She watched his head topple slowly, slowly against the arm of the divan. Lora was relieved. She had not wanted to make a scene, but Boyd Pigeon has been asking for it. She looked over at him now, dead asleep. *Foolish character*, she thought. But there was a lot of truth to what he said about pigeons.

She started to get up. It was too much effort. It was not worth it. She glanced at Arty. He was grinning again. The room spun pleasantly about her. She wanted to laugh, but she was too tired to laugh.

She just felt good. There was nothing wrong with Boyd Collins. He was just silly. Everybody was silly. All her worries were silly.

She nodded her head. It was true. It was a profound thought. Everything was silly. She saw that now. Silly, and she had no troubles any more, no troubles at all.

Chapter 6

Lora woke up slowly. She sat up and looked around, remembering after a moment that she was still in Pete's apartment. The others were just as they had been last night, only now they were inanimate, like wax figures, sprawled in chairs, divans and on the floor.

She was nauseated and thirsty. Her throat was dry. She blinked her eyes. Even the dim light coming through the Venetian blinds made her eyes ache.

She wondered what time it was. She got up, staggered across the room and looked at the sleeping faces. They looked more dead than asleep to her.

Someone was missing. She looked around. It was Peter, the gray-haired host, who sold his guests their sticks. *Oh God!* Lora thought! *What have I started now*?

She told herself angrily it was foolish to think she had started anything. One or two marijuana cigarettes would not hurt her, and besides, she'd had enough. Never again. All she wanted was to get out of this place.

She found the bathroom. When she came out, she had washed her face and combed her hair, but in the bathroom mirror, she had seen something that she had not noticed before.

What had seemed like an aimless tussle last night must have become pretty violent. She could remember only that Boyd Collins had pawed at her and cooed against her face, but that would not explain the way her dress was ripped across the front. How would it explain the scratches on her arm. Boyd had been rough, very rough.

Her hand shook. She had not only lost her sense of time, but all reality had been lost to her.

She shuddered. Well, this was it. Enough! She found her purse and took one last look at Arty. If he got her a job, she would take it, but no more affairs like this. She wondered how he ever got to work.

On her way to the front door, another thought struck her. It would have come sooner, but she realized now that her reactions were slowed down, way down.

What was Ken going to say when he saw her? She had never stayed out all night. What would he do when he saw the scratches on her arm and the ripped dress? Her throat felt drier than ever. She slipped her arms into her light coat and buttoned it closely about her.

She heard somebody moan behind her, but she did not turn around.

Let them moan. Let them die! The whole thing was ugly and depraved.

Lora hoped it was not just her conscience at work. She hoped she meant it. This had been her first and last time. She was not ever coming back.

She was at the door when Pete's voice stopped her. "So long, Lora."

Her hand on the knob, Lora turned. Peter looked like some kind of smiling monster in the morning light. There were big circles under his puffed and red-rimmed eyes. His gray hair looked unclean and stood up like horns because he had not yet combed it. His face sagged, and his mouth hung loosely at the left corner.

"Goodbye," Lora said.

His brow tilted slightly. "Goodbye? You'll come back. Won't you?"

There was no sense answering that. Lora did not want any argument. All she wanted was to get out of there.

"Any time," he said. His voice was soft. "Any time you want to make a score, Lora, you know where to find me."

"A score?"

"Scoring is buying, Lora. I'm here."

She did not say anything.

"I must warn you," he said. "Don't bring anyone with you. Ask me first. We have to be careful, don't we?"

"All right."

"There are so many people who don't want us to enjoy ourselves," his soft voice went on. "We've got to fight them all the time. We've got to be careful."

She twisted the knob. He stepped close and unlocked the door for her. "We have to be very careful," he said. He slid his hand under her coat. She twisted away from him.

She flung the door open and ran through it, her mouth pulled into a red scar of anger. She ran toward the stairwell without even seeing it.

Peter came out of the door behind her, the light gleaming in his soiled gray hair.

She looked back once. He was standing there, watching her. His left brow was raised and his smile was sardonic.

On the street, Lora found a clock. It was early, not yet eight o'clock.

She wandered around aimlessly. She passed cafeterias crowded with people. The thought of food made her ill. She wanted to go home.

Her eyes stung. She kept walking, her purse clutched in her hand, her coat tightly about her. She could not go home yet. She had to wait until Ken was gone. She could face Chris. She could lie to her. She could tell Chris any lie, and Chris would believe her. She could not lie to Ken, though. He believed no lies. Sometimes he did not even believe the truth.

She could not face Ken. She had to wait until he had gone to work. Then she would go in and lie to Chris. She would tell her something about working all night, at some place in Jersey. By the time Ken came home, Lora would have the lie all nailed down around the edges. She would have Chris believing it. Chris would be on her side. She would be ready for Ken.

The time dragged. It looked as though the minutes were twice as long today.

Lora decided at eight-thirty that by the time she walked up to the apartment, Ken would be gone to work. She walked slowly. Her legs dragged. She hated getting there. She hated lying to Chris. Why was it when somebody believed you implicitly, it always made it so much harder for you to lie to them?

Lora let herself in the outer door and climbed the stairs. Her heart was racing. She wondered if there were any way that Chris could look at her and tell about last night? Lora shook her head. She knew better.

Poor innocent Chris. Telltale signs would be the last thing she would look for, anyway.

Lora fumbled in her purse and got out the apartment key. She fit it into the lock, wishing there was some way she could tell if Ken really was gone to work yet. Lora opened the door quietly, stepped inside and closed it behind her. She turned, moving stealthily.

Chris and Ken were across the room, watching her. At first, Lora was afraid she was going to fall.

Chris was dressed, sitting in her wheelchair. Her blonde hair was brushed, and there was nothing in her eyes but anxiety. Anxiety. It was poison to Chris's coronary condition! Lora hated herself. Why didn't she just take a gun and shoot her sister? What a hell of a night Chris must have gone through, worried, anxious, tense, drawn, wondering where Lora was.

Looking at Ken hurt Lora worse than the glare of the light had hurt her when she had first opened her eyes that morning. She had to blink, seeing Ken's face. There was cold anger and accusation there. Lora could stand that. He had no right to run her life, none at all. If only there had been accusation and anger, she could have flared at him, screamed at him, but his face was rotted with misery. He was sick and suffering. She could not stand that. She had no defense against his misery.

"Sneaking in like a goddamn thief!" Ken snarled.

Chris grabbed at his hand, but Ken shook free of her thin fingers.

He was still wearing his pajamas. He was wearing no bathrobe, and he had not combed his dark hair. It was standing on end. His pajamas were wrinkled, and he would have looked ridiculous. Now, the very fact that he did not care what he looked like, added to Lora's hurt. Ken was too sick to think of his appearance.

"Lora, honey," Chris said. "We've been so worried."

Lora ran across the room and fell beside Chris's chair. She ignored Ken. She had to ignore him. "I'm sorry," she muttered to Chris.

"Sorry?" Ken's voice growled at her. "How much do you think we can take? How much worry do you think Chris can stand? If you've got to go hotel-hopping with that grinning jerk of yours, you might at least call and say so."

"Please, Ken," Chris said. "I'm sure it's all right. Lora's all right. Give her a chance. She'll tell us all about it. Won't you, honey?" Chris's voice was soothing.

Lora began to cry, her teeth chattering. "I had to work, Chris."

"Work!" Ken yelled. "Back in Council Falls we used to call it fun."

"Ken, stop it," Chris said. "You've no right."

"I did work," Lora whispered.

"Don't lie, liar!" Ken shouted at her. "You had a date with laughing boy Elliot. You know damned well you did. You went out of here. You went with him."

Chris caught his hand. "Darling, everybody in the place will hear you."

"Let 'em. If this wonderful sister of yours starts running the streets, how long you think it'll be before everybody in the place knows?"

"Ken, please stop!" Lora begged. "I did work." She could feel Chris's slender fingers caressing her hair. "I had a date with Arty, but he said that he had this friend who knew of an open date at a club in Elizabeth–over in Elizabeth–"

"What club?" Ken said.

Lora felt her heart drop. She remembered hearing about the Sylph Club from some singer. She named it.

Ken was silent, but he was withdrawn, she knew, waiting. He was sure she was lying, and he was going to trap her in her lie.

"I sang. Arty was there with me–"

"I'll bet he was."

"Ken, please–!" Chris's voice shook.

"He was there, and I sang. You can ask him," Lora flung at him.

"And you can bet I will, sister," Ken growled.

Lora felt as though the bottom had dropped out of her stomach, out of her world. "I had three shows. One was late, very late. Two o'clock. It was too late to come home, so–"

"So you and Laughing Boy went to a hotel. What hotel, Lora. What hotel did you go to?"

"Chris, please make him stop. I haven't done anything."

"I know you haven't, darling. Ken, you've got to stop. You're upsetting her. I've never seen her so ill."

"You never saw her lying so fast, either."

"Now, Ken, stop it," Chris said. She patted Lora's shoulder, her voice apologetic. "You've got to forgive Ken," Chris said. "We were up all night. We were so worried. Of course, Ken's upset."

"We're waiting," Ken said to Lora.

Lora could feel the whole room spinning around in front of her. Ken and Chris danced and bobbed crazily out before her eyes. The world tilted, and she was afraid she was going to fall. It was in her stomach, though, where the worst agony of all was whirling and forming into a round mass of pain and nausea.

She struggled up on her knees. She slapped her hand over her mouth and tried to run.

Ken grabbed her arms. Fiercely she shook his hands down, twisting away from him, her haggard eyes hating him.

"Ken!" Chris cried.

Ken dropped his hands to his sides and stepped back. Lora pushed by him, feeling her stomach churning. She was going to be sick, sicker than she had ever been in all her life. Miraculously she made it to the bathroom.

Lora stayed there on her knees, unable to get up. She was going to be ill the rest of her life.

Chris, who had moved to the bathroom door to bar Ken's way, was crying. “If I could only do something– If I could only help you.”

Lora only shook her head, too ill to speak.

“Take off your coat,” Chris said. “Take off your coat, Lora.”

Lora, even through the waves of nausea, knew she could not do that. If she took off her coat, Ken would see her ripped dress. He would see the telltale scratches on her arms. She shook her head weakly, violently ill again.

“I’m going to call Dr. Simmons,” Chris said. “I’m going to make an appointment for you. I don’t know what’s the matter, but even if it’s your nerves, you need medical attention.”

Lora shook her head, kept shaking it. If only they would go away and let her alone.

“I’m going to call him,” Chris said. Her voice was determined.

Chris pulled on the wheels of her chair, turning herself around. She started across the room.

Lora turned her head. She saw Ken. He was starting toward the bathroom. She knew he wanted to help her, and she knew he was expert. He had been tending Chris for two years. But Lora did not want him near her.

She jumped up, slamming the bathroom door. She turned the key, and then sank down, laying her fevered face against the cool, sweet tile.

Chapter 7

Lora’s appointment with Dr. Simmons was set for three o’clock that same afternoon. She sat in his reception room, asking herself over and over why she was here.

There was only one reason. Chris had made the appointment. Chris would not take no for an answer, even if Lora could say no to her.

Lora’s mouth twisted with bitter self-recrimination. No, she could not hurt Chris, could not say no to her. All she could do was love Chris’s husband, lie with him and take his kisses and his passion, all behind Chris’s back. She knotted her fists in her lap.

The nurse spoke to Lora twice. She was deep in thought, she had to jerk her head up and stare at the girl in her starched uniform. Lora found herself wondering, *What’s on this girl’s mind? What thoughts is she hiding behind that spotless frock?*

Lora wondered if the nurse’s life was as uncomplicated as the serene expression on her face? Was anybody’s? Or had the nurse learned to wear her face like a mask, during business hours only? Lora shook her head, trying to clear her mind of such thoughts.

It must be a marijuana hangover, she reasoned. She felt ill, terrible.

"Dr. Simmons will see you now, Miss Cassel," the nurse said. There was an edge of impatience on the cutting side of her voice. How many times had she spoken to her, Lora wondered? Twice? Three times?

"All right." Lora tried to smile, but the smile was a failure. She started toward the door to Simmons' office.

"This way, if you please," the nurse said.

Lora followed her into a small dressing room. There, the nurse got a fresh hospital gown from its sterile wrapper. "If you'll just undress and put this on," the nurse said.

Lora looked at her, frowning.

"Your sister said you wanted a complete checkup," the nurse said. "If you'll hurry, please."

Lora took off her dress and removed her underthings. This was all wrong, too. It seemed that her life had become a bad dream, an endless nightmare in which everything continually worsened.

She slipped her arms into the gown the nurse held out for her. Then, barefooted, Lora padded after the girl through another door. The floor in this small room was tile. It felt good and chilled against her feet. There was a white-covered table.

"If you'll lie down, please, Miss Cassel," the nurse said.

Lora lay down, and the nurse fitted her feet into the stirrups. Lora let her gaze wander around the office. Sterilizer, instrument cases, light in dome reflector. The light reminded her of a TV studio. She should not be here. She ought to be out trying to find a job. *Hurry, doctor. Get this test over with. I've got to get out and keep my face in front of the TV people. If you're out of their sight for more than five minutes, they forget you. They talk about wanting talent, but they won't let you demonstrate any talent. They look at you and decide, she's pretty. She couldn't possibly have talent. Pretty woman. Pretty women are a dime a dozen. Get her out of here. Hurry, doctor!*

Lora looked up, and he was there. The doctor was smiling at her and asking, "How are you, Miss Cassel?"

How are you, Miss Cassel? I'm fine. Wonderful. Would I be here if I felt like bandying words with you? No. I'm here because I didn't even feel like bandying words with my sister, Chris.

Lora had seen Dr. Simmons a few times before, always at the apartment when he came to see Chris. Chris was crazy about the doctor.

Lying there, Lora looked at him critically. He did not look like so much to her. Just another very tired young man.

The nurse shook a sterilized sheet out of a cellophane container. Lora listened to the crinkle as the nurse wadded the cellophane and tossed it into a wastebasket. Then she listened to the sibilant whisper as the white sheet was spread over her.

She wondered what was the sheet for? To pull over her face in case she became embarrassed during the examination? She knew she was not trying to be difficult. She knew what was the matter. She was scared. She was afraid there might be something wrong with her. She was so frightened that there was nothing left for her to do but scoff.

At last it was over, all of it. They had samples of every kind of fluid in her body, and he had counted her heartbeats and measured her pulse. There was no part of her with which he was not by now more familiar than she was.

Dr. Simmons was sitting at a small white desk. Lora had not noticed this desk before. She sat up on the table, completely tired.

"Could you come over here?" Dr. Simmons asked.

She nodded. She thought she could make it.

She sat down beside his desk, conscious of the brevity of her hospital gown. How belatedly she became modest, she thought. She knew what was the matter. She was still nervous, and she was more frightened than ever.

"What is it, Dr. Simmons? What's the matter with me?"

"You're in pretty good health. No sign of any heart irregularity, as in the case of your sister–" he said.

No. I have my sister's heart, and I've taken her love from her to mate it.

"There is something wrong?" she whispered at him.

The doctor frowned at her, sitting back in the small chair. "You mean you haven't suspected? Miss Cassel, I can't believe that you didn't have any idea what was the matter."

"I didn't have. What's the matter?"

"You're pregnant."

"I can't be!"

He smiled. His smile did not help much. It did not make him look happy. It made him appear only slightly less tired.

"I don't know why you can't be. All the signs I spent years learning to look for are quite evident. Of course, it could be a Florida orange, but I don't think so."

Sweat had broken out across her forehead. Her mouth sagged open. "But I can't be pregnant."

"Why? Because you're not married?"

"How will I tell Chris?" Lora moaned. "What will I do? What will I say?"

The doctor's tired smile appeared again. "Ah, then you are willing to concede that perhaps–just perhaps–you could be pregnant."

"Dr. Simmons, please don't joke. This is serious."

"I don't doubt it. But it needn't be world shaking. It's not far along. From what you've told me of your cycle, and from my calculations, I'd say not more than two months."

"Two months!" She could hardly speak.

"Well, give or take a little. You examine your own recent past, Miss Cassel. Maybe you can come up with a more accurate estimate. But my point is, that I'm sure your young man will marry you."

"He can't." The words tumbled across her lips before she could stop them.

Dr. Simmons did not smile. He looked a little more tired than ever. "He's already married?" he asked quietly. "Is that why he can't marry you, Lora?"

She nodded. There was no use adding to her lies, not here.

He shook his head. "A beautiful girl like you never was left without more opportunities than one."

"You–mean–just marry anybody?" Lora stared at him.

"I'm not suggesting anything. As far as I'm concerned, whether or not you're married won't affect the birth of your child. I was thinking about the effect on you–psychologically. In our present culture, childbearing is undoubtedly easier on the mother if she's married. That's all."

"Do I–have to have it?"

The doctor sat there, waiting. He drummed his pencil on his desk. He did not look at her.

"Can't you–? There's an operation, isn't there?"

"Yes. But I won't do it."

"Why not?"

"It's illegal. It's dangerous–and I think you'd make a good mother."

Her voice cracked. "A good unmarried mother. I'd be wonderful. I won't marry just anybody. I've got to work. To work I've got to have a figure. I can't have a figure and a baby. I can't get a job looking like a barrel.... Please, Dr. Simmons. In the name of mercy. It's nothing to you, and if I beg you, if I tell you my life will be wrecked unless you help me, won't you please be merciful? Won't you understand that I can't have the baby? It's hard enough getting work–"

"I still won't do it."

Lora felt the tears brim in her eyes. She tilted her head, refusing to let the tears show on her cheeks. "I'll find somebody," she said. "I'll find somebody who will."

He tossed his mechanical pencil on top of the pad he had been filling out. He sighed heavily. He put both his hands against the edge of the desk and sat there a moment, staring at them. He nodded. "All right. You can do that."

She got up from the chair. She walked woodenly out of the room. She knew he was still sitting at his desk. He had not moved. The nurse was not around to help untie the bows at the back of the gown. By the time Lora got out of it, she was crying openly.

Chapter 8

Chris was sitting in the front room in her wheelchair when Lora came in dispiritedly and dropped her hat and purse on the table.

Chris was waiting, smiling, expectant. "What did Dr. Simmons say, Lora? What was the matter?"

Lora shrugged. "Nothing."

"Nothing! As sick as you were?"

"I was just upset. That's all he said, Chris." When you started lying you could never stop, could you?

"Something you ate?" Chris pressed.

Lora could not restrain the bitter smile that tugged down at her mouth. "Just my nerves, Chris. I'm going to be all right."

She turned her face away. There was a lie with no future in it. How long before Chris–and Ken–would know what was the matter? They would be able to see what was wrong with her. Well, she would not think about that now.

Lora smiled at Chris and went across the front room to the small extra bedroom which had been hers since she had followed Chris and Ken to New York.

She sat down on the side of the bed. She could not face what was ahead, here in this apartment. When Chris found out the truth, she would want to know who was Lora's lover, and that Lora could never tell her.

Ken would know, but it would only add to their guilt. This was something that had started because they had been drawn together irresistibly. She had fought against it, and it was like the overwhelming pull of a fast current. The more she fought, the more helpless she was against its strength.

Lora got up and went to the window. A few people were moving along the sidewalk. Two boys were throwing a rubber ball and screaming. Behind her, there was silence in the apartment, and Lora knew that Chris had not moved. Chris was sitting perfectly still in her wheelchair, worried and anxious about Lora.

Lora cursed sharply under her breath and heeled away from the window. She got her suitcase from beneath her bed. She tossed it on the spread and opened it. Then she went to the bureau, opened the drawers and started taking her belongings out of them.

No matter what cruel and dishonest things she had done to Chris until now, she was not going to put her sister through what was ahead for her. Lora could take it alone.

She had gotten into it without any help from Chris, and that was the way she was going to get out of it. Cheating Chris with Ken was one thing. It was an act of passion, of desire that overwhelmed her. No matter what other human beings thought, Lora could not believe that God would hold that against her.

As long as she stayed on here, though, she stood between Chris and Ken. Now her baby, too, would come between them. Lora knew she was the woman who could wreck their lives. The other, passing affairs of Ken's that Lora knew about did not matter. They were an escape from his life as Chris's male nurse.

The affair between him and Lora was much more than that. Lora was right there in Chris's home, and all this time she had been telling herself there was nowhere she could go.

She met her tear-brimmed eyes in her mirror. Would she have gone even if she could? There was no answer to that. It did not matter. She was leaving now.

"Lora." Chris had pulled her narrow wheelchair through the bedroom door.

Lora turned from the mirror, leaning against the dresser. She felt the blood rush out of her face, leaving her pale.

"Lora, what are you doing?" Chris gasped.

"Chris, I can't stay here any more. I'm a burden to you." More lies! More lying! But she could not tell Chris the truth. "I've got to get away."

"Darling, you can't leave me," Chris wailed. "Not feeling despondent, the way I know you do. I'd worry. It makes me all ill inside to think of your going."

Lora moved her head back and forth. "Please, Chris! Don't ask me to stay."

The wheelchair came nearer. Chris's face was stark. "Lora, what's the matter? Is it something I've done? Have I hurt you, or failed you, that you can't tell me the truth any more?"

"You haven't done anything. There's nothing to tell."

"Then why are you leaving, Lora? You're not in any trouble?"

"No." No. *Not yet*. Lora wanted to get out of Chris's sight before the truth gushed out. She could not hold back much longer.

"Then you must talk to me. Put your suitcase away. Put your clothes away. There's nothing so wrong that we can't figure some way out of it."

Lora gestured helplessly. "I'm just tired, Chris. I know I'm not going to make it here. I haven't–haven't got what it takes. Please don't lecture me. Let me be honest with myself at last. Maybe I'd make a good waitress somewhere, or a curb hop, or maybe I could polish up my typing and get a steno job. I don't know. I don't know what I'm good for, but the things I've been trying are all wrong."

Chris caught her hand. Chris's voice was soothing. "You've been trying too hard, and worrying too much. You're all tense. No wonder you're upset. You're going to take it easy for a while. You're not going to answer any telephone calls, or call back, or go tramping out looking for work. Ken makes enough that he can take care of us. If he doesn't, he'll have to make more."

"I'm not going to make Ken support me."

"He'll want to. What kind of monster do you think Ken is? He loves you, Lora–just as I do. We want you happy. You're not a burden–not unless you run away, and make us worry. Why, last night, Ken couldn't sleep. He paced the floor all night. He was worried sick about you. And I was, too. What would we be like if we let you go off somewhere alone?"

Lora did not know when Ken had come in. She was aware of him first, without seeing him. She knew he was standing in her doorway behind them. She was aware of his presence in the room–the way she always was, the way she always must be.

He did not speak. She did not turn to look at him, and yet his face was clearer before her eyes than her sister's face in front of her.

Lora knew. She was not going anywhere.

Ken slipped quietly into Lora's room that night, shortly after Chris had gone to bed. Lora was not surprised when he came. She had hoped he would, hating herself as she longed for him.

"Lora–" he whispered, dropping down beside her. "Chris told me, baby, about you wanting to leave here. Don't, Lora. Don't ever. I'll follow you, no matter where you go. It'll kill Chris, too, if you do."

He stroked her hair gently, soothed her flushed cheeks. Lora's senses flamed at his touch, but she made no move, said not a word.

"Let's forget what happened, Lora," Ken said. "I get so crazy jealous when I think of some other guy–!"

"Don't Ken! There is no other. You know it."

"You're so lovely, Lora. You can't blame me. Don't blame me, honey. Understand me–and don't run away from me." His tone was deep, throaty with emotion.

Ken drew her closer and kissed her. Lora could not fight him a moment longer. She did not even try. She knew the inevitable outcome every time her conscience and her emotions for Ken came into conflict. Ken won every time.

Lora abandoned herself to the pleasure of the moment. She needed this so badly, to be loved, to be treated tenderly. She had taken such a beating from life. She forgot about her qualms, forgot about Chris and all her other problems. She just reveled in Ken's love.

When Ken left, hours later, Lora was assailed, as always, with stabs of conscience, as she thought of her sister. Poor, dear, sweet, trusting Chris. Of all the men in the world, why did it have to be Chris's husband? Why couldn't she have found someone else, anyone else at all in the world?

The sobs caught in Lora's throat until they pained unbearably. Slowly the tears came, bringing only a slight release. Lora buried her face in the pillow and wept until exhaustion won out, and fitful, restless sleep came.

Chapter 9

It was a hot night. The heat came up from the walks and from the bricks of the street. People hung from their windows in their underclothes, like fish gasping out of bowls.

Even in her lightweight frock, Lora was uncomfortable, but she could not blame all of it on the weather, not even the unseasonable heat.

She reached the small village basement cafe and went down the steps. Inside, she saw four men beating out a nameless rhythm, and the devotees were crowded in, against the wall, speechless, numb with whatever thoughts the music conjured in their whirling minds.

Arty was already there. He had a table, and when he saw her come in, he stood up, grinning, and waved to her.

He pulled out her chair for her, and weary and hot, she sat down. She started to speak, but she could tell by the faint frown on Arty's brow that he did not want to talk.

She sighed and sat there, feeling the music hitting against her like giant breakers against boulders on the shore. She closed her mind to its strange, numbing effect.

She glanced at Arty. The smile was gone, and his eyes were faraway. She shivered. Arty lived for nothing but emotional kicks. He worked at the TV studio for one reason, to be able to afford the jolts he felt he needed.

He repelled her. She knew she did not like him. She never had, but before it had been merely a passive distaste that had been groundless.

She had not meant to see him again. She had been sure that the night in Pete's apartment would be the last time she would ever see Arty. She knew now that most people on marijuana got on jags, similar to whiskey, but the people at Pete's that night had purposely gone past that.

Except for Arty, for those people the joints had lost their first kick. They were trying to get the last ounce of jolt from the sticks. Maybe they knew that when they moved on to opium or heroin they were lost forever. Maybe they were trying to keep from admitting that by blowing the joints until they rode out of the world on goofy clouds.

Arty himself was a horrible little man. She had not wanted to see him, but what she wanted was no longer important. It was now a matter of what she needed, needed badly.

The music died on a blue wail that was like a nail scratching across a blackboard, unless you were deep in the spell of it.

Lora sat with her hands clenched in her lap, tense until the sound died away. As there had been the other night, there was a hushed silence when the music ended, and then the place went wild with applause. The musicians seemed not to hear the applauding. They were unaware of the people out in front of the dais. They set their instruments at their sides and dissolved from the small stage without even looking forward across the crowded room.

Arty came back to earth slowly. "Hello, Lora. How are you?"

"All right. How's everything, Arty?"

"Straight, hon. Been meaning to bleep you, but I had no time. Had no time. Things are slow at Taylor-Webson."

"I didn't want to see you about a job, Arty."

He smiled. "I know. I was just wiring you up on the latest. If anything turns, I'll bleep you."

"Arty, is there some place we can talk?"

Arty looked around. "Why not here? We're as alone here as we could be in New York."

The waiter came, and Arty ordered highballs. When the drinks arrived, Lora noticed that he only toyed with his glass. Arty never took more than a sip at a time.

"I want to ask you something, Arty. A favor."

His smile was uncertain. "Sure, hon. Anything."

"It's–about a friend of mine, Arty."

He looked relieved. "Somebody you want to take up to Pete's?"

She wished it was that simple. She saw now that Arty thought she had called him just because she needed the kicks that he could arrange for her at Pete's.

She looked down at her sweated hands. "No. It's something else. You see, this friend of mine, this girl I know, is in trouble."

"The minute you're born a dame, you're in trouble."

"Arty, listen to me. It's serious. She's going to have a baby."

"Tell her to get married."

Lora shook her head. "I did–but she can't. The man–he's already married."

"Like I said, the minute you're born a dame. Trouble."

"Arty, she's got to get rid of it."

He stopped smiling. "It's that bad?"

She nodded. "But she can't find a doctor who'll do it. I thought about you. You know so many people, so many things."

He shook his head. He touched his tongue to his lips. "But a butcher medic." He shook his head again. "I don't know, Lora."

"Please, Arty. There's nobody else I can get to help."

His eyes narrowed. "Why is it so serious with you?"

She spread her hands. "Like I told you, Arty. It's a dear friend of mine. She's going crazy. If she has the baby, she'll lose her figure–almost a year. Her figure is important. She–she's a model. We–we've done a lot of work together. You know how important a figure is, Arty, and besides, she can't tell her family."

"All right, Lora. You sold me." He did not smile. "I don't know anybody–but I guess I can find out for you."

She clutched his hands, tears spilling from her eyes. "Thanks, Arty, I won't forget it."

He remained cool. He still did not smile. "It might take a day or two, Lora. I'll call you. A day or two. That won't matter in a thing like this."

"No."

No, just two more days in hell. Not knowing. Two days. No. It didn't matter at all.

Lora climbed the stairs to Pete's place. She counted the floors. One, two, three, four. She was sure she would turn back. She had just come down here to prove to herself she had the will to resist. She could walk by the place, and it did not matter. She could climb the stairs, and still go away without giving in. Five. She was on the narrow fifth floor corridor. Her steps dragged, and she had no will. It was as though she was standing aside, watching herself knock at Pete's door. But she could not stop herself.

The door opened, and Pete stood there. He looked more sinister and unclean than ever. The lines in his face were lines of evil. When he smiled, he was not smiling at all. He was laughing at her.

Pete did not speak. He jerked his head, beckoning her inside.

The room looked the same, except that the blinds were up, and the people were gone.

"Hello, Lora."

She tried to smile. "I was in the neighborhood."

"Sure, Lora."

"I wondered–"

"How many you want, Lora?"

She shook her head. "I don't know. Could I just stay up here for a little while? I won't be any trouble."

"Sure you can." He went across the room and unlocked the cabinet. He brought back the small, flat pack. He opened it, extended. "Help yourself, Lora."

She took two in her trembling fingers. He told her how much they cost. She smiled, pleased because they were so inexpensive, and she paid him.

He returned the pack to the cabinet and locked it. She watched him drop the key into his vest pocket.

He led her across the living room and opened the bedroom door. It was darker in there. The blinds were drawn. She could hear the vibrant hum of the air conditioner.

"Make yourself at home, Lora."

She nodded. He closed the door. She pulled off her hat and dropped it with the purse on the bed. She looked at the cigarettes in her hand.

If she wanted to, she could crush them in her fist. She shook her head. She did not want to. All she wanted was to buy a reprieve from time. She wanted to forget for a little while. A couple of days, Arty had said.

She could not stand to wait a couple of days. She found a match, lighted the cigarette, tasting it on her tongue.

She walked around the room. She began to be afraid. It was not going to help. Nothing was going to help.

She went to the window. It was wide. The blinds were closed tightly. She tilted one of them and peered out into the sunlit street. She could see a dozen pigeons roosting on the building cornice across the street. She shivered, dropping the slat.

She smiled. He had been silly, that Boyd Collins, the singer, the pigeon. He had been a hateful thought in her dreams, but suddenly she remembered him with kindness. Not even Arty seemed so bad. And Pete. He was vicious, sure, but there was a place in the world for people like Pete, just as there was a place for pigeons. Somebody in this wide world needed them. She needed them.

She was going to be all right. She turned slowly in front of the gray mirror. There was not the slightest sign yet that she was pregnant. There would never be any sign. Two days, Arty had said. Two days, an operation, and her troubles were ended. Hell, her troubles were over, right now. There was more courage in one little stick than in an army.

She swung away from the mirror. The cigarette was just a stub in her fingers. She went into the bathroom and flushed it away. She came back and picked up the other one.

She would save it. She did not need it now. She felt perfect. She felt wonderful. She felt too good to stay in this dark room.

She opened the bedroom door. Pete was sprawled in a club chair. He was reading some thick volume, and he was playing some classical music on his radio console. The sound was rich and low in the room. It was not what she wanted. She wanted life and excitement.

Lora saw Boyd Collins then. He was lying on the divan with his legs crossed. His shirt was open. He looked pale and ill.

She smiled at him. "What's the matter, Boyd?"

"Sick," he said.

"Broke," Pete said coldly from the top of his book.

Lora was bewildered.

"Pete," Boyd's voice cracked. "I'm asking you like a gentleman. Open that cabinet. Just one joint. That's all. My God, we're friends. I've paid you plenty. I don't want to take the key away from you, but I will. So help me God, I will!" Boyd's voice was ragged. He sat up, his hands trembling.

"Go to hell," Pete said without rancor.

Lora looked at Boyd. She felt good, too good. She could not stand to let anyone be so miserable when she felt so good. She fumbled in her purse. She found a dollar and pressed it into Boyd's trembling hand.

She glanced at Pete. He was looking at her, nostrils distended. He said, "Sucker."

She only laughed. It was so silly. It was all so silly.

She started toward the door. Boyd did not even thank her. She looked back over her shoulder. He had flung the bill in Pete's face. For the moment they had forgotten Lora. They stared, their faces cold with hatred.

She shrugged and walked out.

Lora rode a subway. She watched the skaters at Rockefeller Center. She wanted to skate, but she knew that if she did, she would get going swiftly, and sail right over the top of the tallest building. She wanted to laugh aloud at that idea, but she was clever. She had never felt so clever in her life. She knew if she laughed, she would attract attention. She only smiled, quirking her lips a little.

She kept the laughter bottled up inside her. But she was roaring. Inside. Where nobody would know–but where it mattered.

It was about three o'clock in the afternoon when she got back to the apartment. She let herself inside, wanting to dance lightly around the front room, but she knew better. She had to play it cagey. Chris would suspect. Chris would know something was wrong. Lora had been basement-low, and now she was higher than stratosphere. Chris would know how Lora had been when she left here, and she would see that Lora was delirious now.

Chris was sleeping, her afternoon nap. Lora smiled to herself as though this was some magic plan that she had worked out in advance.

She tiptoed into Chris's room. She moved by the bed. She almost bumped the wheelchair. She studied the pad where Chris kept the call backs and the notes. It was bare.

Lora started to turn away. The telephone bleeped behind her, and she jumped, trembling all over. She grabbed the instrument off the hook before it could scream again. She wanted to laugh. It had startled her so. It had scared her silly.

"Hello," she whispered.

"Miss Lora Cassel, please."

"Speaking."

"Miss Cassel, this is the Taylor-Webson agency. We have a female bit part in a production now shooting. Mr. Taylor warmly remembers you. It's a speaking part, but it must be filled immediately, this afternoon. You understand, of course, it's a replacement, but Mr. Taylor asked that we try to get you."

A job, a speaking part. If she got a part like that, they would have to remember her. Even the great Ron Taylor would have to be aware of her. She smiled. It came through the agency. It was not something Arty had arranged. They had remembered. They had called.

Sweat poured off her forehead into her eyes. Her hands were trembling, and her legs felt weak. She was sure she was all right, but she knew that she could never coordinate well enough to follow Ron Taylor's quick-fire direction.

"I'm sorry," she whispered. "But Miss Cassel has an engagement this afternoon. I would appreciate it, though, if you'd tell Mr. Taylor thanks, and have him call again. This time, though, I'm just too busy." Lora held her breath, waiting for an answer.

The girl started to say something else, but Lora dropped the receiver back in its cradle. She had to hang up. In another moment she would accept that job. If she went up to Taylor-Webson in her present condition they would laugh at her, and she would never be called again.

Just the same, she had lost a job she needed, and pay for which she was desperate. She thought about the other cigarette. She needed it now, badly. She could smoke it in the bathroom. Nobody would know. She resisted. Told herself no. It was much too soon. She must not give in too easily. There was the danger.

At least she had known better than take that job in her goofy condition. She smiled. She still had that much sense, anyhow.

The letdown came later for Lora, and it was bad, very bad. She regretted the lost job opportunity and worried herself sick about it. She could use the money, definitely, but more important–would they bother to call her again? She became so depressed that she could think of nothing after a while but another stick. Getting another stick. Until she slipped into the bathroom quietly and locked the door.

Chapter 10

Lora came awake from a dream. It was a sad little dream about a baby. She was watching it die, and she could not do anything to stop it. She wept in her dream. She went everywhere, trying to get help, only nobody would help her. She woke up with her cheeks wet with tears.

Her bedroom door was open. A faint shaft of light glowed from the night light in the living room, the light they kept burning for Chris. That light got all mixed up in Lora's mind with Chris's chances to live. That light had to burn. Lora awoke at night sometimes, going to the living room to be sure the light was still glowing.

Ken was standing beside Lora's bed now. He was looking down at her.

She caught her breath, shaking her head. "Go away," she whispered. "Go back to bed. Let me alone, Ken."

He sat down beside her. He put his arm about her. His hand was chilled against the bed-warmth of her body.

"What's the matter, Lora? Why are you doing this to me?" His voice was ragged, tormented.

"Doing what?" She tried to twist away from him, but her flesh seemed to adhere to his flesh. All the pleasant sensations in her body were confined under his gentle hand.

"You know what you're doing. You're trying to break it off with me. Aren't you? Answer me, Lora. I want an answer."

"It's got to end sometime, Ken. You know that."

"I don't know it. It's never going to end. I'm going to keep you with me until–" His voice stopped abruptly. She caught her breath waiting, but he did not say it. He exhaled sharply. "Until I can have you. And you know it."

"No, Ken. We're cheating Chris. We have no right."

"No right? Look at you. You're going crazy right now, aren't you?" Ken kissed her fiercely.

"You drive me crazy. I can't help it."

"You need me, Lora. Why try to fight it?"

"I don't need you. I don't need anybody. I want you, but I don't need you."

"Don't you?" His laugh was harsh. He pulled his hand from her and she felt herself grow cold as he moved away. She caught his arm, stopping him.

He laughed at her. "You do need me, don't you?"

She turned her face away.

She felt him come closer to her. "Say it, Lora. Say it. Say you need me."

She could hardly breathe. She turned her face back to him. "I need you," she whispered. She sobbed. "I need you, Ken."

The wail of the telephone wakened her the next time. She was alone, but the impression of Ken's body was still beside her. The good, compelling scent of him was there, too.

She got up, hurrying to answer the telephone in the living room. She picked up the receiver, glancing at the table clock. It was ten o'clock in the morning.

It was Arty.

"Lora. Arty. Say, the great Taylor was pretty upset when you didn't show yesterday."

"I'm sorry. I couldn't."

"He blew his stack. Why not?"

"I–" She looked over her shoulder at the closed door of Chris's bedroom. "I had been to–to see Pete, Arty. I was not in shape. I couldn't."

"Oh." She could not tell from that single word what Arty was thinking.

"Well, I got to run, kid." Arty said. "But I found out the man you wanted. You know– For your friend."

There was no question about what Arty meant now. He was not deceived. He knew there was no friend.

"Thanks, Arty. What's his name? Where can I find him?"

"Better meet me at lunch time up here near the garage, Lora," Arty said. "I'll give you all the dope on this guy."

"Sure, Arty." Nervously she settled the details of their meeting, writing down the address of the restaurant he mentioned on the memo pad. Then, assuring him she would be prompt, Lora hung up.

Just as she started back to her bedroom the doorbell rang. She got her negligee, and went to the front door, tying it about her.

She opened the door. It was Dr. Simmons. It was time for his morning call on Chris. She looked at him, feeling the blood suffuse her cheeks.

Simmons smiled at her. He looked tired. His blue-gray eyes were heavy-lidded. Probably he had been out all night, she thought. She did not envy a doctor, no more than she did a TV actress.

"Hello, Lora. How are you?" His tone was gentle, not reproving as she had expected.

"All right."

"Have you done anything yet about–?" Still he was not harsh.

"No." She shook her head, glancing at the closed door. Chris might be awake. "Not yet."

"I wish you wouldn't, Lora. I know a place where you could go. You could work until you didn't feel like it any more. Then you could leave your baby until you were able to care for it, or these people would place it for adoption. The very best–"

"I can't! And please, don't say anything to Chris and Ken about this."

"Haven't you told them?"

"I couldn't. Not yet." Her whisper was tense.

He smiled crookedly and glanced down at the front of her negligee.

"How long is nature going to let you keep your secret, Lora?"

She shook her head. "I don't know. But I'm not going to tell them until I have to. There's–there's no sense worrying Chris. She's got her own troubles. Please, Dr. Simmons, promise me you won't tell them."

He shrugged. "You're no longer my patient, Lora. I've no right to tell them. If you were my patient, I would tell them, and I'd get them to help me make every possible move to assure your safety and good health."

"Then thank God you're not still my doctor."

He smiled, shrugging. "I'm still your friend, Lora. If you ever need me."

The doctor started across the room, his shoulders round. He was so tall, so thin. His medical case seemed to weigh him down. He glanced over his shoulder. "Is Chris awake yet?"

"I don't know."

"It doesn't matter. I'll waken her. I like to see a woman smile when she wakes up in the morning, and Chris always does."

"We can't all be saints."

"No," he agreed. He was at Chris's bedroom door. He smiled again. "Be careful, Lora. Whatever you do, be careful."

She looked at him, but she did not answer.

Lora dressed and slipped out of the house, murmuring some story about an appointment at the agency to Chris.

Lora rode the subway uptown and waited anxiously in front of the restaurant for Arty. She was more than twenty minutes early.

When Arty finally arrived, Lora could scarcely wait until they were seated before she asked him, "Will it be all right, Arty? There–there wouldn't be any trouble about his taking care of–my friend, would there?"

"It's simple, kid. The guy's name is Dr. Klausmiller," Arty said, handing her a slip of paper with the doctor's name and address on it. "You don't have to tell him anybody sent you. Just go in. That's what this guy said. Klausmiller got into some trouble once, and about the only practice he gets anymore is the kind that you said your friend had."

"Thanks, Arty," she said. "I won't forget this–ever."

As she was leaving him, later, Arty said, "Good luck. To your friend, I mean. And, Lora, fly right, kid. That was a speaking part they called you about. When they call you, it might mean something. Keep yourself ready."

"I will, Arty. I promise."

Chapter 11

Pete opened the door for Lora. His eyes glazed over at the sight of her. He jerked his head, motioning her in, and then he closed the door behind her.

"You're getting to be quite a frequent guest," he said.

"What do you care? I pay you, don't I?"

"I don't like too much company, Lora. I thought you had sense enough to understand that."

"Maybe I won't come back."

"For Heaven's sake! You still talking like that?" He gestured. "A party or an occasional visit is all right. I don't think I'm being watched, and I don't want to be."

"I thought you wanted to sell the stuff," she said.

"You want to buy a pack?"

"Where would I keep it?"

"That's up to you. You've got to be smart to stay alive. I'm being smart when I tell you to stop coming up here so much."

She bit her lip. "I can't buy a whole pack this time."

"Bills getting scarce, baby?"

"No. I'm all right. It's just that I need what money I have with me this morning–for something else."

"You don't need anything else worse than you need a pack." Pete said coldly. "I'm telling you I don't want to see you around here for a week. It ain't that I don't like you. I do. But if we're going to stay friends, I got to stay out of trouble."

She gestured. "Sell me–sell me ten?"

He nodded. "All right. I even got an empty pack I'll put 'em in for you."

"You mind if I blow a joint right now?" she said.

"Here?"

"I'm on my way to something. I need courage."

He shrugged. He opened the cabinet, counted out ten sticks, put them in a pack, closed it and brought it back to her. He took her money in exchange and stuffed it into his coat pocket.

She lighted one with trembling fingers. He went back to his club chair and sat down, watching her.

"You're gone," he told her. "You're real gone."

She puffed quickly, nervously. "You're crazy! I'm all right. I can stop–any time I want to."

"Sure you can. Anybody can."

She felt nauseated, but she knew it was going to be all right. Her feet felt lighter, and her body felt lighter. Soon she forgot the way Dr. Simmons had looked at her before he went into Chris's bedroom. Now she was ready for Dr. Klausmiller. Lora felt she was ready for anything.

"See you." She gave Pete a salute.

He did not look up. "But not too soon."

The address Arty had given Lora was on an aged and rundown side street. Gutter peddlers called at her as she pushed by them. People bumped her without seeing her. Old men and old dogs sniffed and poked at battered garbage cans. Children with old, pinched faces stared at her, like masks in a nightmare.

Lora was sure she had made a mistake. She looked again at the slip of paper. Then she looked around and saw a small, faded sign behind a closed ground-floor window. She started up the steps. She could read the sign. Hans Klausmiller, M.D.

She stepped through the opened doorway. The hall was dark leading back into the dank, smelly recesses of the house. There was a large, old-fashioned buzzer on Dr. Klausmiller's door which Lora pressed hard, and fast, feeling she would turn and run, unless the doctor appeared instantly.

That moment, the door was flung open by a middle-aged woman who motioned Lora in. Lora's knees felt watery, and she was afraid they would not support her the rest of the way into the room.

The doctor was standing in the shadows. She could not see him except that he was a round man in his vest, sleeves rolled up and collar open.

"Dr. Klausmiller?" Lora asked, her voice shaking.

"Come in, Madam." They were all madam to Dr. Klausmiller.

She stepped in the room, and he closed the door behind her. She heard the snick of the lock.

The room was gray. The doctor limped across it and turned on a reading lamp over his old-fashioned roll-top desk.

She caught her breath, staring at him. Lora would have been willing to believe that he was some image conjured up by the joint she had blown at Pete's. He looked as old as the street he lived on. Paralysis had struck his left side, leaving it pulled down. His shoulder sagged, and his left eye was closed, although he kept trying to open it. His mouth pulled downward in the left corner.

He sat down at the desk, and motioned her into a chair beside him. "What's your name, Madam?"

"Mrs.– Brown."

He nodded. That satisfied him. He met a lot of Mrs. Browns. He wrote it at the head of her chart.

Dr. Klausmiller asked a few more questions pertaining to age and medical history, then he set the chart aside.

There was a thermometer lying open on his desk. He picked it up and shook it. He told Lora to open her mouth. She stared at the unclean thermometer in horror. He seemed not to notice. He thrust it between her teeth and under her tongue. She thought she was going to gag.

He held her pulse. He looked at the watch on his wrist. She stared at his fingernails. They were dirty, his hands unwashed. She felt her heart racing.

He looked up, trying to force his left eye open. "Have you been on narcotics long?"

Her eyes brimmed with tears. She shook her head.

He removed the thermometer from her mouth. "No use doing this now. It won't tell us anything. How long, Mrs. Brown?"

"About two months."

He nodded. "Are you prepared now?" he asked.

"How bad is it?"

"Pretty bad. You should have brought somebody along. You'll have to go home in a taxi."

"Couldn't I stay here? At least overnight?"

He shook his head. "I'm sorry. No."

She was glad she had blown the joint. She wished for another one. She was going to need plenty of courage.

"Come this way," the doctor said. He got up, and she followed him through a door to a kitchen.

She stared at the smoked and blackened room. This was not real. It was a nightmare. She began to shake her head.

"I can't!" she gasped. "Infection. I might die."

Klausmiller's voice was hard. It was without sympathy. "You won't die. Death is too easy.... I know."

She shook her head, too terrified to speak at first. Then the words gushed out. "I've changed my mind. No! I've changed my mind." She turned around and ran back into his cluttered office. She clutched up her purse. She had to fight at the lock to get the front door open.

Dr. Klausmiller came and stood in the kitchen doorway. He stared after her. He did not say anything.

Lora ran down the steps and kept running along the street, her purse clutched against her roiling stomach. She could see the old faces around her, staring and leering, watching her run.

She slowed down at the corner. She closed her mouth, forcing herself to breathe through her nose, as she went down into the subway kiosk.

She stood on the platform, waiting for the train to rumble in. Well, she had failed that. Not even all the false courage she could summon was enough to save her.

She felt depressed and physically exhausted. Whatever the effect of that marijuana cigarette had been, it was gone. Had there even been any effect?

Well, she had ten more in her purse. They would save her. Ten sticks was all that stood between her and the shakes. They would save her. Either they would save her, or they would blow her straight to Hell.

Chapter 12

Lora was crying. She was alone in her bed, and she had no idea what time it was. She did not care. Time and clocks were in a conspiracy against her, anyhow. Each long hour seemed an eternity as she tried to live through it, and yet the weeks were speeding past.

She was beginning to show. Chris still did not suspect, because Lora's being pregnant was the last thought in Chris's mind, but how much longer was it going to be before Lora's condition would be apparent even to Chris?

None of that, however, was the reason for Lora's crying. The last two sticks, the life saving marijuana she had bought from Pete, were gone. Not only the ten. They had been gone days ago, weeks maybe. She did not know any more. She had gone back to Pete. She had not been able to stay away. He had warned her that he was not going to let her in the door the next time she came if it was within a week.

Pete was frightened for some reason. He wanted her to buy in quantity, and she could not afford it. She had had only one job since her visit to Dr. Klausmiller. Her nerves had been shot. She had managed to get through the single job at the photographer's studio, and he had thanked her. He had said nothing, though, about having her come back.

That was new. Men always made a fuss over her. They had at every job. They made extravagant promises, even if they were never able to keep them.

Her pride was hit, but more to the point, her money was low. She was not down far enough that she would take Chris's money for narcotics. She twisted her head on her tear-stained pillow. *Not yet!*

She had a final and more terrible reason for her tears. The joints gave her nothing any more. If she smoked too many of them, she became nauseated, but there was no more release from the pressures around her, no goofy dreams, no laughter bubbling inside her.

What Pete had said about her was true. She was gone. She was really gone.

The bedroom door opened slowly. She saw that it was Ken. Her heart raced. She dragged her crooked forefinger under her eyes, wiping away the tears.

"Baby?" He sat on the bed beside her. "Are you awake?"

"I'm awake."

"I just came in. I heard you crying."

"I wasn't crying."

"Don't lie to daddy. I heard you. What is it, honey? What's the matter?"

There was no thought of resisting him tonight. It never even occurred to her to try to send him away. How she needed him tonight!

Loneliness. She caught her breath, wondering how she could have stood the awful loneliness another minute. What would have become of her if Ken had not walked through that door?

Loneliness. Didn't that explain everything she had ever done? If people only knew how many tragedies started from there, from the empty, crying need for somebody to care about her.

She had somebody to care. She was all right now. She had Ken.

"Come on, beautiful," he whispered. "Tell me what's the matter."

She pulled herself over and lay her head in his lap. She put her arms around him. "Don't talk, Ken. Please don't talk. I don't want to talk."

He laughed, massaging her scalp with his fingers. "Well, this is a hell of a note, isn't it? Maybe I'm getting old, but it just so happens, I do want to talk. I want to talk to you, baby. About you."

"There's nothing to talk about."

"There's you."

"I'm nobody. I'm nothing. Without you, I'm nothing."

"Well, so many girls tell me that. You'll have to do better."

"Please, Ken. Don't tease. Just love me."

"I'll love you. It's one of the wonders of my life that I should even hear a girl lovely as you begging me to love her."

"I love you."

"All right. Prove you love me. Tell me what's the matter? Why have you been so miserable these last few weeks?"

"There's nothing wrong, Ken. Nothing I can talk about."

"Have I fouled up your life, baby? Is that it?"

"Without you, I couldn't live, Ken."

His voice hardened. "Then what's the matter? You're driving me nuts, sweetheart. Don't you even realize, Lora? Even when I'm in this room, right beside you–in this bed with you, with my arms around you, you're staring past me. You're thinking about something else. Okay. If you don't love me, that's okay. But you say you love me. So what gives?"

She pulled back the covers. "Love me now, Ken. I promise I won't stare. I won't think about anything but you.

She watched him bite his lip, but he slid his arms around her. She could feel her heart slugging so hard it ached in her bosom. But Ken was angered, and no matter what she did to please him, that anger persisted like a shadow in his eyes.

Lora's brief moments with Ken were like finding shaded oases the size of quarters in a desert that engulfed her whole world.

She went uptown to her agent the next morning. He was sorry, but there was nothing for her. Advertising men were screwy. There was one demand that was never filled. New faces. Lora was not a new face any more. He did not say it in so many words. It was worse. He implied it. Lora had been around too long.

As she started from his office, the man stopped her, his voice worried. "Honey, you ain't beginning to let yourself go, are you?"

She stopped as though he had struck her in the small of her back. She looked over her shoulder. "Why?"

He shrugged. "Well, a doll like you–there's always a chance–an opening. Just keep your fingers crossed."

"Why did you ask if I was letting myself go?"

"Well, I hate to say it, hon, but aren't you putting on a little weight?"

Her face colored. She could feel the backs of her legs go weak. Somebody had noticed. She was really beginning to show....

There was no sense in going to any of the other places Lora usually called on when she was uptown, not with the feeling inside her that even casual observers in the street could tell that she was putting on weight. It was better not to be seen by the experts than to appear unfavorably.

Lora started across the street toward the subway. A small white banner caught her eye. The odd name attracted her first, and then she stared.

The banner was soiled with street dust, and with some justice, streaked by the pigeons. Still there was his name in large red letters: "All this Week–BOYD COLLINS, The Voice With the Throb of Violins. Six Shows Daily."

She stopped in the middle of the walk, staring up at the banner. She walked over closer. There were photographs of Boyd Collins, smiling, singing, selling a song.

Lora smiled. At least Boyd was working.

She felt someone grab her arm. Startled, she turned. It was Boyd.

"Admiring me, sweetheart?" he said.

"You look lovely," she said, nodding toward his pictures.

"No matter what I look like, I'm working."

"I'm glad." She smiled. "What do the pigeons do, without you to watch them?"

"Honey, I'm convinced those pigeons don't care if anybody watches them or not. Those fellows live every day like it's their last." He took her arm. "Come on in. We'll talk."

She smiled and entered the club with him. They went down six steps and through a single door that opened on a round foyer which was overcrowded with the doorman and hat-check girl.

Beyond the foyer was a bar, the length of the left wall. Three-quarters of the place was filled with white covered tables around a dime-sized dance floor and bandstand.

"Near the wall," Boyd told the headwaiter.

The man led them to a table for two. Boyd told Lora to order like it was her last day on earth, but she was too upset to eat. She ordered a white-turkey sandwich. Boyd ordered sweet pastries.

"I've been looking for you," he said.

"I'll bet."

"I'm serious. I have," he insisted. "I have tried to find you. I asked Pete where you lived, but he didn't know. He didn't even know your last name."

"Cassel."

"Lora Cassel. How do you do? Well, I went uptown, and I found Arty Elliot. I knew you came to Pete's that first time with him, but Arty wouldn't tell me anything about you. You know I don't think Arty approves of me."

"Maybe he remembers how you scratched me up and ripped my dress the first time you saw me."

"I scratched you? Ripped your dress? You're way off, baby. I wanted to.

I remember it was in my mind, but I got too tired. Right in the middle of it all, I got sleepy."

She stared at him. "That's the way I remember it, too. But the next morning, my dress was torn, and my arm was all scratched."

He shook his head. "You had company during the night, kitten, or I've got rocks in my head. I hated myself, but I didn't touch you." He shrugged. "But that gets us nowhere. What's new with you? What have you been doing? How have you been getting along?"

"Not good."

"Have you–been to see Pete?"

She shook her head. The waiter put the turkey sandwich before her. Boyd plopped a pastry in his mouth.

"No. There's no kick for me, Boyd. Just when I needed it, there was nothing there."

He smiled and leaned toward her. "I got there, too, baby. It took me longer than it did you. When I started with the bands, I took a pod now and then, so the fellows would think I was hep. I never went for them. Then my luck turned sour That's when I started big. It took the place of success. Pretty soon I was down to where I couldn't even buy the things any more. You saved me one day, but I knew I wasn't going to get anywhere like that."

Her heart speeded up. Here was a man who had gone through the hell. He had found the answer, the way out. She put down the untouched triangle of sandwich. "What did you do, Boyd?"

He smiled at her. "I found out that blowing the joint was kid stuff. That's what I did."

"How'd you break away? What did you do?"

"Honey, when I moved up, it was like graduating. The whole world changed. I got this job. Outside, it says, all this week. Hell, I been here almost a month. And baby, what it did for me, it can do for you."

Chapter 13

Boyd's apartment was very nice. You entered through a small, new-smelling kitchen. The bathroom was beyond that. The front room was half-dinette and half-living room. It had two small bedrooms, and Boyd told her that the living room couch opened up into a bed. This was living, he told her. He could throw a ball now whenever he felt like it.

Lora could feel her heart thudding against her ribs. The first thrill of expectancy that she had felt at the supper club with Boyd was gone. She had thought at first that he had gone off the grass, stopped smoking marijuana. Gone square. What a lovely sound that had to Lora.

She knew better now. All Boyd meant was that he had grown up. Sticks were kid stuff. Now he was on H.

Heroin. Even the name had a sick kind of fascination for her. She would have said goodbye to Boyd there in the club, but he looked better. Thinner, but happier. His eyes had life. He was working regularly, making money.

He seemed to have an answer, and that was what Lora had to have. An answer, a way out.

Boyd gestured around the room. The drapes were solid colors, and had an expensive look. The furniture had been chosen with care. Has Boyd found the answer, she wondered.

"As long as I keep working," Boyd told her, "I'm all right. I'm up to here with payments, but I'm cooking now, kid. From the first jolt, I knew I was going to be all right. I was living again."

"What if–if you can't quit, Boyd?"

He shook his head. "I don't want to quit. Hell, I'm hooked. I'm good and hooked. But as long as it pays off, I'm not beefing. When I get low enough, I don't want to breathe, but I can't stop breathing. A jolt makes it easier. That's all."

She wandered around the room while Boyd went into the kitchen. In a moment he returned, and set out on a table before her fascinated eyes the paraphernalia that goes with drug addiction. He kissed a small package in his hand. "My life," he whispered, grinning at Lora. "Probably be my death, too, some day, but now it's my love, my caps."

He went over and dropped the Venetian blind to the sill. He closed it. The room went gray. He snapped on the light. "The pigeons don't care if I watch them," he said. He grinned. "But I don't want them watching me."

Lora knew better. Like every addict, Boyd lived in continual fear of surveillance. The worst part of his nightmare existence was the ever-present terror of being busted, caught and removed from his life-giving caps.

His only protection lay in secrecy. He had to hide. It was not enough that narcotics officers suspected him. They had to catch him with the stuff, or find him using it, or they had no case against him.

"It's okay with me," he said. "It's worth it. I really go for a jolt. They wanta run my life. They wanta tell me what I can't do. Okay. Let 'em tell me. I want to go to Hell my way, not theirs."

Lora had not moved. She was standing still, staring at the implements

Boyd had spread out on the table. She did not want to jolt–no matter what Boyd said. She had seen them, when they got hooked. They were derelicts, hopeless derelicts. There had to be some other way. There must be some other way out for her.

Boyd was looking at her, smiling. "Come on, Lora. Give in. I got the secret here, the life. That's all you got to do. Get started. You're all right, once you get started."

She shook her head. "I'm scared, Boyd. Once I get started. What if I get hooked?"

He looked sad. The smile wavered. He was not trying to be smart.

His voice expressed his own hopelessness. "They all say it, honey. They all say they don't want to. They don't want to get started. They don't want to get hooked. I said it. Hell, what a laugh! All the time I was saying it, my mouth was filling with saliva, and I was empty-bellied. Because all the time I knew that I was hooked. I was already hooked. Hell, baby, I was hooked the first time a guy handed me a pod and I blew a joint. I didn't even want to that time. I didn't even need to. Hell, I was just being sociable."

"It isn't true," Lora whispered. "It isn't true. That's what Pete said about me, but it isn't true."

"Come on, Lora. You did me a favor. You saved my life. I want to do you one."

"No, Boyd, I can't get started. I'm almost broke now. What if I got started. What if I had to have it? I couldn't buy it. I'd go crazy."

He came closer to her.

"Honey, you forgot about me. I'm a punk. Sure, I'm just a punk. I never was anything else. I grew up in the gutter 'cause my old man walked out on Mom and me. Mom worked so much that, hell, half the time I had to look at her twice to be sure I knew her. I grew up looking out for one cookie, Boyd Collins. But you ask anybody, Boyd never forgets a favor. And what you did for me that day when I was nuts up in Pete's place, well, that put you up front in my book. Long as I got it, baby, it's yours. You just take– You don't even have to ask."

She touched his arm, thanking him. "You're a good character, Boyd, but while I'm off it, I better stay that way."

He shook his head. "You're not off it, baby. You're just low. That's all. Take a jolt, and you'll feel better. You'll know you're better than anybody else. How do you think I got my job? I looked down my nose at this guy, and I sang for him, and I knew I had it. Hell, I felt superior. I was superior. He couldn't say no. He knew I was right."

"Okay. But I'm scared. That's why I can't."

"There's nothing to be scared of. It's easy. Look, Lora." He shrugged off his coat. He rolled up the shirt sleeve.

Lora caught her breath. His arm was white as a slug, and rail thin. She could see the small telltale pricks and scratches.

He did not notice how thin his arm was. He was unaware of the scars.

Boyd was crusading now. There was light in his eyes, and there was life about him. "Look, Lora. It's easy. Not only easy, it saves your life. Maybe the first time you upchuck. So what? Afterwards you feel even better. Maybe because there's nothing but good old Charley inside of you then."

"No!"

"I'm not asking you, baby. I'm going to show you."

Before Lora's horrified eyes, Boyd took a cap of heroin from the small box. He was a chemist, a scientist. He was careful. He was taking his time, although anxiety showed in his eyes. His mouth was twitching a little, but his hands were rock steady....

It was over. He was smiling now. Boyd walked around the room. He told her he felt wonderful. "Three or four times a day now," he boasted. "Hell, I know guys that jolt six times a day, but they're hooked, real hooked. I'm not like them. I got it under control. Control. That's what I got it under. Con-con-control. Sure. Know when I need it, and that's all, see. Maybe right now–maybe I wasn't low, but I want you to see how it picks–how it picks you up. Boy, it picks you up. Picks you up. Wonderful. Feel wonderful. You feel wonderful. But you don't see any change, do you? And I don't talk–talk different. Do I talk different? You're damned right I don't. That's why I been wanting you to know–know about this, Lora. Long as you can–con-control it, you got the world."

She could see it happening in his eyes. They were glazing over. His mouth was getting loose. She knew what was happening. She was seeing him go to pieces right in front of her, but he did not believe it. He would not believe it. He was up high. Man, the world was wonderful.

"I can't!" she cried. She was illl, just looking at Boyd.

"Sure you can!" Before his voice had been soft and gentle. Now there was a raging edge to it. He hated her now because she was a square.

"I must run," she said. She touched his cheeks with her lips.

He caught at her. "You won't snitch, Lora?"

She was shivering. She shook her head, and he relaxed visibly. She ran from the apartment, feeling him watching her with his glazed eyes. She knew. Never. She would never jolt, not even the first time.

Chapter 14

Dr. Simmons did not look astonished to see Lora at his office. Maybe he had been surprised when the nurse told him that Miss Cassel was his next patient, but he did not show it when she walked into his office.

The room was spotless. Everything looked polished and new, in sharpest contrast to Dr. Klausmiller's place. Everything, except the young doctor, was bright-looking. Long hours and little sleep were playing havoc with him.

Lora hid the wry smile she felt at the sight of his weary face. Brad Simmons ought to see a doctor. If she did not know him better she would think he was on dope himself.

"I'm back," she said.

He told her to sit down. "I was sure you would be. I was counting on your innate goodness and good sense to bring you back, Lora. People who have those qualities can't fight against them successfully. They can only try."

Lora did not smile. She did not thank him. "Don't count on that too much with me," she warned him. "I'll tell you the truth. This is easier. It was easier to come back to you than to go through with the–the other." She shuddered, remembering the filth and decay of Dr. Klausmiller's kitchen.

"Anyhow, you're back. It's a month since you were last here, and that's as soon as I would have had you back anyhow. So let's just forget the other part. We can forget about you for a while and concentrate on a healthy baby, huh?"

She shrugged. "Looks like we'll have to."

His smile was tired. "A happier outlook would be fine for a starter."

"I don't know where I'd get that," she said bitterly. "This baby means that my figure will be gone–maybe forever. I don't work until after it comes, and maybe they won't want me then."

"I have news for you. A woman isn't really beautiful until she's had a child or two. They're really matured then, really beautiful. Before they're nothing, they're children, playing with dolls. And then they're women, lovely and finished."

"Finished. I can go along with you on that."

He smiled. "Wrong word. I meant complete. You take care of yourself, Lora, as I tell you, and after you've had your baby, you'll be lovelier than ever. And you'll have something you must have wanted, or you'd have never taken that gamble."

She shook her head. "Maybe I was crazy."

He shrugged. "Maybe. But now the way out of it is to go through with it. Isn't it?"

"You're the doctor."

He smiled again. "Well, you're refreshingly different, anyhow. You should see the young expectant mothers that I usually get. They're simpering, grinning, young fools who think it's the first time it ever happened. They want you to agree they're goddesses or something because they're pregnant. A joyful young mother can get a little stale."

"You don't believe that, but you're working like hell to convince me you're on my side."

He laughed. "You do me good, Lora. It always refreshed me to go to see your sister Chris, and in a different way, it does me good to know you. Maybe I'll give you a special rate, or something."

"I could use that."

"What I've been thinking, Lora, is this: Suppose you go to this private hospital for about the last three months. It's out of town, upstate. You work as a nurse's aide, dietitian's helper, in the laundry, the sewing rooms. You can even work in the garden–anything you choose to do. Whatever you do, it helps pay your way up there. They have a nursery for the baby when it comes. The child can stay there while you're waiting to land a job. Of course, you don't have to use the nursery. I'm sure Chris and your brother-in-law will want you and your baby with them–"

"Sure–a screaming baby in the apartment. That's all Chris needs."

"Okay. You decide. You leave the baby up there while you get a job, and a place to take it. Or, and all my advice is against this, you don't have to see the baby, Lora. They'll take it, and place it for adoption. You'll know it has a good home, but you don't ever even have to see it."

She stared at him. She felt as though the bottom had dropped out of her stomach. Not wanting the baby now was one thing, but to have it, and never see it. She felt her eyes brim with tears.

"You don't have to decide any of these things now," Dr. Simmons said. "Don't let them worry you now. First, have you told Chris and Mr. Hunter that you're pregnant?"

"No."

"Well, you want to do that. A slender girl like you usually gets as big as the house. There's no use trying to conceal what's happening to you. They'll want to know. They'll want to help you."

Her voice was bitter. "They'll raise hell, and I won't blame them."

"I know your sister, Lora, and I think you're wrong. But right or wrong, you've got to tell them."

After a few more words of advice and comfort, Dr. Simmons led Lora to the door. She turned to him, and said, "Thanks. Maybe I can sleep tonight. I can use it."

The supper club where Boyd Collins sang his six shows daily was called The Lowdown. It was listed in the smart New York magazines. It offered tasteful decor, good food, and a floor show.

Boyd's first show went on at five in the afternoon. Three days after she had been to Dr. Simmons' office, Lora was at the Lowdown.

She asked the headwaiter to take a note back to Boyd Collins. The man showed her to a small table and went away. He said that Mr. Collins sent word that he would join her after his show, and in the meantime, anything she wanted would be brought to her as Mr. Collins' guest.

She ordered a cocktail, just so she would have some excuse for occupying a table during this busy hour.

The m.c. made a big thing of introducing Boyd Collins. The applause did not match the buildup. Lora sat and watched Boyd come out into the spotlight. They brought him a mike, and his singing was really an act with the microphone as his partner. It was his love, his confidant, his confessor. Boyd was the sobbing-type ballad man. The voice with the throb of violins was really a weepy cello.

Lora could not tell if Boyd had a good voice or not. His singing was all an act. Maybe nobody sang any more. Just as books could be hits without a hero to admire or respect, with only weepy, sad and frustrated little characters afraid of their own shadows, a singer got in front of present-day audiences, and bellowed, or bawled or sobbed.

When the exhibition was over, Boyd joined her at the table.

He did not ask her if she liked his singing. He did not mention it. She saw that he was real gone. His eyes were glazed, and he did not really look at her. That was fine for now. How long was he going to last like that?

"Hello, baby." His voice was low and intimate. Maybe it was the coo he had learned from mating pigeons. "Four whole days. You stayed away longer than I thought. Want to go up to my place now?"

She caught her breath. He was not fooled. He was not going to pretend he was. "All right," she shrugged.

He grinned at her, triumphant. "Got another show at eight," he said. "I'll make it easy."

He signed a tab, and they left the Lowdown. They got into a taxi in front of the club, and Boyd sat back beside her, laughing. "They signed me for another drag. I don't know how long it'll last. I ask no questions. I just have fun."

She bit her lip. "You looked a little rocky up there, Boyd. Hadn't you better take it easy?"

He laughed again. "Don't preach. You can't take it easy. You take it the way it wants you to take it. Haven't you found that out yet, baby?"

"I'm not going on it," she said. "I'm not going to get hooked."

He turned his head, looking at her. "You're not? Why are you here? What do you want?"

"Just once. Just this once," she whispered. "I've got something I've got to do. I've got to tell my family something–something I don't want to tell them. It's something they don't want to hear, either. I've got to have something inside me–something I haven't got. Courage. I went back to Pete, and I tried sticks. I get depressed, and that's all I get."

"This will fix you, baby. A jolt will fix you. You won't be afraid of anything."

"That's what I want. That's what I've got to have."

Strength. That was what she needed, the strength and the courage to face Chris and Ken, especially Ken. He would yell and rage at her. It was more than she could take. She had promised Dr. Simmons that she would tell Chris and Ken about the baby, but she had delayed, hour after hour, day after day. He knew she could delay no longer. Dr. Simmons would visit Chris tomorrow. If she had not told Chris by that time, Dr. Simmons would tell them.

Damn him! Damn everybody in the world who would not let people live the way they wanted to.

Still Lora could not hate Dr. Simmons. He was thinking about what was best for the baby. He had told her a dozen times that it was time to start thinking about the baby.

It might have been easier if she was married, if she had planned for the baby, expected it, but that was not so. The pregnancy was a catastrophe. It was the worst possible accident that could befall her. It struck her career, her whole life. She could not think of it as a baby, a new life, as the doctor could. All she could see was a tragedy befalling her.

Lora had to tell Chris and Ken today. Marijuana would not help, and whiskey left her cold. She had known for three days there was one answer: a date with Charley, a good stiff jolt. Yes, the answer was in Boyd Collins' home.

Boyd let them into his apartment. He told her to make herself at home, and then he went across the room and let down the Venetian blind, closed it. He walked unsteadily.

"Boyd, when was the last time you've eaten?"

"Honey, I don't want to eat. You won't, either. This cap, that's all I need."

"You're looking like a scarecrow."

"Flattery will get you nowhere."

She opened the electric icebox. It was bare. She heard him laugh. He was preparing the equipment, fondling the cap of heroin.

"Come on, honey. This is where you graduate," he called out.

She pulled off her coat and extended her arm towards him. He touched her hand. "Like ice, he told her. "Relax. This is good."

"It better be good." She gritted her teeth.

"I'll fix you this one, baby," he said, "but it won't be long before you can do it yourself."

She spoke through her gritted teeth. "No. Just this time. I swear it. I swear it."

"Sure. Sure." His voice was placating.

Her eyes closed, and she bit her underlip as she felt a sharp, stinging pain.

At first she was sure she was going to be sick. She could feel the nerves in her stomach bunching up and a choking sensation in her throat. She sat down on a straight chair, her hand pressed hard against her mouth.

"Go ahead, kid," Boyd whispered. "If you're going to be sick, let it go."

She shook her head. She was not going to be sick. It took a few minutes for it to hit her. Boyd told her that he had given it to her right mainline, perfect.

Her feet felt light, and she felt giddy. She wanted to laugh. She felt as she had the first time she had tried a joint in Pete's apartment, only this was much better. It lifted her up out of herself, way up, out of reach of her troubles.

I can tell them, she thought. I can tell them because no matter what they say, it won't reach me. They can't reach me where I am now. And if they do, I won't care. Because up here where I am, nothing matters.

She wanted to dance around Boyd's apartment. He shook his head. "No time, baby, I got to get back. Got a big show this time. Wanta see it?"

"Sure. I wanta see your show. You'll be wonderful."

He was looking at her, thoughtfully. "Maybe I better hit it," he said. "I don't wanta let down in the middle of a show. That's all that ever worries me now, that I'll let down in the middle of one. I want to stay up high. I'm up there where I can look down on those people listening to me. Up where

I am, I can see 'em liking it, see 'em eatin' it up. That's where I want to stay, high, up high."

She wandered around the apartment while Boyd fixed a cap for himself and took a jolt. He put everything away, very carefully. It seemed no matter how high Boyd sailed, he never forgot to clean up.

"Gettin' busted. That gives me the horrors. I'm a kid that's gotta stay free," he told her.

She took his arm, and they went out of his apartment, laughing.

The Lowdown was crowded when Lora and Boyd got back there but Boyd got her a table. He was imperious. He would not take no for an answer. He was wonderful, and when he was on the floor, he laid them in the aisles. He really put on a show. He was gone, real gone.

Lora stayed for three more shows. The time was nothing. She was not even aware of the passing of time. She was not aware of the people changing, coming and going. She was up there high with Boyd, looking down on the people who came into the Lowdown, the jerks, the squares, trying to share whatever magic it was that Boyd Collins had. That was a laugh. They never could, because they did not know Boyd Collins' secret.

At midnight, she made up her mind that she could tell Chris and Ken. When Boyd came to her table, staggering slightly, looking starved, the circles under his eyes darkening, she told him she was leaving.

"Take care," she told him. "Get something to eat, Boyd."

"Eat." He made a face at her. "I don't need to eat."

Poor Boyd. She thought he needed her to take care of him. If only Ken were a little like Boyd, if only he ever needed her. But Ken was so strong. He took care of Chris, and he held his job, and he had his secret life that Chris did not even suspect, and that Lora could only guess at. Poor Boyd. If somebody did not help him, he was not going to make many more shows.

"Thanks, Boyd. Thanks for everything."

"I'll see you again, honey," he said.

"No. I'm not going to get hooked."

He shrugged, grinning at her. "If you change your mind, baby, I'm there. I'm always there."

Ken and Chris were up when Lora got home. She knew they were going to be. She was thankful for the jolt. She was ready now for Ken, ready for his accusations and his snarling contempt. There was no way for him to reach her now.

"I have something to tell you," Lora said. She laid her coat and purse across a chair very carefully, very deliberately. She felt as if she was floating, but she had to play it smart. She had to keep them from guessing. "But I won't tell you, unless you promise to be glad–unless both of you promise to be glad."

Ken said. "What's the matter with you? Are you drunk?"

Poor Ken. Poor dear innocent Ken. Drunk. That was Ken's idea of a ball. Get drunk and go out on the town with some bleached blonde. Poor baby.

"I'm not drunk. I'm all right," Lora said.

"Where have you been?" Ken demanded, his dark eyes glinting.

"Where have you been? Where have you been?" she mocked him. "I'm a big girl. I can go where I want to go."

"Lora," Chris said. "Ken's worried about you. He isn't trying to be cruel."

"Maybe I ought to be cruel," Ken said. "That's the trouble. She's been spoiled. All her life she's been spoiled. Now she's got the idea she doesn't have to behave."

"I behave. I'm as good as you are," Lora taunted.

Chris's voice was very soft. "Baby, we've known for some time there has been something on your mind. We want you to tell us. Maybe we can help you."

Lora laughed. It was a cruel and sharp laugh. She had no right to laugh at Chris like that. "All right," she said. Her voice was cold. "I'm going to have a baby."

Neither Chris nor Ken spoke. Chris turned white, even whiter than her normal light color.

Lora looked directly at Ken. His face, too, was white. She was startled. She saw something she had not expected to see. Ken was not going to yell at her. He was not going to doubt her, or accuse her. He knew. No matter how he raged at her about running around, he knew. Inside, he realized to whom Lora Cassel belonged, body and soul.

Lora felt her eyes fill with tears. Ken knew she loved only him. His raging at her was the only way he could express his misery at the wrong and confusion of their muddled lives. Poor Ken.

"Lora, baby," Chris whispered. "You–you're–going to have a baby?"

Lora nodded, trying to blink away the tears, to camouflage them behind harsh laughter. "Yes. I wasn't very careful. That's what Dr. Simmons told me."

"And that's why you–couldn't tell us." Tears slid down Chris's white cheeks. "Who was it, Lora? He'll marry you, won't he?"

Lora tried to laugh again. Her face ached with the pain of laughing. "I hope you won't kick me out in the snow when I tell you. He can't marry me. He's already married."

"Oh, God!" Chris whispered. "But he must do something. He'll have to."

"I don't want him to do anything!" Lora's voice was defiant.

"Maybe you don't," Chris whispered. "But you have your baby to think about."

"Don't keep after her," Ken said.

"It's all right," Lora said. "Dr. Simmons has it all fixed. I'm to go to a private hospital some place upstate. I don't even–have to see the baby. Then–they'll put it out for adoption right away."

"No!" Chris breathed. "No, Lora, bring it here. It's part of you, darling. That makes it part of us. You mustn't feel alone, or feel that we won't help you."

"Chris is right," Ken could hardly speak. "You don't even have to go away, Lora. Whatever we can do, we'll do it."

Lora began to cry. "Why don't you yell at me?" she wept at Chris. "Tell me what I am. I know. I know. Pretending won't change it. Say it, Chris. I'm no good. You don't have to do anything for me."

Chris put out her arms. Lora fell to her knees beside the chair. Chris's voice was very low. "We're in this together, baby. All of us–all the way."

Chapter 15

Ken came into Lora's room about three-thirty that morning. Lora had lain awake for what seemed hours to her, and she must have just fallen asleep. She awoke with Ken caressing her.

"Wake up–mother," Ken's voice was soft. He was gentle. She had never heard him like this. Always before she had been a little afraid of him. He had great strength. Now she feared his gentleness. She could not say why, but she felt the stirring of panic, deep in her stomach.

"You're beautiful when you wake up," Ken said. "I wish I could be with you every time you wake up."

She pressed her fingers against his cheek. "I wish you would be." She could see the line of his square jaw harden in the faint light from the living room.

"Maybe I will," he said. His voice remained gentle.

The panic swirled faster. She could feel it like a real thing now. "What are you talking about, Ken?"

"About us. I've let you go through this alone long enough. I'm going to tell Chris the truth."

"Ken, don't even talk like that in this house! She might hear you."

"She's got to hear me. We've played enough hell like this. I'm going to tell Chris the truth."

"Played hell?" Lora's voice was full of awe. "Ken, how blind are you? If you think we've played hell before, just wait until you tell her. Ken, I can't hate us for what we've done until now. Maybe we've been wrong, but sometimes the pull between two people is stronger than a lot of laws and conventions–and even moral standards–"

"Stop the lecture, baby. It sounds like hell coming from a beautiful woman."

She pulled away from him. "You've got to listen. There might be some justification for what we've done, but there can never be any justification for telling Chris–making her see it–breaking her heart. Why, we'd be killing her."

"I've thought that until I'm nuts, baby. We can't help it. We've got to live. This is my baby that you're going to have. I can't go on standing around like a brother-in-law with nothing but thumbs on both hands."

"You won't have to, Ken. Just seeing you, just knowing you're near is all I need. If I didn't have that, I couldn't stand it."

"What are you going to do about the baby?"

"I'm going to have it. I've got to."

"And then?"

"I don't know, Ken. I don't know yet."

"Poor nameless little thing. Just because I haven't got guts enough to tell the truth."

She pressed her fingers over his mouth, hard. "Stop, Ken. Do you think it would take guts to tell the truth? What kind of courage would it take to tell poor little Chris that we've been faithless in her home for months? What could she do? How could she hit back? She couldn't. If we'd had the guts we talk about, we'd have stayed away from each other that very first time."

His hands caressed her hair. "There wasn't any first time, baby. There was just never any time when I didn't want you. During the day, working, I thought about you. When you were around, I saw no one else. I heard nobody else."

She pressed closer. "It was like that with me, Ken."

"All right then, damn it!" His voice growled. "You think feeling like that is something we just made up ourselves, like bathtub gin? Well, I don't. There's some reason behind it, and the only reason I know is that we belong together. We belong together like this."

She shook her head, tears spilling against his hand. "No, we don't. No matter how terribly we want each other, there's Chris."

"I'll take care of Chris. I won't walk out on her, but I've got to think about you–and about a baby that I'm responsible for."

"That's it. You're not. You're just responsible for Chris. You're not making sense, Ken. You're not thinking. Do you pretend to believe that Chris would let you take care of her after you told her about us? Even if she went on living, do you think she'd even see us?"

"I can't help it."

"There's nothing we can do, but go on as we are. If you told her, I'd hate you. If you ever let her find out the truth, I'd hate you."

"What am I to do?"

"Nothing. I was crazy about you. I still am. I got myself in a jam. I'll get out of it."

"You're not going to marry somebody else, Lora. I'm damned if you are. I'll kill you before I'll let anybody else touch you."

She smiled. He was like a small boy in the night. She put her arms around him. "I won't, Ken. Because after you, there is no other man. I couldn't."

"I'm going to take care of you, Lora. Somehow, I'm going to take care of you."

She kissed his throat. "Just hold me, Ken–for as long as we have, hold me. That's the way you can take care of me."

His arms went around her, pulling her against him. As always, her heart started pounding crazily at the touch of his hands. She pressed closer. It was as though she could not be near enough to him. No matter how tightly his arms held her, something was pulling her away from him–with an irresistible pull.

She was frightened. She was losing him, and she did not know how. She knew they loved each other more at this moment than they ever had, maybe more than they would ever again. Yet, it was as though she was already cold, because he was gone and lost to her.

Her mouth parted. Her frightened eyes were hungry, staring across his shoulder, trying to find what it was that was chilling her, even close in his arms like this. It could not be true. She could not lose him. Nothing but his love could save her from whatever Hell lay ahead of her.

The next morning at breakfast, Ken sat across the small kitchenette table from her. His face was set. His eyes were bleak.

"Ken, what's the matter?" She had to whisper. Chris was awake in her bedroom. She might be listening.

"Nothing. I've been thinking about what we talked about. I can't promise I won't tell Chris, Lora. No matter what I think, I keep coming back to that. It's what I've got to do."

"If you do, I'll hate you!"

He just looked at her. After a moment, he shrugged. He got up, shoving his arms in his coat. He kept his voice light. "So long, Lora. Got to run. I'm late to work now."

She did not look up. She sat at the table, motionless. She heard him in the bedroom with Chris. Then he went out the front door.

Now she was more afraid than ever. Ken would think all day. He would take a few drinks. He did not drink very much, and a few would be poison to him in his mood. What would happen when he came home like that? What would he say to Chris?

Lora tried to talk herself out of it. Ken was smart. He was intelligent enough to know that he might kill Chris if he told her the truth about himself and Lora. Still the nagging worry remained, the terrible anxiety. Did Ken care any more what happened when he told the truth?

Lora got up from the table, leaving her breakfast untouched. She went into the bedroom.

Chris turned up her wan cheek for a kiss. Lora touched her with her lips. Chris's flesh was cold.

Poor Chris. Ill as she was, she could not stand all this heartbreak. Tension and anxiety were as deadly to Chris as bullets from a gun.

"You mustn't worry too much, honey," Chris was saying. "A baby without a name. That isn't ever easy, but we'll make it as easy as we can. We don't know many people here. It won't be nearly as bad as it would be back in Council Falls. You couldn't keep a secret in that town. Why, they're like they live in the Dark Ages. I thought last night, Lora, that if anyone asks we can say you're married. Just say it. Your husband could be dead, for all anybody knows. You can say you use your name because unmarried girls have a better chance as models."

Lora laughed. "Unmarried mothers have a hell of a time as models–especially when they get fat."

"I've told you that you don't have to worry about a job."

"Ken has more than he can do, taking care of you."

Chris bit her lip. "I think we can manage."

Lora fell beside Chris's chair. "Oh, god, darling! I didn't mean anything by that–only that Ken has enough to do. He wants to take care of you."

Chris's voice was empty. "Yes. Of course, he does."

"He does, Chris! You never heard him complain."

"All right, Lora. Help me get ready. Dr. Simmons will be here soon. I've got to look pretty. It–it isn't every day a girl gets an eligible young bachelor like Brad Simmons to call on her."

Dr. Simmons was late. Lora's nerves were stretched taut by the time the doorbell rang. She practically ran from Chris's bedroom to answer it.

The tired young doctor dropped his hat on the foyer table. His dark hair was wrinkled over his forehead. He ran his hands through it. "Sorry, I'm late," he said. "Looks like everybody got sick last night, with illnesses ranging from migraine headaches to acid indigestion. Of course, they were all dying and had to see me immediately. I prescribed bicarbonate of soda and a psychiatrist at the last house."

Lora tried to smile. It was a failure. She was too tense.

He looked at her. "Have you told them?"

She nodded.

"It wasn't as bad as you thought it was going to be, was it?" he asked gently.

"No. They took it beautifully. I'm the one who's ready to blow my top."

"Remind me. I'll give you a sedative before I leave."

He winked at her, and for a moment he lost the perpetually tired look. He pressed Lora's hand in a gesture of approval, and walked into Chris's bedroom.

Lora stood there, listening to her sister and her doctor exchange compliments, thinking that Dr. Simmons was a very attractive man when he smiled. She supposed the doctor loved Chris as much as any patient he had. Chris had come to look forward to his calls.

The doctor brought her news, and gossip, and sometimes a new joke. Lora wished she could be like that, but she was all wrapped up in her own woes. It would be wonderful to get all unsnarled, and able to think about something else. What magic would work a trick like that?

She dialed Boyd Collins' apartment. The telephone rang a dozen times. Just when she decided that he was not in, he answered. His voice was odd, but when she told him it was Lora, he laughed.

"That was quick. Come on over, baby. We'll have a ball. I don't have my first show until five o'clock. I got all day to live."

Lora was trembling with anxiety under the shower. Nothing would go right. It seemed to take her an hour to dress. She went to Chris's door. Dr. Simmons was still there.

"I'm going out," Lora said. "I'll be gone all day." With that she heeled around, hurrying out before Chris could protest.

Boyd opened his apartment door for her the first time she rang. He had combed his hair and shaved, but he had not bothered to dress. His pajamas were expensive broadcloth, and his robe over them was a Chinese red silk. Boyd was living high.

He had everything laid out on the table. He grinned at her, his mouth pulling wide. "I had a hell of a time waiting, baby. I almost had one jolt while I was waiting for you. I feel low this morning, mighty low."

"You've got to take it easy, Boyd. You can't stand so many jolts."

He laughed, taking off her coat. He was hurrying her.

"When was the last time you ate?" Lora asked him, ashamed of her own eagerness, and trying to cover it by preaching to Boyd.

"Eat? I don't need to eat. I'm on top of the world. When you're on top of the world, you don't need anything but this–"

He handed her a cap. "You fix this one, Lora, and hit yourself. You got to learn some time. It might as well be now."

She hesitated, repelled at the thought, but then she reached for it, feeling she could not wait. She could not take time to argue with Boyd, to coax him. Sweat beaded her forehead. She tried but she could not do it.

Boyd laughed at her. "Here–I'll do it." She stared, fascinated. There was the red, swollen mark from yesterday. Now there were two marks on her arm, two notches.

The dope took effect on her quickly. She wandered around the apartment while Boyd fixed his cap. Almost before she could believe it was over, he was behind her, his arms around her, his hands caressing her.

"We need each other, Lora," he was saying against her hair. "I'm on top of the world. I got everything–except you. If I had you, they couldn't stop me. They couldn't ever stop me."

She turned, trying to twist away from him. "I don't love you," she said.

"Love?" Boyd was laughing at the word. "Honey, what we got is better. We got the craving. The hunger. We're a couple of gone kids."

"I'm not going to get hooked." That was some stranger saying that. Boyd was laughing at the stranger and Lora found her derisive laughter mingling with his. They were laughing at the stupid little square who thought she wasn't going to be hooked. They knew better. She was already hooked. She was already going with Charley. Steady.

The weeks whipped past like a fast ride on a roller coaster. Lora got by with Ken by refusing to talk seriously with him. That was easy. Heroin, her constant companion, made it easier. She felt high, and Ken's anger only made her laugh.

Ken was so funny. He never even suspected. It never occurred to him or Chris about H. Those two were simple, when you thought about it. They had come to New York, but they still lived the way they would in Council Falls. Addicts were something they read about in the Daily Mirror or the News. Addiction was not something that could happen in their circle, not in their family.

They thought she acted odd because she was upset and nervous about her pregnancy.

It was sad in a way, though. It was an empty kind of existence. Lora lived with Boyd Collins. He did not need her. He never really wanted her. Even that first morning she had gone up there. He had kept after her, and he had talked her into having an affair with him. Nothing had happened, though, because Boyd was without desire.

He thought she was wonderful, and he swore he wanted her. Yet it was all a part of the wild dream he was living. His desire was dead. Charley had killed it.

One morning, Lora put her head inside the doorway of Chris's bedroom. "I'm going out," she said. "I don't know what time I'll be back. Tell Ken not to wait up for me. I'm tired of fighting with him. I don't know what time I'll be in."

"Lora."

Lora had already started out of the apartment. She stood, feeling a hot flush of impatience. "All right, what is it?"

"You had an appointment with Dr. Simmons yesterday afternoon. A checkup. You didn't go."

Lora bit her lip. She had forgotten Dr. Simmons. "I forgot."

"Yes. That's what I told him. He said he wants to see you this morning. Before you go–before you go wherever it is you go."

"All right," Lora said. "I'll go there now."

She knew she had better go. She could let Simmons make his checkup, and she would not be very late. She smiled wryly. Boyd would not wait for her anyhow. He was crazy about jolting.

When she arrived at Dr. Simmons' office, the room was crowded. "I can't wait," she told the receptionist.

"Just a moment, Miss Cassel," the receptionist said. She spoke through the intercom. "Dr. Simmons, Miss Cassel is here, but says she can't wait."

Dr. Simmons answered. The receptionist nodded toward the dressing room. "If you'll go in, Miss Cassel." She smiled apologetically at the waiting people. "Miss Cassel works, and I'm sure you folks won't mind the few moments it will take Dr. Simmons to see her."

Lora went into the dressing room. She undressed hurriedly, slipping her pocked left arm quickly into the sleeve of the gown. The sleeve was short. She was sure that Dr. Simmons would see those red scars. Well, there was just one thing to do, keep her arm bent.

Dr. Simmons came in, The first thing he saw was the girdle on the chair. He picked it up and threw it into the wastebasket. "You leave that damned thing there when you go," he said. "And don't get another one."

He told her to get off the table and go to the scales. He weighed her, and the nurse marked the weight on the chart.

Lora went back to the table. She could hear the nurse whispering to Dr. Simmons. They were bent over the chart. They spoke to each other, glancing at Lora.

She knew she had lost weight. Despite the baby, she was losing weight.

Dr. Simmons came to the table. "Lie down," he told her.

He was apparently satisfied with the examination. He tossed the covers down over her and reached for her wrist. She tried to give him her right arm. He shoved it aside. He took her left wrist, counting her pulse. He did not look at her.

When he was through, he held her left hand in one of his, and with the other he slid roughly up her arm, all the way to her armpit. He brought it down again on the inside of her arm. He still did not look at her. His face was cold.

"I've got news for you," he said at last. His voice was hard. "You're going up to that hospital–now."

"Today?"

"Right now. We're going to your apartment and pack you a suitcase. God knows you won't need much up there. We're taking a train out of Grand Central as soon as we can make it."

Chris did not offer any objections. Whatever Dr. Brad Simmons wanted to do was perfect with Chris. He stood in the bedroom with Lora, supervising her packing. She was not alone for a minute.

She supposed he was waiting for her to attempt to hide caps or the hype in her bag. The joke was on him. She did not even own them. Or was the joke on him?

He did not even leave her alone long enough so she could call Boyd. She wondered if Boyd was waiting for her in his apartment.

Chapter 16

Lora waited beside Dr. Simmons for the train. She was beginning to feel low, cellar low, basement, cave, black pit. Her hands were shaking for no good reason.

It seemed to her that the people around them knew what was the matter with her. They knew she was drawn tighter than a fiddle string. She should be with Boyd now. She should have the life saving cap. Oh, God! She bit down on her lip.

From the corner of her dry eyes she stared at Dr. Brad Simmons. He was ignoring her. He seemed to be unaware of what was happening to her–purposely.

She looked around the crowded platform. Weren't the people looking at her, pointing, talking about her? What were they saying? They were looking wise and saying, "That girl's an addict, an addict, an addict. She's drawn all taut, and she's going to break down and go to pieces right here in front of us. Watch her. Watch her. Watch her!"

Perspiration broke out across Lora's forehead. This was a nightmare, another nightmare. Brad said something to her. She had to ask him to repeat it.

"I said, do you want something to read on the train?"

Read? Oh, God, no. She shook her head.

"We won't be on the train long anyhow," he told her.

Their train was called. They went with the crowd and boarded it. Dr. Simmons had bought tickets for the day coach. He was determined to keep her surrounded by people. What was he, some sort of devil, intent upon putting her through hell on earth?

"You mustn't think that you're unique in any way–in what's happening to you, I mean," Brad Simmons told her. "I've made this trip often, with other girls who thought they had the first trouble in the world."

"I don't think that. All I know is that it's the first trouble that has floored me."

"Maybe not. Most things have a reason for happening. I've found that out. Your baby might be the thing that will save you."

She knew what would save her–this moment. She thought about Boyd, lying in his club chair, dreaming. He needed nobody.

"I don't see how," she whined. "I can't work and take care of the baby, and yet I can't stand the thought of putting it out for adoption."

"You have plenty of time to think about that, Lora. You'll meet other girls riding the same boat with you. You'll get all kinds of advice. You'll work it out."

"It's pretty easy to say that, isn't it? It's my trouble, not yours."

He smiled wearily. "Honey, I was born with trouble. Want to hear some of mine? I was too poor even to attempt to become an M.D., but I was burning up with ambition. I went in hock for it. I studied days, and I worked nights. I wouldn't advise it for anyone, but I know what it is to be alone, and to think you're beat."

"I'm sorry."

His smile made him almost handsome. "Why should you be? You thought I'd never had a moment's trouble in my life. I had you fooled, didn't I? That's what you'll have to learn to do. Learn to fool people. There are only a very fortunate few who have a smooth time of it in this life."

Dr. Simmons' arriving with Lora made everything easier and smoother at the hospital. She was deeply grateful to him, through all her misery.

She had the idea that the place would be out in the country. It was not. It sat on the edge of a small, quiet town. The front of the building was flush with the sidewalk. The building was a squared U-shape, with grounds on both sides and extending down an incline to a brook. The inside was not pretty, and it looked old. The corridors were polished and spotless, but cold-looking.

Brad Simmons talked to her continually as they entered. The place was almost a shrine to him, and he wanted her to share his pride.

She could not. The sound of his voice stretched her nerves tighter and tighter. If they were going to keep her from the caps that would save her, she prayed that they would leave her alone. She wanted to go crazy. She would try to do all her screaming inside her mind but she had to start screaming soon. She could not stand it much longer.

Everybody was interested in her. At the reception desk, they asked her a hundred questions, and Brad Simmons let her answer them.

They went along the corridor then. The deeper they got into the hospital, the stronger was the odor of disinfectant. Lora pressed the back of her hand against her nostrils. The smell penetrated. She could feel her stomach roiling.

They had to wait for the elevator. They got off on the ground floor. They stood at a desk presided over by a Mrs. Mullins.

Lora looked right at Mrs. Mullins and could not say too clearly what she looked like. Lora got a vague impression of a tall woman with gray hair and sharp, bony shoulders. Mrs. Mullins had more questions than the receptionist. She asked Brad Simmons what he would suggest as Mrs. Cassel's tour of duty.

"She's young and healthy," Brad said. "She ought to be able to do almost anything. She's a singer, though, Mrs. Mullins. That's her profession. I think if you worked her in on the entertainment."

"Wonderful. Wonderful!" Mrs. Mullins beamed. "We never get enough good entertainers."

At last it was over. They showed Lora a room. It was a cell. Lora could feel the walls pressing in on her. Mrs. Mullins and Brad stayed for an eternity. Lora sat on the edge of her chair. She was not looking at them. In her mind she was saying over and over, *Send them away. Make them get out of here. I've a right to go insane in privacy.*

She knew that Dr. Simmons and Mrs. Mullins were standing in her doorway, talking about her, but she no longer cared.

Lora got up and wandered around the room. She stood at the small window with her back to them. Their voices were meaningless, anyhow. She could see lights below her in the streets. The lights wheeled and skidded crazily before her eyes.

They were gone at last. She knew without turning around. Dr. Simmons had not said goodbye, or indicated when he would be back. Maybe he had. She was too sick to know, too sick to care.

She turned and shambled over to the door. She ached all over. Her head ached, and her eyes felt as though they would burst out of her head.

She moaned aloud. She heard herself moan. She did not want to moan, but she was so ill she could not help it. She felt stiff and sore across her shoulders. She staggered to the bed and fell across it. She bit the back of her hand to keep from screaming.

Lora had heard about the withdrawal period. Whenever she and Boyd got around other hypos, the talk always turned to those who got busted and thrown in jail where they could not get a fix. That was the hell all the addicts dreaded. All of them lived in constant terror of being busted, and they knew that when they were caught, the police would let them die before they would give them even enough junk to help them through the agony.

Lora expected that from the police, but she was in a hospital. Relieving suffering was supposed to be their reason for being. Saving life was their alleged aim. Yet, they were letting her die in agony.

She heard the door open. She tried to lie still on the bed. She could not. It was as though she was lying on rocks.

Somebody spoke to her. She felt her arm being lifted, the sudden cold smear of alcohol, the sharp jab of a needle. She relaxed, falling against the pillow. They turned off the lights, and she lay there feeling the agony subside.

It was not junk that they had shot in her arm. She was sure it was a synthetic drug. It was the stuff they gave you when you started a cure. Still, it eased the agony, and she was grateful for it. After a while she slept.

Boyd Collins came up to see her the first Sunday she was at the hospital. They told her he was there, and she went downstairs in the elevator, wearing the drab, gray smock they furnished in the hospital.

Boyd was sitting in the waiting room. He was surrounded by the simple, ordinary people who had come to visit. In his own world, he seemed quite normal, but here, with his flared lapels, his colored shirt, tinted tie and his forty-dollar oxfords, he seemed from out of the world. His hair was plastered down, glistening with oil. His ears seemed more protuberant than ever.

He got up, grinning at her. "God, what a place!" he said. He shivered. "I get the creeps, man. The creeps."

"Let's go outside. We can walk," she said.

"Are you kidding? I walked all the way in here from the taxi. We can sit on the grass, though. I want to get out of this place. I can't stand the smell."

They walked together out in the sunlight. Boyd picked up his trousers and sat on the grass. She sat down beside him.

"Man, I had a ball trying to find you," he said. "I called your house, and some guy answered. I got nowhere with him."

Ken, Lora thought. Ken would not approve of Boyd Collins, not even over the telephone.

Boyd laughed. "I had to find out your doctor's name and call him."

Boyd looked around the yard, shuddering. "Man," he whispered. "I don't know how you stand this place."

"There's nothing else I can do."

"How about a fix? Can you get a jolt up here?"

She shook her head. "Nothing."

"You want me to bring you some caps, baby?" he asked.

"I couldn't keep them, Boyd. They watch me too closely. When I get down, they give me a shot of something that's supposed to take the place of caps."

She saw him shiver visibly. He glanced around, wishing he was out of there. "How'd you get up here? Why'd you come?"

"I went to my doctor for a checkup. He found out that I was losing weight. Even with the baby I was losing weight. He must have known I was on the junk. He didn't say anything, but he must have known. I guess he saw my arm. He wouldn't even let me alone long enough to call you."

"Yeah, man! I got the shakes, worrying about you. I thought you had been busted, sure. I didn't know how it could happen. I knew you didn't even own any caps, but that's the only thing I could think. You'd got busted, and there was no way for you to get word to me." His eyes traveled over the yard. "And that's just about what happened."

She tried to smile. "I've got to stay here until the baby is born."

"Man, that's bone yard talk. I don't know how you'll take it. You better let me try to get some caps to you. We could get to somebody–a nurse, or somebody."

"No, Boyd. I'm scared. I'm all right, except nights. The nights are hell. Maybe I won't even need a jolt any more when I'm out."

He laughed. "Baby, that's suicide talk. Why, if I couldn't have a ball, I wouldn't want to live."

"How have you been, Boyd?"

"Oh, up there high. I missed one show, one lousy, damned show. You'd have thought I burned the joint down or something, the way that manager talked. Hell, you'd think he couldn't serve his damned cut-liquor if I wasn't there to sing. I asked him, I said, 'How come if I'm such a big attraction I can't get a lift in stipend?' That stopped him. He started yelling about my contract. It was in my contract. Every show, six shows. Hell, all I missed was one lousy show."

"You've got to be careful, Boyd."

"Baby, I am careful. It was just that one time I couldn't see going down there and singing for those peasants. I had a ball, a real ball. Maybe I took a couple of extra hits that day. Anyhow I was all right. All right? I was wonderful. But I didn't want to sing. Hell, I didn't sing."

She touched his arm. "Boyd, you've got to be careful. If you lose this job, you lose everything. You won't be able to buy any caps."

His eyes darkened. "That ain't going to happen to me, baby. Never any more. When I get low, I'll find a way to get money. I won't beg, the way I did with that damned Pete."

The look on his face frightened her. "Just take it easy," she said, "until I get back. Keep singing, make all those shows."

"Don't worry about me, Lora. As long as I got H, I'm all right. I'll make the shows. Don't worry about taking care of me. I'm all right. When you come back, we'll have a real ball."

Those were his words to her, but he seemed unaware of her. He had come down to the hospital, remembering the way it had been for those weeks together in his apartment, but it was not like that. She was like a stranger, a stranger in hospital gray.

Lora had felt sympathy for Boyd, and a desire to help him. It made her feel stronger for those moments when she had thoughts that Boyd was in trouble and needed her.

She knew better. He had what he needed. It was killing him, but it was the way he wanted to die. He was satisfied. He did not need her. He had almost forgotten her.

She saw Ken come out of the hospital door and start across the lawn toward them. How tall he was, and how clean and good he looked. How she had missed him!

Boyd followed the direction of her gaze. "More company for you?"

"My brother-in-law."

"The one I talked to over the phone?"

Lora smiled, "Yes."

Boyd got up. "Look, I'll run, baby. Take care, and when you get back to town, you look me up. You hear? And if you need anything, you call me. You know where to find me."

"Be careful, Boyd."

"I'm careful, baby. I know I got to be."

"Don't miss any more shows."

"I got it made, baby. You're the one. You take care."

Boyd started across the lawn. He seemed almost scurrying, he was so anxious to get away from there. She knew that he would not come back to see her here. He would want to, but the odor of disinfectant, and the creepy feel of the place would linger in his mind. He would not come back. He had what he needed in the caps that he kept in his apartment.

She watched him pass Ken on the lawn. He waved and bowed exaggeratedly. Ken would not know what to think of Boyd. Boyd was on a ball, right now.

Maybe he had to be. Maybe he had had to find the courage even to make a trip up here.

Lora stood up. Ken came hurrying forward. He had a box of candy for her. He tossed it on the ground beside her and put out his arms.

It was wonderful to feel his arms around her. It lifted her up, like nothing else ever could. She pressed herself against him. In that moment, nothing was real but his arms about her, the good feel of him, the wonderful smell of him. There was nothing, no one like Ken. There never would be.

They both stepped back simultaneously and spoke in unison. "Let me look at you!"

They laughed.

"You look fat," he said.

"You look beautiful," she told him.

"Well, naturally. I dressed up to come to see you."

"How's Chris?"

"Good, honey. She sends you her love. We've got a woman who comes in days now to look after her. She stays until I get home."

Lora could not resist asking. "Is she pretty?"

"Who? Chris?"

"No. The woman."

"Honey, I wouldn't know. I've stopped looking at women–except you. I save my eyes so when I come up here, I can stare at you longer."

"You haven't–haven't said anything to Chris?"

His shoulders sagged. "I wanted to, Lora–but I couldn't. I look at her. I start to tell her–and I can't."

"You never can, Ken." She took his hand. She bent over and picked up the box of candy. She kissed his hand, thanking him. They started walking slowly toward the stream.

He was silent a long time. At last he said, "Aside from that, everything is fine. I got a raise."

"Another one? That's wonderful, Ken!"

"Sure. I feel like a damned heel. They talk about me down at the company. The solid-type citizen, the man most likely to succeed–and all the time, I know what I am–the gutless wonder."

"You're not! You're as wonderful as they say you are. You're almost as wonderful as I think you are. You–you can't help it if you're such a good salesman."

She smiled, looking up at him. She thought the double meaning would please him.

He frowned. "Is that what you think, Lora? That I sold you a bill of goods?"

"It doesn't matter."

"It does matter. You think if I could that I wouldn't marry you? Take care of you?"

"I know you would, Ken."

"Sure. That's what you say, but do you believe it?"

"I believe it–and somehow, that frightens me. You don't need me. I don't even believe you really want me–"

"That's a hell of a way to talk!"

"All right. You want me–as much as you want any one of a dozen other girls, but you don't need me. You'd be better off if I was out of the way."

They had stopped beside the stream. Lora stood looking down at her reflection in the water. She waited for Ken to answer her. She glanced at him. He was silent, his mouth taut. He was staring along the creek, and he did not meet her eyes.

It was true! She had been talking, hoping to be reassured. What had she wanted to hear? That he was lonely for her in the nights? That it was the same hell for him away from her that it was for her?

She had wanted to hear him say that he did need her.

He was not going to say it. Ken did not believe it. He did not need her. He was the solid citizen, the good salesman, the man most likely to succeed. She could be part of his life. Probably he wanted her as part of it, but he did not need her. Secretly, he surely felt that he would be better off if she was out of the way.

The ripples on the stream obscured her reflection. There was a sudden breeze. She shivered, scrubbing her hands along her arms. "I'm cold, Ken. Let's go back. Do you mind?"

That night was the worst one she had. She had all the pains and ills of withdrawal. Not even the synthetic drug they administered could make her sleep. She stared, tired and hollow-eyed, at the ceiling. She lay perfectly still, as though she was in a trance, too tired to move. When morning came, she still had not slept.

It was four endless days before Dr. Simmons came up to the hospital. Lora was ecstatic when she first saw him and wondered why she should be so moved by the sight of him.

He walked with her out on the lawn. His voice was harsh, surprising her. "What is the matter, Lora? The nurses say you haven't slept ten hours in the last four days."

"Maybe I'm not sleepy."

"Well, that certainly isn't normal. Most women in your condition practically hibernate at this time of their lives."

"Maybe they're happy. Maybe they're married. Maybe they want to be mothers."

"It's something else, Lora. It started last Sunday. Something happened. You'd better tell me about it."

"There's nothing to tell."

He shrugged. "You're not helping anything, Lora, acting like this."

"I'm all right."

"I'm prescribing some sleeping tablets, Lora. You can get them as you need them from your nurse."

She did not thank him. "Sure, I know how they hand things out here. Their idea of what I need."

He shook his head. "It won't be that way. You've got to sleep. I'll give definite orders. You're to be the sole judge of what you need, Lora."

After that, it was better.

Ken came regularly every Sunday, but Lora no longer looked forward to his visits. At least she no longer dreaded them. The sleeping pills were wonderful. They knocked her out at night, and when she got up in the morning, she insisted on being given two more pills. She took one in the morning, and one in the afternoon. She lived, and worked and moved through a state that was neither waking nor sleeping. She knew what was going on around her, but she just did not care.

Her baby was born at eleven o'clock Saturday night. That pleased her. She would have something to tell Ken the next day when he came. It had been so hard to think of nice things to say to Ken.

She planned how she would tell him that she had her baby on Saturday night so that he could see it when he came to visit on Sunday.

They showed her the baby for a moment before she fell asleep. Dr. Simmons was happy. He told her it was a beautiful girl.

A girl, Lora thought, a poor little girl.

It did not look beautiful to her, but Dr. Simmons told her that no new baby ever looked pretty unless you understood it. "I understand them," he said. "That's why I can see how beautiful she is."

Lora went to sleep with the thought from somewhere that the baby would be gone when she woke up.

Her sleep was restless. When she woke, the sun was high. It was Sunday morning. Ken was sitting across the room. The nurse was there, too.

Lora looked around wildly for the baby. She was there. The nurse was feeding her from a bottle.

Lora stared. "Don't I–don't I feed my baby?" she cried.

The nurse smiled, shaking her head.

"I'm no good!" Lora wept. "I'm no good. Not even for my baby."

Ken came across and held her hand. "It's all right, Lora. When you get her home, you can take care of her."

She believed that for a while, but it did not work out that way. The nurses bathed the baby, fed her, pushed her over to the window for her sunlight. Lora was in the way. They did not need her. The baby did not need her.

She looked at the child, crying behind her dry eyes. Poor little stranger. She did not need Lora, either.

Chapter 17

Chris very carefully explained to the hired nurse about Lora and the baby. The way Chris told it, Lora's had been a brief but romantic affair. The boy had been a young soldier. He had met Lora while she was singing in a club. He had been sent to Korea, and they had received word from the War Department that Richard–Chris had chosen that name by herself–had been killed. Lora, according to Chris, had continued to use her maiden name because it was by this name that she was best known as a singer.

The nurse was a solemn-faced woman named Louise. Whether she believed the story or not, you could not tell by looking at her.

Lora did not object to the story because she was sure it made the situation easier for Chris. Chris felt that the nurse would repeat the story, and it would spread in the neighborhood and be accepted as true. All that mattered to Lora was being sure that Chris was content.

Lora had been shocked when she came back from the hospital. Chris had suffered a heart attack. Her face was more ashen than ever. It looked difficult even for Chris to smile any more.

Lora was angered that Ken had not told her. When she asked him why, he just shrugged. "I could handle it. You had troubles of your own."

There it was again. They did not need her. They did not count on her for anything.

She had hoped that when she got back to the apartment she would be forced to take care of her baby, but Chris had all that arranged.

"You'll have to be looking for work before long anyhow, honey, and we might as well let Louise and the baby get used to each other right from the first."

It did not matter what Lora wanted. Louise was the kind of woman who took over anyway. Lora could stand around, but it was as it had been at the hospital. She was in the way. Louise did not mind telling her so.

Lora took the baby's diapers to the corner laundry. She put them in the automatic washers and stood by helplessly. The manager would not think of letting her move the diapers from the washer to the dryer, and she stood by helplessly again while the diapers dried.

The manager wrapped the dried clothes in brown paper for her, and Lora told herself she had won a minor victory. She carried the clothes home alone.

She unwrapped the laundry bundle and opened the bureau drawer to put the baby's underthings away. The baby was asleep in the bed that Chris had bought and put in Lora's room, next to Lora's bed.

"Don't worry, honey," she said, tiptoeing to the crib. "Tomorrow I'm going to find a job. I'll make money for you. I'll take care of you."

She had gained too much weight at the hospital, and she knew she ought to lose some of it before she tried to get work. They remembered her–if they remembered her at all–as a slender girl.

The inactivity was boring, and Lora needed money. Maybe that would save her. Maybe if she got work to do, she could forget the persistent, gnawing hunger inside her, the hunger that she could not keep out of her mind, the craving for narcotics.

She admitted it. She had not been off it. She had been given just enough to keep her from going insane. She had taken nothing but the sleeping pills that she had gotten from Dr. Simmons. She still had some of them. They were not going to last much longer. She told herself she did not have the courage to face Dr. Simmons for more.

But nobody had to tell her. There was nothing you would not do when the hunger got bad enough....

The bedroom door opened. Ken stepped inside it and closed it behind him.

Lora turned around. "What do you want?" she whispered. "You know Chris is still awake."

His face was cold and angered. He had something in his hand. He kept it turned just so that Lora could not see what it was.

"Never mind Chris," he said.

"You'll wake the baby."

"Never mind the baby, either. Nameless brat!"

She flushed. "What's the matter with you? You know who that baby belongs to."

"Do I?" His mouth twisted. "Do I know, or do I just think I know? Maybe I don't know anything about you, but I'm going to know. You're going to tell me, or I'm going to beat hell out of you–here and now."

Her face twisted, she stared at him. "Ken, what's the matter?"

"Nothing. I'm just a jerk, that's all. Just a guy who believed a cheap little tramp. Let her live in my house while she–"

She yelled at him. "What are you talking about?"

The baby whimpered, stirred on her bed. Lora bit her lip.

Ken's voice was tense, but he kept it very low. "This is what I'm talking about." He flung the paper he was carrying. It settled on her bed, face up.

It was a nude photograph. Lora felt herself go weak and cold all over. The feeling of illness started at the backs of her legs and flowed upward.

It was a picture of Lora. At first, she could not even speak. She could only stare at the photograph. In her mind, she tried to imagine when it could have been taken. Where?

She felt with a flash of horror that it might have happened while she was high on heroin, but she knew better. It was a professional photograph, the kind she had posed for a hundred times, in undies, in bathing suits, in dresses, but never in the nude.

She shook her head. "Where'd you get it?"

His voice remained hard. "So that's important? Well, I got it at the office. Nude photographs have a way of getting around, baby. You should have thought of that when you had it made. What else have you done, Lora? That's what I want to know? This was just a start, wasn't it? Nothing for a girl who can smile into a camera looking like September Morn."

She picked up the photograph in her trembling fingers. In dim outline, she could see tables and chairs and painted out figures of men.

"This–this has been retouched," she whispered.

"So?"

"Well, don't you see? I never posed for a photo like this! I had something on. It must have been at the Sleeping Beauty sales dinner when I modeled a bra set. That's got to be it. I was paid for pictures–but not for a nude."

He was not convinced. "No, you couldn't get paid for a shot like that. When you pose like that, you have to want to do it."

The door behind Ken opened. Chris was there in her wheelchair. Her knotted right hand was pressed against her breast, and her colorless face was taut. "Ken," she whispered. "What is it? What are you shouting about? What's the matter?"

With her eyes, Lora begged Ken not to show Chris this photograph, but Ken was beyond caring about appeals. He snatched the glossy print from Lora's lifeless fingers.

"I'll tell you what's the matter," he snarled at Chris. "This lovely sister of yours, this wonderful, beautiful thing that could do no wrong. This whoring little slut! Posing for nudes. It must have been some kind of stag party. She brags that the men in the picture have been painted out–"

Lora's voice was a wail. "No! My clothes– They've been touched out. You can see it!"

Chris took the picture. She looked at it a long time. She looked up, her eyes wet. "How did it happen, Lora baby? Where?"

"Let me get myself together, Chris–!"

Ken raged. "Sure. Take up for her!"

"She'll tell you, Ken," Chris whispered. "If you'll let her, won't you, baby?"

Lora was crying. "I tried to." She tilted her head. "He won't believe me."

"Why should I believe you? This picture is all over town. Hell, it's probably all over the country. Look at that brazen smile. I've seen smiles like that–you know in what kind of dives."

Chris stared at him, her face pulled with hatred. "Stop talking like that Ken. Now. Or get out."

Lora shook her head. She knew what was the matter with Ken. It was misery. Doubt and suspicion had him sick. It was not cruelty. It was, but he was being as cruel to himself as he was to them.

"I'll go," she said. "I've caused you enough trouble."

Ken growled at her. "Nobody wants you to go. I just want to hear the truth out of you."

"I told you. I posed for a picture in a bra set at the Sleeping Beauty company. That's the truth. Somebody has touched this picture up. You can see it. They've painted out the set."

"You've got a reputable agent," Ken snarled at her. "I know. I looked him up a long time ago. Chris wanted me to, and I wanted to. He would not send you into anything like that."

Lora spread her hands helplessly. "I'll see him."

"I think you'd better," Ken shouted. "If you're telling the truth, we'll sue. And if you're lying, I'll beat hell out of you–with my own fists."

"If you touch her," Chris whispered, "if you ever touch her, I'll kill you."

Ken turned on Chris, his eyes wild, brimmed with tears. His voice was vibrant with anguish. "How many of her lies will you take, Chris? How many will you believe?"

"She's telling the truth. I know she is."

"And I know she's lying. She posed for this picture, all right, and she posed for it just the way it was taken."

"I'm not lying!"

"Wait, Ken, Lora will see her agent. Won't you, baby?"

Lora nodded.

"Sure, he mocked. "And come back with more lies. Well, you can believe them. I won't."

Lora stared at him in horror. Her mouth opened. She whispered. "You won't believe me, because you don't want to. You want to believe I'm lying, don't you? You want me to be lying!"

He wheeled back around, facing her. In his eyes she could see the torment he was living in. It must have started when they passed this glossy print around at his office this morning. He had had to stand there. He had to listen to the talk, knowing it was Lora. He had had to take it, and now he could not take it any more.

"Your lies are rotten enough," he said. "Don't accuse me of being as rotten as you are!"

Lora shook her head. "You want to believe it! It makes it so much easier for you, doesn't it?"

He struck her across the face with the back of his hand.

Chapter 18

Lora carried the imprint of Ken's hand across her cheek when she went to her agent's office the next day.

He was surprised to see her. He had tried to keep her waiting, but Lora had told his secretary she was not going to wait. Whatever else it was Jerry had to do, that could wait. Something in her voice convinced the secretary.

Lora was shown into Jerry's cluttered office. An astonished club manager stared at her as he passed, on his way out.

When she was alone with her agent, Lora took the glossy print from her envelope and laid it, face up, on his desk.

He swallowed twice, looking at it. He looked up at her, and his face was flushed. He gestured helplessly. "A beautiful girl, Lora. That's all I can say."

"You'd better be able to say a lot more than that."

"I can't, Lora."

"I suppose you didn't know about this?"

"I'm not going to lie to you. I knew. I raised hell, with Sleeping Beauty, the photographers, everybody. You're not the only one, Lora. It just happened that they got a better picture of you to work on, that's all. And you were the loveliest girl there. Maybe that's why whoever did it was careful to get the best shots of you."

She stared at him, her mouth pulled. "Whoever did it? Am I supposed to fall for that?"

"I hope you will, Lora–because it's the truth."

"How could it be? You know the owners of Sleeping Beauty. You know the photographers."

"All right, baby. Here's what I found out: Sleeping Beauty hired the photographers. The photos delivered to Sleeping Beauty are above reproach. The photographer claims that the prints were stolen by a part-time employee. They've tried every way to trace him, but they can't find him. He's made plenty on this deal, but he's a dead duck in this town."

"And I'm not?"

"It's a rotten break, kid. A dirty, rotten break."

"It's worse than that. Something has got to be done."

"Lora, I wish there was something that could be done, but there isn't. A stolen negative, a touched-up print, and the dirty crook who did it has disappeared. There's nothing any of us can do."

"I've got to have work. What kind can I get with those pictures out?"

"You'll just have to take it, Lora. I'll get you what work I can. After a while, the thing will die down. You'll be all right."

"I'll be all right. You mean I might as well quit, don't you?"

He swallowed again, his eyes clouded. At last, he cleared his throat. "You've been away a long time, Lora."

She felt empty and lost. She tried to find some assurance in Jerry's eyes, but there was none.

"You mean there's nothing for me?"

"Not now, kid. Not right now. I'm sorry, Lora."

She gestured. "Will you do me a favor, Jerry?"

He looked worried. She knew he was afraid she was going to try to borrow money. "What is it, Lora?"

"You've got a good reputation, Jerry. If anybody got a letter from you, people would believe it, wouldn't they?"

He smiled doubtfully. "They might. I'm honest–but only as honest as I can afford to be."

"I want a letter from you, saying that I was hired by Sleeping Beauty, through this agency, and that I posed for them, along with a dozen other models, and that the pictures now circulating were taken then, during that show, and retouched."

He bit his lip. "You poor kid. Sure." He called in his secretary. He dictated the letter that Lora wanted. He told his secretary to type it in triplicate, give Lora two copies and keep one for the office.

Lora said nothing. She wanted only one copy of the letter, but she would take two. One for her souvenirs, her career as a model and singer, and the way it ended.

The manager of the Lowdown Club did not smile when Lora entered his office. He was a small, dark man with sleek hair and a flushed round face. "You're looking for Boyd Collins, eh?" His eyes went over her. "You don't mind if I ask you why? Why should a girl like you want a no-good like Collins?"

"I want to see him. I thought you might know where he lives. I went up to his apartment, but he had moved. The super of the building said he didn't know where."

"You can bet what he meant was, he didn't care."

"The sign out front says that he sings here."

"Signs lie. Let's say that once in a while, he sings here. Let's say that when it pleases the genius, he makes an appearance. Sometimes when he makes the appearance, he looks decent enough to go out there before my customers. Mostly, he doesn't."

"He must be ill."

"Ill? He's ill, all right. Anybody that don't know what's the matter with him is the one that's ill. I'd break his contract. I'd break his neck. But my lawyer says it's easier to fill in for him, and when his contract ends, he's washed out. It's quieter that way."

It had happened. What Lora had warned Boyd was going to happen to him, had come to pass, with a vengeance. He had started out, making H work for him, give him a lift, a charge, and now it had him. The worst kind of slavery, and there was no way he could fight it.

"Do you know where I could find him?" she asked.

The man nodded. He opened a pad on his desk, and wrote an address on a slip of paper. He handed it to her. He frowned. "Aren't you the girl who used to come in here with Collins a few months ago?"

She nodded.

"Well, if he means anything to you, you better see if you can make him fly right. He's washed up here when his contract ends, but he's also through everywhere, unless somebody does something for him."

It took Lora an hour to reach the address the Lowdown Club's manager had given her. It was a squalid neighborhood. The rooming house where Boyd was supposed to live was only a court order away from condemnation.

She climbed three flights of stairs. A dim light, suspended from the ceiling, burned constantly in the smelly corridor.

She found Boyd's door. She knocked three times. Just when she decided that he was not home, she heard movement inside. She knocked again.

The door opened cautiously, just the length of the guard latch.

"Who is it?" Boyd whispered.

"Boyd, it's Lora." She heard his sigh of relief.

Boyd threw open the door and grabbed her hands. He tugged her inside and slammed the door. He set the latch and locked it. He leaned against the door then, looking at her and breathing through his mouth at the exertion. "Got to keep it locked," he said. "Nosey people."

She stared at him. His face was only a skull, with yellowed flesh drawn across it. His dry eyes stared at her, pupils dilated.

He had always been slender, but now he had lost weight until his chest looked sunken. His hands showed the structure of his bones.

She looked around the shabby room. A bed, a hot plate on a rickety table, a few chairs. There was nothing left of the expensive furnishings he had bought for the other apartment.

"Boyd, what's happened to you?"

He smiled and shook his head. "What always happens. You need more of the stuff than you can afford. You buy it with money you don't have. First thing you know, you've lost what you did have." He laughed. "Remember when I said it was my slave? Well, doll, what's happened is that there's been a revolution. Boyd Collins now works for Charley."

He slumped into a club chair. Lora sat down across from him. "But that's it. I was talking to the manager of the Lowdown–"

"That mangy crumb! What lies did he tell you about me?"

"He said you don't show up for work half the time."

"Half the time is twice as much as he deserves! Why, I doubled his business. Hell, he'd admit that. There were bigger crowds when I was going to sing than he had all the rest of the day. Then, just because I wanted a raise. Hell, it was like I told him. It wasn't just that I wanted it. I had to have it. He turned me down. Got me tossed out of my apartment, and I lost all my furniture. Just because he was too stinking cheap to give me a raise!"

"It's worse than that, Boyd. He's letting you out when your contract expires."

"Letting me out? Why, damn his soul! Is that what he told you? Look, I wouldn't sing there a moment longer than I had to–"

"Boyd, listen to me. He says if you don't finish your contract, you're through everywhere."

Boyd's shoulders sagged. He looked up at her as though he was punch drunk. "I know, Lora. I know. I can't help it."

"But can't you just sing, Boyd? If you'll show up, at least you can get on at another club. Maybe less money, but–"

"Hell, I can't get along on what the Lowdown pays me."

"But you won't have *anything*. Just make your shows, Boyd. I don't want to see you go like this. You've been good to me, Boyd. You've been my friend. I want to help you if I can."

He shook his head. "Make the shows, Lora? Look at me. I'm beat. Six shows. Hell, I couldn't. I just couldn't." His voice broke. "Look at me. I'm filled with it now. I had a fix just a little while before you got here. I'm up right now. Good Lord, you ought to see me, Lora, when it wears off, when I'm down. It's all I can do to make a fix. Hell, you know what's going to happen? Some day I'm going to be in this room, down low, low–and I'm going to need a fix, and there's not gonna be a cap. I'm going nuts before I can make a contact. I know it. I wake up in the night crazy–knowing it's gonna happen."

She got up and stood beside his chair. "That's why you've got to work, so you can buy the caps." She pushed his dry hair back from his forehead. "I'll help you."

He nodded, staring up at her, wanting to use her strength. "Sure. You can help me. That's what's happened, Lora. We made a game out of it when you were here. I took a cap for a laugh, but when you were gone, I took 'em for every kind of reason. Sometimes for no reason. But if you'll stay with me, I can whip it. I can, Lora. I swear it. Help me. Please God, help me!"

Boyd refused to eat anything. She went out and brought in some pastry, and he ate that at about four in the afternoon. She talked him into appearing at the five o'clock show at the Lowdown.

She got him dressed. His newest dress suit seemed to hang on him. By the time he was ready to go, he had the shakes so badly he could hardly stand. She was forced to wait until he had a fix. He made her a hundred promises. It would be all he needed. It would get him through the night.

She watched him and she began to breathe heavily. There it was. For the first time in months her hands trembled.

Boyd was standing there, looking at her. She swallowed hard. "I need it," she whispered. "Just this time."

Boyd handed her a cap. He stood watching her fix it. His mouth twisted into a leer. He began to laugh. He laughed until tears fell from his eyes. "You came back to help me, eh, Lora? What a laugh! I know why you came back. It had nothing to do with me. It was Charley. All the time I thought you came back to help me."

She turned away, grabbing her purse and coat. "I don't want it, Boyd. Come on. Let's get out of here."

They left. The last thing she saw was the cap, lying there. She had not won. Only Boyd's contempt had stopped her. Would anything stop her next time?

Chapter 19

Lora and Boyd walked into the Lowdown Club at ten minutes before five. Lora went ahead of him into the manager's office.

The little man's round mouth opened in surprise. "I don't know how you did it, sister." He looked Boyd over, contempt pulling at his face. "You might as well get out there so the m.c. can know you're going to fulfill the terms of your contract–one more time."

"He's going to make his shows," Lora said.

The manager laughed. "If I was a betting man, I'd lay you odds on that, but I don't want to take your money."

"Go to hell," Boyd said.

The manager waved him out of the room.

When the door closed behind Boyd, the manager looked at Lora. "You his sister or something, to care what happens to that slob?"

"He needs help."

"No. He's beyond help."

"He's here. If you'll keep him here until the next show, I'll be back. He'll be all right. He'll make his six shows."

"Why should I look after him?"

"He's your singer–and it's your contract. Just keep him here at the club until I get back. I'll see that he makes the rest of the shows."

The manager regarded her, puzzled. Finally he shrugged. "I'll do what I can."

Chris and Ken were in the living room of the apartment when Lora arrived there at six. Chris had been crying. Ken's eyes were cold, and he merely nodded when Lora came in.

"I had the nurse stay with the baby," Chris said. "I didn't know when you'd get back."

Lora nodded. "I want her to stay. I'm not going to be here for a while. I came to get some clothes."

Chris sobbed. "Lora, you're not going to leave?"

"Where do you think you're going?" Ken said.

"I'm not going to tell you," Lora said. She took Jerry's letter from her purse. "That's all I have to say to you, Ken." Her hand trembled as she extended the letter.

He took it, opened and read it, slowly.

Chris put out her hand. Ken gave her the letter. "Satisfied?"

"I'm sorry, kid," Ken said.

"Sure."

"You don't have to pull a sore act," he said. "I was upset. All right, I admit it–and I'm sorry."

Chris folded the letter. "I don't blame you for wanting to leave, Lora," she said. "Maybe I wouldn't want to stay here, either–but, what will you do?"

"I'll be all right. When I get some job. I'll come for the baby. Until then, Chris, I guess you'll have to keep her for me."

"I want to–but I want you to stay."

"Wait a minute!" Ken's voice snapped at them. "Why do you have to go? I've said I was sorry. What else do you want me to say?"

Chris just looked at him. "You've said too much, Ken. Don't say anything else."

Lora kissed Chris's cheek. She whispered, "I'm so sorry, Chris. For everything."

Lora packed a light bag and carried it with her to the Lowdown Club.

It was almost eight when she got back there. The manager said that Boyd was in a small private office.

Lora went in there. Boyd was sprawled out on a divan in his dress suit. It looked wrinkled.

She shook him. He turned over, staring up at her. In that moment she saw that Boyd had made a contact. Somebody had brought in junk to him here in this room.

"Boyd, you promised."

He grinned at her. "I got low, Lora. Low, Lora. 'lo, Lora. Now I'm ready."

"You're all messed up. You can't go out there like this."

"I'm going."

"You're crazy!"

"I'm supreme, baby. Supreme!"

"Boyd, you're ruining yourself. You don't care, do you. You're not going to try."

"That's right, Lora. I'm not gonna try. You and me, just alike. We ain't gonna try."

"You'll end up like a tramp. You won't even be able to find a fix," she warned him.

"That worry you, Lora? You got to keep Boyd going, so you won't lose out, don't you, Lora?"

"I'm trying to help you. I thought you wanted me to help you." She pleaded with him, prayed he'd believe her.

He just lolled back on the divan and grinned at her.

She sighed. "I'm sorry, Boyd. I made another mistake. I thought you needed me. I thought you would try if I helped you."

"I told you, baby, that I got what I need–Charley. That's all I ever need. Old Charley takes care of me."

Someone knocked on the door. "You're on, Mr. Collins."

"Boyd, you can't go out there. You're crazy if you try!"

A cunning look moved across his face. "Got to. Got to be there. Contract. You know contract. Boyd Collins has got to fill out his contract."

She picked up her suitcase. "I won't see you again, Boyd. Good luck."

He wheeled around facing her. His mouth was tight. His eyes were cold. "You're not going anywhere. You chant about me needin' you. Hell, you need me, baby. You always have."

"I'm not coming back."

"You're not going anywhere!" He caught her arms. "We're in this together. I don't know what you call it, but I guess it's love. I love you."

"You don't love anybody. You couldn't."

His hands tightened. His eyes hated her, but she realized that he was talking of love, his brand of love, the only kind possible to him.

"You stayed with me when I had it, baby. You let me think you felt about me just the way I felt about you. Well, you're not going to walk out just because things are tough for me."

"It's no use, Boyd. I can't help you. I thought I could."

"Help me? I can help you. Your soul, if any–and your heart–if you ever had one, they belong to me–or they belong to what I can get for you."

She turned her head away. He shook her, his hands twisting the flesh of her shoulders, hurting it, burning it.

"You're hurting me, Boyd. Let me go!"

"You can't go–and you know it. I'm your life, baby. I'm your source of supply. You can't get along without me. In twenty hours you'd be stark raving crazy."

She would not face him, but she felt lost inside. She knew her eyes admitted the truth. He owned her. She had come back looking for quick forgetfulness, driven by a craving that would not leave her, even when she looked at Boyd and saw what it had done to him.

Somebody knocked at the door again, impatiently. "Hey, Collins! You gonna make it, or not?" a grating voice called.

"Comin' man, coming!" Boyd said. He looked at Lora. "You'll be here when I finish this show. We'll go up to my place. I'll give you a fix, baby. You'll feel better."

She just looked at him. She did not answer. He laughed at her and went out of the door.

Lora stopped near the front door as the m.c. announced Boyd Collins. There was a smattering of applause and some uneasy laughter.

She frowned. Why did they laugh like that? The headwaiter led her to a table. She sat there in this strange crowd, puzzled, frightened as Boyd came out into the spotlight.

Her eyes filled with tears. He was thin, just bones and taut-stretched parchment skin under his wrinkled suit.

He gave them his professional smile. Again that uneasy titter of laughter swept the room.

Why did they let him up there? The manager could have replaced him. There were a dozen ways he could have broken Boyd's contract. Why did he want him to appear?

Watching, Lora began to be ill. Boyd caught the microphone in his left fist. He missed once and had to grab again. Laughter. He grinned, sheepishly.

The music began, and Boyd started to sing. How could he even sing? She wondered where he found the strength and the will to stand there. He had enough heroin in him to kill an ordinary man. He knew they were laughing at him. How long had he known it?

He did not miss a note, or a word. And yet it was all just off, wrong. The audience applauded when he finished his first number.

She looked around, hating them. They felt the wrong, they knew that Boyd was ill, dying, but this thing had the fascination of evil. It was something they watched, while they felt repelled.

Maybe some of them did not even understand. They were trying to keep Boyd up there until they solved the riddle of what there was about this mild, sick looking little man that repulsed and attracted them at the same moment.

There was no mystery left in Lora's mind, though. She knew why they did not break Boyd's contract. She saw why they let him go out there as often as he could make it, and she knew they'd let him appear as long as he was able to stand.

The manager sat down across the table. He smiled at her. "You see? You still want to bet he makes the rest of the night?"

"There's a word for people as low as you are," Lora told him. "But I don't know what it is."

He shrugged. "Boyd signed with me to sing. Hell, let him sing."

Boyd's song ended, and he started out of the spotlight. He staggered at the arch. Lora heard the uneasy laughter, and she stood up quickly.

"Where are you going?" the manager said. "Out of here? That's what you'll do, if you're smart."

"I'm going to take him home," Lora said.

The manager gestured. "Might as well. I don't think little Boyd would make it all the way through another one tonight."

Lora found Boyd sitting on a straight wicker chair in the corridor. One of the waiters had brought it for him from the kitchen.

"Come on, Boyd," she said. "I'm going to take you home."

He looked up at her, his smile crafty. "I knew you wouldn't run out, baby. Like I told you, you can't run out on ol' Boyd Collins." But he made no move to get up.

She helped Boyd to his feet. She did not say anything. She could feel the manager's eyes on them as they went out the rear exit to the alley.

Boyd could walk only as far as the end of the gangway. When they reached the street, he leaned against the building. "Long walk, kid."

"Have you any money, Boyd?"

He tried to joke. "A little bit. What do you want, a newspaper?" He laughed foolishly.

"Have you enough for a taxi?"

"A whole taxi? For two?" He grinned. He shoved his hands into his trouser pockets. He fished out two wrinkled dollar bills. "Two bucks. No good. Not 'nough to buy a cap. Sure. Call a cab. We'll squander it. We'll go home in style."

Lora helped Boyd across the walk. She signaled a cab. When it pulled up to the curb, she shoved her suitcase in ahead of them and then helped Boyd in. He stumbled and sprawled across the back seat. Boyd looked more dead than alive. For a moment Lora thought he might die, and she grew panicky. Then a foolish grin spread over his face, and she was relieved.

The cab driver looked at him. "Really loaded, ain't he?" he asked Lora.

She said nothing, merely got in and slammed the door.

The driver stared at them a moment. "Say, ain't he Boyd Collins, the character that–pardon the expression–sings at the Lowdown?"

"Yes."

"Thought I knew him." His eyes moved over her. "And I think I know you, too." His smile was a leer.

Lora felt her heart sink. It was as though the world had dropped out from under her. She was not ever going to forget the leer on the driver's face. He sat there, looking her over. He recognized her from the nude photograph, and the fact that she was with Boyd did not matter. That photo had made her public property.

"Drive," she said. Her voice shook. She gave Boyd's address.

"I got you, lady," the driver smirked, ground his gears and then took off.

She had to get away. She had to escape. Either she would use the cap at Boyd's apartment, or she would have to run away, catching a ride, trucks, cars, freights, anything. She had to get away. It would not matter how she got away, or where she went, just that she got away from here.

In her mind as the taxi moved through the darkened streets, Lora could see herself, standing on a highway, a wide, clean avenue. A car stopped. There was a clean man at the wheel, a decent man, giving her a lift toward a decent life.

She shook her head. She knew better. There was just one kind of escape for her. That escape lay in Boyd's apartment. She could not take any more of this, men staring at her, leering, recognizing her. It was not only this city that was out-of-bounds for her. It was the whole tough world. Only a cap could take her out of it.

She half-carried Boyd up the steps. She had the key to his apartment in her purse. She opened the door, thinking it was odd that they had left the lights on. That was when she saw the two men.

Lora was too startled to cry out.

One of the men was short and stocky. He was wearing a tan suit and black shoes. She saw this as he slid past her, grabbing Boyd's arm. He tugged Boyd into the room and closed the door behind them.

The other man was tall. His hair was blonde. He turned back the lapel of his coat, showing her a shield that glittered in the light. The tall man spoke to Boyd. "Your name Boyd Collins?"

This is it, Lora thought. *Finished!*

Boyd knew he was busted. His eternal nightmare had been realized. He was limp against the stocky detective. He nodded.

"You live here?" the detective pressed.

Boyd nodded again.

"Her, too?"

Boyd shook his head. "No," he breathed faintly.

"You're under arrest," the tall man said. "I guess you both better come along."

Boyd tried to stand straight. "What's the matter?"

A brave try, Lora thought, *but useless.*

"You're goofy with what's the matter, fella, but you're under arrest for possessing narcotics. I guess this stuff on the table is all the evidence we need."

Lora's eyes moved past the detective to the array of equipment on the table. It was all there, complete, including the cap she had left untouched that afternoon, the one she had not fixed. That was the evidence that was to be used against them. The tall cop gathered it up carefully.

"All right," he said. "Let's go."

Chapter 20

In Lora's nightmare, there were crowds of men standing behind her. They wore masks. They wore them so that she could not recognize them. They were watching her. It was some kind of fascinating show to them. They could not take their eyes off her. She was screaming for the merciful release of just one fix, one more fix.

The men watched the doctor come forward to the chair in which Lora sat. They watched his hand close over her bicep. He lifted the hypo, needle gleaming in the light.

She stared at the doctor, sweating, panting, her eyes begging. The needle plunged into her arm. Now! It was in her bloodstream. It would work quickly. It would save her. She could open her eyes now. The nightmare would end....

She lay face down on the cell cot. She was suddenly afraid to open her eyes. Would the nightmare end? Or would it just begin?

Would they be standing around, staring at her, the way they had been when they brought her into the women's tank last night from Boyd's apartment?

She had thought she would never sleep, but fatigue and anxiety had knocked her out. Because she had been picked up with Boyd, they had sent a doctor in to see her. He had given her a small shot of morphine that was supposed to get her through the night.

The other women in the tank had drawn away from her. Drunks, thieves, streetwalkers, they would not get near her. She was different. She was an addict. She was a junker, a hype. They whispered together, their eyes on her.

She had lain there, wondering what Chris would say when she heard this. What would Ken believe? He would think that she had forged Jerry's letter, or stolen it, or paid to have it typed.

Lora had fallen asleep. The nightmare had been too terrible, and she woke up. The other women in the tank were sprawled on their cots, sleeping.

A matron came up to the bars. Lora was sitting up on the side of the cot. "You all right?" the woman asked.

Lora nodded.

The woman laughed. "Got something for you." She folded a tabloid and tossed it to Lora.

Lora opened it. Her own picture and Boyd's stared up at her from the front page. The headlines filled the rest of the page. They were bold and black. "Model, Singer Nabbed in Narcotics Raid." They were followed by the inevitable italics: *See page three.*

Lora's hands trembled as she opened the tabloid. "Entertainers Jumped with Junk. Night Club Singer and Undress Model Caught in Latter's Apartment. Just Friend, Singer Says of Girl."

She read the story. It suggested much about the sort of modeling that Lora had allegedly done. The front-page picture had come from the model agency, but there was no mention of the agent. Jerry had some influence.

Boyd had taken the rap. He declared that Lora was innocent, that she had just come from the club with him. As far as he knew, she had never used or possessed the junk.

Lora laid back on the cot. She felt physically exhausted. Boyd had known he did not have a chance. He was trying to keep her out of it.

She stared at her front-page picture. There was no keeping her out of it. If she had not been dead before professionally, she was now.

At nine o'clock the matron took her upstairs to the office of the lieutenant in charge of the narcotics squad. He questioned her. She told him that she had once used narcotics, but had stopped months before. This was checked at the hospital upstate by telephone. The hospital gave Lora a clean bill of health. Evidently they did not even mention the sleeping pills.

"We're holding your friend," the lieutenant said. "He says you're in the clear, but we've got your name, your address, your agency address. We can pick you up when we want to–and this is it. Keep going, and we'll want to."

Then the officer asked her if there was anybody she wanted to call. She thought for some moments. Nobody tried to hurry her.

The lieutenant spoke. "Kind of in a hell of a mess, aren't you?"

She tilted her head. "I'm all right," she said. "There's just no one I want to call."

When Lora walked into Dr. Simmons' office, the secretary buzzed him. This time, she did not apologize to the waiting people. She just motioned Lora into a small office to the right of the reception room.

Lora set her bag beside the door. She sat down beside a small white desk and looked around the room without really seeing any of it.

Dr. Simmons came in at once. He looked more tired than she ever remembered seeing him, but she was too wrapped in her own grief to think how weary he was.

"Hello, Lora." He sat down, looking at her. "Are you all right?"

"I am now. They held me overnight. They let me go this morning."

"Yes, I know. I called as soon as I heard about it. They said you were being released."

"Thanks for calling."

"I tried to see you. They said you were being questioned, and that you would be released. I called Ken Hunter, and I told him to call me if you went back home."

"I haven't been there yet. I don't know if I can go."

"Are you worried about Chris? The world isn't over. She'll understand."

She clasped her hands in her lap. "That's it. What is there to understand? They let me go, Dr. Simmons. They let me go, but you know, I have been on it."

"What are you going to do?"

"I don't know. That's why I came to you. I want you to tell me something. Can I be cured, Brad? Can I get over wanting it? Can I ever be all right again?"

He sat there a long time. She began to feel more lost than ever. He was trying to find an easy way to tell her it was hopeless.

"There's no easy way, Lora. It's hard, hard all the way. There's only one way to stop, the hard way. That's why most people never make it. It's too tough for ordinary human beings. They're too frail. They can't stand it."

"But is there a chance? Any chance at all?"

"Yes. If you'll go back to that hospital. You'll be in a different ward.

They'll treat you differently. Most of the medics will be mental specialists. It's long, and it's tough–and it's expensive. When you get out, you're in hock, whether you're cured or not."

"But they will take me?"

"They'll take you–because I'll go up there with you and see that you get in. But don't expect any sleeping pills, Lora. Don't expect any mercy. There won't be any. You'll think you're going to die, and maybe you'll wish you would die. But that's the only way I know."

"I've got to know if I'll be cured. If I won't, I'm not going on living. I won't. I'm no good like this. I'm useless, and worse than useless. If I can't be cured, Brad, I don't want to live."

"We're not up to that yet, Lora. You've got time to think about that later–and maybe you'll never have to. Maybe you'll make it. I'll help you. I'll do whatever I can."

Lora moved closer to him and clasped his hand. "I'll never forget what you've done for me, Brad. I hate to drag you into this, to take your time–maybe to waste your time, but I have no one else–"

The tears flowed freely now, and Lora found release in them and some measure of comfort. Brad said nothing, did nothing, but stroke her blonde hair, which was crushed against the white of his coat. He let her cry....

Dr. Simmons called the Hunter apartment and learned that Ken was still there. He had not gone into work. The two men talked for a long time. Dr. Simmons told Ken that Lora was going back to the same private hospital where she had her baby, but there would be no visitors, not until she was released. The doctor promised to get in touch with them every time there was news of Lora. He said he would bring news to her of Chris and the baby.

Lora sat numbly while Brad made arrangements to leave with her. He called another doctor and arranged to have him see the patients now in his office. At that Lora protested, but he would not listen. Then he and Lora went out into the street and caught a taxi to Grand Central.

Brad Simmons had warned Lora that it would be hard, but he had not told her it would be hell. Maybe no one could ever tell what it was like.

The psychologists spent hours and days, probing at her thoughts, trying to help her find the basic cause of her insecurity. They put her on a special diet. They kept her occupied all the time.

Sometimes Lora thought she was dying. When she came out of it, it always seemed to her that she had come back from death. She told herself there was nothing to go on living for. Still she could not die. She never wanted to die, really. She was always sure there was some reason for living, some good ahead for her, if only she could find it.

The psychologists got nowhere. They told her repeatedly they could do nothing for her. They could only help her search in her own mind for a way to help herself.

Dr. Simmons came to see her three times a week, every single week. From the first, she knew this was unusual. He had managed one trip every week when she had been up here before, but now three times every week, he walked into her room. He brought a warmth and a glow with him that was now the only bright thing in her life.

He never brought her any real news from home. Everything was fine. The baby was fine. Chris, Ken, himself. Sometimes she thought he did not even call the Hunters. He was so busy.

"Can you really spare the time to come up here?" she said. He looked haggard. She knew his practice would be suffering badly, and it disturbed her. She did not want him hurt because of her.

"I want to come, Lora. I thought you knew. You stopped being a patient of mine some time ago. Then I used to try to find some way to cure you, but now I stand on the sides and pray for it. I need you to be cured more than you need it."

She stared at him. She had not known. How would she know? Wrapped up in her own tragedy, she had seen him as some shadowy kind of father-image, and now he was telling her that he loved her.

"I want you to marry me, Lora. I want to take care of you," he said. "I love you."

"Knowing me? Knowing all you know about me?"

"All I know is that you're lovely–and I want you."

She shook her head. There had been no thought of any man but Ken. Now, she saw Brad Simmons as a man in love with her, but she knew better than to let herself go. She knew what she was, even if Brad would not admit it. Maybe she would never be cured. If not, no matter what man she was with, her love was divided–between the man in her arms and her craving for her deadly lover.

Brad said no more about his love for her during that visit, and Lora knew why. It was easy to see that the most important single object in his life was keeping her emotions at an even keel. The doctors wanted her to suffer no upsets during the period of her attempted cure. They felt that her addiction was a result, and they were still probing into her unconscious for the cause.

They told her that obviously she had been seeking an escape from an emotional upheaval. She did not answer, but she thought, *Not one, but a hundred upheavals.*

"There is no cure," they told her. "You can never be sure. You could be sure if someone could promise you an even, uneventful life, with no crises that you couldn't face with a smile. No one knows when there will come some situation so terrible that you'll have to escape, no matter how heroically you struggle against it, and the easiest escape will be the easiest escape that you remember. Back to narcotics."

Lora's appetite returned, and slowly she began to gain weight. She was sure that she was recovering when she began to miss her baby. She became more anxious to see the child than to pacify the urges that made her body itch with craving and need. She began to look forward to Brad's visits, with new interest and eagerness. She started watching to see him come along the hospital walk. She began to act and feel like a girl in love.

As she slowly returned to normal, the restrictions on her were removed. When Brad came, they went for walks on the grounds and along the creek below the hospital.

She began to feel good. Whatever cravings she had when she had come here, they were replaced by the desire for simple laughter, and small pleasures she could share with Brad.

The realization of the change in her brought her up sharply. She knew where that was leading. It was a matter of will. She had lacked courage and will, and she had started on the junk, and now because she was happy with Brad, she overlooked the fact that caring for him was a short, dead-end road.

Lora was walking along the creek with him. The morning sunlight made something fresh and new of the old world that she had overlooked so often before. Brad had said something. She did not even know what, and she had laughed. Part of that laughter had been in response to his words, but most of it had been the good feeling that bubbled up in her just because she was near him. Another part came from just wanting to laugh. Just being with him made her happy.

She stopped laughing abruptly. "We'd better go back," she said.

He turned frowning. "Why? What's the matter?"

"Nothing's the matter. I'm just tired. That's all."

"You're amazing! You just said you could walk forever–over the top of the hills and right on out."

"I've changed my mind." Her voice was cold.

She turned on her heel and started back. She could see the gray hospital building ahead of her. The light was gone from the morning, from the world. The hospital was an ugly building, with narrow walls and many cells all filled with human suffering.

Brad caught her arm. "Come here to me."

Before she could protest, he had pulled her back against him. There was the sudden, antiseptic smell of him, the way his face grew larger coming close, the way his lips quivered, and then he was kissing her hungrily. "You're not going to run away from me, Lora. You're not!"

"Let me go!"

"Am I that hateful to you, Lora?"

"What difference does it make?"

"I love you, Lora!"

"Are you crazy? Haven't you had enough trouble from me?"

He tried to smile. "I'll tell you. When I kiss you, I get an ache across my nose. I feel weak, and good at the same time. There's pleasurable agony at the nape of my neck. Don't you feel anything, Lora, when you kiss me?"

"Yes. You smell like a hospital."

First, he frowned. Then he laughed. "You're like a child, trying to strike out with the first thing that comes to your mind."

"You kissed me. I didn't ask you to."

"I'm an unprincipled character. Few girls have to ask me to kiss them."

"And it doesn't matter whether they want you to or not?"

He smiled. "No. The ones I decide to kiss, I don't care whether they want it or not."

She was forced to smile at him. She shook her head. "Please let me alone, Brad."

"So it wasn't so bad, was it?"

She shrugged, and started walking again, but her steps were slower. He moved along beside her, tall and thin, and silent. There was not the excitement she had known with Ken. Maybe she would never have that again.

Suddenly she remembered something, or thought of something that had not occurred to her before. Maybe it was the work of the psychologists. They may have gotten her mind to working on itself. She remembered something about the way she had fallen in love with Ken.

She had been first drawn to Ken by what she felt was his need for her. Before he had married Chris, he had been in an accident, and she had been afraid he was going to die. He never seemed to be cared for as constantly as she would have cared for him.

Later, when Chris had suffered her first attack, and was left an invalid, rugged Ken needed a woman as alive as he was. Lora had been sure he needed her. Afterwards came the thrill of being near him, a thrill that superseded the desire to aid him.

Lora had found Ken could get dozens of women. He did not really need her. He never had. Hadn't her feeling of insecurity begun to overwhelm her when she found out she was not needed?

Every person she had ever been attracted to had been someone whom she had felt had needed her, and each time when she found that there was actually no dependence on her, she had felt alone, and useless, caught in a life without direction. She had run to heroin for escape, for purpose in living.

Even her baby. Lora had been addicted by the time the baby was born. She had been irresponsible, unreliable. She had been in the way, unable even to feed her own baby. Even the baby had not needed her.

Her thoughts returned to Brad Simmons. There was no sense of need with him. He was too thin, too tired, but that was overwork. That was the years he had to work too hard to get where he wanted to be in the medical profession.

No, if she married him, she would be a burden to him. Suppose she started on the junk again? That would be the end of his career. The doctor's wife, a junkie! They had told her there was no certain cure. She could never be sure. She was not going to hurt him. She knew what she had been, and what she had done. Brad Simmons deserved better.

Her steps hurried, but he caught her arm.

"Will you listen to me?" he demanded.

"What is it?"

"I want you to marry me."

"No."

"You will!"

"No!"

His arms went around her. He ran his fingers up the back of her neck, into her hair, rumpling it. She felt a shiver of pleasure. She steeled herself against it.

His mouth was against her face. "We're just going to stay right here, until you change your mind."

"Brad, stop! It's no good."

He kissed her mouth stopping her words. She could feel the world spinning around her. She was hungry for love, starved for it. It was not fair. She tingled, feeling warm all over with his mouth moving against hers.

He was breathless when he released her. She stepped back. She tried to laugh. "You went into the wrong profession."

"There's no money in being a gigolo."

"Think of the fun you could have had."

"I don't like loving women. I just like loving you. You won't get away from me, Lora. I know all the accusations you're hurling against yourself, all the doubts you have. I still want you."

"Do you have a comb?"

He found one, handed it to her. She ran it through her hair. She could feel his eyes on her. It was so wonderful to feel alive again, the way he made her feel. She felt young and attractive. It was a better tonic than his medicine.

She returned his comb. She made her voice casual. "This is all very nice, I'm sure, Dr. Simmons, but I'm afraid I'll never be able to pay my bill when you send it. All these extras."

"Don't be flippant, Lora. That was love I gave you, and it was love that you returned to me. Fight it, if you must, but you can't win. You can put me off for a while, but not for long. I won't force myself on you, Lora. I'll let you seek me out–whenever you're ready."

Chapter 21

Lora was released from the hospital at eleven o'clock in the morning, a week after her last visit from Brad. She knew that Brad had been consulted. It was not possible that she could leave the place without his knowledge. She dressed and packed, and yet he did not come.

She tried to deny that she felt any sense of loss. This was undoubtedly more of the doctors' ego therapy. They wanted her to rely on herself, return to town alone, take up her life where she had left off.

She had refused to marry Brad. She had not seen him for a week. Even the fact that she was to be released had not shortened the time. She missed him. She had not known that she would miss him so much. She kept looking for him as she left the hospital.

She had not realized how disappointed she would be when he did not come to ride back to the city with her. She had been sure he would say the event called for a celebration, but there was none.

The streets were quiet. The town was somnolent. There was no singing, no dancing in the street. Lora Cassel was released from the hospital today. The world shrugged its shoulders. So?

Maybe even, the world was thinking, how long before she'll be back up there? Hadn't they warned her there was no cure? She shivered.

At the train station, she bought a ticket. She wandered along the platform. Her gaze kept moving to the parking lot. She told herself that Brad had gone to the hospital. He had missed her. He would be there before the train came.

He was not. The train was on time. Lora boarded it, and the ride was uneventful back to Grand Central.

Lora came out on Forty-second Street, the traffic noises striking her like thundering breakers. She could feel herself tremble. After the hospital this was bedlam.

She found a taxi. The car moved across town. In a few moments, the apartment, Chris, the baby, Ken.

Ken. He had been out of her mind, out of her thoughts. What would it be like to see him again? She felt a surge of emotion at the thought of him.

The cab turned, speeding downtown on the West Side. The driver began to hit the lights just right. They moved steadily with the one-way traffic.

The taxi stopped before the apartment house. It looked the same. Lora was sure that if she had been gone ten years, she would have returned to find the same people in the same windows, the same peddlers along the curb, the same children in the street.

She let herself into the apartment house and climbed the stairs, carrying her suitcase. At the door, she started to put the key in the lock, and changed her mind. She rang the doorbell, three long rings. She stood back, expectantly.

It took forever, Lora thought. They should have come running. They should have been as excited as she was.

At last the door was opened. Ken stood there. She started to cry out, laughing. Something in his face stopped her, his ashen face. Her gaze pulled downward, drawn like a magnet to the black band on his sleeve.

Her lips moved numbly. "Chris?" she whispered.

Ken's voice was level. "Chris is dead, Lora."

She started across the threshold. She felt the world spin out from beneath her. She fainted, crumpling forward.

Ken caught her in his arms.

Ken made Lora sip some hot tea. He made her comfortable on the sofa and began to talk.

"It happened weeks ago," Ken said. "We wanted to tell you, but

Simmons wasn't sure if you could take the news. He left it up to your doctors at the hospital, Lora. They decided not to tell you."

"But to–to leave it–to hit me like this."

"I'm sorry, Lora. It had to hit you. There wasn't any way to make it easy."

"Can I–can we visit her grave?"

"I took her home, Lora. She was buried at home. I don't know. I wouldn't have come back. The job wasn't worth it any more. Old man Hargrave wanted me in his wholesale company back in Council Falls. I told him I'd let him know, but I had to come back. I knew if I didn't, you'd be alone."

"Thanks, Ken."

Lora looked around the apartment, the bare and empty apartment without Chris. To think that Lora had thought nothing had changed! It had changed, all right. All the life was gone out of it, all the reason for being here. This apartment was nothing now. It had been home, and now it was just another flat, owned by a stranger in a strange town.

"Where's the baby?"

She saw Ken's eyes flicker. Anger. She could read his thoughts. He thought her interest in her baby came belatedly. No matter how understanding Ken was, he did not accept her addiction as illness. Chris had been ill, but she saw what Ken thought of her. Lora had been weak, evil.

"Louise is taking care of her. She thought she could do better in her own apartment. I agreed. She's very good to the baby, but she wants it named. She thinks it should be christened. She thinks there's something a little barbaric about calling a teething child 'Baby.'"

Lora looked at Ken, feeling the cold disapproval in his voice. "And what do you think about it, Ken?"

"What difference does it make what I think?"

"It's your baby, too, remember?"

He flushed. He gestured. "Well, I couldn't tell her what I wanted to name it. After all, I'm just supposed to be the brother-in-law."

"You've never forgiven me, have you, Ken?"

"Forgiven you? What's there to forgive?"

"Nothing." She shrugged. "I want to see the baby. I'll take her, naturally. I've no right to expect you to go on paying Louise to take care of it."

His voice snapped. "Let's not fight, Lora, not the first few minutes. You've put me in my place. It's my baby as well as yours. We'll pay Louise to take care of it–until we're settled."

"Settled?" She was aware her teeth were chattering.

"Yes. We'll have to wait a while, but we'll be married. Then we can bring the baby here and–"

Her teeth stuck together. She grabbed her chin, but she was unable to stop the chattering of her teeth. Her shoulders began shaking, and she was shivering all over.

Ken grabbed her. "My God, Lora! What's the matter?"

He held her tightly against him. It seemed to Lora that the chill would never stop. Chris was dead. She had hurt Chris, cheated her, and yet she had loved Chris more than anything on earth, needed her more. The baby was with Louise. Ken was a cold-faced stranger trying to be polite, trying to do the right thing, trying to overlook his own desires. The shivering increased! His own lack of desire!

At last the chill subsided. Gradually the shaking ceased. She lay back against the divan, exhausted.

Ken was looking at her, amazed. "Ken," she whispered. "What's happened to me? I don't have attacks at all. My God, it was just everything at once. It ganged up on me. It knocked me out. I'm sorry."

"Sure. I understand."

But he did not understand, not at all. To Ken, she had become some creature who was different, a person apart, a woman who had come back from some kind of cure. Lora knew it, and while it hurt, it made it more evident that she and Ken were through.

He looked around helplessly. "You want a drink of rye, Lora?" He bit his lip. "Or do you think you better?"

She forced herself to smile. "I don't want it, Ken, but you can stop worrying. It wouldn't matter if I did have it. It wouldn't affect me. It wouldn't ruin me."

He gestured. "I'm sorry, Lora. You must think I'm nuts, acting like this. It's just that I'm not sure about you."

"I'm all right, Ken. I'm as well as I'm ever going to be."

He stood up. "Then what's the matter with us? Why do we act like this? It's as though there was a wall between us."

Lora smiled at him. Her smile was sad. It was not a wall, but she couldn't explain that to Ken. There was nothing she could say to him to make him understand. Chris had never kept them apart while she lived. Maybe even, in her gentle wisdom, she had known about them, and the terrible pull, and she had said nothing. Now that she was dead, it was as though she stood between them, there in the room, and she would always be between them.

It was five o'clock in the afternoon when Ken and Lora came out of Louise's small apartment. They walked silently. Lora was thinking about how lovely her baby was, and she was looking forward to the moment when she could have the child with her again.

She wondered if Ken was pleased that she had named the baby Christine. It had to be named for Chris. Maybe Chris's name would be magic protection for it, and keep it happy.

When they reached the corner where a newsboy was hawking papers, Lora stopped. She put out her hand. "Well, Ken, it's been nice."

He stared at her. People passed them on both sides. The newsboy shouted.

"What are you talking about? What's been nice?" he demanded. "What gives, Lora?"

"Everything. Us."

"So? Let's go home. Everything is still going to be nice."

"I'm not going back to your apartment."

"It's our apartment."

"No. Not any more. It's yours. Yours to close, sublease, whatever you want to do so you can go back to Old Man Hargrave and the job he had for you. It doesn't belong to us. Not any more. Maybe it never did."

"Lora, not here. Stop talking like this!"

"I'm trying to keep it casual, Ken–because that's the way it is now."

"You mean, it's all over between us?"

"You mean, you didn't know?"

"But what about the baby?"

"What kind of life would she have with parents who didn't love each other?"

"God, Lora, I'm sorry."

"So am I." Actually she was not. It was something that had mattered once, but did not matter any more.

"What will you do?" he asked.

"I'll get a job. Not in anything I was in. That's not for me, and I know it. I'll be all right."

"I'll send you money, Lora, for the baby–"

"All right. I'd be a fool not to take it." It seemed the newsboy was shouting right in her ear.

Ken said, "But you've got no place to stay. Come back to the apartment. If you don't care for me, it's a place to stay. It won't matter."

"That's why I can't go back." Why was that news vendor's voice so loud? Something about a narcotics nab. Another one? "Because it won't matter.

We might try to make it matter. That wouldn't help anything–right now."

"You've become a pretty wise little cookie, Lora. You're more like Chris than ever."

Her eyes filled with tears. "I hope so. Maybe that will save me." God knew, something had to.

The newsboy's voice was louder than ever. "Doctor nabbed by Narcotics Squad. Young M.D. forges Dope Prescriptions for Personal Use."

She turned, looking at the newspaper the boy was waving.

The world spun crazily about her. That was Brad Simmons' picture on the front page. The headlines were about him!

The lieutenant of the Narcotics Squad remembered Lora. He smiled. "So you took the cure, Miss Cassel? That's wonderful. I hope it'll take."

"It's got to," she said. "But I didn't come about that. You arrested Dr. Brad Simmons. Could I see him?"

"That was this morning, Miss Cassel. He arranged bond, so we didn't hold him. He'll go before a judge. But he has a wonderful record. When we first got the tip on him, even we wouldn't believe it. We had to prove it to ourselves. We're going light on him. He'll be on probation for a year or so."

"Where is he?"

The lieutenant frowned. "Why do you want him? He's not responsible for starting you, is he?"

"Oh no!" The shocked look on Lora's face convinced the detective. "He saved me. He put me on the cure. He kept me on it. He saved me–and all the time he was suffering himself."

The lieutenant stood up. He nodded. "Maybe that's why he worked so hard to save you, Miss Cassel. He's a brilliant man. He knew what could happen to you. So be smart. Don't let his sacrifice be wasted on you."

"No. I won't. I promise I won't. But I've got to find him. Maybe I can help him. If anybody can help him, maybe I can."

He stared at her. For a moment there was silence in the office. "Yeah." His voice was thoughtful. "Maybe you can. According to his story, he got on the stuff, light, when he was an intern. He was broke, and lonely, and insecure, overworked all to hell. He took tablets to sleep. Benzedrine to keep him going twenty hours a day. If there was ever extenuating circumstances, they're there in his case! His whole life had been spent helping other people. Come to think of it, I guess nobody has ever helped him. They used his strength. So he had to get it–the hard way."

"Will you tell me where he is?"

"You love him, eh?"

"What's the difference?"

"I guess you do. You must."

"Yes. I never knew, maybe, how much, until I read the paper. Until I saw he needed me. Please–tell me where I can find him!"

"You got a worthwhile job there, Miss, saving that wonderful guy for the world."

Her voice quavered. "I'll do it. If you'll just tell me where to find him."

The lieutenant smiled. He reached for his hat. He slapped an intercom switch and ordered a cruiser. "I want a fast one," he snapped. "One with sirens on it, good and loud."

He straightened up, grinning at Lora. "You're gonna save him, and you want me to tell you where he is? I'm gonna do better than that. Come on. I'm going to take you to him–right now."

Lora's lips trembled, and she fought back the tears as she climbed into the car. They took off instantly. She could hear the siren wailing, and it was like the sound of Brad crying for her, needing her.

"*I'll be with you soon, darling*," she whispered to herself. "*Be patient, darling. I'll be there....*"

THE END

WINTER GIRL

by Harry Whittington

Revised by David Laurence Wilson

Chapter 1

An hour after I met Lu Ann again that winter, I knew I was headed for deep, serious trouble. Only I had no idea how deep, how serious....

I saw Mr. Berlinger was hooked on my Irish setter from the moment he spotted her.

"A man can tell from the start when he sees something different," Pa said out of the side of his mouth to me.

"Fanny's different, all right." I felt sharp pride because Fanny was different from all the other hunting dogs, and better, and she was mine.

I whistled sharply just because I felt good with the chilled November wind cutting through me. Fifty yards away in the jackoaks, Fanny tensed, stood waiting. Six other men in Mr. Berlinger's hunting party, but Fanny knew my whistle. It stopped her and held her.

Mr. Berlinger saw it, too. He knew hunting and dogs. I could almost see his mouth watering, he wanted her so bad.

Only owning Fanny's papers wouldn't do Mr. Berlinger any good. But when I tried to explain this, nobody listened. They thought they could get from her all that I did. They figured I was trying to jack up the price because everybody in Cottonseed County knew my Pa would sell anything he owned, or anything he could con you into thinking he owned. Everybody knew Lutz Fenton, all right.

Only there was a wide difference between me and Pa. When he got mad at me, he'd yell that I took after ma's people.

Fanny came to heel and Mr. Berlinger never took his eyes off her.

This fenced preserve belonged to Mr. Berlinger and though Pa was his hunting guide and the caretaker of his big winter house, this was the first time I'd brought Fanny on his land. Maybe all along I'd known that when Mr. Berlinger saw Fanny he was going to want her.

He was a man used to getting what he wanted. At fifty, he was a lawyer worth millions.

Fanny came in to heel and pressed against my leg. Mr. Berlinger's close-working pointers were casting in widening circles. He had all three classes of dogs in his kennels: close-workers, medium, and far-rangers. He always used these close-workers when his Sunday-hunter friends were along so they would at least know what was going on.

Mr. Berlinger watched me and Fanny, forgetting his other dogs.

I waved my arm in a wide-sweeping pattern. Fanny sprang away as if her legs were steel springs, moving in an exact pattern I'd outlined from my hand to the crest of a jackoak knoll.

Most of Mr. Berlinger's friends watched Fanny, too. They knew something was going on. There was this tension between Mr. Berlinger and me. And there was fascination in following Fanny's mahogany coat slicing from dappled shadows into sudden sunlight, abruptly lighting a broomstraw flat.

Fanny kept to the pattern I'd projected for her. Nothing could turn her from it, no distraction, or sudden noise.

Mr. Berlinger came over to me, his $2,500 Ithaca Model 37 20-gauge shotgun with raised matte surface sighting rib, in the crook of his arm. That gun would knock your eye out. Hand-engraved 14 carat gold-embossed game-figures on his walnut stock, anti-glare surfacing on the top-stripping of its receiver, a Williams FP rear peep-sight that corrected barrel pitchdown to Mr. Berlinger's personality, physique, weight, height, drop at heel, and length of pull.

His peaked-bill hunting cap was pushed up on his high forehead. He wore a khaki hunting jacket, tan breeches in calf-length boots. He looked like what he was, all right, a million dollars taking time out to shoot quail in a seeded preserve.

He gave me a smile that would have made you think we were fraternity brothers, though he'd barely looked at me in all the eighteen years of my life. "That's some setter you got there, Calder."

I nodded, watching Fanny.

"I want her," he said, still smiling.

I felt chill. "Sorry, Mr. Berlinger. Fanny's not for sale."

"Boy, I'm not talking peanuts. This is the best-looking dog I've seen in ten–twenty years. Always been partial to setters. She's got everything." He spoke over his shoulder, laughing, to Pa. "Hey, Lutz. That's some setter. How long you had her in hiding?"

"That's Calder's dog, Mr. Frank," Pa said.

"Don't give me that, Lutz. You raised that dog here on my property." He winked at his fat-cat friends. "That dog is mine by rights, but I want you happy. I'll buy her."

"That there's Calder's dog, Mr. Frank." There wasn't much force in Pa's protesting, but I hadn't expected there would be. Pa wasn't about to oppose Frank Berlinger in anything.

"I want the dog," Berlinger's voice hardened. "And I don't want you two robbing me on it."

Fanny had frozen to a point–in the very area where the other dogs had missed birds.

Mr. Berlinger caught his breath, held it. We all did. You'll never see anything more beautiful than a setter at point, settled down, breathless, sun slanting orange and sharp on her coat, her fine nose and feathered tail in perfect alignment.

"I'll give you five hundred dollars," Berlinger whispered across his shoulder. "It's settled. Now let's drop it."

He strode away, bringing his gun up across his chest.

His friends took out after him, boots rustling dry leaves, ground reverberating. Even the fat-bellied quail sensed something wrong and flushed, whirring upward, scattering low over the underbrush. There were five in the covey.

Mr. Berlinger threw up his gun and fired. He got one.

Pa said, "I marked two or three of them down in the wire grass, Mr. Frank."

Berlinger grinned. "Fetch, Fanny."

Fanny stared up at him, wagging her tail. She didn't move. "Fetch!" His voice hardened.

Fanny waited until I said, "Fetch, Fanny."

She sprang into smooth action, going through the undergrowth. When she returned with the quail, she held it so gently that there were no teeth-prints marking its ruffled feathers.

She came directly to me. Berlinger spoke her name sharply but she appeared not to hear him.

"That dog deaf, Calder?" he asked.

"No, sir." I took the quail from Fanny's mouth, tossed it to Mr. Berlinger. "She doesn't know anything except to retrieve to me."

He dropped the bird into the game pocket of his khaki jacket. "I still want her. She'll obey me–she'll learn."

"No sir. You see, I trained her. I–"

"All right boy, I see that. You've done a fine job. You're even better with dogs than Lutz, and I never thought I'd meet the man who could handle dogs better than your Pa. But I'm paying you well for your time."

"Calder's got a lot of patience with a dog," Pa said to nobody in particular, trying to steer Berlinger off that tune.

But Mr. Berlinger never made millions being sidetracked from what he wanted. He said, "Five hundred. That's a lot of money." He spoke to me, but peered at Pa as if saying a hundred other things with his chilled blue eyes, all of them ominous.

Pa shook his head, his gaze sagging. "You'll have to dicker with Calder,

Mr. Frank."

I sent Fanny in another long cast. "She won't hunt for you, Mr. Berlinger. Ask Pa. Other men have tried. She won't do it."

"Calder's got a lot of patience with a dog," Pa said again.

"A dog will hunt for anybody. You train a dog, you train it right. Breed hunters. Some are better, better scent, better tracking, better reflexes, that's all. Now it's settled, Calder. I have been good to you people. You. Your folks. You people *live* off me."

"I'm sorry."

Berlinger's face flushed red. But at that moment we heard a jeep engine roaring through the flats.

We turned, watching the four-wheel-drive racing between the jackoaks at forty miles an hour–like something in a Bugs Bunny cartoon.

For the moment Frank Berlinger forgot me and Fanny. He glared at the jeep and then laughed because he recognized his daughter at the wheel, and he had never learned to stay angry at Lu Ann.

She raced to within ten feet of us, slammed on brakes, spewing sand from all four tires.

"What's the idea, Lu Ann?" Berlinger's voice rang.

"I got bored," she said.

"Come racing out here. Scaring birds out of the fields. Haven't you got anything better to do with yourself?"

She laughed at her father, but she wasn't really looking at him. She was staring at me.

There was nothing hidden about her gaze. It was open, direct and interested.

I couldn't take my eyes off her.

I'd seen her every winter as she grew up, but she'd never looked like this before.

She looked like what the right genes, diet, blood, breeding and ten million dollars could do to any red-blooded American girl in eighteen years.

She was slender, maybe a little too thin, but she had a little extra of everything she needed; class, polish, finish–she had it all. It was like something they poured over her every morning, or put in her bath water.

She swung out of the jeep, and the oldest man in the crowd caught his breath along with the rest of us. Or maybe when she appeared there weren't any old men any more. There were just males gawking at something too beautiful to touch, too rare.

Her dark hair bounced loosely in lustrous waves. Her face was high-planed and her almond-shaped eyes slanted upward in some strange way she seemed to have invented, under curved lines of her brows.

She modeled her perfection for us. Her high-standing breasts were unencumbered by any bra and they shifted against the fabric of a white, form-tapered shirt. Her hunting pants accented the line of her long legs and the rise at her thighs as if poured on her as hot liquid and allowed to dry like adhesive.

Her boots were so bright, expensive; they reminded you of miniature silver slippers.

"Bring in that dog, Calder," Berlinger said to me. "I'll show you I can put her to heel in five minutes."

I barely heard him. I stared at his daughter. It was as if I'd never seen her before. Of course I had, every winter as long as I could remember. But now in this bright slanting sunlight everything was different, and I felt as if somebody had shoved her father's shotgun up my left nostril and pressed the trigger.

"Calder!"

I moved my head as if awakened suddenly. "Yeah, Pa?"

"Didn't you hear Mr. Berlinger?"

One of Berlinger's friends laughed. "He's never seen a pretty girl before."

"Bring in that dog, Calder," Mr. Berlinger ordered. He glanced at his daughter. "Lu Ann, watch this. If you can watch this dog and stay bored, you're hopeless."

"I don't exactly have a thing for dogs, Daddy," Lu Ann said. She winked at me. "Hi, Calder."

"Hello, Lu Ann."

Angered, Berlinger put his fingers between his teeth and bit off a shrill whistle in Fanny's direction.

She didn't know he was alive.

But Berlinger wasn't a man who believed everything he saw. "Boy! Get that dog in here!"

Still gazing at Lu Ann, I nodded. I whistled low. Out in the sunlight Fanny hesitated, lifted her head, ears pricked. It was beautiful. Until Lu Ann rode up, it was the finest sight I'd ever encountered.

I whistled low again. Fanny broke pattern and came across the wire grass to me in a perfect line. She could have stepped on quail and never paused. Everybody watching knew this.

She came directly to me, pressed against my leg, her red tongue lolling out, head tilted, gaze fixed on my face.

"Isn't that the cutest thing?" Lu Ann said.

"Cute?" Her father roared. "Cute? Is that what they teach you? Cute?"

Lu Ann knelt beside me. I smelled the scent of her hair, and I ached smelling it, and smelling the fine clean fragrance of *her*.

Lu Ann caressed Fanny and Fanny wriggled with pleasure, pressing close to her.

"What a beautiful dog, Calder," Lu Ann said.

Berlinger said, "I'm buying her. How about that, Calder? Lu Ann likes your dog. Want to sell her to me – for Lu Ann?"

"Don't let Daddy con you," Lu Ann said. "He knows I hate dogs."

I smiled at her. I wasn't listening to her father anyhow. I was gaping at the way the sun glinted in her black hair, making it seem purple, and then pale blue, and then flashing colors through it that I had no name for.

"Watch Fanny," I said to Lu Ann.

She nodded, straightening. She stood beside me so her shoulder brushed my arm with the lightest touch. I trembled inside as if I'd bumped 120-volts head-on. I wondered if my eyes lighted up–or my nose.

I put Fanny through her paces.

Fanny went into a point, trancelike, rigid. I called her off of it. I let her flush two quail into the air and I got both of them, swinging my gun up easily, knowing Lu Ann was watching.

Berlinger raged. "Nobody ought to let any dog flush a point. It ruins the dog, and makes them jump-happy so you can't depend on them to hold a point."

Fanny retrieved my birds, barely holding them between her teeth.

The older men tried to head her off, making a joke of trying to take the birds from her. But Fanny sidestepped them, coming to me with the birds no matter how they tried to turn her.

I heard Frank Berlinger's increased breathing. I didn't blame him. I knew how he felt about Fanny, because Lu Ann affected me even worse, and suddenly I saw that from now on everything was going to be different. Everything.

Fanny rode on the seat of the jeep between Lu Ann and me.

"Where do you want to go?" Lu Ann yelled above the roar of the wide-open engine, the rasp of the wind.

I hung on, gritting my teeth. "It doesn't matter," I shouted. "We wouldn't make it anyway."

Lu Ann smiled. "You're cute, Calder. How'd you get so cute, all of a sudden?"

"It came in the mail," I said, hanging on. "In a plain wrapper.... Lu Ann, watch the road. I'm too cute to die."

She laughed, slowing slightly. "You think this is fast? Up home, I've got a 300SL. Four forward speeds. Goes faster in low gear than this jeep in high. You'd love it."

"I bet it's cute," I said.

She drove like a maniac, as if she hated cars, or herself, or the world.

She talked and drove and studied me in that bold way. She was different from anybody I'd ever known. I didn't complain about her driving any more. She didn't listen to me; I was with her, and at the moment I couldn't think of a better way to die.

She slowed the jeep when we hit a hard-surfaced road and we rolled along, letting the engine cool down to white hot.

"Look, Calder," Lu Ann said. "I hate to offend you, pet, but can't we get rid of this shaggy animal? She breathes with her mouth open. Of course you don't mind that, but she slobbers on me. And look at the way she grins, sitting there so I can't even see you."

"You don't like her," I said. "No sense fighting with me about it, you just don't like her."

"Like I told Daddy, I got no big thing for any animals, and I hate dogs."

"Any girl that hates dogs can't be all bad," I said. "If you'll drive me home, I'll put her in the kennel."

When I came back out to her jeep from the wired run, Lu Ann was slouched under the wheel waiting for me. I hadn't believed she would be. I hardly believed it when I saw her there, her glazed eyes consciously shutting out the view.

I couldn't blame her for that. The home we lived in would never make *Better Homes*. It probably would have been condemned, only nobody cared.

Five rooms, paint-peeled frame, black cypress roofing. The yard was bare sand, with flowers in old tire-casing beds. Chickens clucked under the chinaberry tree. The sagging barn had never been painted. Beside it were the dog runs where Pa held as many as thirteen pups in training sometimes. Our kitchen garden looked pretty pitiful.

It was as if somebody ripped scales from my eyes and I really saw that place for the first time. "Some estate," I said. "Some real beautiful place."

"Any home's a dump, Calder, and don't you doubt it. Any time it's got parents in it, it's a real pesthole." She didn't even look at the house.

She didn't care, and I quit caring because I was looking at her. She'd unbuttoned that white blouse deep down between her breasts, and I gazed at the golden rising of them.

My heart pounded raggedly. I'd been with very few girls, but I knew I'd never seen anything like this before. I could follow the outline of those uptilted breasts under the sheer fabric of her shirt, the nipples peaking it.

She hardly noticed the way I stared at her. It didn't please her. It didn't bore her. It was something that happened all the time.

"Let's flake off, boy," she said. "Where you want to go?"

"You want to ride into town, maybe we can have a drink?" I suggested.

"Come off it! Who'd sell us a drink? You don't think you look twenty-one, do you? You even shave yet?"

"Lord, Lu Ann. I meant a Coke."

She laughed at me. "You are young. But young. Do you know about the girl bees yet, Calder? Or is Fanny the only female you traffic with?"

I straightened, hating the way she laughed at me. I didn't like anyone's laughing at me, but it was triple murder when Lu Ann did it.

"Forget it," I said. "Nice knowing you. Real nice."

She burst into laughter. "Now I know why I flip for you, Calder. It's that stiff-necked pride. Boy, have you got pride. Proud. And kind to animals. What a parlay. Come on, Calder. Smile. What's it going to get you to be hot-tempered with me? Come on. We'll go have a drink somewhere."

I hesitated, staring at her because she was totally unlike any girls around Oak Bluff.

"You're wasting my time, Calder." She put a chill in her voice even while she was still smiling. "I'll run back to Daddy's shoot-out and pick up Homer Carmack. At least he's old enough to buy a girl a fifth of Scotch and a tin of protection."

I shivered at the way she talked. But I got into her jeep, my gaze fixed on her.

"Homer Carmack?" This was all I could say.

I scowled, remembering him. Homer Carmack was one of those over dressed hunters. I knew which one he was, all right. Tall, blonde, with a straight profile, he looked like an aging actor. He had a Scotch-flushed face, and manicured hands. He was getting gray and beginning a pot belly.

"Sure, Homer." Lu Ann shrugged. "Homer went along hunting unwillingly. He wanted to stay with me, but Daddy suspected. I promised Homer I'd rescue him."

"He's older than your father!"

"So?" She started the engine, goosing a roar out of it, and threw the jeep into reverse. She hit the road in front of our place doing forty.

"You mean you came out there this afternoon looking for–that old guy?"

"Let's not beat it to death, Calder," she warned, staring me down. "Face facts, boy. A mature man is much more exciting than a callow boy whose hand you have to hold so he can find his way around."

I shook my head, feeling ill inside. "You came out there–looking for Homer Carmack?"

"Don't sound dull-witted, Calder. Of course I did. He's fun. You don't think I somehow heard *you* were out there giving Daddy a rough time and came looking for you, do you?"

"It doesn't sound any crazier than the truth," I said.

Her tone softened. "I just flipped when I saw you, Calder. That's all. You looked so *new*... untouched. You looked like a new-minted penny that nobody had spent yet." She laughed. "I wanted to spend you, Calder. And spend you, and spend you, and spend you."

I didn't say anything because I didn't even know what she was talking about. I concentrated on the graceful cut of her neck, the tilt of her chin, the full underlip. She was so lovely it got inside you and shook you, just looking at her.

She reached under the seat and fished up a fifth of Scotch. She held it out to me. "Have a drink, Calder. Maybe you loosen up when you drink."

"Straight?" I made a face involuntarily. "I'd as soon drink kerosene."

She made a clucking sound of disapproval. "Status, Calder. Something you've got to learn. Acquire the taste. Don't be backwoodsy. Everybody who is hip drinks Scotch, Calder."

"Like Homer Carmack," I said.

Her face tightened. "I warned you. Don't beat it to death. I didn't hog tie you, you came willingly. Now be nice. Make me laugh, Calder. I came down here this winter to have fun. I could be bored up home with boys just as pretty as you."

I tried to think of something to say. I couldn't think at all. "Just one thing, Lu Ann, about Carmack. Then I'll drop it."

"You better." Her voice was cold. "I warn you, Calder. I get interested fast, but I lose interest a lot faster."

"Carmack," I persisted. "What does your father think about you–drinking–with a man as old as he is?"

Lu Ann twisted the cap off the bottle, took a long drink. She stared at me with her upslanted eyes cold with contempt.

"The devil with my father. You got that, boy? And the devil with you."

She slammed on the brakes. Her face was set and her chin was lifted. I'd thought she was beautiful before, but I'd never seen *anything* as lovely as she was now. I got all empty just looking at her.

"Get out," she said. "Why don't you get out, Calder?"

I forced a laugh and took the bottle from her. "Now we're even," I said. "Look who's got a stiff neck now."

She thawed slowly, finally smiled in a way that was only a compromise. "Well, you can be human," she said. "Almost, anyhow."

I gagged on the liquor. I was wrong about the Scotch. It was worse than kerosene.

"No status at all," she taunted. "A real nothing."

She stopped the car and slid over. "Why don't you drive, Calder? You look so helpless sitting there."

I got under the wheel, put the car in gear, headed toward Oak Bluff for no better reason than that it was three miles away and I thought three miles was fine for being alone with her, but it wasn't much. It raced by on the wind.

"Lu Ann," I said.

"What?"

"Nothing. I was just saying your name. I like it." I smiled at her. "It's got status."

She slid over close to me. When my arm moved I bumped her breasts. They were full and they gave under my arm. They were upsettingly full for such a young, slender girl. She enclosed my arm inside hers, pressing it against her. I could hardly see the road.

"You're nice, Calder." She talked against my face, the Scotch smelling good on her breath. It made me hungry. I wanted to drink in her breath as long as I could, until I was wildly drunk. "I like you when you're nice," she said. "Do you like me, Calder?"

I let the car grind to a stop on the lonely, late-afternoon road.

For a long time we didn't move. Then I slipped my hand up, unbuttoned her blouse. I had been right. She wore no slip under it. I covered her breast with my fingers.

"You do like me, don't you?" she whispered.

I shuddered, pulling away from her. I had never seen anyone as lovely, never felt anything like her in my life. It was as if she was burning up, and the fire from her body burned me.

But I knew what her father would do to me if he heard about this–and I knew he would hear if anyone saw us on this road.

I pulled away from her, shaking all over. "We better get on in to town."

"Why?" She didn't move. Her eyes opened, peering at me wildly.

"We better. We can't do this, Lu Ann. You'll hate me if we do."

"Are you a fool? I'll hate you if we don't!"

Chapter 2

I was shaking all over. Lu Ann twisted her body, turning on her side and letting one of her legs move across me.

"Hold me, Calder. Hold me."

I lifted my head, looking both ways along the road. I was sure I heard a car in the distance. The very thought that somebody would catch us like this left me weak.

She thrust her parted mouth over mine. Her eyes were like a baby's, sleepy, fighting against sleep, rolling up in their sockets–only, of course, Lu Ann wasn't sleepy at all.

And me? I felt like I'd never sleep again–I'd always be haunted by this moment–by the need and the fear that was all mixed up in it for me.

She pushed her blouse away from her golden body and her breasts thrust upward, taut, quivering. I trembled looking at the loveliness.

"Touch them," she said in a long sigh.

I was her slave. I had to do what she wanted–because it was what I wanted, even when I couldn't forget what they would do to me if they caught me with her like this.

I shuddered. For no good reason I remembered a mongrel that had leaped the kennel house and gotten to one of the purebred hunting dogs. They killed the mongrel without even thinking twice about it.

I was pretty sure that's what Lu Ann's father would do to me.

"What's the matter with you?" Lu Ann said.

She pulled me closer on the uncomfortable, divided seat. She didn't care about the discomfort, the road. She pressed against me, working her rigid breasts against my chest. She cried out and whimpered in her throat. She was wild, abandoned. I'd never been with a girl like her. All the girls I had known had fought me–or at least pretended to fight.

And suddenly I knew I could never go back to any of those girls again. Lu Ann had spoiled me for them. Maybe she had spoiled me for all other girls.

I could not imagine wanting any body except hers.

I kissed her, sick with need for her. She had driven me clear out of my mind. My breath hurt and burned in my throat. I moved my hands hungrily along her supple back, holding her rounded bottom in my hands, working her against me.

But when she tried to pull away her pants, moving them from between us, I straightened.

My face was gray. I knew I looked scared. I was.

She stared at me a moment, her eyes barely focusing. It was as if she didn't know where she was.

Abruptly she lunged away from me. Her face was gray and rigid, the pallor showing in the high planes of her cheeks.

Her upslanted eyes were dead, as if the wild fires had suddenly burned out.

"Oh, you fool," she wailed. "Why don't you get out of here!"

She hit at me with both fists, striking my face and my chest.

"Lu Ann!"

"Get out of here! Get out of here and let me alone–"

"Lu Ann–"

"Get out of this car and get away from me and don't ever come near me again. I'd hate to have a nothing like you happen to me–even by accident."

I sat unable to move, staring at her. There was no sense trying to talk to her, she would not even listen. I could only gaze at that beauty and know it was truly lost to me.

She made no effort to cover her nakedness. Those breasts stood taut as if laughing at me, because they could have been mine and now I could never have them.

I shook my head, unable to pull my gaze from her bared breasts.

"Go on!" she screamed. "Get out. Get out."

She hit me in the face with her fists. Dazed already, I barely felt the blows.

I nodded. Then I got out of the jeep and stood beside it in the late afternoon sunlight.

"Lu Ann."

She didn't even hear me. As soon as I got out of the car, she jumped in under the wheel, turned the key to the ignition and started the engine.

I gazed at her, but she threw me one look full of contempt–and then she was looking right through me.

I shivered, lonely, regretting something I'd never had, would never have now.

We had made a quick short circle.

We were right back where we always had been every other winter when she came down here. She didn't know I was alive.

The jeep roared away, dust powdering back over me. It was as if I were a piece of litter she had discarded.

She never looked back.

It was dark when I got back home. I was in no hurry. I ached in my guts, and I felt sad with a kind of sadness I'd never even thought about before.

When I came into the house the TV was blaring in the front room.

I stood for a long time barely conscious of the rise and fall of Mom's and Pa's voices out in the kitchen.

I stared at the TV set but didn't really see it. I was seeing Lu Ann. I couldn't forget the way she had pressed her body upon mine.

I tried to laugh at myself. I had calmed down on the long walk home, but I was probably going to have a heart murmur and high blood pressure the rest of my life. She had really charged me up. I didn't know you could need anything as badly as I needed her.

I shivered. No matter how long I lived, or what I did, I was never going to have kisses as hot and sweet tasting as Lu Ann's. They would never be the same with anyone else, with that wild, fierce need and sweet Scotch-tainted taste. Status. Her kisses gave you status all right. But when you got status like that, what did you do with it?

Sweat beaded my forehead. Nothing made sense. I wanted to be with Lu Ann, and here I was back in this lousy house, and Lu Ann was–she was out wherever she was.

It was less than two miles to her big winter house up on Dead Indian River, but it was too far from here for me. I couldn't make it in a million light years.

I kept telling myself it was better this way, even if I felt as if I were going to vomit. It had to be better. She was nothing but trouble for me.

That didn't stop me from wanting her.

I drew the back of my hand across my mouth, gagging.

I stared at the television set. For the first time I noticed that the picture was fuzzy, with sound waves fluttering across it.

Not even thinking what I was doing, I bent down in front of the set, fine-tuned in a glass-clear picture. Mom thought I was a genius when I did it for her. Mom wasn't really ready for the telephone, and TV was something she had to accept without thinking about it. She snapped it on, happy and pleased with any kind of lousy picture she got.

Finally their yelling got through to me.

My parents were yelling at each other in the kitchen. They didn't know I was in the house.

They may have been yelling when I first came in, or maybe they had been building up to this. I didn't know. I was too wound up in my own thoughts and what Lu Ann had done to me; I didn't hear anything.

Slowly, I straightened up in the darkened front room with the pictures jumping like gray shadows on the TV tube, vague light lunging in the dark corners of the pine-paneled walls.

My stomach twisted, tied in knots. Don't ever let anybody tell you that country boys can't develop ulcers. I had a stomach that only the Maalox people could love. My first memories were of hearing Mom's crying and Pa's swearing at her, his voice slurring. Then I'd hear him hit her in the face with his fist, with that sound that makes you sick when you hear it. Then I'd hear him crying, bawling, begging her to forgive him, and my stomach would cramp in knots, and if I ate anything for the next two days, I couldn't keep the food down.

I stared around that dimly lighted room, wanting to clear out. But I didn't. I went on standing where I was, my fists clenched and my stomach nerves knotted, waiting.

I could tell myself I didn't know what I was waiting for, but I knew better. I was waiting for Pa to hit Mom. I had it set in my mind, the next time he hit her, I was going to beat him as long as I could stand up.

It made me ill, thinking that. Pa was good to me, and he always had been, and even when he hit Mom and you heard his crying and pleading with her to forgive him, you got the empty feeling that he had done something bad that he never wanted to do, something he couldn't help doing because he was driven to it.

But I wasn't going to let him do it, not any more. He was drinking, potted; he must have started tanking it on as soon as the Berlinger hunt broke up. This might be an excuse from him that Mom could accept, but I couldn't buy it any more.

I had seen this meanness for a long time, among the country men Pa hunted with, and in the winter people up at Berlinger's big house: Any man that was mean when he drank was mean all the time, only he couldn't hide it when he was drunk.

I clenched my fists. Pa couldn't take out his meanness that got all bottled up in him on Mom, not any more. Not when I was around.

I knew something else. Even drinking, Pa was more than a match for me. He was muscular, big. But it would get through the liquor fumes in his brain. As often as he hit her, I was going to hit him, even if I finally got my brains stomped out.

I shivered, thinking about it, hating it, but hating what he did to her worse.

There was music in Mom's voice, even when she was crying.

"Lutz," Mom was saying, "I haven't said anything to you for a long time, but now you've got to listen to me."

His voice rode over hers. "You heard me, Molly. I told you. I don't want to talk to you. I ain't got time. I got to eat my supper and get out of here–"

"That's what we've got to talk about, Lutz."

"About me getting out? Woman, I can't clear out fast enough. What kind of life you think I got, Molly, taking crap from Berlinger all day, and coming home to more crap from you at night–"

"That's not true, Lutz. I've said nothing to you for months now–"

"No. You ain't really talked to me for years. All drawn up against me inside. You used to care when I drank, you used to care what happened to me. You don't even care any more."

"I can't help that, Lutz. You killed all that in me. I couldn't let myself go crazy worrying about you running around, drinking, fighting–"

"What's a man supposed to do?"

"I don't know, Lutz. I used to think I knew. I used to think all men were like my father–"

"Don't bring him into it! Not when I'm eating!"

"My father provided a good home, and food, and clothes for his family–"

"You ain't naked, are you? You missed any meals lately?"

"–but even more than that, Lutz, my father provided us with a good name. A name we weren't ashamed of, a name that people respected and looked up to. I guess that's mostly what he provided us. I guess that's what I thought men were supposed to do."

"You think there's a better name than Fenton in this country? You ask anybody. Nobody takes Lutz Fenton for anything. A man wants the best hunting dog, who does he go to? Lutz Fenton–"

"Yes!" Her voice rose. "And the best moonshine liquor, and the best dirty stories, and the man who owes everybody that will let him. What a lovely name you've made. But I don't care about that. Not any more. I'm resigned to all that, Lutz. I'm Mrs. Lutz Fenton and I've got to accept what that means."

I heard his chair scrape back and knew he had lunged up to his feet. My stomach shook.

"What does that mean, woman? What's so bad about that?"

There was a long silence as if Mom had withdrawn again, the way she had for so long, as if she didn't care what Pa did any more, or what happened to us.

Finally she spoke softly, tense: "I can't live like this, Lutz. Not like this.

I'm a Calder. No matter what you've made of me, no matter what you've done to me; I am a Calder, and my name–my people–are as good as anybody. You must owe me something–"

"I don't know what you're talking about! No more than you do! I give you things." His hand slammed down on the kitchen table. "Didn't I give you that TV set in there?"

"Yes. You got drunk and sold some of Mr. Berlinger's dogs and you bought me a TV set."

"And that stove there! Electric stove, ain't it. I'm not rich. I give you what I can. I ain't no prissy Calder, thank God, but I give you what I can."

"Don't you understand, I don't want things you buy when you're drunk and trying to make up to me for some terrible thing that you've done to me.... I don't want that, Lutz!"

"Let's get together then, woman. Why don't you tell me what it is you do want?"

"A good name!" She sobbed it. "You want to know? I don't want you chasing after the widow Goldie Hampsden. People are laughing and gossiping about us all over the county–you chasing after a woman whose husband's barely cold in his grave–and her such trash she carries on with you–right in public."

His laughter erupted. "So that's it. Jealous! You're jealous! You are a real dog in the manger, ain't you, Molly? You don't want me–but I ain't supposed to have no other woman? What am I supposed to do, beat my head against them fence posts out there? I'm a man! I can't live like no lily-livered, bloodless saint. I ain't no saint, and I never said I was. But I do get hungers. I get hungry in my guts–with a hunger you can't even know anything about–and you're too good for me; I got to get it somewhere."

"Your dogs are like that, too, aren't they, Lutz? Does that make you any better than they are? I want you to be decent. You don't care. You could wallow with the pigs and be happy. Not even for me–but you owe it to Calder to be decent. Don't you know everybody is talking about you and the widow Hampsden?"

"Let 'em talk. If they're talking about me, they're letting some other poor devil rest!"

"She's trashy, no good. You're dragging us down with you, Lutz. Can't I make you see? I have nothing. I don't care. Not any more. But it's the shame of what you're doing in front of Calder's friends, and mine."

"You know Goldie Hampsden don't mean nothing to me."

"Oh, I know that. No woman means anything. You're like a dog, running after anything–"

"Look, Molly, if it makes you feel better to rip me up, you go ahead. But you're a little wrong when you mix up calling a man a dog–a male dog lives quiet and easy, Molly, until he gets the scent of some female in heat–it's them females that run loose and got to get it when they need it–"

"You got the scent of Goldie Hampsden?"

"Maybe I have, Molly. But it don't have to touch you."

"Touch me? It shames me! I'm sick with shame."

"It don't touch you, Molly. It ain't got nothing to do with you."

"I don't want people talking my name and Goldie's in the same breath–"

"They don't, Molly. You know they don't–"

"When it's my husband they laugh and whisper about–then it's me, and it's my son they talk about."

"You know better, Molly. Maybe I take a few drinks with Goldie. Maybe I laugh some with her. Lord knows, there's little enough to laugh about around here...."

"If my husband's trash, then I'm trash, too."

"Nobody talks about you, Molly. I'd kill the man talked about you."

"Don't think that makes me feel any better. That makes me no better or different from your Goldie."

"It's not the same! I married you," Pa said.

"What's that supposed to mean?"

"I married you!" He yelled it.

"How does that make me any different?"

"I married *you*!"

"Why? Because you had no respect for me? Because you wanted everybody to laugh at a woman fool enough to stay with a man who ruts with every pig in the county?"

Pa's voice shook the house. "Stop it, Molly. If you don't see it, I can't tell you. Stop hammering at me. I don't want to hit you, Molly, but so help me, you drive me, you drive me!" His voice broke, trembling. "You drive a man, Molly, right out of his mind!"

The kitchen door slammed and Pa strode though it, going down the steps and across the yard.

I didn't move. I knew where he was going. He kept his liquor in the barn.

"Calder."

I trembled because Mom had walked into the living room, and I hadn't even known she was here until she spoke my name.

She said, "When did you come home, Calder?"

"A little while ago, Mom."

She came to me and touched my arm. Her eyes were bleak. "Are you hungry? Supper's ready. I've a nice supper for you, Calder."

I swallowed hard, shook my head. "I'm not hungry, Mom. I couldn't eat."

"You're so thin, Calder. You must eat." She stared up at me.

She was pretty thin, herself, but I didn't say anything about that. I had grown tall quickly. I still had an odd feeling when I looked down at the top of *her* head. Her hair was a honey-brown with gray in it, though she was only thirty-three.

Mom was fifteen when she ran away from home and married Pa. Sometimes she looked a lot older than thirty-three. Tonight she did.

Her pale blue eyes had no life in them, and they were red-rimmed from her crying. Her mouth pulled down at the corners even when she smiled. "I want you to be a fine man, Calder. I want to be proud of you."

I didn't answer. What was there to say? I'd heard the same line since I was three years old. Maybe she'd said it to me to stop my crying when the doctor slapped me on the bottom, delivering me.

I knew what she wanted, all right. Her father and her grandfather had been lawyers. Two uncles on her mother's side of the family had been doctors. She never let me forget it. She didn't have much. I guess she had to cling to what she had, and to keep thinking about it, and talking about it, I don't know.

"There are good people, Calder. Real good people. The simple kind of good that doesn't get in newspapers."

I smiled at her and moved away toward the front door.

Her voice sounded frightened. "Where are you going, Calder? You haven't eaten any supper."

"I want to go down and feed Fanny," I said. "Maybe then I'll feel more like eating."

"All right." She let me get to the front door. She spoke my name again. I turned, glancing across my shoulder. "Your father doesn't have it easy, Calder. It isn't easy for him, working for Mr. Berlinger."

"I'll go feed Fanny."

But I didn't go to the kennel runs.

I pushed open the barn door, let it close behind me. Pa had lighted a lantern and hung it on a nail in a two-by-four upright.

He sat in the front seat of his old car, the door swung open, his booted legs hanging out. He was drinking white moonshine from a quart mason jar.

He watched me walk across the straw-littered flooring. The barn smelled of old hay, old leather, old gasoline. Mice skittered in the loft. The place was stacked with broken furniture, junk of all kinds.

I stared at Pa, sprawled half out of his car. I looked away because it hurt to see him like this.

Mom was right about him. I knew it as well as she did, better, because he used to take me on some of his parties. Usually he'd start out not even meaning to party, but somebody would give him a drink, and it ended the same way, with me waiting in his old car outside some house where they were laughing and yelling and wenching–and finally fighting.

"Pa, I want to talk to you."

"Sure, son." He took a long pull at the mason jar and from hospitable habit offered it to me before he remembered I wasn't a friend, I was his son. "What's on your mind?"

I looked at him again and winced because it's senseless to go on admiring a man when you know as much about him as I know about Pa.

But there was a look about him. There was the width of his shoulders and the depth of his chest, and the tilt of his head when he was away from Berlinger.

Pa was ten years older than Mom. He was in his early forties and losing his hair, so it winged back from his forehead. Otherwise it was hard to tell he was getting old, except when you looked in his eyes.

The look in his eyes was *old*. Old hurts. Anguish. The pained light in his gray eyes said everything had gone wrong for him. Everything always went wrong, no matter how fine it started out. But only his eyes wept. I never heard Pa whine. That was why it beat me to see him hold his hat in his hands when he talked to Frank Berlinger.

"Speak up, Good-looking," he said. He tilted the wide-mouthed jar, drinking again. He smacked his mouth, exhaled. "If this stuff was mother's milk, I'd be nursing yet, boy.... Hey, boy, you and me got to go hunting one of these days. I mean just you and me. A real hunting trip–on the other side of the world from them baited fields."

"Pa–"

"You and me ain't been anywhere together lately, boy.... I don't want to lose you, son. I sure don't want to lose *you*–"

"Listen to me, Pa–"

"Well, that's it, boy, you ain't saying nothing. I figure I'd just as soon listen to myself as to sit here and stare at that look in your face." He took another drink.

"I know all about it, Pa, and you got to quit. I ain't had guts enough to talk to you about it before, but I'm talking to you now."

"That's fine. Now all we got to do is figure what you're talking about–"

"You know what I mean, Pa. I'm talking about *her*, Mrs. Hampsden. That's what I'm talking about."

"You loco, boy? Ain't you kind of mixed up? I had the idea I'm the father–the man around this house. I don't have to take talk like this from you."

"Listen to me! People are talking. And they're laughing. Maybe you are my father–but you couldn't prove it by the way you act. You sure don't act like it."

"How am I supposed to act, boy?" He watched me with those anguished eyes cold. He took a drink, never moving his gaze from my face.

I waved my arm. "I heard you and Mom in the house. She's right–her friends are talking about you. Only it's a lot worse because she doesn't know how bad it is."

His voice was flat. "How bad is it?"

"You know what they're saying. You're doing everything they say you're doing. You don't care about anybody. But you've got to care about Mom."

He took another long drink. "I care about your mother, boy."

"You sure don't act like it!"

"Calder. You don't want trouble with me, do you? So why don't you drop this and walk out of here?"

"Because you're breaking her heart. You're killing her. You're making an old woman out of her and she's only thirty-three. It ain't worth it, Pa. Nothing you get ain't worth that."

He stared at his clenched fist for a long time, and then moved his gaze to the mason jar. It was less than a quarter full now. He exhaled deeply and then drank, letting his hand relax on his leg.

At last he looked up, his eyes burning with the heat of moonshine.

"Look, Calder. You figure I owe you something. All right. So I'm going to tell you–and this is what I owe you–to tell you the *facts* of life.

"Not life like your ma wants to think it should be, or the way they talk in church, or school, or anywhere else that they make a dime by lying to you about what life is like, or what it ought to be, if only God had made us all bloodless namby-pambies, and rich and honest, and without something inside that sets you wild with hunger, with needs that won't let you be, won't let you rest.

"A man is born hungry, Calder, and that is all he's born. Some men it don't take much to satisfy. Some men get spoon-fed all their lives and never know what it is to get hungrier and hungrier every day of their lives.

"Some men are born with everything, and some take it from other people, and some can't ever get it. Men like me, Calder, go through life like a scavenger, taking the leavings of other men. Maybe you won't be like me, Calder. I pray that you won't.... Why, I'll get right down on my knees with you right now, and we'll both pray that you won't ever in this world be hungry like I am."

He stared up at me and the look in his eyes was painful. I had to turn away from it.

He laughed. "Just as well you don't want to pray. If I ever get down on my knees like I am right now, I'll never get up."

"Pa. I know it ain't easy. But you got to think about Mom."

He was finishing off the mason jar of shine and wasn't looking at me.

"What do you think there is in life for a man like me, Calder? What? I ain't educated to be anything. I could farm, but I've hated farming since my pa used to whip me out of bed at four-thirty every morning to start the chores.

"Where farm work is concerned they give me a yellow belly instead of a green thumb! I ain't nobody, Calder. I ain't nothing. Maybe that's the hardest thing a man has to say to his own son. Maybe it's the hardest thing for him to accept.... I ain't a Calder like your ma.... Thank God, I ain't a Calder....

"You want to know what there is for me, boy? There's nothing in my life but a little moonshine to drink, a woman every now and then, a few laughs if I can think up something to laugh about.

"I can't live like they teach in Sunday School." Pa shook his head. "Because the world ain't like they say. I do what I have to to stay alive. I learned early. You take what you can get. You get so you figure it don't matter, and then you can settle back and enjoy it–even the bad things–because it don't matter. The rich own everything worthwhile. If they don't, they'll take it.... I don't even blame them any more. That's what life is. Only I know it now. I look it straight in the ugly face and I know it, and I laugh at it, and I take another drink."

Pa stared into the empty mason jar, hurled it across the barn, smashing it against the wall.

"You could be better to Mom, Pa. Looks like you could be better to her."

He slid out of the car but he couldn't stand straight. He leaned against the door, staring at me as if I were only a blur.

"Why? What would that buy me? What would it buy Lutz Fenton to try to be what your ma wants? *I couldn't do it, boy*. It's that simple. I found that out before you were born. I ran away with your ma when she was a fifteen-year-old, and already carrying you inside her because we loved each other so terrible we couldn't wait."

"You loved her then. Looks like you could remember–"

"Remember, my memory ain't as strong as my needs, boy. Them Calders wanted me put in the state pen for statutory rape. Molly swore she wanted me to have her, but even so it would have got me twenty years in prison. I talked her into running away and marrying me. A man could take his wife to bed, no matter ... That's what I thought."

He laughed, licking at his mouth. "That's what I thought. I thought I'd get a job and your ma and me would live happy like they do in the movies.

"Only nobody would hire me because the Calders and Judge Stark used influence against me. Don't hire Lutz Fenton."

Pa laughed again, the sound bitter and hurt.

"It still would have been fine with me and Molly–if only them Calders would of let us alone. I could run shine, steal cars; I could do anything to keep Molly and me alive. I wasn't scared of nobody when I was twenty-five.... Now I reckon I'm scared of everybody–not physically–but afraid of what they can do to you with their sneaking and lying.

"But them Calders came to Molly everyday when I wasn't there, telling her that she was a Calder and I wasn't good enough to lick her shoes. Finally got so she believed them, and she wouldn't let me lick her shoes. I'm a man just by nature got to have a woman.

"Your ma was too good for me–but I went on living somehow. Other women didn't think they were too good. I'm what I am–whether I'm proud of it or not. Now, get out of here, boy, and let me alone. I need a drink."

He straightened from the car, turned and aimed himself with deep concentration toward the hay bin where he cached his shine.

He took one long step, staggered, and plunged forward to his knees.

I moved to help him, but he twisted around, his face rutted and his eyes wild.

"Get out of here, boy! Let me alone! Don't come near me. Don't touch me."

I stood, my stomach twisted, watching him half-topple, half crawl to the hay bin. A mouse leaped out when he dug around in the straw.

He came up with a mason jar of shine and then sagged against the bin. It took him ten minutes to twist the cap off, but I didn't speak or offer to help. He didn't look my way again.

Finally, he began to drink, thirstily, gagging, smiling, the shine staining his shirtfront. He didn't know I was in the world. He didn't even know he was.

Chapter 3

I swung down off the school-bus the next afternoon at four o'clock, walked alone toward home, in no hurry to get there.

I didn't look up because I didn't care anything about seeing the ugly house, or Mom's standing on the front porch waiting for me every afternoon. She always wanted to know the news from Oak Bluffs, as if I'd spent the day gossiping.

I decided what I'd do was go hunting. I'd take Fanny and spend the afternoon in the woods. Ma said I was like Pa when I ran away from things like that. But when I could go hunting, things would look better when I came back. "Don't run away from things, Calder," Mom said. "That's what your Pa does. You got to face things, you got to work them out."

I glanced toward the house and Mom stood on the edge of the porch, in the reach of the sun, an arm around an upright, watching me come along the road.

I winced, hurting inside in a way I couldn't even explain.

I waved to Mom and turned toward the kennels. I hated doing it. She had nothing to look forward to. Pa hadn't even come home last night. Maybe he hadn't come home all day. I was hurting her now. I hated myself. Why didn't I just walk up there and hit her in the face, like Pa did? He didn't want to hurt her, either, but he did.

I was sweating and feverish. The last thing I'd eaten was sometime yesterday, and the last I'd held in my stomach was that drink of straight Scotch in Lu Ann's car.

A memory of her bared breasts flared through my mind, the golden color of her naked flesh, the fiery burn of her frantic breathing.

I jerked my mind away from her. That got me nowhere, either.

I was almost to the kennels before I realized Fanny wasn't barking.

Mom called something to me.

I ran toward the kennel runs. The run was empty. Then I saw the long rip in the wire.

Mom came down the steps and stood in the sun. She shaded her eyes with her upraised arm.

"Calder–"

I only shook my head at her as I ran past, going toward the hardroad.

My eyes were blurred with tears. I could barely see her.

I heard her whisper after me, "Oh, Calder...."

I didn't look back.

It was four miles from our house into the Cypress Bar on Main Street in Oak Bluffs. Maybe I didn't run all the way. I don't remember how I got there. A man in a pickup truck offered me a ride. I shook my head and kept running. When my chest started burning and my throat hurt from breathing through my opened mouth, I'd stop running and stride along, taking long steps, and then suddenly I'd be running again.

Pa sat at a table near the rear of the room in the Cypress Bar. The fat blonde woman who tended bar was talking to a couple men. The room was dark, with cheap tables covered with red-and-white checked cloths and candles in bottles on each table.

The juke box was wailing. Mrs. Hampsden was with Pa.

They watched me walk between the tables toward them.

"Pa," I said. "Pa–"

"Hello, Calder." There was pain in his eyes to match mine. Only suddenly I didn't care. For the first time I figured maybe Pa didn't really hate hurting Mom the way he swore he did. Maybe he said it because it made him feel better.

"Where is she, Pa? Where's Fanny?"

"Sit down, boy. You look bushed. You been chasing rabbits?"

"Where is she, Pa?"

Mrs. Hampsden stared at me, letting her pale blue eyes crawl over me as if I were something on a notions counter and she had a notion to buy me.

I don't know how old she was. She was proud of her long, curved legs and she stuck them out from the table for everybody to see. There was a look of boldness about her, the full breasts, the broad hips, the perfume. She wore her dyed-blonde hair fluffed up. She had a wide-lipped mouth, bright rounded cheeks. I knew all the men in the place thought she was a good-looking woman, and they all envied Pa.

Goldie said, smiling, "Hello there, Calder."

My voice shook. "Where is she, Pa?"

"Say hello to Mrs. Hampsden, Calder," Pa said. "You got to learn to be polite, boy."

I stared at them. It was as if they were inside one of those mirrors that distorted everything–they were or I was.

"You can say hello," Goldie said, smiling. "But don't you dare call me

Mrs. Hampsden, Calder. You call me Goldie. I'm not that much older than you are."

Pa laughed. "You best keep your eyes this way, Goldie. I'm the one paying for your beer. Remember? Calder may be prettier than me, but I've forgot things that boy will never learn–he's too much like his Ma."

Goldie laughed, still lapping at me with those pale blue eyes.

"I never realized Calder had grown so tall, Lutz. Why he's a handsome young man."

I leaned forward, catching Pa's shirt in my hand. "Where is she, Pa? Where's Fanny? What did you do with her?"

Pa twisted free of my hands. He held my wrists in a touch so gentle I barely felt the pressure, yet was like steel bands. He guided me into the chair directly in front of him.

"I meant to be home when you got there to tell you. I got delayed. I sure meant to–"

"Where is she?"

"I don't know, boy."

"Pa. Please! Don't lie, Pa. Please!"

He sucked in a deep breath. He said, "Count yourself fortunate, son. I realize you're upset. You don't know what you're saying–"

"I know what I'm saying–"

"Don't do this, boy. They's a few dead men that called me a liar to my face, but not a living soul. Now I feel bad as you about that dog. I know what she meant to you. I done what I could. I heard them thieves out there, and I ran from the house. But they got away before I could get there. They took her–two men in a black pickup truck–they got clean away boy, before I could stop them."

"Why, Pa? Who got away?"

"I told you, Calder. I feel worse than you–"

"Who was it, Pa?"

"I don't know! I wanted to get the license number for sure. I mean, men can't come right in your yard–"

"In broad daylight?" I said.

"That's right. Ain't that the worse thing you ever heard, Miss Goldie?"

"Calder, you look pale," Goldie said. "You better have a beer or something."

I glanced at her, shook my head. "Why was the fence cut, Pa."

"In broad daylight? They rode past the house to get the dog out."

"In broad daylight? They rode past the house to get to the kennels. They took time to cut the fence? The gate was unlocked, Pa."

"Maybe they didn't know that–"

"They had to walk by the gate, Pa, to get where they cut the fence." My voice shook. "Why was the fence cut, Pa?"

"I don't know, boy. I swear to you. It tears me up about that dog of yours. I heard that pickup truck. Black–"

"Like two hundred other black pickup trucks around here, Pa?"

Pa's face went cold. "I done what I could, Calder. I run out there. I saw two strangers. Wasn't anybody I know around the county, I'd swear that. They stole Fanny and drove off."

"They'd have to pass the house, Pa–"

"I told you, I'm sorry!"

I stared at him, feeling my eyes distend and my face twist into ruts.

I stood up. He caught at my arm, saying my name, but I jerked free and lunged away from him. I was running by the time I hit the street.

Nothing was clear to me. My eyes were blurred with tears. I felt helpless and lost.

I almost bowled over two people.

I heard the man shout something and the young girl with him gasped.

I straightened, glancing at the girl and the old man with her. I recognized Willi Ruth Stark. She was in my class at school. There was a kind of fresh loveliness about her, she had a scrubbed look, and yet it was soft, as if she'd been grown under glass. Maybe she had. She had full breasts, but you could not think about any boy getting to play with them. It was impossible to imagine Willi Ruth panting with passion. She was Judge Stark's daughter, and she looked it.

Judge Stark was tall, soldierly, gray, with the most forbidding look I ever saw about a man. You could believe the old Salem judges looked like him, presiding at witch trials. He stared at me as if ready to sentence me to a public flogging.

He said, "Look out there, young man."

He glanced up and saw that I'd just come out of the Cypress Bar. You could read in his face what he thought of anybody who went into the Cypress Bar. He never entered it himself, except in the weeks before each election, when he suddenly became a great fellow and went everywhere and slapped everybody on the back.

I caught my balance and tried to move around them.

Judge Stark said, "Are you drunk, young man?"

Then he stared at me, figuring my age, my social status. It was years before election time. He said, "You're too young to frequent bars."

He caught my arm, but I twisted free and shoved past him.

I glanced back across my shoulder.

"Go to hell," I told him. When his daughter gasped again, I remembered how she never knew I was alive in any of the classes we had at school. I said it even louder. "You go to hell, too, Willi Ruth...."

Judge Stark's face went as gray as his brows, and he looked as if he were going to run after me and drag me off to jail personally. It crossed my mind that I'd be in a bind if I ever came before him in court, but I figured if that happened, I'd be in a bind anyhow.

I strode away from them and kept walking. It was all mixed up in my mind, all the reasons I had for hating Judge Vasco Stark and his stuck-up daughter. I'd hated her all through school, and I hated him for what he had done to Pa before I was born, but even while I was hating him for this, I couldn't really blame him. That's how fouled up I was.

It was deep dark, after nine o'clock, and I was plodding around Berlinger's yard at his winter house on Dead Indian River.

I had a flashlight, but I didn't even remember where I'd gotten it. I was checking out his place without even knowing what I saw. I didn't need to see anything. Fanny would smell me. Fanny would bark. I'd find Fanny all right, if I got anywhere near her.

Some distance away, and beyond the bluff where Berlinger's big house stood lighted and loud, I could hear the swirl and flow of the fast moving river.

Suddenly lights erupted from every corner of the yard lighting the place up like a revival tent.

I stood blinking against the light.

I heard men spilling out of the house, all of them talking, some carrying shotguns. Berlinger and his friends wouldn't bother asking questions about what I was doing on his lands.

"Calder!" Frank Berlinger's voice struck at me like 20-gauge shot from his Ithaca 37.

He strode toward me, his gun in the crook of his arm.

"What are you doing out here in my yard, Calder?" he said. "You trying to get yourself killed, prowling around like this?"

"I'm looking for Fanny, Mr. Berlinger," I said.

"Your setter? What you looking around here for?"

"She's gone. Pa took her and sold her to somebody."

"Your Pa wouldn't do that to you."

"He would if the price was right, Mr. Berlinger. And your price was right–for him."

The others stood in a half-circle some feet away from us.

I glanced at them. Most were puzzled, all of them had been drinking, and none was really concerned about what was going on out here. They had come running, armed to the teeth, because it sounded exciting.

But there was this blank look in their faces, and Berlinger stared at me coldly. I almost gave up. I decided I was wrong–about Pa and Mr. Berlinger and that phony wire-cutting job in Fanny's kennel run.

Then my gaze struck against Homer Carmack's. As I said, he was a handsome man growing old. Something in his face held my gaze.

"You better get on home, Calder, and sleep it off," Berlinger said.

I stared at Homer Carmack. He smiled as if he just couldn't swallow the secret pleasure that showed in his face. Maybe the other guests didn't know what had happened to Fanny, but he knew.

"Pa sold Fanny to you, Mr. Berlinger." I sounded wild and scared, because I was. "I want her back. I'll pay you–I don't know how–but I will–"

"How old are you, boy?"

"What difference does it make?"

"I'm just trying to remember you're a kid, talking to me like this, Calder."

"I *trained* her, Mr. Berlinger. From a puppy." My voice rose.

Even saying those words had an empty sound because you couldn't put what Fanny meant to me in words. No words I knew.

You didn't *train* a dog like Fanny. What you did was you patiently showed her everything you know, and with an instinct nobody understands, she took it from there.

Pa was the best trainer in the county and he taught me all he knew: the ways to pull a dog off a point, the way to break a dog from pouncing on wounded game when he got the scent of fresh blood. Some dogs will point meadowlarks. Some will point rattlesnakes. Fanny was born knowing better.

"I trained that dog, Mr. Berlinger–"

"Stop it, boy. You're upset." He turned, smiling, and lifted his voice. "Why don't you fellows go back inside and hit the Scotch? Young Calder is upset. Nothing to it. I'll be in in a moment."

They turned and trooped toward the house. But Carmack took only a few steps with them, then he paused, watching us, smiling.

I said, "Please, Mr. Berlinger. Pa had no right to sell you my dog–no matter what he said."

Berlinger tried to smile. "You're right. The dog was mine in the first place. All dogs are mine when they come from this place, Calder, no matter what your Pa said to you. But Fanny isn't here–"

"You wanted her!"

Berlinger's face went cold. He stopped smiling. "I ought to take a whip to you."

My voice shook. "Pa had no right to sell her to you–"

"You impudent trash. Lutz Fenton ought to spend less time teaching his dogs obedience and beat a little common decency into you, teach you respect–"

"Respect for what?"

"Get out of here. I ought to run you off the place and fire your old man–"

"Pa doesn't know I'm here."

"No. You've flipped your wig." He shrugged, relenting. "Go, boy, take a light. Check my kennels."

"I already did."

Homer Carmack laughed. Berlinger glanced coldly toward him, then said to me: "Stay off my land, boy, all of it. From now on. Or I'll have you arrested for trespassing."

"What's the matter, Calder?" It was Lu Ann's voice.

Both Mr. Berlinger and I jerked our heads around.

I went empty at the sight of her, her beauty eating through the agony in me like an acid. She wore an ice-blue dress that was cut well above her knees and deep between her full breasts.

"Go back in the house, Lu Ann," her father said.

Homer Carmack caught at her bared arm as she walked past. She sidestepped, never even looking at him. He stopped smiling then.

Lu Ann laughed at her father. "You must be confused in this light, Daddy. This is Lu Ann, not one of your servants."

"Go back in the house," he said again.

Lu Ann glanced at him. She reached up and touched his cheek with her palm as if he were a backward child. Then she looked at me. "You got all the lights on out here, Calder. You must have come on big."

"He's prowling around the yard," Berlinger said.

Lu Ann laughed. "Come on, Daddy. Calder's been prowling your yard as long as I can remember. Maybe he came to see me–"

"He didn't come to see you. He's accused me of stealing his dog!"

"Fanny? Well, give her back to him, Daddy. You can buy other dogs–even if they're not quite that perfect–whatever it is you see in her. Still you can afford dozens of other dogs."

Berlinger nodded. "This kid ought to have sense enough to realize that. He knows I could buy a hundred dogs like his."

"There's only one," I said, my voice quavering.

Lu Ann jerked her head around as if seeing me for the first time, really looking at me. Her face softened and I saw her in a different light, too, as if I'd never really seen her before.

She said, "You really are upset, Calder. Why, you can barely talk."

I tried to speak but I couldn't. I wasn't going to break down in front of her.

She said, "Well, come on, Calder. We'll get a jeep. You and I will go looking for your dog–"

"Stay out of this, Lu Ann," Berlinger ordered.

"–if she's not around here, there are plenty other places she could be. Daddy has land–and hunting cottages all along the river."

"Lu Ann!" Berlinger's voice lashed at her. "I'm warning you. I won't be treated this way–by my daughter and backwoods trash. If I say I don't have his dog, that's good enough. You understand? I would have let him look–anywhere he liked. But not now. It's over. If he sets foot on a piece of my ground, I'll have him jailed. Now, you get in the house. I've taken plenty from you, but I won't take this."

He caught her arm, turned her, and walked her back toward the house. When they reached Homer Carmack, he fell into step beside them as if this were the funniest scene he'd ever witnessed. I stood without moving until every light was doused and the yard was black dark again.

A little past midnight I was almost three miles down river from Berlinger's winter house. One of his cottages was on a wide turn in the stream. I plodded along the dusty road toward it.

Headlights suddenly flared ahead and I paused, blinded by their brilliance.

The car rolled toward me. It stopped. I opened my eyes. I was not surprised to see it was a green and white sheriff's cruiser. "Sheriff Williams Gill" and a big star was painted on the door in gold on green.

The two deputies got out of the car and came to where I stood beside the narrow road.

One was Ben Sawyer, a stocky man in his late twenties, his khaki hat pushed back on his head. The other one was Truman Lahey. Talk around high school was that Truman had a thing for young boys. He was sloppy, but huge, all his muscles gone to lard. His face was pimpled, and fat-cheeked.

"What you doing out here, Calder?" Truman asked.

"Forget it, Tru," Sawyer said when I didn't answer. "We know what he's doing. He's trespassing on Mr. Frank Berlinger's property. We know the charge. All we got to do is take him in. Get in the car, boy."

"All I ask is," I said, staring at Truman's pudgy face, "is that you let me ride in the back seat alone."

Truman caught his breath and Sawyer laughed. They knew what I meant all right. If Lahey hadn't been a sheriff's deputy, he'd have been doing time a long time ago.

They drove me into Oak Bluffs. All the way in, I felt beat, but I was going back out there as soon as I could.

They put me in a cell with three other men. They told me to lie down on the unused army cot and keep quiet.

Nothing they said really got through to me. I thought about Fanny, and Pa, and the way Ma would be worried. That couldn't be helped. Then I thought about Lu Ann, the way I had held her naked breasts in my hands. It was better than thinking about where I was. I lay face down on that cot, barely aware of the smells, or the noise, or the deputies walking outside, laughing and talking in quiet undertones down the corridor.

Chapter 4

Judge Vasco Stark watched me from behind his desk when I entered his courthouse office the next morning at eight-thirty.

The sheriff's bailiff who was with me closed the door and waited outside.

I walked across the room and stood before the judge's desk, but I didn't say anything.

Judge Stark continued staring at me from behind his rimless glasses. He'd been judge for so long in this circuit that he truly believed he was slightly elevated above the people who voted for or against him. He'd held the power of life and death for a long time. It showed in his face.

"A lot of people have spent much time this morning, Calder, concerning themselves with you," he said at last.

I waited.

"Don't you care, Calder? I've been up since five this morning, learning all I could about you. Do you want to know why? Because I have to know what a young boy is like–what his friends and neighbors think of him–when he comes before me. Because when a boy finds himself in my courtroom, he's usually in serious trouble."

I glanced around. He seemed to read my thoughts: this was his office, not the circuit courtroom.

"I don't have to hear boys like you–young boys–in my court if I believe justice can be best served with a talk in the privacy of my office."

He didn't ask me to sit down. I watched a fly light on a stack of papers before him, wander around lost, take off.

Judge Stark's voice sharpened. "What were you doing out there on Frank Berlinger's property, Calder? Midnight. Prowling. With a flashlight."

"If you know I was there, Judge, you know why I was there."

"Don't take a rebellious tone with me, Calder. I don't tolerate such behavior in my chambers. You remember that."

"I was looking for my dog. Somebody stole my dog. Yesterday some time. And I was looking for her."

"On Frank Berlinger's property? You were prowling; you were trespassing. Berlinger had to call for police protection. Trespassing. That's what concerns us here."

"That figures."

His head snapped up. He glared at me. "What's that?"

"I said that figures."

"I warned you about your tone, young man. You be thankful we're in my office, not in that courtroom. You ever speak to me in public like that, I'll throw the book at you–"

"I'm sure of it."

"–for contempt."

"And also, I'm Lutz Fenton's son. No use either one of us pretending to forget that."

He stared at me, his gaze fixed on me, a graying, hard-eyed man with those rimless glasses. "Is that fact supposed to make some difference, one way or the other?"

I shrugged.

"I'm waiting for an explanation."

"Why I was out there, why I was trespassing, that wouldn't matter to you, would it?"

"Are you accusing Mr. Frank Berlinger of stealing your dog?"

"I thought my dog was on his land. I was looking for her. That's the whole truth."

"I asked you a question. Are you accusing–?"

"Maybe Mr. Berlinger didn't steal Fanny. He paid for her. But he has her out there–somewhere."

Judge Stark exhaled heavily, sat back in his judge's chair. "One moment, young man. Do you expect me to take seriously the charge that a man with Frank Berlinger's money, position, would buy a stolen dog when he could buy any dog he wanted?"

I glanced around the room, more helpless than ever. Finally I said, "Yes, sir. I do."

"Don't you realize you'd have to prove such a charge in a courtroom?"

"I know what happened."

"Mr. Berlinger is a multimillionaire. He could buy Irish setters by the gross. Before you find yourself in serious trouble, young man, you'd better withdraw such noxious charges."

"Judge Stark, if I'm wrong, I'll apologize to Mr. Berlinger in front of this courthouse–"

"I'm afraid that wouldn't be good enough. It doesn't make sense that a rich man would steal–condone stealing–or buy stolen property of such little value."

"Not to you. Not unless you knew Fanny. Or unless you really knew Mr. Berlinger."

"Do you know him, boy? Intimately? Socially?" His scathing voice asked questions he didn't expect answered.

"Judge, may I say something?"

He sat back in his chair. "You were brought here for a talk between you and me. I'm trying to be fair. We all are. You're making it difficult. You may speak, but I warn you that I make tape recordings of all such hearings like this."

"I'm not saying anything I'm ashamed of, sir."

He waited and I said, "Whether Mr. Berlinger would buy Fanny is not what matters. Like you say, Berlinger could buy any dog. But if he did, he still wouldn't have Fanny–the instincts Fanny has, the intelligence, the–I don't know what it is that makes one dog a hundred light years better than any other dog–but Fanny has all of it, and I trained her–and nobody, Mr. Berlinger, or you, or anybody could get a dog like Fanny. That's the whole thing. There aren't any more like her–and Mr. Berlinger wanted *her*."

"Still, he could buy better dogs."

"Judge, it takes something besides money to get a dog trained and responding like Fanny. It takes time and patience–and a lot more. It takes a dog that's got everything in the first place–to understand what you're teaching, and more."

"And you believe this was the only such dog available to Mr. Berlinger?"

"The only one around here."

I fell silent, giving up. If a man didn't understand about a dog like Fanny the first instant, you could spend your life without being able to explain her to him.

"Fanny may be a fine animal, Calder. But to suggest that Mr. Berlinger would enter into any conspiracy to–"

"You believe what you want to, Judge Stark." I lifted my hand, let it fall at my side. "Your mind's made up–"

"Take it easy, young man–"

"Why? What difference will it make? Will what I say change what you've decided to do? I'll tell you this. Mr. Berlinger figured Fanny belonged to him anyhow. He says she was born on his land, to a dog my father was hired to tend and train. He thinks Fanny is his by rights. He wanted her and he took her."

He wrote something on a yellow pad. At last he glanced up under those gray brows. "Can you prove this?"

"No, sir."

"I've warned you about making irresponsible charges against respected citizens."

"I could prove it if I could find Fanny."

"You prowled–you trespassed on Frank Berlinger's land. You didn't find your dog. You found no trace. No evidence to support your claims. I'm not going to waste any more time with you this morning, Calder. You find yourself standing on a threshold, young man, before two doors. You can go on being stubborn and rebellious and suspicious like this, and you will end up in trouble. Or you can become a decent young man with respect for his elders."

I waited and he stared across his desk at me.

"Here's my decision, young man. You have no previous record with the police, the sheriff, or my juvenile investigator. Your high school principal says you do well in school. Now I don't like your attitude–not toward the arresting officers last night, not toward me, and certainly not toward Mr. Berlinger. I'm going to place you on probation, on your good behavior, for one year. Now, you stay away from Mr. Berlinger's property, you behave yourself. You stay out of public drinking places. You stay out of trouble, or I'll sentence you without a qualm. Now, go home and behave yourself. And stay away from Frank Berlinger's."

He stared at me a moment, then looked down at his papers, dismissing me.

I gazed at him, but I didn't say anything. He looked up, as if surprised to find me still standing before his desk. Something in his eyes dared me to speak. But I didn't. I turned and walked out.

When I came out into the sunlight, Lu Ann Berlinger was sitting across the street from the courthouse in a jeep. I glanced at her, but turned on the walk, heading out of town toward home.

She touched her car horn, beeping at me.

I walked across the street. She grinned up at me.

"How'd you make out with the fuzz, Calder?"

I shrugged. "Who makes out, ever?"

"You're in the sunlight, boy. It could have been worse. You should have heard my father explaining the law to Judge Stark for two hours. Whatever else my father is, he's a very good lawyer."

"Yes," I said. "I'm out. I'm real lucky."

"What are you going to do now?"

I glanced up at the courthouse clock. I had been longer in the judge's office than it seemed, even.

"Maybe go to school. I'm late, but I'm on their list."

"Nobody will expect you at school today, Calder."

I shrugged, glancing along the street. I knew what I was going to do, all right.

"Why don't you let me help you look for your dog, Calder?"

"Why should you?"

"I hate dogs, but I don't hate you, Calder. Come on, we'll check every hunting shack Daddy owns. If he has your dog on his land, we'll find her."

"I'm on probation. I step on Berlinger property and the world falls in on me."

"It's only a matter of time until the world falls in on you anyway, Calder. You're one of those helpless proud people who think the world ought to be better than it is. Well, it's never going to be. So relax and enjoy it, the way it is."

"I'd better not take you with me."

"Why not? Nobody will say anything about your being on Berlinger property as long as you're with me. Not even Daddy. Nobody has to know we're looking for Fanny."

I stared at her a moment, nodded. "If I got anywhere near her, she'd start barking." I said, beginning to hope.

"Sure she would," Lu Ann laughed. "I know just how she feels."

I got in the jeep with her. She whipped out into Main Street, tires screaming. Everybody stood watching us tear along the road out of town.

"Why are you doing this?" I asked her.

"Do I have to have a reason?"

"Maybe not. But I keep thinking you do."

She laughed. "Maybe Daddy *doesn't* have your dog. Have you stopped to think about that? What a kick in the head it will be to both of us to search everywhere and find out he doesn't have it!"

"That's a fine reason," I said.

"Sure. And hasn't got a thing to do with it."

She drove us recklessly along the highways, secondary roads and back country lanes.

People in fields, along the lanes, in the yards of the farmhouses watched us pass. It couldn't be any secret that we were covering all the property Mr. Berlinger had acquired in this end of the state over the past fifteen years. Nobody stopped us.

We spent the whole morning but we found no trace of Fanny.

At noon Lu Ann sped into town, roared into Pete's Bar-B-Q Drive In, blew the horn for service.

The curb boy came running. I glanced at the car parked beside us. I caught my breath, shaking my head. Judge Stark stared at me from behind the wheel. Beyond him, I saw his daughter.

Lu Ann glanced at me. "What's the matter?"

I inclined my head. "Judge Stark. And his daughter."

She stared at them. "She seems pretty," she said. "But plain. She isn't taking her eyes off you."

I shrugged. "Probably her old man's telling her how I turned out."

"Would she care?"

"No. She's as big a snob as he is. She had a crush on me when we were in the first grade. Then she got old enough to realize she is a Stark and I'm Lutz Fenton's son."

Lu Ann went on staring at the judge and Willi Ruth. Their gazes must have touched hers because she waved. "Good morning, Judge Stark," she called.

I didn't hear him answer.

Lu Ann laughed. "He didn't roll up his window, Calder. But he looks like he wants to."

"Afraid I'll contaminate his daughter. Don't worry. As soon as he gets to a telephone, your father will hear you were with me, too."

She smiled. "You've got to learn, pet. I don't care what my father hears about me. He's got his life, I've got mine. And never the twain.... I'm going to give you a book to read. On the facts of life. You've got to know before you're hurt so bad nobody can patch it up. It's called The Care and Feeding of the Living Bra."

"Sounds cute," I said, trying to go along with her mood. "Like it has real status."

At four o'clock that afternoon we climbed a sand road to the crest of a hill. Lu Ann killed the engine. We could see for miles in every direction. The sun glittered on the short-leaf pines, on the river in the distance.

Below us was a small house enclosed inside a sagging wire fence. A no-trespass sign was nailed to the gate.

"Daddy doesn't own this place, Calder," she said. "You want to go down there and check?"

I shook my head, staring at the little house. It overlooked Dead Indian River. It was in cleared land that had gone back to fennel and wire grass and blackberry patches. I knew her father didn't own it. The house and the land was mine, willed to me by Mom's father.

Grandfather Calder had lived out here alone. He left the place to me because I was named for him. This was the only reason he gave in his will.

Mom said he meant for me to sell it so I could go to the university. This was her favorite topic. I had to sell grandpa's place and go to the university. The whole farm wasn't worth a thousand dollars, fifteen miles from Oak Bluffs. I never bothered pointing this out to Mom.

"We might as well go back," I said to Lu Ann. "We're not going to find Fanny."

I didn't want to go down to that old house. It always made me sad to go near it. I knew it would bore Lu Ann. And Fanny wasn't down there. She would have heard the car, smelled me. She would have barked.

She shook her head. "We've beat the bushes. Maybe your Dad was telling the truth, Calder–"

"Sure–"

"Well, maybe." She laughed. "It *could* happen."

But I couldn't laugh. "The fence was cut, Lu Ann. They had to drive past the house both ways. They had to walk past the unlocked gate to cut the fence.... I know Pa. I've known him too long. He wanted me to think that fence was cut by strangers.... Nobody stole Fanny. No men in a black pickup truck anyhow."

"We've been everywhere."

"You've been fine," I said. "I couldn't have looked everywhere, the way I did, without you. I can't ever thank you enough, Lu Ann."

"Oh, you could, too, if you tried."

She reached over and took an army blanket from under the seat. She swung out of the car and stood smiling invitingly at me.

I stared at her standing in the sunlight. My heart began to pound irregularly, and I felt the excitement making me empty, putting everything else out of my mind except the way she looked, her body supple and tantalizing, her breasts standing full under that shirt. I swung out of the car and ran toward her.

Lu Ann waited for me.

For a moment we clung together, locked in a breathless embrace. I felt our hearts hammering against each other, out of rhythm. Her breath was hot against my face.

We walked like that to the thicket of loblolly pines. I threw my shirt over a low hanging limb. It was cool and shadowy under the trees. I felt like the first man, alone with his woman in some primeval cave.

She spread the blanket on the thick pine needles and sank down on it, watching me.

I sank to the ground beside her. I undressed her. I was trembling with the need to hurry, but I forced myself to take my time. I didn't know what gods had arranged my being here like this with Lu Ann, I didn't believe it would ever happen again. I had to have all of it this time. All of it.

My fingers shaking, I removed her shirt.

She unbuttoned my shirt, moving swiftly as if activated by some desperate driving passions. Her breasts rose and sank with her frantic breathing. She loosened my belt and then she was moving closer to me, insinuating her bared body upon me.

I felt her breasts crush against my bared chest and it was like the charge of raw electricity. She pulled my head down to her face, opening her mouth to take my tongue deeply between her lips.

"You're so wonderful," she cried. "You make me feel so wonderful. So wonderful. I can't stand it, Calder."

She was crying out all sorts of things, and none of them made sense. They were words, disjointed words that she'd heard, made-up, or dreamed. I crouched above her, sweated with trembling need for release and I watched her sweat-filmed body quivering and undulating, every muscle begging for relief.

I had her. I had dreamed of women. I had had fumbling moments with silly girls, but I had never even dreamed that it could be like this. I touched all the delightful parts of her body that she offered up to me.

She was talking to me, but I could not speak, and the blood pounded in my temples so that I couldn't even hear what she was saying. It didn't matter.

Nothing mattered any more except what we were doing to each other. We were destroying each other.

Suddenly she screamed out. "Oh, Calder, I–"

She didn't finish it. Her voice rose to that keening wail and stopped as if she could no longer breathe.

She panted out the sweetness, crooning it.

She thrust herself upward and stayed as if locked to me, as if we truly became one in the sweetness of our embrace, as if the heat of what we were doing welded us in this wild clutching hold.

"Oh, yes–"

"No more, darling. No more."

It was as if our violence and burning would ignite the shadows and the trees and the underbrush. A strange silence stretched suspended through the pine hammock as if the world hesitated before the violence of this moment between us.

And in a kind of blinding sweet hotness it was over for us.

We went on clinging to each other.

But we were no longer mindless animals caught in a hurricane of lust, we were like babes lost in the soft shadows of the forest. There was only gentleness left in this moment for us, the pleasure and wonder of fulfillment, her breasts pressed shapeless upon my chest, our hands moving with faint caresses in an orgy of contentment.

It was getting dark as Lu Ann sped the jeep along the highway to the gate outside my house.

She stepped hard on the brakes. The wheels locked and skidded on the rough pavement, all four tires screeched, laying down rubber in long black lines.

I clung to her a moment. I didn't want to let her go. I don't mean for that night–I didn't want her to leave again ever. I believed that we were made for each other–it had been meant for us to be together, hadn't it?

We were so perfect together.

This was all I could think.

But Lu Ann's mind seemed somewhere else already. She was in a hurry to be away.

Her kiss was almost perfunctory.

I got out of the jeep and watched her barrel away down the highway toward her winter house on the river.

I felt empty and lonely away from her.

I told myself this was nuts because I'd see her tomorrow. But I didn't feel better because I didn't really believe it.

I stood unmoving until her little car was out of sight.

I saw Mom and Pa on the back porch. I walked around the house in the dusk toward them.

When I came up on the steps I stopped, my breath hurting in my throat.

"No," I whispered, staring.

Pa turned, smiling. He swung his arm, indicating the automatic washer-dryer combination. It was gleaming new, shining white. All I could think was it must have cost five hundred dollars.

I wanted Ma to have it, but all I could really think was where the money came from. I pressed the back of my hand over my mouth to keep from vomiting. I leaned against an upright.

Pa said, "How you like this, Calder? Bought it for your ma. Paid cash. Like I told her, she don't have to worry about no bill-collector coming around trying to take this here play-toy away from her."

"Pa," I whispered.

"You like it, Molly?" Pa turned away from me. "I got all upset, the way you and me had words yesterday, Molly. I was plumb sorry. Sick. I figured you'd like this here new washer-dryer."

"Yes, Lutz," Ma said.

"Nobody in Oak Falls got a better one. Nothing too good for the girl that Lutz Fenton married. Lutz Fenton's wife has things good as anybody."

Mom stood looking at the combination washer-dryer.

"How do you like it, Molly?" Pa kept saying.

She only shook her head.

I said, "Where'd you get the money, Pa?"

He heeled around, staring at me. "What's that, boy? You asking me questions after all the trouble you stirred up, worrying about Ma, getting yourself on probation in Judge Stark's office?"

"Where'd you get it, Pa?"

"What kind of question is that to ask your father?"

I straightened, bracing my shoulders against the upright.

I stared at Pa, too sick to speak. Our gazes met, clashed. I was trembling, but Pa's eyes were cold, dangerous, daring me to say it, and I stood, not saying anything because even then I couldn't bring myself to put in words what I knew he was.

Chapter 5

I got out of there. I walked down the steps and across the yard and when I reached the hardroad, I turned away from Oak Bluffs. I didn't want to see anybody. One thing I couldn't stand in that moment, people.

I walked fifteen miles to the place Grandpa Calder had willed to me. There were no lights down there, but I didn't want any. I was so tired and so beat when I walked across the old yard I didn't hear the flow of the river, the mournful cry of owls, or skittering of field mice in the house walls. I fell across a bare mattress on an old-fashioned iron four-poster bed. I pressed my face down hard into its dry musty ticking. I fell asleep at once.

When I woke up the sun was high and it laid a dusty runner from the window to the bed. I reached out, put my hand into the streamer of sunlight, warming it.

I got up finally. I went out into the yard, walked to the river. I found an empty tin can, picked blackberries to fill it. I returned to the house, sat on the steps in the sun and ate the blackberries. Then I threw the can across the yard.

I spent the afternoon fixing up the house. I tried to figure how it would be to farm down there. I'd have a horse, a couple of dogs–nothing fancy, no dogs anybody would want to steal, just mutts, vicious mongrels that would chew the tail off any human being who got within a mile of the place. I'd put up no-trespassing signs, get a gun to enforce them.

I felt better, thinking how it would be. I slept well that night, ate blackberries the next day, caught a fish, cleaned and cooked it on Grandpa's old wood stove.

Grandpa had been dead two days before anybody even came along and found him. I hoped I'd be dead at least two weeks before anyone came near me.

I didn't sleep at all that night. I heard every sound, every cry on the wind; I was lonely and had no notion what I was lonely for. I knew Mom was worried and I got up at daybreak, walked home and told Mom I was sorry I'd troubled her. I spent the whole day around the house. I didn't bother anybody and no one bothered me. I felt Mom watching me, her eyes troubled, but she didn't say anything. About six o'clock Lu Ann's jeep wheeled into the yard and I went hurrying out there.

I looked at her, feeling my heart slugging crazily.

I knew suddenly what I had missed down on the river.

The road was paved, maybe twenty feet wide, rolling up one country hill and down another, around one long slanted curve as if even the people who built it knew this highway wasn't going anywhere.

Lu Ann drove along it slowly and we listened to the music on her transistor radio.

"I missed you," she said. "I didn't know what had happened. It scared me."

"I was scared too," I said, smiling at her. "Away from you."

"I never met anybody like you, Calder."

"Makes it like mutual."

"You drove me wild."

I saw the color flush up into her cheeks and her pale eyes got a strange look in them.

She cut the engine, let the car roll to a stop in the middle of the dark, unused highway.

"Maybe–after the other day, I'm not the same person, Calder. If I'm not, it's your fault.... That day I first saw you, you were cute and that's all I really thought.

"When I'm down here every winter, Calder, away from all the people I know, I figure I ought to have fun. The more fun I could have down here every winter, the more I could stand all the things I don't like to have to do at home all the rest of the year."

She laughed, moving her hand on me as if unable to stay away. "That's what I thought. But you weren't like that. You were different and I wanted to be different. This isn't something that happened this winter and that I won't even be able to remember next spring."

"I get all empty when I look at you, Calder. I can't think anything except how good you were, how wonderful, and the way you drove me wild. The way I feel about you, I never felt about anybody else."

She came closer to me, her eyes sleepy, and the warmth from her face warming me. When I reached for her, she pulled away and swung lightly out of the car.

"Come on. Come dance with me, Calder."

She turned up the volume on the radio. She moved against me and we danced in the headlights. I was already sweated with need and pulsing with excitement. My body pressed in close to hers and she sighed because we fit so perfectly.

It was as if we were made for each other.

I was heated when she was pressed close to me, and I got chilled when she moved away. I wanted her so bad I was aching, breathless, in a stricture of sweet agony.

I felt stronger than Atlas, able to hold the world on my shoulders because I knew I was going to have her. Nothing was going to stop us, and the thought that she could not resist now even if she had wanted to, made me wilder with desire than ever.

All the need since the last time I'd had her, the pressures of our bodies, the excitement she felt holding me was all taking effect now. Her breathing was rapid and her eyes were heavy-lidded. She sagged in against me.

I looked for the blanket but I couldn't find it. I sweated.

She said drowsily, "What's the matter, doll?"

"The blanket. I can't find it."

"It doesn't matter."

"We need it."

"It doesn't matter."

She took my hand and we went off the road, leaving the jeep in the middle of the highway. We half-slid down the clay embankment to a sump near a dry creek-bed.

She pressed herself upon me, fitting her body to me.

"Darling," she murmured.

"You drive me crazy."

We sank to the clay together. She was right. It didn't matter about the blanket. It was as if we floated in soft, fleecy clouds.

I removed her clothes, kissing all of her lovely young body as I bared it. She trembled when my mouth touched her skin. I felt wild with need for her. It was as if I wanted to devour her.

"Oh," she cried out. "I can't stand it! You drive me insane!"

"Yes. That's the way I want you. Crazy! As crazy as I am!"

It was as if this were the first time I'd had her. It was as though I'd never had her body before–almost as though no one had ever had quite what we were sharing on the sump of that clay ditch.

I clung to her and our bodies heaved, desire and pressures building up in me. I heard her wail out three or four times and knew she had reached that many climaxes ahead of me, but I did not release her, and she didn't attempt to pull away.

What I wanted, this was what she wanted. And that's what we had. I lifted my head, seeing the lonely shafts of yellow light up on the highway. I was thinking nothing except that I could not endure the agonizing sweetness of what was happening to me, and I was being carried upward, high above the shafts of the light, into the darkened sky, only the sky wasn't dark any more, it was rent by lightning, brighter than any lightning the world had ever known before.

And then I sagged into her, unable to move at all.

"When will I see you again, Calder?" Lu Ann whispered, pressing her cheek against mine when I stopped her jeep outside my gate.

"Tomorrow?"

"When? How early? I want to be with you all day."

"I better hit school."

"Why?"

I laughed. "That's a good question. What time will you come by?"

"Soon as I wake up."

"I'll be out at the front gate, waiting."

I walked tiredly into the house.

I lay awake remembering her, trying to recreate in my mind the way it had been with her.

I exhaled, my throat dry. Memory wasn't good enough. Having Lu Ann wasn't something you could dream up. You had to have her body, naked and frantic in your hands, or you had nothing.

I was out at the front gate at eight the next morning. At ten she came barreling down the highway.

As soon as I was in her car, she grabbed my face in both her hands and kissed me on the mouth, hard. Her lips were sweet and moist and hot. I shivered involuntarily at the savage sweetness.

"I overslept," she confessed. "Oh, Calder, I hate myself. Please forgive me."

She drove directly to a secluded place on the river. We bumped over a sand logging road, emerged on a bluff that had just enough sunlight, just enough shadow.

"I had our cook prepare us a lunch, and enough for dinner if we want it," Lu Ann said. "We can stay here all day. We'll never go back if you don't want to."

I took her in my arms, but she wanted to swim. She acted restless.

"There are alligators bigger than your jeep in that river," I protested.

But she wasn't afraid of alligators. "They're cowards," she said. She stripped away her clothing and I watched her, aching with desire. "I'm not afraid of alligators, are you?"

"Yes."

She laughed at me, a sound containing all the magic in the world. Before I could move, she spun and ran across the bluff.

I yelled at her but she didn't even look back.

She dived outward, glinting and gold in the sun, eighteen feet into the river.

I ran across the bluff, stood on the brink of it. She sliced through the air like something unreal, a wraith, cutting into the water with barely a splash to mark the place.

I hesitated on the rim of the bluff. Across the narrow river, sweetbay, gum, wild magnolias and elders were all tangled together in dark green masses, and their shadows turned the river black.

I undressed as swiftly as I could. I didn't try to dive. I leaped outward.

The current was swift. I surfaced fifteen feet downstream. I watched Lu Ann swimming easily against the current, thrusting herself through it.

I swam to her and reached for her. My hands closed on her breasts, but she eluded me like a sleek little otter, swimming all around me. The racing torrent hurtled us along with it.

When we finally got to shore and worked our way back up to the cleared bluff, I staggered to the blanket and toppled across it, breathing through my mouth.

"You call that fun?" I panted.

She was barely winded. Her eyes glowed. "I've swam alone in that river for hours, Calder. It's wonderful. A challenge. It's something worth doing. I'd glad the natives around here are afraid of it. It leaves it all for me. You were afraid. I could see it in your face."

"You can have it. I wanted to be with you." I rested my forehead on my arms.

"I know," she whispered. "That made it so wonderful. I knew you hated it, but I knew you were doing it for me. You'd do anything for me, wouldn't you?"

"Anything."

She pressed her sleek, wet body upon mine, kissing me between the shoulder blades. Charges of excitement flared out from the place where her lips touched. "I'll teach you to love it," she whispered. "Because I want you to love everything I love, Calder."

I rolled over, staring at her. She wouldn't have to teach me that because I was already ill with the way I loved everything about her. All I wanted was to stay like this with her, away from other people, forever.

She cried out in delight and fell upon me, kissing me, making little gurgling noises deep in her throat.

I had to pull her away. "I can't stand it," I whispered. "You'll kill me."

"We've got all day," she protested, fighting to get back to me. I saw her eyes were heavy-lidded, her face was red, her lips swollen. The excitement flared through me, making me shiver.

She came slowly down to me and I kissed her mouth. We stayed like that a moment until I felt her body quivering almost uncontrollably.

Then I slid her sleek damp body under mine on the blanket. Our wet bodies clung, kissing where we touched.

She screamed out, the sound coming back in a passionate echo from the swamp across the river.

"Talk," she wailed, "talk. Tell me how wonderful I am. Tell me what you're doing to me. Say it. Say it. Say it. Oh, Calder! Say it!"

But I couldn't talk at all. I couldn't barely breathe, but I didn't worry about it because I didn't care. I had what I wanted.

And I knew something better than that. I would have her all day, just like this, as many times as I wanted her.

It was after eight that night when she rolled up to the gate before my house and let me out. I kissed her for a long time. We were gentle now with each other. We had gentled each other. It hadn't been easy.

When I walked across the yard, Pa was waiting for me on the porch. Faint light touched him from the hallway.

I glanced at him, wincing. I had stayed away from him as much as I could. This was the way it had to be.

I started past toward the inside of the house.

"Calder."

He stood up from the rocking chair.

I paused in the light from the hallway through the front screen door. "Yeah, Pa."

"I got to talk to you, son."

"What about, Pa?"

"Nothing pleasant. Nothing I want to talk about. I'd like it powerful if things were like they used to be between us, when you was a young 'un. I could talk to you then."

I looked at him. "What you want, Pa."

He gazed at his hands, finally drew a deep breath. "Judge Stark," he said.

"What about him?" My heart sank.

"He sent Truman Lahey out from the sheriff's office to talk to you today, Calder. You weren't here. Truman said I was to give you a message from Judge Stark."

"All right."

"The judge says the high school principal called him. You ain't been to school all week."

"No."

"Now, son, I don't care, one way or the other. I figure you know what you want to do. I never got near the education you've already had, and I've done all right. I've done fine. But the judge sent word to you that you could get to school or go on the work gang."

I nodded. My stomach muscles trembled. I had heard the truth from Pa. You couldn't beat 'em, you joined them.

I went back to school the next morning. The principal wanted me to stay in every afternoon for a week to make up the work I'd missed.

"I won't do it," I said. All I could think was I had to see Lu Ann. "I'll go on the work gang first."

He shook his head. "Nobody wants you to go on the work gang, Calder. You're a smart boy. We want you to get the most out of school."

I didn't say anything.

He argued until he talked himself out of it. He finally agreed if I didn't miss any more school he wouldn't insist on my making up work. But he looked wounded. "We're trying to help you, Calder."

When I came out of school Lu Ann was parked out front in her jeep.

"I hate you," she said. "You made me wait all day for you."

I shrugged. "I don't have to go to school."

"Then don't."

"They only let you visit me weekends on the work gang."

Her lips parted. "Who did that to you, Calder?"

"They're doing it for my own good," I told her.

"I need a drink." Her voice was hard.

I looked around helplessly. "I don't know where to get you one."

She laughed. "Don't worry about that. I do. Get in."

She sped out of town and headed north on Highway 301. "Where you going, Lu Ann? I mean, if we had any chance of making it alive?"

She patted my leg, not slowing down. "I know the sweetest little place," she said. "They don't care about anything except money. If you've got cash, you're automatically twenty-one years old."

Bar 301 was a dark green frame shack set in a paved parking area and well back from the highway.

By the time we got there the men who drove the big trucks for the contractors, gravel and construction firms were just getting off work. Their cars were parked thick outside.

I followed Lu Ann through the screen door. Flies buzzed up from it when it slammed behind us.

There were men at the bar, the tables, at the jukebox, the brightly lighted pinball machines. The place smelled wetly of beer. There were a few women but they looked tougher and older and meatier than the men.

When Lu Ann walked in everybody in the place laid their eyes on her.

We found a table and Lu Ann called the owner. "Hey, Lonzo, bring us two of my specials."

He grinned, waving his bar rag. "You bet, Miss Lu Ann."

I sat on the chair, feeling as if it were a board of nails.

Lu Ann took my hand on the linoleum table top and squeezed it. "Relax, doll," she said. "You're all right. You're with Lu Ann. I'll hold your hand."

"If I were sure I could take you along to the county jail to hold my hand, I'd feel better," I said.

She laughed. Lonzo was a big-bellied man in dark slacks, denim shirt and soiled apron. He brought us beer laced with whiskey.

The men along the bar had watched Lonzo prepare the boilermakers. They stopped whatever they were doing and stared at Lu Ann. They gave her a cheer when she tossed off her drink.

Lonzo stood beside her chair, grinning. She smiled up at him, exhaling heavily. "Lonzo, you better bring us another round," she said.

I tried to drink my boilermaker, but I felt it strike at the pit of my nervous stomach and bounce against my skull at the same time.

She reached over, took my glass, drank deeply. "I really needed that."

Lonzo brought her a refill, and I saw her eyes change, saw the strange lights flare up in them. The irises were blank and when she looked at me, it was as if she didn't really see me.

She snapped her fingers, moving her bottom around in her chair and glancing restlessly around the room.

"Drink up, Calder," she whispered. "Let's have fun."

She signaled for another round. I hadn't finished my first boilermaker and the second sat waiting for me.

While Lonzo was bringing her a fresh drink, Lu Ann took a long pull at my glass. Her voice was low, tense.

"Drink up, Calder. People are staring. It looks bad for you to sip at a boilermaker. You want them to think you're a kid?"

I took a deep drink, holding my breath. I gagged. I gasped at her, "I'll look a lot more childish if I throw up."

She glanced around impatiently, fought in her pocketbook and found some quarters.

She got up and paced along the rows of men at the bar to the jukebox. Then men around the juke fell away as if it were her personal property. They never took their gazes off her trim bottom when she leaned over to make her selection. It was as if they undressed her. They grinned, nudged each other and winked.

Lu Ann appeared unaware that they were alive.

I sweated, seeing the way they looked at her, feeling trouble building.

She punched in some quarters and returned to our table, through the hot gauntlet of eyes.

One of the men at the bar pushed his way into her path. He said something to her, but she stepped around him and ignored him.

He swore, and gazed after her, his face rutted.

He spoke loudly. "They do make them more delicious every year, Lonzo! Bring me some gloves. You know I couldn't touch that with my hands!"

Everybody in the place roared with laughter because they had to laugh or burst.

All I was thinking was we had to get out.

Lu Ann heeled around at our table, glaring at the loudmouth. He stood, gazing back at her, licking his mouth and smacking his lips in an exaggerated way.

Her face was rigid, white, and her eyes blazed. She sat down slowly and took up her drink.

"We better get out of here," I said.

"Oh, shut up." Those boilermakers had really slugged her. Rage chewed at her insides. "I can go anywhere I want to go. I'm not responsible for slobs like that." She shook her head violently as if dismissing the whole business.

She listened to the music, snapping her fingers.

"Let's dance, Calder," she said.

"Let's stay where we are. Or better yet, let's get out of here."

Her eyes flashed. "If you want to go, you go. I'm not running away from anything."

Miserable, I stayed where I was.

The loudmouth at the bar talked earnestly to the men around him, drinking as fast as he could fill a shot glass and toss it off, straight.

He turned, his gaze grazing over the lushness of Lu Ann.

He spoke to the men around him again, emphatically, as if trying to convince them of something.

Their grins doubted him.

"I want to dance, Calder," Lu Ann said sharply. She pretended the noise at the bar behind her did not even reach her.

"Please, let's clear out–"

"Don't be a child or an old woman. I'm disappointed in you, Calder. You're not what I thought you were at all. I want to dance. Are you going to dance with me, or–"

We both looked up at the same moment. The big trucker staggered from the bar, his mouth twisted into a sweated grin.

"You want to dance, baby? Come on, Johnny'll dance with you. Then we can get out of here–like before, huh? You and me? Huh, baby?" He glanced in contempt at me. "Never take a boy to do a man's work, honey. Looks like you'd know that."

"Get away, you drunken slob," Lu Ann said, gazing coldly up into the sweated, rutted face.

"Is that any way to talk to me, baby, after–"

"I never saw your rotten face before!" Lu Ann raged. She spoke so sharply that everyone stopped talking, watching us. "Get away from me. You stink."

He staggered back as if she'd struck him. He shook his head, his slack mouth working, trying to form some answer.

He didn't say anything because Lonzo and two other men grabbed him and dragged him, yelling, back to the bar.

I breathed out, slowly. "Let's get out of here."

"Don't be a child. That animal insulted me, Calder–"

"We can still clear out–"

"You've got to beat him up, Calder."

"What?"

"You've got to beat him up. You can't let men like him talk to me that way."

I drew the back of my hand across my sweated forehead. I stared at her disbelievingly. Where was the girl who'd spent a day helping me look for a lost dog? Where was the girl who'd pressed closer and closer into my arms, and danced with me in the headlights of her jeep? Where was the gentle girl who'd spent a day with me on a picnic?

She was nowhere to be found. The girl beside me in this dim barroom was compounded of boilermakers, rage and cold fury.

"Go hit him, Calder. You've got to–or I can't live around here."

"Good lord, Lu Ann. I'm in trouble enough, just being in this place."

She jerked her head up, and all her contempt and anger was spewing all over me like corrosive acid. Her voice held the same tone that had ripped at Johnny. "If you want trouble with me, let men act like that slob just did."

She drew a deep breath, held it, staring at me, her mouth twisted.

Johnny lunged away from the men holding him at the bar and charged toward our table again.

His eyes were tormented, fixed on Lu Ann. He raged out, "You dirty little–"

"Calder!" Lu Ann screamed it, beating her fists on the table.

I stood up. My stomach felt empty. I felt the gazes of all the people fixed on me.

I pushed away from the table and met the big man coming toward me.

He swung at me with the back of his hand and missed. This turned him awkwardly toward me and left him open. I slammed my fist into his beer belly as hard as I could. My fingers seemed to crumple under the impact, and my arm was jarred to its shoulder socket.

I stood waiting for him to recover, and I tried to remember if I had a decent suit to be buried in.

There was absolute silence in that room except for the jukebox. The music blared away, but it had no reality, seemed to come from some distant place.

The big man kept plowing toward me for a moment, then his knees buckled and he stumbled, sprawling to the floor.

He struck a chair, knocked it over as he fell. He landed hard and the room trembled.

I stood against the table, waiting. Lu Ann was poised on the edge of her chair, her mouth twisted with violent pleasure, watching him.

I had been lucky. The big trucker was so drunk that he fell quite heavily.

After what seemed an eternity he rolled over, shaking his head. He looked like a glob of lard on the floor, in his work clothes and muddy boots.

He shook his head trying to clear it. He wiped the back of his hand across his mouth.

He straightened and steadied himself on his elbow. He had forgotten Lu Ann for the moment and he looked at me, his sweated face twisted as if he were going to cry.

He impaled me with his gaze, his slack mouth quivering. I had no idea what I expected him to say–curse, threat, I didn't know.

He said, "You going to fight 'em all, kid?"

It was as if he'd kicked me in the belly.

I stared down at him, sick at my stomach. I was aware of Lu Ann's lunging up suddenly, grabbing my arm. And then fat Lonzo was helping her and they pushed a way through the crowd, and then we were outside.

Distantly, I heard a sheriff's car siren.

I heard Lu Ann telling Lonzo to send a bill to her father, for the drinks and any wreckage, but I was only vaguely aware of what they were saying.

We stood outside the dingy car in the parking area. I kept seeing Johnny's twisted face, the way he looked as if he was going to cry, the quivering mouth.

Lu Ann tried to talk on the long drive back to Oak Bluffs, but I was too sick to talk. My right hand felt as if it were broken, but I didn't even think about that. I couldn't think about my fist, or Lu Ann, or anything. I couldn't get the way that big man stared up at me from the floor as if he were even sorrier for me than he was for himself.

You going to fight 'em all, kid?

Chapter 6

I wasn't going to fight any of them.

But if I didn't, I had to fight myself. I figured this was easier.

I didn't see Lu Ann for a week. She didn't come back and I didn't call her. I had to stay away from her. If I got to thinking about her–about her breasts and her body, and the way I was cold away from the warmth of her loving– I checked my right hand; it was swollen like a half-cooked ham.

I lay awake at night, thinking about her, wanting her, and knowing I was going to stay away from her because I had to, unless I wanted to end up on the work gang. One thing I admitted. She was too much for me. Too rich for my blood. She was a rich winter girl, and I had to let it go at that. She was too many different people, all of them dangerous, and I didn't understand any of them. Just when I thought I knew her, or had found the girl she really was and that I wanted, she spun into a new light, and she wasn't like that at all.

About the eighth day it got rugged trying to stay away from her.

I woke up that morning, sweated, as if a raging fever had broken, and I felt calm and yet excited at the same time. I was going up to her winter house to see her. I had tried staying away from her. It was no good. It didn't work.

I caught the school bus, went to my classes, but I didn't really hear anything they said. If I thought about the people around me, I pitied them. I knew wonderful things they didn't know, something some of them might never know. I knew what it was to love a girl so much that it was illness being away from her.

Time went slowly, and yet it built with intensity and anticipation. As time drew nearer for school to end, I sat trying to figure what I'd say to her, the way I would beg her to take me back.

When I came out of the school building that afternoon, Lu Ann was parked across the street in that jeep.

I saw her like a sunburst all that distance, the green dress she wore, the way she wore her hair brushed back from her face.

I tried not to run, tried to keep the exultance from my face. Someone else knew what it was to be in love and lonely, too.

Lu Ann said, "Hello, Calder."

I stared at her, feeling a sense of wrong, but a kind of wrong I had no words for, couldn't understand.

There was a look of fatigue and emptiness about her. Her face was bloodlessly pale, drained, tired. I couldn't figure it out. I gave it up.

"It's really no good," I said, trying to show some sense even when I was burning with need for her.

"Don't do this, Calder," she said in a tired voice. "We've had trouble enough, we don't need any more. Come on, get in. Let's get out of here."

I went around the jeep and got in. That emptiness spread in my belly. It wasn't going to work–there was too much difference between us. But I wanted to hear her say she'd missed me, that she wouldn't go ape and drag me into any more of those senseless nightmares like the 301 Bar. I needed to hear her say it. We had to have something we could trust between us, or we had nothing.

"I'll be good, Calder," she said in a flat tone.

I tried to smile, teasing. "Good with you is kind of relative."

"I know what you want," she said. "I'll be that."

She drove deeply into the woods. She had a blanket with her. She didn't say much. We got out of the car and she spread the blanket under the low-hanging branches of a loblolly.

I kissed her and we sank down on the blanket together. She let me undress her. She lay with her head on my lap watching me silently.

I moved my hands over her breasts, caressing them. Then I moved my hand across her flat-planed stomach to the dark rise at her thighs.

"I missed you," she said, looking up at me.

"I nearly went nuts without you."

"I thought you'd call me."

"Let's don't fight about it now."

"No," she said. "Let's don't fight now."

I moved my hand, loving her with my caresses until she began to stir, breathlessly excited.

"Do you like me?" she said.

"I'm out of my mind."

"You could have fooled me."

I felt that emptiness again at the flat quality of her tone. I said, breathless, "What do I have to do?"

"Don't you know?" she was teasing me, but chilled about it.

I sank my head down to the upthrust pillows of her breasts, burying my face in them. The chill was gone and she was reaching for me, whimpering.

Suddenly everything changed and it was as it had been the first time.

Anything that would excite and thrill me was what she insisted on doing.

I was weak with longing. I whispered something. I didn't even know what, just words.

"You like it?"

"Lord yes."

"You think I'm worth it–no matter what?"

"I know you are."

She was talking to me then as she loved me with her hands and her mouth and her body. It was all as natural with her as if she'd been born knowing every wild and passionate thing a woman could do to drive a man out of his mind.

I didn't know what was ahead for us. I knew only that I had never been so excited in my life.

The painful pleasure increased. It rose to such a frantic pitch that it became something else. It was neither pain nor desire any more, it was a need to become one with her, to intrude deeply into her until we were no longer two but a whole and complete being.

The world dissolved into a pattern of sweet, swirling images, and we lay still, and we did not move.

We spent the afternoon like that.

Fanny came home that night.

Mom had just called Pa and me into the kitchen to supper.

We sat down at the table and she brought hot dishes, collard greens, side meat, field beans. I felt good for the first time in days, whole again, as if I could eat and keep food in my stomach.

I heard a whining, a crying outside the kitchen door.

I jumped up from the table, knocking over my chair. I knew what that sound was, I recognized that cry.

Mom stood tense beside the table, not looking at Pa or me. Pa watched me. He said, "Calder."

I didn't answer him. I didn't even look at him. I ran across the room, slapped the door open, letting it slam behind me. Mom and Pa came to the door and stood there silently.

I crossed the back porch in two strides.

At the steps I stopped as if stunned.

It wasn't quite dark yet, the yard was lighted, but maybe darkness would have been kinder.

Fanny hadn't climbed the steps because the front of them was as far as she could make it.

Her sleek coat was torn and matted. Her paws were blistered, swollen and cut. She was bleeding. She was trembling so she could hardly stand up.

"Fanny." It just gushed out of me, and I swallowed the sickness.

She lifted her head. She did it slowly, taking a long time, but at the sound of my voice she looked up, her mouth stretched in that way she had, grinning, and she shook all over trying to get up enough strength to move to me.

I went down the steps, sat on the lowest one.

Fanny pressed against my leg. She went on quivering with pain and fear, but she stopped whining. She must have believed she was all right. She was back home.

I said, "Fanny. Where you been, girl?"

Her mouth stretched and she wriggled, pressing harder against my leg. She went tense all over, working her head as if trying to speak, and dying because she could not.

"It's all right, Fanny," I promised. "It's all right, girl. You're all right now."

Pa came out on the back porch. He said, "Calder–"

I didn't even look up. I just set my shoulders, bracing myself against anything he was going to say. "I don't want to hear it, Pa–"

"You best listen, boy–"

"No." I saw where Fanny had gashed her neck breaking some barbed leash. Whoever had her had meant to break her spirit, all right. I stopped, not letting myself think about that any more.

"I'm going to fix you up, Fanny," I said soothingly. I moved my hand over her, wondering as I said it if I really could.

She was almost dead. Somebody had beaten her with chains, and the way she had been beaten she could have been bleeding internally. When I touched her ribs she fretted, too weak to lunge, but in agony, as if they might be broken.

"Calder." But whatever Pa was going to say, he didn't say it because a jeep drove into the yard.

We watched the land rover slow down out front and then roll slowly across the yard toward where we were.

I recognized Frank Berlinger at the wheel of the jeep. I felt no surprise. I looked beyond him at Cletis Lahey, one of his tenant farmers. It figured Berlinger had kept Fanny on Lahey's place where he tried to 'break' her.

Cletis Lahey stayed in the jeep. He was a brother of the pot-bellied sheriff, Truman Lahey, and looked something like him.

Berlinger swung out of the jeep. He carried his expensive Ithaca loosely. He wore hunting clothes. He walked toward me.

I stood up and Fanny pressed against my leg, shuddering.

"It's all right," I said to her under my breath. "It's all right now, girl."

If you've ever seen a dog cower and cringe with its tail between its legs and try to turn into itself with fear, you know how Fanny looked when Berlinger came near us.

He stopped a few feet away.

Pa came to the edge of the porch. "Fanny's here, Mr. Berlinger. She just came in. We was just planning on bringing her–"

"Never mind, Lutz," Berlinger slashed at the air with the side of his hand.

He stared at Fanny.

"This dog got away from me," Berlinger said. "I knew where I'd find her." He gazed at me.

I met his gaze evenly. "She won't stay with you, Mr. Berlinger." I was amazed at how cold and flat my voice sounded. Inside I was shaking and yelling with rage. I went on in that same cold way. "I tried to tell you."

"I know. She won't stay away from here. She's broken loose four or five times–even from her barbed leashes." He stared down at her. "She's no good to me."

"How much did you pay Pa for her?"

"What difference does it make? I gave him five hundred like I said."

"I haven't got five hundred. I've–got some land–"

"I've got all the land I want."

"I'll pay you along as I can."

"For what?"

"For Fanny. She won't stay with you. I'll buy her back."

His voice was flat. "She's not for sale–"

"But you just said it, Mr. Berlinger! She won't stay with you. Even when you almost kill her. She won't obey you. She–"

"I know." His mouth twisted and his eyes raked across my face, to Pa, and back. "You got a neat gimmick, boy. You work it fine, you and your pa. You show a man a dog he wants, you sell her, only she keeps coming home–"

"I tried to tell you–"

"Oh, sure you did. Part of the sales pitch, eh? Cletis tells me that's what you tell 'em all. I hear you've sold Fanny before–"

"Never. I never sold her. I never sold her this time–"

"Only when the sucker finds out she won't obey, she won't stay away from here, you get her back, and they let you have her. That's what Cletis says. Now, I want to hear you or your Pa deny that, boy. You sold her before?"

"I never did–"

"–and she always comes back, and your suckers are disgusted and let you have her back?"

"I tried to tell you–"

"Nobody makes a sucker out of me, boy." He jerked his head, gazing at Pa. "I thought you'd have better sense, Lutz. I thought you knew me better than to pull something like this."

"Honest to God, Mr. Frank!" Pa took a step down toward where we stood, then stopped. "I've sold her before. The boy didn't even know–she never stayed that long. But I thought you could handle her. I mean, a man like you, Mr. Frank. Like you said, you got a way with dogs."

Berlinger's face tightened. "Nobody's got a way with this dog but you two crackers. And don't try to soft-talk me, Lutz. It won't work. You pulled a fast deal on me, but you're not going to get away with it. Not this time. It's a matter of pride with me–"

"Mr. Frank!" Pa came down the steps, voice shaking. "You know I wouldn't try a deal on you–"

"You'd try a deal on your own mother!"

"No, sir. No, sir, Mr. Frank. I need that job with you too bad to do anything like that–"

"Oh, you got the job. Until I catch you pulling another trick on me like this one." He jerked his head toward Fanny. "Or until I can find an honest cracker that knows dogs."

"Oh no, Mr. Frank–"

"I begged you not to buy Fanny, Mr. Berlinger," I said. "I told you she was my dog. She never came from a litter on your place. And I trained her. I tried to tell you she wouldn't hunt for you."

"Oh, sure. You made me want her so bad I itched. Oh, I give you that.

You're the spit and image of your Pa, all right–you're a schemer boy–"

"I tried to tell you!"

"You and your pa. Real neat. Should have seen your Pa when he took my five hundred dollars, telling me how your heart was breaking–as if you both didn't know this bitch would cut for this place the minute she broke free."

"I knew if she was alive she'd come home," I said. "But I told you that. She's back home now. I'll pay you."

He shook his head, staring at Fanny cringing against my leg. "Hell with that. Didn't you hear me, boy?" He turned, shouted across his shoulder. "Hey, Cletis, bring that leash." He turned back, lowered his voice. "Didn't you hear me, boy? This bitch is not for sale."

"She won't do you any good," I cried out helplessly.

"No." He watched Cletis slip a leash on Fanny and drag her across the yard. Fanny fell to her belly, straining against the leash. "But she won't be any good for you to sell again, either. I paid five hundred for her, I figure to get five hundred in satisfaction."

Before I could move, he tilted the gun on his arm, pressed the trigger. Startled, Cletis dropped the leash as the gunfire rocked the yard.

Fanny was knocked two feet along the dirt, but she was already turning, crawling back toward me.

Berlinger stood with the gun in his hand and watched her. She left a wide trail of blood. He had shot the side of her head away. But she made it. She didn't whine or make a sound but she got back to me, and Fanny died the way she had lived, pressed hard against my leg.

Chapter 7

I stood for a long time holding the shovel after I'd buried Fanny in the field behind our barn. The silence was deep, unbroken. It was as if I were isolated inside the rim of lantern light. This was the way I wanted it.

I picked up the lantern, blew it out. I stood in the silence and darkness until my eyes became accustomed to the black night. I walked out of the field.

I saw Mom and Pa standing on the lighted back porch. The rest of the house was dimly lit. I heard music from the TV set, the rage of gunfire, the sounds of violence.

I shook my head. I couldn't go back in there, not now.

I replaced the shovel and lantern in the barn. I waited, hoping Mom and Pa would go in the house. But when I came out of the barn door, they were still waiting, silent.

I walked across the yard away from them, going toward the highway. Pa came down the steps and called to me.

I kept walking.

I saw the headlamps of a car coming toward me on the road. I paused a moment at the gate. Probably Judge Stark would send Deputy Lahey down to the farm to get me and drag me off to school or to the work gang. That's what they'd have to do.

I walked toward the river, toward Grandpa's old house. The carlights picked me up. The jeep bucked to a halt beside me.

"Calder."

I paused, staring in at Lu Ann.

"I came as soon as I could, Calder. As soon as I heard."

I nodded.

"I'm sorry, Calder. I can't tell you how sorry I am."

I stood waiting for her to drive away.

She bit her lip. "Don't hate me, too, Calder."

"No, I don't hate you." I didn't even recognize my own voice.

"He was enraged, Calder. He doesn't want anybody to take advantage of him. He can't admit he's wrong. He can't admit there's anything he can't do–can't bend to his will."

"I don't want to hear excuses for him."

Her laugh was sharp. "You don't know me at all, do you?"

"No."

"Get in, Calder. Please."

After a moment, I got in. She drove fast, lost in thought.

"I'm not what Daddy wants, Calder. He wanted a son–or a Sweet Sue sort of girl. We fight all the time. Under the surface. He has a strong will. So do I."

"I don't want to talk about him."

Her voice lashed at me. "You mind if I talk about him? I've got to talk about it, or burst. I can't keep rage bottled up. If I could, I could get along with him. He doesn't care what I think as long as I act sweet and stupid."

"You're smart enough to fool him. Why don't you?"

"Because I don't want to! I've a right to be what I am, as much as he has. He can't change me–he can only make me hate him when he tries."

"Hate him then."

"I do hate him. I hate him for the things he does–to you and your poor stupid dog. He doesn't care about other people or even think about them.

He fights with me because he can't break me, any more than he could poor little Fanny. I hate him because he won't stop trying. I started smoking because he hated for me to do it."

We rode in silence.

"You know when I stopped smoking, Calder? As soon as I learned that he hated to see me drink even worse. Wonderful. Liquor I loved. It was easy to start drinking and stop smoking."

She stared straight ahead, her eyes glinting with diamond-hard tears.

"Every mean thing I do, even when I do them to other people, I do when I'm full of hate for him." She laughed emptily. "I get so full of hate for him I've got to let it erupt, or I'll burst."

She laid her hand on my leg. "That day at the 301 Bar, Calder. I was full of hate when we got there. Daddy and I had fought about you and your dog. I knew he had Fanny at Lahey's farm. I'd have told you, but Daddy had told Cletis to shoot you if you came near, and I knew that stupid farmer would do it. They couldn't control Fanny, they whipped her when she broke loose–"

"I don't want to hear about it."

"I told Daddy he couldn't break her, any more than he could me. He could kill her but he couldn't break her. We yelled and fought and I ran out, looking for you. But all I really wanted was to get that hatred out of me before I got sick."

"You got it," I said.

"But I didn't mean to hurt you, Calder. I was trying to get even with Daddy, not get you in trouble."

"It doesn't matter," I said. "Not any more."

She turned, looking at me. "You want a drink, Calder?"

"You got any kerosene with you?" I asked.

She laughed. "You mean Scotch?"

"It comes out of the same tank. I'd love some."

"We'll go to the 301 Bar." She laughed again. "We don't have to go in. I'll get us a couple of bottles. We'll have a picnic. We'll have Scotch sandwiches, Scotch canapes, Scotch broth."

"I like Scotch Baked Alaska."

"My favorite. My very first favorite." She smacked her lips and stepped down hard on the accelerator. She barely slowed wheeling into the parking area outside the bar.

"Wait here, doll," she said. "Mama will be right back with the groceries."

She went inside the car. I sat looking around. She was gone a long time. Other cars rolled into the parking lot. I felt empty. I was going to have to go in and get her. I figured that big slob trucker I'd fought with would be there. Nothing was ever easy.

Then I saw her carrying a sack of bottles. A man followed her between the tables. He talked urgently to her, trailing her like a hungry mongrel. He was in shadow. I didn't recognize him. Lu Ann wasn't even listening to him. She let the door slam in his face.

She set the bottles on the seat between us, got in under the wheel. I waited but she offered no explanation for having stayed so long.

"Well, come on," she said. "Break it open."

She'd bought potato chips, fiery-hot spiced sausages, pickled fish, five bottles of Scotch.

"You know what happened at the Alamo," she said. "They ran out of ammunition and lost the battle."

"They'll never take us alive," I said, opening a bottle.

I held it out to her. She drank thirstily. "I had a couple inside there," she said. "It was a dry night. I couldn't wait."

I drank deeply. The liquor burned and I gagged. Lu Ann laughed but I kept drinking.

I didn't feel anything.

"Got a lot of hatred inside me. Guess it'll take a lot to wash it away."

"We got a lot," she said. By now we each had our own bottle because it took too long to pass one bottle back and forth between us. "You just keep working at it, boy."

I lifted my bottle in a toast. "Here's to the bastards," I said. "They've inherited the earth."

"Inherited it? They invented it."

"I wonder who invented Scotch?"

"Nobody invented Scotch. They cracked it. Out of coal tar."

She touched my arm. "I like you, Calder. Never cared for anybody the way I do you. What are we going to do, Calder?"

"About what?"

"About my liking you."

I took a deep drink. "There's nothing we can do about it. You got to live with it. It's like having pointy ears. You know I wouldn't marry you, Lu Ann. Not for anything."

"Who asked you?"

"I asked me. But I couldn't do it. If we had a kid and it looked like your old man, I'd get up every morning and kick his teeth out."

She drank, spilling it. She'd had enough, too much, but I knew her too well to say so.

"If we got married, we wouldn't have kids," Lu Ann said. "I promise you. And I know all the pills–all the tricks."

"There ain't any trick to it–"

"Trick is not having any. And those are the tricks I know. Don't have to worry about me, Calder.... Calder, did your mother ever tell you you have two noses?"

"She wouldn't dare."

"Calder, we got to go somewhere."

"Where do you want to go?"

"Know a nice motel. Down the highway."

"You trying to get me killed?" I shook my head. "I'm on probation."

"Probation has been repealed," she said. "Way before we were born."

"Everybody knows your car."

"All right, chicken. Not everybody knows you're with me. I've a right to sleep where I want to."

She started the engine, wheeled the car out, banging a couple of parked cars on the way. "Just keep drinking."

I did drink, all the way to the motel. I finished off the bottle and hurled it out into the darkness as we sped along the highway.

She skidded to a stop before the motel office. I saw a man inside. He looked up, peering through the picture window. He had gray hair, a pink face, sharp features.

"He doesn't look like he ought to be in the motel business," I said. "He doesn't look very broad-minded."

"You worry too much." She pressed some bills into my hand. "Nobody in the motel business these days can afford to be anything but broad-minded."

Lu Ann was right. The manager didn't like the way I looked or the way I smelled, but he took the money and the card I sprawled my name on. I. W. Harper, I think. And wife.

He gave me a key. "You kids be quiet," he said, "we got people trying to sleep here."

I nodded, turned and walked as straight as I could out the door. I read the number on the key and Lu Ann put the car in gear, roaring forward into the court. Four other cars were parked in there, all with local licenses.

"He said be quiet," I said above the roar of the engine.

"I hope you told him where to go," she said. She parked the jeep. "Bring our luggage, darling," she called over her shoulder. "Don't spill a drop of it."

The old man was standing outside his office, staring at us.

Lu Ann filled water glasses with Scotch. A look of wildness altered her face. She was more than high, beyond that.

She undressed, flinging her clothing to all parts of the room. I sat on the bed. I smoothed my hands along the supple nakedness of her legs and thighs and bottom, caressing her.

"Don't be gentle!" she cried. "I'll kill you!"

She pushed me back on the bed, lying down on top of me. She clung to her glass, sipping at it between kisses. I grew breathless and excited. When I moved her she spilled Scotch on the bed.

She tossed her glass to the floor and lay back, putting up her arms to me. "Show me how much you love me, Calder."

I placed my glass on the nightstand, drew her to me. Her breathing was loud, ragged.

She shoved me away suddenly, reached out for my glass, spilling Scotch along her arm.

"Calder, you don't know much about loving a girl, do you?"

"Sorry!"

"Stop apologizing!" She spoke loudly. "It's just that you're–not rough enough."

"What do you want me to do? Beat you?"

She giggled. "Yes."

"Oh, come on now."

"It's not your fault, Calder. You're just young. You don't know enough about using your hands. I'll teach you how to love me with your hands. Your fingers. And your mouth. Nobody will ever laugh at you after tonight, Calder–"

"You laugh tonight and I will beat you!"

"That sounds good!" she cried out. "But not right now. Later. Don't rush me, Calder. I like a man who takes his time."

She got up, went into the bathroom. I lay on the bed listening to her sing in there. There was no tune, nothing I'd ever heard before.

She came back slowly, the lights gleaming on her faintly perspiring nude body.

She was like something you never saw outside a dream.

"There ought to be a law," I whispered.

"There is," she said. "But you'd only break it anyway."

I reached for her. She threw herself upon me, kissing me, trailing her hair across my face, my throat, my chest.

"It's going to be a long night." Her voice rose to a toneless wailing. "Love me, love me, love me."

I moved my hands on her, trying to do all the things she had taught me, feeling the heat of her, the way she responded.

She was talking, but I couldn't hear what she said. There was only the shouting of her words. They spun inside my head and drummed at my temples. Then she was screaming and clinging to me, and then we sagged silently into the mattress, but it seemed to me that her screams still banged against the walls of the room.

"Don't stop loving me, Calder."

There wasn't anything she didn't know, not anything she didn't want. Her excitement ignited me and even when I thought I could not move any more, I was suddenly loving her again, responding to something new she was doing, something I'd never dreamed.

Time raced past, only neither of us cared about time, or thought about it. I was unable to think. She was too loud. Her sweetly agonized cries rose louder and louder all the time.

I kissed her hard, covering her mouth with mine to keep her from crying out.

We fell asleep in each others' arms. I don't know how long we slept. I woke, feeling drugged. Her warm mouth moved on me, tantalizingly.

I caught her head, clinging to her, and she wriggled free, her eyes distended.

She stared at me, her eyes glittering.

She crouched naked on the rumpled bed, her hair wild about her face.

Her voice shook. "I want you to beat me now, Calder–"

"What?"

"Beat me. Now. I want you to. With your belt."

"Are you crazy?"

"You do what I tell you!" she screamed.

"Now you sound like your old man–"

"And you sound like a prude.... I want to feel good, Calder. I want what makes me feel good. You hear? Beat me!" Her voice rose. "What's the matter with you?"

"I was just going to ask *you* that."

"I want you to know what excitement is, what pleases me. I want you to change, Calder. Change–"

"Change? Beat you. With my belt."

"It's what I want!" she cried. "Anything's right–and good–if that's what you want. And that's what I want. You hear me? I want you to *hurt* me!"

She grabbed up my belt, hitting at me with it, wildly.

"Where'd you ever hear of this?"

Her eyes blazed. "What do you think I am? A child like you?" Her laughter wailed upward. "Must I lie on my back–in the same old way–all the time–?"

"That's wild enough for me."

She swung the belt, screaming. "It's not what you want that matters. It's what *I* want!"

She swung that belt buckle again and I caught it, wrenching it from her hand.

"Beat me!" she screamed. "If you don't beat me right now, you'll never have me again. None of me. Nothing! If you won't give me what I want, I'll find some man who will–"

She swung around and ran naked to the door, fighting at it.

I caught her and spun her back across the bed.

I stood over her, my head throbbing. "You talk like that and I will beat you."

She lay on her back and stared up at me defiantly. She laughed, raging with laughter at the top of her voice. Her wild eyes dared me to hit her with that belt, dared me not to.

"Lu Ann, you're crazy! You're ruining us. You're ruining everything!"

"Am I? Hit me. Hit me, Calder. If I'm crazy it's just that I'm crazy to be loved... the way I want... is that so wrong?"

"Not the way you tell it."

"Hit me! Hit me! Hit me!"

She was screaming at the top of her voice.

I hurled the belt aside and fell on top of her. I wrestled her to the mattress, held her quietly.

I heard people running and calling to each other outside our room.

I clapped my hand over Lu Ann's mouth.

"Please, Lu Ann! Show a little sense."

She bit my palm until it bled. When I jerked my hand away she screamed again.

Her screams melted into the wail of police sirens. I wasn't even astonished.

The manager pounded on the door. I threw a spread across Lu Ann's naked body and stepped into my pants.

I was coldly sober. Sick.

By the time the sheriff's deputies were beating on the door with clubs I had stopped shaking.

I heard Truman Lahey shouting outside. "Open up in there, or I'll tear it down."

I unlocked the door, opened it, and stepped back, staring at them.

"What kept you?" I said.

Maybe I sounded tough and hard to them and as if I didn't care, but that wasn't the way I felt. I was sick and empty and sober. But I knew I didn't have a chance now, and I gave up.

Lu Ann giggled on the bed.

She sat up on the mattress, letting the spread fall away from her magnificent breasts. She took up a glass of Scotch and raised her arm in a toast.

The silent people stared in at her.

"I ask you all to join me," she cried out, "and drink a toast with me. To my daddy!"

Chapter 8

I finally fell asleep on the army cot in the county jail at Oak Bluffs. About nine o'clock the next morning the bailiff woke me by scraping his nightstick across the bars.

Pa was with him.

"Come on, son," Pa said. "I come for you."

The bailiff unlocked the cell and I followed Pa out. I didn't say anything until we got out to Pa's old car at the curb.

"How'd you do it, Pa?"

"You can thank Mr. Frank Berlinger that you ain't on your way to the chain gang this morning." He went on. Mr. Frank had paid fines, costs, damages, and probably plenty on the side.

"Mr. Frank wants it all hushed up and forgot," Pa said. "And as far as we're concerned, that's what it is. You hear?"

"Nothing like money," I said. "Buy anything. Stolen bird dogs. Circuit court judges–"

"You simmer down, boy. You thank God–"

"And Frank Berlinger–"

"*Mister* Frank Berlinger. You thank God you didn't have to appear before Judge Stark today. He was plenty wild when he heard what you done with that fine young Berlinger girl–almost as wild as Mr. Frank himself. A sweet young girl like that! I ought to beat you."

I held my breath. "Don't try it, Pa."

He stared at me. "Sometimes I think I don't even know you. My own son! Trying to get me fired. Messing around with the daughter of Frank Berlinger. Taking her to a motel!"

Pa started the old car. "Mr. Frank had to pay that motel man plenty. But he shut him up. Old Judge Stark wanted him to press charges against you this morning. But he said as long as everything was paid for, he wanted to keep it quiet, too. Bad publicity hurts everybody."

We rolled along the street and Pa parked his old jalopy outside the high school. "This is where you get out."

I stared up at the school. It was silent, all classes busy through the windows.

"They know you're coming and that you'll be late," Pa said. "Go on in. That's part of it, boy. You keep your nose clean. You go everyday to school. You stay in school until you graduate. And you stay away from Lu Ann Berlinger!"

"Is that part of the deal too?"

"That's part of it. Mr. Frank said he'd kill you if you came near her again. Ever." I swung out of the car. Pa said, "I know I've hurt you bad, selling your dog and all. But a man has to stay alive, son. He has to get money somewhere–no matter who he hurts. I don't mean to hurt you."

"So long, Pa."

"Don't go near Berlinger's, son. It'll only be trouble. The worst. And anyhow–she ain't out there."

I stared at him. "Where is she?"

"Mr. Frank sent her home, Calder. This morning. We took Lu Ann across to Jacksonville and put her on a plane north."

I went back to school and stayed there. I couldn't get Lu Ann out of my mind. I could close my eyes and see her sitting in that motel bed, naked and pink-glazed skin glowing and lovely, her hair wilder than her eyes, drinking a toast, "To my daddy!"

Hunting season closed and Berlinger returned north. Pa closed the old winter house. I prowled around the huge mansion, looking for some sign that Lu Ann had been there. There was nothing.

I walked out, lonelier than ever. The wind was cold off the river. The whole country was turning brown. Leaves spun and rolled across the yard. Dogs yowled in the kennel runs. I shivered. It was as if Lu Ann had never been here at all.

Weeks passed slowly. I wrote to her. My letters were returned unopened. She didn't write to me at all.

I walked all the roads where we had ridden together, but it wasn't the same.

I kept to myself because I hated everybody. I wandered around town alone at noon.

"Calder."

It was Goldie Hampsden. She smiled at me in the noon sunlight on Main Street. "I see you in town everyday at noon when you're off from school. Why don't you come by and have lunch with me? I could fix you a hotter lunch than you'd ever get at school."

"Yes. Thanks."

"A growing boy like you needs hot lunches, Calder. A lot of hot lunches."

I nodded, letting it go at that. But I never went near her.

I was graduated from high school the last of May. The next morning I was outside Oak Bluffs, on 301, hitchhiking north.

A car pulled to the shoulder of the highway. It was a girl alone. "Hello, Calder."

I scowled, recognizing Willi Ruth Stark.

"I'm going pretty far," I said.

"It doesn't matter, Calder. I'm not doing anything. I just dropped Daddy at the courthouse."

I shrugged and got in. I sat far across the seat from her. I could smell her, the good clean scent. Hate at first sight. She had full breasts, and good-looking legs. But I wasn't interested. I told myself she could have been naked and I wouldn't have cared.

I realized she was talking. "What?"

"Did you ever find your dog?"

"Yes. It came home."

"I'm glad."

I didn't tell her Berlinger had shot its head off. Willi Ruth was the type who liked happy endings on all television shows. It was just as cheap to let her have her happy ending. I didn't want to talk about it.

We rode for miles in silence. She was uncomfortable, unable to think of anything I'd talk with her about. Any time she got tired slumming she could let me out.

"You don't like me, do you, Calder?"

"Am I supposed to?"

"We live in the same town."

I shrugged and stared through the window. After a moment she said in a soft voice, "I was in love with you in the first grade, Calder."

"I blush for you now. The shame."

"Oh, no. I used to talk about you all the time. At home. They teased me. Calder Fenton. Calder Fenton."

"I bet it would get a big laugh today."

She smiled but didn't say anything. At last she said, "You don't like my father, either, do you?"

"I never think about him much. Sometimes I'll go a whole day and never even think about him."

She laughed. "Oh, Calder. Why won't you be friendly?"

"All right. I'll do something friendly for you now. I'll tell you I'm going to New York."

"New York!"

"That's right. So if you want to let me out and turn around, why that will be just fine. I'll understand."

She let her car roll to a stop in the blazing Spring sunlight. I got out and nodded, thanking her.

"Hope I see you when you get back, Calder," she said.

I closed the door and walked away. I stood in that open country for two hours before a trucker let me crawl up in his big semi. He dropped me about three o'clock the next morning in some town in Carolina.

I washed up, shaved, put on the clean shirt I'd saved for the moment when I arrived in the little up-the-Hudson town where Lu Ann lived.

I asked directions, my heart banging with excitement, anticipation.

I rang the doorbell.

"Miss Lu Ann is out," the servant said.

"When will she be back?"

He shrugged. "She went horseback riding earlier. Perhaps she'll be home soon."

He didn't invite me to wait but he didn't order me off the property, either, so I sat down on the front steps. I felt shaky, feverish, sitting in the sunlight. I'd been riding so far, standing, waiting, running to hop rides. I couldn't believe I was here at the house where Lu Ann lived.

A car swung into the drive. Lu Ann got out. Five or six others yelled at her from the open convertible. I didn't even see them. I stood up. The car skidded in reverse, blasted off. Lu Ann turned, walking toward me in a riding habit.

I had never seen anything so beautiful. I started toward her. She stopped cold, staring at me. The color drained from her face.

She glanced around the drive. "How'd you get here?"

"I hitchhiked."

"From Oak Bluffs? You're joking."

"I missed you. I wrote to you. They returned my letters."

She looked all around again. She came forward slowly, but she didn't come into my arms or put out her hands. She said, "Are you hungry?"

I shrugged. "I haven't thought about it."

"Come on around to the kitchen, Calder. I'll get you something to eat–while we talk."

We went around the side of the house and through the rear door. Two servants were working in the kitchen. Lu Ann motioned them out. "We want to talk awhile."

She leaned against the stove and stared at me when we were alone. "Why did you do this?"

"I wanted to see you. I thought you wanted to see me."

She bit her lip. "Didn't you see enough of me–that last time?" She laughed casually and poured coffee into cups. She told me to sit down at the kitchen table. She brought cream, sugar, half a roasted chicken, rye bread. She placed it before me, deep in thought. "What do you want, Calder?"

"I told you. I want to see you."

"Yes. But what for?"

"What for? I love you. I thought you wanted to see me."

She winced. "Drink your coffee. You better eat something. You look dead tired. You have any money?"

"It doesn't matter, Lu Ann. I'll get a job."

"They'll arrest you for vagrancy in this town." She shook her head. "Wouldn't Daddy love to get you like that?"

"I'm not afraid of him."

"I know. You haven't been smart about anything, have you? Don't you know he was ready to kill you? That night down there–"

"I don't want to talk about him, Lu Ann. I want to talk about us."

She sat down, stirring her coffee impatiently. She glanced up at me. "What about us?"

"That's it. I love you. I came up here to be with you."

"What for?"

I shook my head. "You said you loved me–"

"That was–months ago. Last winter."

I drew the back of my hand across my mouth, feeling dizzy and empty. "You said in that motel–"

"Don't ever mention that place in this house–"

"You said you loved what we did, you loved me–we–were made for each other."

She laughed, exasperated. "Oh, Calder! I might have said that. Everybody is made for each other. At some time."

"That's not what you said." I could hardly see her.

"What did I say?"

"You said we were made for each other, we felt right, and good. We belonged."

"Calder, everybody says that."

I felt more feverish than ever. "I kept remembering–all winter. The good things."

"Well, don't."

"I can't forget, Lu Ann. The way we swam in the river together. The way we made love–"

"Don't, Calder."

"And I looked at you. And I never saw anything so lovely. And all we wanted was to be together–"

"Don't talk this way, Calder."

"Why not?"

"I don't want to hear it." She drank. "I'd hate for anybody–even the servants–to hear you talking like this."

"But I love you. You meant everything to me."

"Stop. Please. I'm ashamed enough–"

"Ashamed?"

"Yes. I hate for you to come here like this and remind me of all that."

"I didn't do anything I'm ashamed of."

"Maybe you didn't. I did. I don't want to be reminded." She stared into her coffee. She spoke in a tense tone, as if to herself. "Everybody does things they're ashamed of. But they don't have to be reminded all the time."

"I didn't come here to shame you."

"But you do. You remind me of–ugly things. Things I don't want to remember. Things I hate to remember. Things that made me feel all dirty."

"Dirty?"

"You make me feel dirty–coming here like this."

"What are you talking about?"

"About you. Following me up here. Broke. Hungry–"

"I don't care about that–"

"What did you want? What did you expect?"

"I only wanted to see you! I got lonely. I thought about you all the time. I wanted to see you."

She sat back in her chair, her mouth pulled as if she'd tasted something bitter. "Well, now you've seen me."

"Lu Ann. I came all this way."

"I'm sorry about that."

"I missed you."

"I'm sorry about that, too. I thought you had sense enough to know–it ended down there."

"No. I never thought that."

She gestured impatiently. "Are you for real?"

"I love you. I thought you loved me."

"Oh, Calder. Don't make me be unkind. All right, *I loved you*. Then. Down there. Those weeks. Those nights. If that makes you feel any better. I'm sorry now about the whole thing. But I can't help it. That's the end of it."

I stared at her. "You never cared at all."

"Keep your voice down. All right. Maybe I never cared, the way you mean. I got away from there. And I got to thinking. I'd done some other things I was ashamed of. And I realized how lucky I was to get away–nobody hurt."

The room wheeled around me. I held on to the table.

"That's the way it was, Calder. Nobody cares, not the way you mean. You might as well learn that. Nobody really means what they say. Maybe for the moment, but not later ...I didn't know you'd follow me up here, Calder."

"That makes us even."

"Even?"

"I didn't know you could be like this."

"I'm trying to tell you the truth. I'm sorry if you're hurt. I'm sorry you came way up here. Hitchhiking. Good lord. I'm sorry. But that's it. People do things they are sorry for. And I'm sorry. But that's the end of it."

I stared at her helplessly. I was never going to see her again, but really, I had never seen her before. "You didn't even care."

"Don't beat it to death, Calder. Now I'll give you some money. You catch a bus back home. Hitchhiking is for the birds. I liked you, Calder. But I've liked a lot of people. A lot of boys. None of them were so foolish as you. Wait. I'll get you some money and than I'll drive you down to the bus station so you can get started back home."

"I don't want any money. What's it to you?"

"I'm trying to be nice."

Chapter 9

I walked past Miller's Department Store on Main Street as Willi Ruth came out the front door of the shop.

I didn't bother to speak. I was almost to the Oak Bluffs Cafe next door when she called after me. "Calder."

I hesitated and turned around. She came toward me, frowning slightly. "I'm glad you're back home," she said. "When did you get back?"

"I've been home about a week."

"I haven't seen you."

"No."

She smiled uncertainly. "Where do you keep yourself, Calder?"

"When?"

She laughed. "You don't make it any easier, do you? You've been home a week and I've not even seen you in this little town."

"I've been down on my Grandpa's farm."

"Are you working down there, Calder?"

"Sure," I said. I saw the fennel and the blackberry patches, the whole place desolate in the sun. "A big estate. We raise race horses. Forty or fifty slaves singing in the cotton fields all day. Raising race horses and cotton fields and singing slaves. And cantaloupes. We raise a lot of cantaloupes."

"They don't raise cantaloupes around here–"

"Wait until I tell Grandpa that!"

She burst out laughing. "Oh, Calder! Why don't you be nice?"

Three truckers coming through the doors at the cafe stopped on the walk near us. One said, in a falsetto voice, "Now, Calder, you be nice!"

Willi Ruth blushed. I jerked my head around. She caught my arm. "Calder, don't pay any attention. You'll only get in trouble."

"That's right, Calder," one of the truckers said. "You'll only get in trouble, and you'll never take me like you did when I was drunk."

Willi Ruth's hand tightened on my arm. "Please, Calder."

I moved away from her, watching the big trucker. But he shook his head and laughed. "Not this time, sonny. I didn't realize you were just a kid." He waved his arm. "I don't want to fight you. I owe you plenty. I owe you one of the hottest weeks I ever had in my life." He winked at his pals. "I can tell you, kid, that Lu Ann was prime. Young and willing."

"You're a liar."

"No, kid, I'm not lying. She came back that night and picked me up. Said she was sorry you hit me like that." He laughed. "Didn't she ever tell you about her Johnny-Cake? That's what she called me, Johnny-Cake. Real touching. We spent almost a week at the Starlighter Motel."

He laughed, remembering, and his pals laughed with him. I wondered sickly if Lu Ann and I got the same room she'd shared with Johnny-Cake. "We sure warmed up that dump. We'd be there yet, but I'm just human. I found that out. I really found out how human I was. A man can take just so much–"

"Liar!"

"No. Just going over my memories." He laughed. "I'd buy you a beer in the Cypress Bar, kid, to show no hard feelings, only you ain't old enough to drink beer."

He turned and the three of them walked into the Cypress Bar.

Willi Ruth clung to my arm. I kept seeing Lu Ann's face before me, the way she'd looked, waiting for me outside the high school after that long week apart. No wonder she'd looked so white, so drained. A week at the Starlighter Motel with Johnny-Cake.

"Don't listen to them, Calder," Willi Ruth said. "They're dirty, ugly men."

"Let me alone, Willi Ruth." I pulled free of her hand. "You don't owe me anything, and I don't owe you anything, and let's keep it that way."

She nodded. She studied my face a moment. "Calder, the reason I called to you. My father is going to give me a party. All my friends–"

"Sounds swank."

"Will you come?"

"I don't think I'll be in town that day."

"You didn't even wait to hear what day it is."

"Yes," I said. "That's what I mean."

She exhaled heavily. "Good-bye, Calder."

I nodded without looking at her. She walked away from me. I heard her heels clicking on the concrete.

Everybody looked up when I walked into the Cypress Bar. The stout blonde woman who ran the place said, "You Calder Fenton?" And when I nodded, she jerked her head toward the street. "You're too young to be in here. You're trouble. Get out."

I stared at the big trucker's laughing face. "I came to talk to somebody," I said.

The blonde woman reached for the phone. "Get out or I'll call the sheriff."

Pa came running from the back of the room. I saw Goldie back there with him. He said, "Hold it, Mamie, don't call the law."

She paused, hand on the phone. "Sorry, Lutz, they warned me what they'd do if I let him come in here again and didn't call them."

"I'll get him out of here, Mamie," Pa said.

Pa caught my arm, walking me along the bar toward the rear of the saloon. I heard the truckers laugh. I tried to break free. "You trying to get on the road gang, boy?" Pa said to me, his voice tense.

I heard a siren in the street, and Pa shoved me, moving me faster toward the alley. "Get out of here, boy. And don't come back."

Pa kept dancing me along toward that rear door. When we were almost there, he shoved me and I hit against the door-facing hard.

The door swung open and I sprawled out into the dirt of the alley. The last thing I saw in that room was Johnny and his friends leaning against the bar laughing.

I heard the sheriff's car stop out front. I stood up, brushing mud from my clothes. I walked down the alley toward the street.

"Calder!" Willi Ruth pulled her car into the mouth of the alley.

"What do you want?"

The alley door to the bar swung open behind me. I heard Willi Ruth cry out something. I glanced across my shoulder. Truman Lahey was coming out into the alley.

I got into Willi Ruth's car. She got out of there fast. "Your father's going to be real proud of the new friends you're making this summer," I said.

She didn't answer. She broke speed laws getting us out of Oak Bluff town limits. She hit the Dead Indian River Road and slowed the car. "Where do you want to go, Calder?"

I shrugged.

"You better get out of town," she said. "Or are you trying to get hurt? It's none of my business, but–"

"You're right about that."

We drove five minutes in silence. I said, "You can drop me off anywhere along here."

"What will you do out here?"

"You've not really taking me to raise, are you?"

"Like I said, it's none of my business. But I've talked to my father about you. I know what trouble you've been in, what kind you can get in if they take you before my father for being in that bar."

"Looks like you'd get away from me as fast as you could then."

"Yes," Willi Ruth said. "It looks like it, doesn't it?"

I looked at her. "Did it ever occur to you that maybe I didn't want you to help me?"

She just kept driving at fifty, watching the road.

"Has it ever occurred to you what your father will do to you if Truman Lahey catches me in the same car with you?"

"My father is not like you," she said defiantly. "He wants me to be happy–whether he approves of what I do or not."

"He'd draw the line just this side of Lutz Fenton's son."

After a moment she sighed. "Who was that girl? What was she like?"

"I know so many girls–"

"The one you and your friends were discussing in the street. Lu Ann. Wasn't that her name? Queen of the Starlighter Motel?"

"Shut up."

"She really tied you in knots, didn't she? Made you hate everybody. Going to fight everybody. Wreck a beer hall. She really tied you in knots."

"People will think you're jealous," I said.

She didn't say anything and concentrated on her driving, putting miles between me and the sheriff's deputies at Oak Bluffs.

She didn't seem to realize they would follow me anywhere in the county. I didn't tell her. I felt a grudging admiration and appreciation for what she was doing for me. A judge's daughter, she was taking more chance than I was.

"Sorry I was rugged toward you," I said.

She smiled. "What happened to the old Calder Fenton?"

"Let me out anywhere along here," I told her. "Go back to town. Tell them I forced you to drive me out here. They'll believe you."

"Sure they will," she said.

"You don't have to get in trouble because of me. Tell them I forced you–"

"Sure. Why don't you break my nose to make it look better?"

Over the next rise was the turnoff that led, across a hard-surfaced road, a rutted lane, and finally a cowpath, to Grandpa's old farm on the river.

I said, "Slow down. The road up there leads to Grandpa's farm–"

"Race horses," she said. "Singing in the cotton. Cantaloupes."

"A good place to hide," I said. "Nobody lives out here. Maybe they'll cool off by the time they find me down here."

"I better run you down there." She turned the car off on the secondary road. "They might use rubber hoses on me. Brainwash me. I might break. I might tell them where I took you."

She parked her car in a clump of pines near the gate at Grandpa's place. We got out. I lifted her in my arms and set her down over the fence. My hand closed over one of her breasts. It was as if a charge of electricity raged through me.

When I set her on her feet we didn't say anything for a few moments. She didn't look at me. Silence pressed in around us.

At last, she said, "Oh, Calder, it's beautiful."

I looked around, seeing the run-down farm.

"It's like something from a hundred years ago," she said.

"At least."

"So lovely, so serene, and quiet."

"Them cantaloupes singing all the day," I said.

She looked up at me, smiling. Her eyes were lighted with pleasure. Looking at her like that, I felt my stomach go empty with a terrible kind of longing. I saw for the first time how lovely she was, clean and fresh and dainty, untouched. Her complexion was clear and her dark hair lay softly about her face. Her eyes were deep, almost violet blue.

I heeled around and walked away. I'd been on one merry go round like this. If Frank Berlinger's daughter was impossibly far above me, Judge Stark's only child belonged in another galaxy.

I wouldn't have had it any other way.

"Why?" I said. We'd searched the whole place, picked a can of blackberries. We sat on the front steps, eating them. Her legs were scratched by the briars and so were her hands. "Why did you stick your neck out like this for me?"

"I think you've been hurt enough," she said. Her mouth was stained with blackberry juice. I wanted to kiss her. I looked away.

"Why should you care? Judge Stark's daughter. The kindly judge with the steel gray eyes behind the rimless glasses. He'd break my neck for speaking to you. Why don't you leave it that way?"

"Do you want to?"

I winced, staring at her. It was building in me fiercely, what I really wanted. "We got troubles enough without getting mixed up with each other."

She glanced around. "This lovely old place. You could restore it to perfect condition–"

"Sure I could. With a couple old rusty nails and fifty thousand dollars." I stood up. "That's what I mean. You don't even know what it is to have no money–nothing."

"You could get some."

"I could rob a bank."

"Yes. And you could work, too. What you could do with this lovely old home with some work. Those rusty nails–and some paint. A plow out in those fields."

"Money."

"You need money? Look at those lovely stands of pines. Your grandfather planted those pines for you. You could plant seedlings, sell those trees, the way he did. You'd have money then to restore this place, money to go to the university next fall."

"You make it sound easy."

"No. I didn't say it was easy. You'd have to work. Maybe you couldn't do that. But it isn't impossible. You could do anything you wanted to."

I stared at her. Her eyes were filled with tears and her hands trembled.

"Oh, Calder," she said. Her voice broke and she stepped forward until she was pressed hard against me, her face on my shirt. "Why can't you be the way I want you?"

"I didn't even know you wanted me," I said. I felt the fever, the need. It was different from with Lu Ann, but it was a raging desire just the same. I felt protective and lustful all at once.

I let my arms move along the small of her back. I cupped my hands on her buttocks and pulled her up on me, forcing her body to fit against mine. I was having trouble breathing.

We both were.

My heart racketed against hers. I kept thinking this was Judge Stark's daughter. His pride. Kindly Judge Stark with the steel gray eyes. The hanging judge.

But he was not here now. And Willi Ruth was.

I moved my hands on her supple bottom. I heard her breathing go faster. I wanted her. There was nobody to keep me from having her. She'd followed me down here. Maybe next time she'd stay away from me. Nobody to stop me. I'd have every breathless thing I'd had with Lu Ann, only I would have more because Willi Ruth was mine. I could tell, holding her like that, she was mine to have any way I wanted.

"Calder," her voice came as if from across the river. I could barely hear her, barely see her. I felt the blood throbbing behind my eyes. My breath was hot across my parched lips.

I moved her against me, and I moved my hands on her. Her eyes had a frightened, sleepy look in them. Looking at her like that, sunken helplessly against me, made me wilder than ever.

I pushed my hand down into her dress, cupping her heated breast, feeling the slugging of her heart. My hand closed tighter.

"Calder," she whispered again.

I could not speak.

"Calder, I won't stop you... I can't stop you... I'll let you... if you want to... but I don't think you ought to do it–not like this."

"Why not? Who's to stop me?"

"Nobody, Calder. But I better tell you. I've–never done it before. No one ever touched me like this. And this isn't the way–not for us–"

"You know a better way?"

"No. I don't know anything. Only it'll spoil everything if we do it–wild like this–when we don't even really know each other. It could be so nice for us. It could mean so much."

"It'll mean all it'll ever mean to me–right now."

"All right." She sagged against me, putting her head back. She did not protest any more. "You can do what you want, Calder. Only, I've got to tell you. I'll hate you. I'll hate both of us. And I won't see you any more. I couldn't. I'd be too ashamed."

I could hardly breathe. "Why would you want to see me again anyway?"

"I don't know," she whispered, and I felt her tears hot against my face. "But I just wish I could–I do want to see you again. I do. It could be so nice. We could have everything."

Chapter 10

She trembled in my arms. "Oh, please, Calder." She could beg me not to do it to her, but the fact was she was starved for love without even knowing what it was really like.

She was beautiful when you looked at her. And I looked.

Her face was flushed with the excitement that rushed through her, making her helpless. I put my hand on her leg above her knee and moved it upward, taking her dress with it.

I knew now I could have her. Nothing could stop me. She shivered, her body going lax under my hands.

I felt excitement unlike any I'd ever known, too, and I warned myself about control, relax, or I'd spoil it all. It wasn't easy.

"It's all so wrong, Calder–darling."

"You've never had it, angel, don't knock it." I kissed her mouth. It was so soft, and fresh and tasting of blackberries that I almost retreated.

It was more than wanting her now. I was crazy for it.

But when I looked down at her, she looked so young and helpless and frightened, I knotted up inside.

I closed my eyes and kissed her mouth, her eyes, her cheeks, along her throat.

She had no strength left to fight me.

But when I opened my eyes and looked down at her, her eyes were brimmed with tears and she'd bitten her lip until it bled....

I was drawn taut, my stomach tied in knots, when Willi Ruth stopped the car outside my gate.

She gave me a pale, wan smile. She touched my hand, clinging to it. Her fingers were like ice. "You won't be sorry you waited," she whispered.

I drew my hand away. I was ambulating agony. It was nothing she'd understand.

"Don't hate me, Calder."

"Why should I hate you? You don't want to bed down with a guy like me. Why should you?"

"It's not that at all!" Her eyes filled with tears. "I'm going to see you tomorrow!"

"If you can't stop, just wave," I said.

"It isn't something to have and then forget, Calder. Not with us. It'll be so much better when we learn to want each other.

"I'd almost learned."

She leaned forward, pressed her face against mine, kissed me gently, her lips fever-hot. I shivered.

I got out. I heard the canned music, the framed violence erupting from Mom's TV set. Pa's dogs barked in the kennels.

But when she was gone, and I stood in the darkness, I glanced toward the house and knew I'd be sick if I went in there. I couldn't talk to anybody. I didn't want to hear Mom or Pa arguing, or crying, or even speaking. My nerves were raw.

I turned away from the house toward Oak Bluffs and kept walking. I strode through the darkness carefully keeping my mind empty, blank.

The town was quieting down when I got there, a saffron glow outside the State Theater, a few display windows glowing faintly on the night street, a flat flare of light from the double doorways at the Cypress Bar. I didn't go near the place. I turned off Main Street and kept walking.

The house was a small place, on a street of cottages. Only one light burned in the back windows.

I went along the walk holding my breath and knocked on the door. I don't know how long I waited. I finally heard Mrs. Hampsden stirring around in there, and then I watched her through the front door glass, walking along the hall, tying some kind of bathrobe about her. She wasn't fat. I thanked God that at least she hadn't started getting fat.

She opened the front door without turning on the front porch light. I was glad of this, then I realized the widow Hampsden had learned not to light up her visitors.

Goldie Hampsden's mouth parted. I couldn't say she was pleased to see me, but she was astonished. That showed.

"Calder," she said.

I licked my dry mouth. "You said to come by sometime–for lunch," I said.

"Lunch–" She frowned. "Aren't you kind of mixed up?"

But at least she didn't shut the door.

"I get hungry at crazy times," I said.

"Don't you, though?" She went on standing in the doorway, staring at me.

I said, "Can I come in, Goldie?"

She stared at me a minute longer, then something happened in her face, as if a light snapped off, giving it a bedroom glow, and she nodded. She stepped back.

I came through the door and walked close against her. She hadn't started getting fat at all. She was like a girl. She hadn't lied about that.

"You finally got hungry," she said.

I hated to waste time talking, but knew I had to. I nodded. "Yes. I got hungry."

"You act hungry. You act starved."

I tilted her head, kissed her mouth, parting my mouth the way Lu Ann taught me. I felt the aching need start at my toes and work upward, agonizingly. Goldie's body was warm, with the warmth of her bed like a heady scent around her. I felt I'd die of chill if I didn't get closer.

She wiggled against me and laughed, talking against my mouth. "Why, Calder! I think you've finally grown up!"

"Yes," I panted. "I think I really have."

It was easy getting her gown off her. It was like taking it off and tossing it behind her. Being naked was nothing new to her, but it excited her being nude before me.

She worked at my clothing. She was expert. I was glad because this was what I needed in the agony Willi Ruth had left me in.

I stepped out of my trousers, left them on the floor. She gazed as if fascinated by me, and reached for me, and I sighed because it was going to be all right. I heard her whimpering faintly.

We sank to her couch together. For a moment I felt as if I were drowning in the cheap perfume she used, but she moved faster and faster beneath me, and suddenly I didn't care.

Her head rolled back and forth on the divan. She kept telling me how young I was, how good I was, and I felt exultant, because she was fighting, but not fighting me.

She was fighting for *it*.

And she got it.

I was working in the afternoon sun, repairing the kennels when Willi Ruth drove into the yard. She came across to me. Her face flushed as if she had not been able to forget what I'd done to her at the farm.

She came close to me and pressed my hand in hers. "Oh, Calder, I couldn't sleep all night."

"Take some of your father's sleeping pills. A judge with all he has on his conscience must take pills–"

"He has sleeping pills, Calder, but he's a wonderful man. If only you'd get to know him and what he's like."

"We've met. We just didn't hit it off."

"Give him another chance. Come to my party–I told father last night I'd have the party if he'd invite you."

"I'd love to have seen that."

"He wasn't overjoyed. But you're invited–or there's no party."

"Willi Ruth, you're a big girl. You know better than this. Look at that house. I was born there, lived there all my life."

"Let's go down to the farm."

I stared at her. "You'd put me through that torture again?"

"It's just as bad on me. Worse. You know I love you, Calder. I have–all my life. Even when I was a snob and pretended I didn't. I never thought about any other boy. Never wanted anyone else. We've got to get used to being alone with each other."

"Why?"

"Because that's the way it is. Be glad about it, Calder. It's so much easier this way."

"Sure. Relax and enjoy it."

We spent the afternoon at the farm. When I touched her, even accidentally, it was as if the air were charged with lightning. I could smell the fresh cleanliness of her. It drove me wild.

We walked all over the place. She made cottage talk. There were clinging vines and mortgages in everything she said.

The rage grew in me, and this was good. It made it easier to keep my hands off her.

She talked about my clearing the pine stands, saving the money for the university. As far as she was concerned, it was settled that I'd go to college that fall.

She waved her arm across the fields of wire grass and fennel. "We could clear this and put in a good crop, one that would pay off before fall."

"We're not playing dolls, Willi Ruth. I've no money."

"You could be anything. Go to school. I could help you. We'd get married–"

"*What*?"

"We could rent one of those apartments for married couples–"

"Come on now! I told you. I'm broke."

"You'll work. Out here. I have some money. And Daddy will help us."

"Yeah. I can see Daddy figuring out ways to help us now!"

"Stop hating and start thinking."

"All right. I'll start thinking. This is what I think. You better get somebody else to play your games with you."

"Is it so terrible for me to want to help you be something?"

"I don't want you to help!"

Her eyes flashed. "No. All you want is to take me down and–use me–and then forget me."

I went back to see Goldie again that night. I was too young to go with her to the Cypress Bar. She brought beer and we drank it in her kitchen. I kept her naked, making her do all the exciting things Lu Ann had done for me.

I got home about three the next morning.

The next day I went to see an old Negro woodcutter named Clem Robbins. He lived with his wife. He owned a saw that worked off the rear wheel of his old Ford truck. "I cut pines with your Grandpa every year," he said.

I told him I wanted to pay him when we sold the pine logs to the paper mills.

"That's fine. I've worked on shares. I'm pleased to work that way with you, Calder. You're your Grandpa's son."

"Most people say I'm like Pa."

We started cutting pines and it didn't take me long to see that Uncle Clem was worth a lot more at this job than I'd ever be. There wasn't a day he didn't outwork me. We spent all that month cutting pines and hauling them out.

The second day Willi Ruth came out at lunch with a picnic basket. We sat on the river bank and ate. I was too tired and sore to reach for her.

I sprawled on my back, listening to her plans for us. I stared at her and wondered how she'd lived with Judge Stark and knew him so little.

One noon she arrived with a new oxford gray suit. "For you," she said. "From me. Your birthday present."

"My birthday's in February."

"So I'm a little late this year. I want you to knock them dead at my party."

"I told you I wasn't going to that party."

She smiled. "You weren't going to be able to clear these pines, either, but just look."

Another day she said to Uncle Clem, "We need a good crop of some kind. Isn't there some crop we could put in that would pay off before fall?"

He nodded. "There's tomatoes, Miss Willi Ruth," he said. "But you take a terrible gamble when you plant them. Water can be pumped from the river with a little jerk-pump, but the sun is a problem in the summer, and root-knot will kill them off and no way to save them."

"Isn't it worth that gamble, Uncle Clem?"

She sold him, too. He appeared as excited as she did, and they yakked about planting and picking and selling, on shares. They already had the money in the bank.

Still, Uncle Clem tried to warn her. "You may hate me and them tomatoes before this summer ends."

"Never!" Willi Ruth cried. "Can we start tomorrow?"

"Tomorrow is just fine with me," Uncle Clem said.

So with Willi Ruth spurring us, Uncle Clem and I cleared the flat field between the old house and the stand of pines. Mornings we cleared logs and afternoons we plowed, harrowed and used the discs that Uncle Clem owned. With some of the money we got from selling pine logs to the mills, we bought tomato seedlings, fertilizer and sprays. Sometimes I thought I couldn't get up off my knees, or straighten my back if I pushed another damned seedling in that hot, dry earth.

I didn't believe it anyway. Or I kept telling myself I didn't. Willi Ruth was playing house. And she'd conned Uncle Clem Robbins and me into joining her games. Uncle Clem should have had better sense. I should have had better sense. She should have had better sense. You could keep playing that tune. Only, she was too full of excitement about it, you got infected, and pretty soon, you forgot the facts of life, and you began to see the world the way Willi Ruth saw it: a lovely place where you got what you wanted if you only worked hard enough.

God knew I worked hard enough. I staggered out of the pine stands into the fields, and from the fields onto the porch of the old house and sprawled there until I got energy enough to make it home to bed. Only seeing brown, wiry little Uncle Clem bouncing along ahead of me kept me moving at all in the tomato fields.

"Oh, Calder! Uncle Clem! It's the loveliest sight I ever saw." Willi Ruth's face glowed and her eyes glittered with pleasure. The three of us stood in the shade of the water oak beside the house, gazing across the small heaped rows, palely green with three-inch tomato plants all the way to the bare cropped pine hill.

"Yes'm, Missy," Uncle Clem said, "but remember, putting tomatoes in the ground is the easiest part–"

"Don't say that, Uncle Clem," I said, "I know you're right, but just don't say it. Not right now. There's got to be something easy about this."

"No. I never found anything easy. Not in my whole life. I wouldn't want to mislead you young folks any. We water them plants, get them up, they get tomatoes, a storm hits–we'll lose them shorely, if the root-knot don't strike from the soil."

"God wouldn't let that happen," Willi Ruth said. "Not to us."

And I went to her party. Sure, I did. I had worked so hard, put money in the bank, paid Uncle Clem, I began to feel I had a right to play house with Willi Ruth. Her games looked like fun, and suddenly I wanted to play them with her, her way.

Judge Stark shook hands with me. His voice was polite but his kindly gray eyes stripped the skin off me, and I was laughing about something about eleven when he tapped me on the shoulder. "When this party's over, Calder, I'd like to talk to you, over in my courthouse office. Can you be there?"

Don't think there was any tone of invitation in his voice. He smiled, and everybody around us saw him smiling, but he had learned a soft-voiced kind of savagery that carried no further than the person he spoke to. When I said good night to Willi Ruth, at her front door, with the Judge looking on, smiling, I walked down to the courthouse.

The old building was like a tomb after midnight, full of shadows, rustling and echoing. After a while I heard the hard tread of Judge Stark's heels on the corridor tiles. We went into his office. He nodded toward a chair and I sat down.

"I won't waste any time, Calder," he said. "I want you to stay away from

Willi Ruth."

"Just like that?"

"Is there any other way? You know some other way, boy? A quick, sharp cut, and final. That's best."

"Have you talked to Willi Ruth about this?"

To show you how much he hated me–or hated the idea of my being in the same breathing area with his daughter–he winced when I spoke her name. He said, "I don't think I have to speak to Willi Ruth. I'm sure you and I can settle this. Here and now."

"I've found out she's pretty stubborn when she makes up her mind about anything, Judge."

He had a sarcastic way of speaking that would rip your ears off if you let him get to you. "I'm sure you have. I'm also aware that you had her sneaking off down to that farm of yours to see you. Did you think I wouldn't find out, Calder?"

"This is going to shock hell out of you, but I didn't think about you at all."

He leaned forward, his judge's chair squealing drily in the tomblike silence. "I think you did. You know I wouldn't permit you to get near my daughter, and you thought you could hide down there–take her down there. Well, that's over. My daughter is a young, impressionable girl. She's too young to know her own mind. You're like a stray cat. A stray alley cat. You appeal to her for this reason. Many young girls are caught in such traps. But my daughter won't be. She's been my whole life–and I've had the responsibility of rearing her since her mother died. I've done well so far, and I won't let her throw herself away on something like you."

"What do you know about me?"

"My God. I know all about you. I know about you and what you did to that Berlinger girl. I get cold sweats to think that next you and Willi Ruth might be caught in such a–a sickening situation. No. It won't happen, because after tonight you are not to go near Willi Ruth. If I see you with her, Calder, or hear that you were with her, you'll go to the work gang. Don't forget you're still on probation."

I stared at him, helpless with rage. "Probation? How long am I on probation with you?"

He met my gaze. "As long as I say you are! And you had better learn your place, young fellow, and stay in it. Because I'll teach you that I mean what I say. Is that clear? You stay away from Willi Ruth, or I'll throw you on the gang until you learn some sense."

I stood up. "I don't believe you can do it. This may be a fouled up world, but I'm damned if I believe a man like you can throw me in prison for no better reason than that you want to."

He remained seated. He spoke softly, but with that cutting edge. "Don't make me prove it to you, Calder."

I turned and walked out of there. I was trembling. Everything rushed back over me. The way Fanny had crawled back, pressing against my leg to die. The way I'd been pushed around, shoved. I ran along the streets, and then along the silent country road. But I couldn't run fast enough. I sweated, feeling the hatred all in me. I couldn't stand to think about it. I strode across our yard into the barn. I struck a match, lighted the lantern, hung it on a nail. I fought into the hay bin and came up with a mason jar of Pa's corn whiskey. I opened the car door, sprawled against the seat, and lying there drank, and kept drinking. I began to see why Pa hit these bottles, and kept hitting them.

The corn whiskey burned into me. It seared a streak into my belly and from there exploded against the crown of my head. Pa could drink and lie here until he passed out. I couldn't do it. I wasn't like Pa. No matter what people thought, I wasn't like Pa. The moonshine made me restless. I had to get out of there.

In less than forty minutes I was banging on Goldie Hampden's front door. I had three mason jars of corn whiskey under my arm. "Goldie!" I yelled. "Goldie. Let me in. I'm grown up again! I'm more grown up than hell, and I want to get in."

It stayed dark. I began to be afraid she wasn't there. I knew better. She had to be there. She was my kind of people, and she had to be there. God, I couldn't stand it if she wasn't there.

"Goldie! Let me in!"

Finally, a light showed dimly in the rear of the house. She came sleepily toward the front door. She opened it, angry, telling me to be quiet.

"What the hell do I want to be quiet for?" I said. "Ain't I got a right to be here if I want to? I got a right to be somewhere, and it might as well be here!"

"What do you want?"

I roared with laughter at that. "You know what I want. You damn well know what I want."

"Sure, keep yelling. Let the whole town know!" She grabbed my arm, pulled me inside into the vaguely lighted hall, shut the door. "You got to stop coming around here like this, Calder! I've got to live in this town. Maybe you don't care what people think–but I've got to live in this town. Now, I want you to stay away from here."

"Oh, no." I shook my head, wanting to bawl like a baby. She took the quart mason jars, set them on a table. I reached for her, pulled her against me. "Let me stay, Goldie. God, please let me stay. I'll be good. I'll be quiet. Only let me stay. My God, where would I go if I couldn't come here?"

"I don't know," she said, holding her body rigid. "You better think of something. Ask the sweet little Stark girl. You ain't going to run around with her, and then come running to me with your hot pants."

"No," I said, panting, shaking with panic. "No, I'm not going to see her, Goldie. Not any more. Please.... Only be good to me. Anything you say, Goldie, only don't send me away."

She stroked my hair with her hand. "All right. You can stay. Tonight. Just tonight, Calder. You hear?"

"Sure, Goldie. Sure. Anything. Sure."

She pulled me against her, and I staggered. She swore. "I'm not taking care of you like a baby. You stand up."

I laughed. "I'm standing up, Goldie. For you. Don't you worry about that. I'm standing up."

She wanted me to go home the next morning, but I refused. I wouldn't leave her and the mason jars of Pa's moonshine. When I got away from Goldie and corn whiskey, I began to think again. Nobody could make me do that.

She stayed angry most of the day. The only way I could get her to smile was to get her in bed. She was all right when she was in bed with me. But about five the next afternoon, she was like a cat; she wanted to prowl; she wanted to visit her friends in the bars. "Go ahead," I told her. "I'll just sleep here awhile."

I sprawled across her bed. "You're making me mad, Calder. Real mad. Now why don't you go on home? You hear me, Calder? I don't want you to be here when I get back. You understand?"

I looked at her through a haze of moonshine. "I'll be here, Goldie. I'll be right here. Because you're my kind of people. My kind of people."

She stared down at me, her face gray and set. I watched her get dressed and powdered and perfumed until I could hardly breathe in that room. When she went out, I fell asleep. It was after eleven when I woke up and I heard noises. She had some man with her. I sweated, hearing them laugh and talk together, hearing them struggle, and then listening to the silences from the front room. I lay there, gagging.

It was hours later. He was gone. She came into the bedroom as if I didn't exist. She was only half dressed, her make-up smeared, her mouth looking big and swollen and misshapen.

She stared at me, daring me to speak. "I got my own life, Calder, and you're not going to come around messing it up, a kid like you. I got my own self to think about."

I made it to the bathroom. When I finally came out, she was calmly removing the make-up from her face. She wore an old bathrobe, and had a towel around her shoulder. She looked like hell.

I staggered toward the door. She laughed. "Come back again, Calder," she said. "Come back when you're sober. When you know what you're doing."

At home, I lay sick in bed all the next day. Mom tried to talk to me, but I begged her to let me alone. She went away, and I heard the gunfire and music crescendo from her television set. I couldn't sleep that night. But I stayed in bed until daybreak, then I dressed, not knowing what I was going to do with myself. The house was silent. I went out on the front porch. It was oddly still and chilled in the false dawn.

"Calder."

Pa had come around the yard from the kennels. He wore dungarees stuffed in old boots and his denim shirt buttoned at the throat.

"I guess I owe you something for the moonshine, Pa. I'll pay you."

"No. That's all right, boy. Like the man says, I can always get more of that. It's you I'm troubled about. You."

"What about me?"

"You and Miss Goldie, son. A young boy like you. She can be trouble for a young boy."

I laughed at him. "What's the matter? You jealous?"

His jaw was a taut line, his gray eyes hard. "No. I ain't jealous. It's you I'm thinking about. Don't get yourself in trouble you can't get yourself out of."

"Why, Pa," I said. "I thought you wanted me to be like you. Seems to me I'm just like you. Even like the same kind of women."

He winced, then stood there as if there was a lot more he wanted to say, but then he shook his head, turned and walked away, back around the house.

I sat on the steps, empty-bellied, sick.

I didn't move when Willi Ruth's car pulled into the yard a couple hours later. It was full daylight, the sun blazing on the yard, the hens clucking around the wilted flower beds.

Willi Ruth got out of the car, came running across the yard. She grabbed my hands, sank to the lower steps, pressed against my legs. "Oh, Calder. What's the matter? Where have you been? Poor Uncle Clem's been working so hard down there, trying to do it all alone. I've been ill, looking for you."

"It's all over, Willi Ruth. You take your toys and get on home. We're not playing house any more."

"Why, Calder? What have I done?"

"Nothing. I'm just tired playing that's all."

"You've got somebody else? Another girl?" Her voice sounded empty, frightened.

"Sure. I thought you knew that. Everybody else does."

"No." She shook her head. "I didn't know. Tell me, Calder. Who is it? What's she like?"

I stared at her. "I'll tell you want she's like. She's like a big girl. If I want to go to bed with her, she does it. She don't play house–it's no game the way she plays it. And I'm tired of playing, Willi Ruth, so go on home."

"I'll do it, Calder," she said quietly.

I felt sweat crawl up my face. "You'll do what?"

"Anything, Calder. Anything you want. Anything I have to do to keep you." She clung to my hands.

"Maybe you couldn't keep me anyway."

"I don't believe that! Anyway, I don't care. Come down to the farm with me, Calder. Now. Please. That's where I–want us to do it."

Chapter 11

I walked into that old farmhouse with Willi Ruth, and I was running a temperature.

When she was in my arms I forgot everything else. What I'd had with Lu Ann was what the animals had, and it would never have been different because this was all Lu Ann knew. And she'd had everything until the only thrill left was danger or hurting. And Goldie gave nothing because she had nothing left to give. She was willing to do anything as long as she could believe some new man thought her pretty and young.

With Willi Ruth's hands on me, her mouth parted to me, her breasts bared to my loving, I burned with fever and I'd never had a girl until this moment with her.

"Hold me tighter, Calder. There. Like that. Oh, your hand is so nice. Do

I feel good, Calder? Oh, Calder! Don't let me go. Please don't ever let me go."

"Your father. He'll come for you, Willi Ruth. With guns and writs and deputies and bloodhounds."

Distantly I heard Uncle Clem's singing in the tomato fields. There was quiet beauty in his deep voice. It was as if he crooned to us, lulling us, telling us how right we were for the first time in our lives.

"Darling, Daddy isn't that cruel. He loves me. Worries about me. But he wouldn't do anything to hurt me. He knows how badly I want you. I told him."

"Ho boy!"

"Darling, it's just that he's been so unhappy. My mother committed suicide. He never got over it. He thinks I'm as weak as she was. He's convinced everyone's weak except him, and he has to be strong for us all, make decisions, judgments–"

"That sounds like the man I know."

"You don't know him at all."

One of us didn't.

I kissed her. She believed in happy endings. I knew better. But even worse, I knew this was the last time I'd ever have her. I couldn't waste the time talking about her father.

Willi Ruth went away at five that afternoon. I stayed at the farm because I wanted to get to work early the next day. I owed Uncle Clem that much.

I walked out to the fields. He glanced up at me, smiling. "God lets mighty few of his children be purely happy, and sometimes then only for a little while," he said.

"You a preacher, Uncle Clem?"

"Only on Sundays."

I stared at him. "After working all week like this?"

"I don't have much else to give to the Lord. So I give him my time and what I think He'd purely like me to say to folks. I owe him."

"For what? You work harder than any mule. White people treat you like trash."

"Some do. But I learned there are good people, and bad, and the color of their skin don't have much to do with it. The good. The bad. Every time there's one good soul on this earth–like Miss Willi Ruth, why the world is that much better for it, and she purely leaves it a little better than when she came into it. About all a man can do. Be as good as he knows how."

"Sometimes they won't let you be good, Uncle Clem."

"*They* don't have anything to do with it. It's inside you. That's where you do what's good or what's wrong. You do it expecting no reward or praise."

"What good?"

"You've already had it. You've had the good. Maybe you won't ever see that girl again–like you say. There is them that can keep you apart. But maybe God has already given you in one day more that's purely good than some folks ever know in all their lives on this earth. You got to think hard on that."

Willi Ruth didn't come back the next day. I tried to prepare myself, knowing Judge Stark wasn't going to let her return to me. But I was sick with disappointment when she didn't come.

Uncle Clem and I weeded, watered, sprayed and watched the sun and the clouds. We didn't mention Willi Ruth. As long as we acted as if we were thinking about something else, she might come back.

On Saturday, I caught a ride on a lumber truck into town. It was almost dark when I got home. Mom handed me a letter from Willi Ruth.

"I've given in to him for a while, darling. Please don't worry. There isn't anything on earth can stop me from coming back to you. You're all I have. But I'm all Daddy has. He says if I'll stay with Aunt Helen in Virginia for a few weeks, he won't oppose us when I come back. Believe me, darling, he's good and wise, but he thinks I'll forget you. We know better. I love you with all my heart. Be patient, don't hate him. I'll never be happy away from your arms, your love."

There was more. Willi Ruth still believed in good, in the happy ending. I felt helpless. I walked out to the barn. When I'd finished off a mason jar of white moonshine, I felt better. I didn't care as much.

Goldie opened her door the third time I knocked. She was straightening her dress, her hair. I knew there had been a man with her. I couldn't care less.

Something flickered across her face, then she smiled. "Come on in, Calder. I've missed you."

I took her into my arms, pulled her up off her toes and waltzed her like that into her bedroom. "Oh, Calder, don't you ever think about anything else, for five minutes?"

"Yes, I did once. For five minutes."

"Like father. Like son," she giggled.

We toppled across her bed. I heard movement in the house.

"Maybe I better go lock the doors, Calder."

"Forget it. They'll have to wait. They'll just have to wait."

She drew me tightly upon her heated nakedness, talking against my face. "Listen, Calder. No matter what happens. No matter what you hear. I really cared for you. I never wanted to hurt you."

"You only hurt me when you talk," I said. "Do you have to talk so much?"

Suddenly something struck me across the head.

I struggled up, crying out. It was as if a bolt of lightning had ripped into the room. Goldie was pulled away from me and shoved across the room. She toppled against the wall and stayed huddled where she was.

Truman Lahey brought those handcuffs across my head again. I lunged upward, hitting at him. Ben Sawyer was behind him. Truman's fist caught me on the jaw, rocking my head.

When I opened my eyes again they had the handcuffs on me. My face bled. I stared up at them.

"On your feet," Lahey said. "Let's go."

"You're under arrest, kid," Ben Sawyer said. "Don't make any trouble."

Truman said, "You know what you've done, kid. If you got to have a name for the charge you're being arrested under, how about unlawful cohabitation. That sound legal enough for you?"

"Sure," I said around the blood filling my mouth. "As long as it's legal."

"How long am I going to be in here?" I said.

Suddenly Lahey swung around and hit me in the mouth. I tumbled against the cell wall, my face bleeding.

I cursed him. He hit me again with the back of his hand, rocking my head.

"Begin to get the idea?" he said. "You stay here until you learn to keep your mouth shut. Until you're smart enough to do what you're told. We'll tell you when you get out."

"You tell Judge Stark I want to see him."

Before I could blink, Lahey hit me again, back and forth across the head.

"Keep your mouth shut, kid," Ben Sawyer said from behind Lahey. "You're only making it tougher on yourself." His face was green. He was gray around the mouth.

"Let him talk," Truman said. "I don't mind teaching him. Let him learn what being on the gang is like."

I was still there two mornings later.

On the fourth day, Lahey came in and sat on the edge of my bunk. He said, "Now, if you're smart enough to listen, here's the word. You got two choices. You can get out of this town. Keep your mouth shut and get out of this county."

He waited but I didn't say anything. He grinned, pleased. "When you get it through your head what you got to do, you let us know."

"How do I let you know without talking?"

He'd been waiting. He caught my shirt front and battered me back and forth across the face until he got tired. This was a good substitute for his favored way of getting kicks. He breathed through his mouth and his eyes glazed over.

He shoved me against the wall. He turned and walked to the bars. He stared at me. "Get the idea? You don't have to talk. When you get smart enough to just nod your head, we'll know what you mean."

I stared at him through bloodied eyes. I couldn't take much more of this. I had to get out of there. I nodded. Once I started nodding, I couldn't stop.

It wasn't that easy.

They couldn't turn me out, battered as I was. Not even Judge Stark could get away with that. They moved me into a clean cell, a clean bunk. They fed me three times a day. The only time I opened my mouth was to eat.

On the tenth day after I'd dropped by to see Goldie Hampsden, they gave me back my shoes, my belt and my money. They opened a rear door at the jail and told me to get out.

I walked along Main Street, my legs as trembly as a colt's. The sun was blazing hot. I glanced up, my eyes smarting, watering. This sun must have burned up all the tomatoes. No sense in going down there to see. There was nothing around here for me anymore.

I tried to put some sense in it, but I couldn't do it. They were running me out of here, but where would I go? It seemed to me Judge Stark had outsmarted himself. That night I went back to see Goldie, I had given up. I'd made up my mind I wasn't going to see Willi Ruth anymore.

I reached the end of Main Street, I passed people without seeing them. I heard people speak my name, but I didn't look at them. I had learned to keep my mouth shut in this land of the free. I kept walking.

I turned off on the road home. I don't know why. I had to clear out, but now I was too tired. I wanted to go back home first. What did they care when I went, as long as I cleared out?

A car skidded to a stop beside me. Trembling involuntarily, I turned, setting myself.

The car door was flung open. Willi Ruth thrust herself out, sobbing. She ran to me, caught me in her arms. She clung to me, trembling.

"Oh, Calder. I came back. Eight days ago. I've been looking for you. I've been so sick. So frightened."

"How did you find me?"

"I don't know. Somebody. I don't know. Came to the house, said they saw you. Walking. On Main Street." She shook, laughing and crying in an hysterical way. "I didn't believe it. I was afraid to believe it."

"It's me," I said.

"Where have you been?"

"Ask your dad, Willi Ruth–"

"I have. Oh, I have, Calder. He didn't know."

I straightened, going rigid. "You still buying his lies, Willi Ruth? I've been in jail. In his jail. With his boys helping me make up my mind whether I wanted to stay away from you–or go to the chain gang."

She stared at me, shaking her head. But at last she believed me.

"So that's it," I said. "You go back and tell him he wins. I can't take it, Willi Ruth. You cost too much. We couldn't make it anyway, but I'm not going to try any more."

Willi Ruth stood for some moments as if stunned. It wasn't easy for her to get it clear in her own mind that the man she'd loved and respected all her life was kindly Judge Stark, the hanging judge to other people.

"What are you going to do?" she asked.

"I'm getting to hell out of here–"

"What about me, what about the farm, Uncle Clem, the tomatoes–?"

"What about your old man, his security cells in that jail, his boys like Truman Lahey–?" I dropped my arms from around her, let them fall to my sides. "I'm sorry, Willi Ruth. I've had it. I couldn't take any more."

"And you're just going to run away?"

"That's right."

"You're going to prove to them they're right about you. You're scared, and you'll run."

"You don't know your old man like I do."

She swallowed hard. "But I know I love you. And you can stay–"

"No."

"They can't hurt you any more, Calder–"

"They don't have to."

"I didn't know where you were before. I know now. You can go down to the farm, you can work there, stay there. Come on, let me take you down there now."

I hesitated, looking at her, looking along the empty road. I didn't want to run, but I didn't have the guts to oppose them any more. They had taught me what it was to be scared in the belly by men with power.

"Please, Calder. I'll come to you there. I promise I will. You'll be all right."

At that moment a sheriff's department cruiser sped past where Willi Ruth was parked. One man was alone at the wheel. He stepped on the brakes, sliding to a halt about a hundred feet down the pavement. He pulled over on the shoulder and sat there, staring through the rear window at us. I recognized Truman Lahey.

"Get in your car," I said. "Go on home. They're not going to let me ride anywhere with you."

She stared at the cruiser. Her face was gray. "I'll come to you, Calder. Please go down there. I'll come to you. As soon as I can."

I nodded. I would have told her anything to get her in her car and away from me. She started the car, crying. She turned it around and drove back into town. I stood there and watched her until she was out of sight.

I felt lonely and sick. Finally, I walked along the side of the road. I went past the cruiser without speaking, or looking in it. I hoped Lahey would get out because I wasn't handcuffed. But he had his orders. He didn't move. He just sat there watching me.

I walked slowly. Finally Lahey started the cruiser, drove back into Oak Bluffs. I felt better because I'd seen Willi Ruth again.

I was less than a quarter of a mile from Pa's house when I heard a car behind me. I turned on the side of the road and watched Willi Ruth's car catching up.

Judge Stark was at the wheel.

At first I didn't see Willi Ruth. She was huddled in the back seat, crying.

He stopped the car, reached over, swung open the door, told me to get in. "You've lied to Willi Ruth. I want that straightened out."

I watched Willi Ruth. "What's he done to you?"

She shook her head. "You lied to me, Calder. You were with–that woman and were arrested by sheriff's deputies. My father had nothing to do with it."

I stared at him, shocked that he'd lied like that.

He winced slightly, but shrugged. "She came home hysterical, accusing me of having had you arrested, beaten. You tried to turn my daughter against me. The deputies have told her the truth. Now I want you to tell her."

Willi Ruth said, "You went to her–and you lied–you blamed Daddy. I don't want to see you any more, Calder."

I stared at her for a long time. Her father was silent, very patient now that he had won. I said, "Is that what you believe, Willi Ruth?"

She nodded. She didn't speak. I got out of the car. They drove away. That weekend I read in the Oak Bluffs newspaper that Willi Ruth Stark had gone north to Richmond Virginia to spend the summer with relatives before entering a New England college that winter.

Chapter 12

In the deepest hours of dark, I plodded across the yard at Grandpa's old house on the river.

I fell across the bed and slept until Uncle Clem's Ford woke me next morning.

I went out to work with him in the tomatoes. He looked worried. "Hear you had trouble in town, with the law?"

"They don't care what I do. I'm not going to see Willi Ruth again. That's all they care."

"It can be tough, staying in a place where they don't want you. I know."

I shrugged, no longer caring. "They warned me out. Let them run me out."

I stayed on the farm all of July and August of that summer, working in the tomatoes with Uncle Clem. I didn't go near Oak Bluffs. I didn't want to go. I had been there.

Pa came out a couple times a month and brought a box of basic grub and I gave him a check for it against my account in the Oak Bluffs bank. Sometimes Ma came with him, but it was better when she didn't come.

Pa stowed in a mason jar of moonshine in every grocery box. I stacked the bottles in the kitchen pantry. The time would come when I'd need those jars of whiskey.

Nights I'd wonder why I didn't break out the bottles. What was I waiting for?

Sometimes working in the tomatoes, alone, or with Uncle Clem a few yards from me, I'd heard a distant engine, struggling through the deep sandy hummock above my place.

I straightened, listening. Maybe it was Willi Ruth. Or more likely, Truman Lahey sent out by Judge Stark.

I had a lot of time to think, even though this was the last thing I wanted to do.

I understood Pa at last, the reasons why he was resentful, driven to retaliate against all who hurt him, taking everything he could. Like father like son. One little break, and I'd be all right, different, better. Only I never got the break.

Still, every morning I got up and went out to fight all the obstacles that stood between me and a bumper crop of tomatoes.

Working those tomatoes under a sun that scorched the life out of the sand itself, Uncle Clem and I talked.

"One break, I'd be all right. It's like the old boys in the Bible, looking for God to give them some little sign that He was *up there,* that He gave a damn what happened to them."

"You mean the load might be a little easier for you to tote?" Uncle Clem said.

"Yes. Like not impossible, just that easy."

"Ain't nothing ever easy. But no matter how tough it gets. You got to be tougher. That's the only sign there is."

I straightened, massaging my back. I glanced toward the metallic sun. "I'll buy your sermon, Reverend. That sun up there is like the eye of hell–crisping very leaf, burning the roots. We jack-pump water, if we get a little rain and a few clouds to shade them, they'll grow. I figure it's up to God. All out of my hands. Tomatoes come in, I have money, I'll go to the university. That'll get me out of this county, pleasing its leading citizens."

"If the tomatoes come in," Uncle Clem said.

I shrugged. It was like saying *if* Willi Ruth came back.

Suddenly those tomatoes came in. I awoke one morning and the whole field flared pink. Rows and rows of pink tomatoes stretched from barnyard to pine hammock.

"Oh, Lawdy," Uncle Clem said when he saw it.

"We'll never make it, Uncle Clem."

"We got a couple days. I'll get my congregation here. In the morning. I'll go right now and start rounding them up."

"And how do we pay them?"

"We pay them when you get paid," Uncle Clem said. "My people understand. We done reached that place, Calder, we don't have to say no more *if them tomatoes come in!*"

Uncle Clem chugged away in his ancient truck and I fell-to in the fields. I worked without looking up. I swore at the tomatoes, the sun, the brassy sky. Those fields turned redder every time I lifted my head.

That afternoon a few Negroes showed up and fell to picking, talking and laughing as if they had the rest of the year. Panic swirled through me and

I wanted to scream like a maniac. But I bit my mouth and said nothing. These people were saving my skin. I had to let them do it their own way.

Night came and we hadn't even made a difference in the color of that field. Everything was red, the earth, the sky, the heaps of tomatoes waiting to be trucked out of here, and those darkening on the staked-up vines.

The summer storm broke about four the next morning. I heard the hale and the pound of rain on the roof, the oaks screaming against the wind. Only the tomatoes were quiet about it. They died silently, beat into the ground, ripped out of the hills, washed out, stakes broken, spines twisted. Lightning cracked, snapping white and terrible where I stood in the doorway. I don't think I even blinked against it. I pulled my gaze off the field, the torrents of water inundating it, washing it out in long, jagged gullies where split and broken tomatoes turned the raging pools as red as blood.

It stormed all day, fourteen hours exactly, as if tolled off on some celestial time-clock.

At precisely six o'clock that afternoon the rain stopped. Why not? What was left out there but deep, twisted gullies, standing full of red water and ruined tomatoes.

Uncle Clem didn't come near me. I was glad. I walked across the ruined field. The havoc was beautiful in its own way. You had to admire its complete destruction. God was up there, all right, and He thought big. He just didn't think my way, that was all.

Then I walked up and down the rows, slogging through the gullies as if by some miracle I might find a few bushes standing. There wasn't anything but I kept walking anyway. Finally I went into the house and fell across the bed in my wet clothes and slept, exhausted.

I didn't turn on any lights, but I dreamed that all the lamps were lit, and that Willi Ruth was shaking me, begging me to wake up, but it just didn't seem worth the effort.

At last I rolled over, shivering with chill, and Willi Ruth was sitting beside me.

"Oh, Calder, I love you."

I stared at her. My teeth chattered. My eyes burned and my throat ached.

"I came back to you," she said. "If you want me."

My teeth were chattering. I couldn't speak. I got up, tore off my wet clothes, pulled on dry ones and went into the kitchen. The lights were on in here, too. I built a roaring fire in the wood stove. Willi Ruth followed, close behind me.

"I'm sorry I stayed away so long," she said.

I didn't speak.

She caught my arm, held it. "I'm sorry for everything, Calder. The way I treated you. I believed my father, Calder, instead of you. I'm sorry. But before I went away I went to see her–Mrs. Hampsden. I had to. I couldn't stand it. She told me they had it planned, if you came near her, for any reason, they were going to arrest you, so my father could prove to me you were no good. Only you went when I left you and you didn't think I was coming back. And they lied to me, and I believed them. I'm sorry."

I rubbed my hands across the stove, trying to warm them.

"You've known all this time I was framed?" I said.

"I was hurt, Calder. I tried to be fair to father. I tried to stay away from you. I couldn't. I've come back and we can go away together, Calder. If we can get away and get married, there isn't anything they can do about it, Calder. Please, I love you and I'll spend all the rest of my life proving it to you."

The stove began to throw off a little heat. My teeth stopped chattering. "We'd have to run," I said. "I've got no car."

"I have one. Hidden up in the pine thicket. I bought it in Virginia. It's mine. They won't find it."

Suddenly I nodded. "Yes. Let's go. Let's get out of here."

But we weren't quick enough. All we needed was that one break, only we didn't get it. We heard the front door slam and Judge Stark's voice, raging.

"Fenton! Calder Fenton! Where are you?"

I moved past Willi Ruth and went into the front room. Judge Stark stood with a shotgun across his chest. His trousers were muddied, wet to the knees. He wore no hat and his rimless glasses were gone. He looked like a maniac.

His voice lashed across the room. "Where is she, Fenton? Where's my daughter? What have you done to her? She ran away from my people up in Virginia. She came back here to me. Where is she? Tell me, or I'm going to kill you."

Willi Ruth stepped out of the kitchen, stood close behind me. "Here I am, Daddy," she said.

Relief flooded through the rage in his face. He looked as if he were going to be ill in reaction.

But his rage returned and he pulled his gaze from her, staring at me. "I'm going to kill you, trash," he said. "You lied to her. You brought her back here. You made trash of her. Trash like you are."

"Nobody lied to me, Daddy, but you–"

"Stay out of this, Willi Ruth. There's just one way to keep him away from you, and you away from him, and that's to kill him. And that's what I'm going to do."

"What will it get you?" she cried.

"You've hurt me enough, Willi Ruth. You've dragged me down before the people I must live among."

"I'd hate you as long as I lived."

"You're trash! Just like he is. You ran after trash, until you became trash like him. You couldn't stay away from him. You let him make you pregnant!"

Staring at her, I didn't hear Judge Stark's raging voice. I turned slowly and put out my arms.

She smiled, crying at the same time.

"Stay away from her, trash!" Judge Stark said. He tilted the gun, his hand trembling on the triggers.

"I'm going to kill you boy."

But I wasn't looking at him. I was staring at Willi Ruth. She spoke quietly. "I love him, Daddy. If you kill him, you kill me. I won't live without him."

I heard Judge Stark's agonized sob. I waited, seeing the way he raised the gun, and the way his body shook.

His eyes brimmed with tears, lids drawn out of shape, face twisted. He sobbed again, deep in his throat.

He brought the gun up, fixed on me. I didn't move. Once I set myself to jump him.

He stared at me, waiting for me to whine, or plead, or run. And I didn't move.

Willi Ruth stood beside me, her face gray and set against him.

Judge Stark's gaze fell to the gun in his hands. Revulsion washed up across his face, making it as gray as death.

He shook his head, moaning, and threw the gun away from him across the room, wiping his played hands hard down his pants.

None of us moved.

He shook his head, crying. "You've destroyed her. I ought to kill you." His voice sank to a hoarse whisper. "I thought I could kill you. I knew I had to. I thought I could judge you and execute you." He shook his head. "I can't do it. I hate you too much. I've lived by the law too long...."

He stepped toward me, arms upraised, fists clenched. "You've killed my daughter," he sobbed. "She's dead. My daughter is dead."

He held those arms upraised, but he didn't bring them down. He stayed like that a moment, tears streaming across his rutted cheeks. Then he heeled around and strode across the room not looking at either of us again. His big shoulders struck the door jamb so hard that the room rattled as he went out. The door slammed behind him.

Willi Ruth pressed close to me. She was crying. I saw how deeply she loved him, how the loss hurt her. But she put her arms around me. "It's over," she said. "We're all right now."

We sat in the ancient front-room rocker. I held her in my arms.

"I missed you," she whispered. "So terribly. I've so much lost time to make up."

I smiled at her because I knew that things were all right for us–for the moment at least. Maybe the things we wanted would never be easy. But suddenly I didn't care.

I had her. I had what I wanted.

Maybe you couldn't have everything. Even so, with Willi Ruth in my arms, it looked like I was the winner.

THE END

STRICTLY FOR THE BOYS

by Harry Whittington

Chapter 1

The taxi driver's eyes undressed her. Amy felt young and flustered under his unblinking gaze. She wished she had the poise to ignore him, tell him to flake off, but she didn't. She fumbled in her purse for change, feeling her suitcase hard against the side of her leg.

In her mind there was one quick, fleeting thought: Burt would hate the way this man looked at her. Burt hated for any man to look at her.

"Want I should carry up your bag, sugar?" He leaned toward her across the front seat of the cab.

She felt her face flush hot. "No."

"I'm real strong, honey."

Amy shook her head again and turned abruptly, bending to pick up her suitcase. She heard the driver's sharp whistled intake of breath. She stiffened but did not turn. Amy straightened and went away from him across the walk, a tall girl, slender, at the moment weary and tired. It was a wonder the cab driver even looked at her, she thought, no amount of powder could conceal the circles under her eyes, the faint lines at the corners of her mouth.

Her mouth pulled and she thought bitterly, I'm so old—when I met Burt I was fourteen, and now I'm married and I'm seventeen and old and filled with bitterness, hating no one any more than I hate myself.

She entered the apartment house foyer and climbed the darkened stairway slowly, breathing raggedly through her mouth as if she'd been running for a mile.

She had not run at all. She'd walked in a cold trancelike way from the Greyhound bus out to the taxi at the street. On the bus a man had tried for a hundred miles to pick her up, but she ignored him. Still, it was true, men did like to look at her. And it wasn't her fault, no matter what Burt said.

Her head tilted. Once it had excited her when grown men looked at her—that began when she was thirteen, when she realized she was growing up. That was such a long time ago.

Amy came off the stairs and walked along the corridor, her steps slowing involuntarily. She thought about her mother, and about Burt, and about the way the cab driver looked at her, the way men always looked at her. A long time ago it had been fun. But everything good was such a long time ago. Once she would have laughed at the hungry way that cab driver drooled over her. Now all she could think was she was running from Burt, and the way he'd hurt her, and the way he'd hated for men even to look at her.

Suddenly, through her mind raced the thought of Al, the boy at the supermarket. A long, lost time ago—ten months ago, just after she and Burt were married....

When the boy at the supermarket asked her for a date, it gave her a sense of excitement to tell him she was married. At first he wouldn't believe it. He was cute, with muscles that pulled like coiled steel when he hefted heavy market baskets. She felt herself grow hotly liquid when his gaze moved over her and he dampened his lips with the tip of his tongue.

She had thought it such an amusing little incident that she told Burt about it that night at dinner.

He sat across the table from her. They had pork chops and canned green peas and instant mashed potatoes and instant chocolate pudding for dessert. She served it all with the new silver, and on the pattern plates that had been wedding gifts. And then, sitting across from him in their beautiful new apartment, she told him about the boy at the supermarket.

Burt stopped eating, holding his fork before his mouth. He didn't think it was funny at all. He got an odd look in his eyes and kept watching her face all through the meal. She could not think what he was trying to find there but she felt herself flush under his probing gaze.

After dinner, Burt poured himself a drink. He flopped down on the divan and told her to come to him. She protested she had to do the dishes. But there was such a note of repressed excitement in Burt's voice that she felt her body and her will respond to him, and she gave him a wan smile, tugging off the apron and letting it fall in a chair.

His hands on her were rough, rougher than they had ever been. He pressed her down on the divan. She shivered, emitted a small gasp.

"Oh, golly, Burt."

"What was he like?" Burt talked against her ear, his breath hot.

"Who?"

"Oh, come on now. The boy that got you so excited."

"You excite me."

"Like the guy at the supermarket?"

His hand moved on her and she cried out. "Like nobody."

He stopped moving his hand and she relaxed heavily, trembling, waiting for him.

"He got you real excited," Burt said. "I never saw you so excited like this."

"Burt, I don't know what you're talking about." She reached up, caressing his face with heated hands. "You get me excited. You drive me crazy. You act so excited, that's why."

"Did he act excited, too?"

She pressed herself against Burt, tried to laugh. "I think you're jealous."

His hand thrust inside her dress, hurting her. "Should I be, Amy?"

"You know better."

"He sure got you excited. I never saw you like this."

"Burt."

"My own wife, and I never saw her so excited until she meets some guy at the supermarket."

"Burt, don't say that."

"Why not? It's true, ain't it? When did you ever get so charged up with me before? Oh, no. Took this new guy, didn't it? Gave you a real ache. Down at the supermarket. Did he bring the groceries home for you?"

"No. Of course not."

His hand moved again, nothing tender or gentle in the way he touched her. There was cruelty and anger in his touch but the sound of his voice, the heat of his breath against her ear was making her more excited than she had known a woman could be. The lights in the room swam before her eyes. Desire, suddenly like anguish surged through her, and throbbing in her brain was the terrible thought that the more excited she became, the more raging Burt got—and he was not believing he had anything to do with the way her body writhed and burned under his hand.

"You sure?" It could not be real but she was aware he was yelling at her. "You sure he didn't bring those groceries home for you?"

"Oh, no. No. No. No."

"Did he bring them home, Amy? Right into the bedroom for you?"

She tried to spin her body away from him but she could not. She knew his anger was building but her body was betraying her. She had every right to be angry, yet all she could think was that she would go insane unless Burt hurried, quickly, wildly....

Now Amy stood outside her mother's apartment door and fumbled in her purse for her key. She still did not know what she was going to tell her mother. All the way on the bus she'd told herself she wouldn't lie any more, but now—she wasn't sure.

She found the key and inserted it into the lock. She bit back her tears, angered at the way her fingers trembled.

Amy heard movement inside the apartment and she paused, puzzled and upset. Mom should be at work in the middle of the morning like this.

Her mother spoke through the closed door.

"Who is that? Who's there?"

"Mom."

It was all Amy could say. Her throat was taut with all the tears she had not shed.

She set the suitcase beside her leg and put out her arms as her mother opened the door.

Her mother's eyes and mouth formed three round o's. Amy let her gaze race across her mother, seeing the new lines, the chill of bitterness about her mouth. It had been only a few months, yet her mother looked older. She was still lovely—she'd always been prettier and smarter than any other girl's mother—but now she looked so tired.

"Don't just stare at me." Amy tried to laugh.

"What are you doing here?"

"May I come in?"

Her mother still did not move for a second. Her eyes flicked over the suitcase, then darted around as if she were looking for an escape, a quick exit so she wouldn't even have to listen. Finally she nodded. "Yes. Come in."

Amy lifted the suitcase and walked past her mother into the small apartment. There was the remembered scent of the toilet water her mother always bought at discount from the drugstore where she worked. Through an opened door she saw the unwashed breakfast dishes piled on the kitchen drain. Beyond, in the single bedroom, her mother's bed was unmade.

Amy set her suitcase at the end of the divan and pulled off her hat. She stared at her mother, thinking they had not even kissed. She studied her mother's face, trying to see if she were well. At that, she thought, this may be a good sign. I'm thinking about Mom—about somebody besides myself. Maybe I'm growing up a little bit. Or maybe I'm afraid if she isn't well, she won't let me stay.

Well, she's got to let me stay.

"Why are you home this time of the morning?" Amy asked.

Her mother moved her shoulders in a faint shrug. "I took the day off."

Amy sighed. "I was afraid—"

Her mother laughed. "As long as I've been there? What would old man Troxler do without me?"

"He'd never be able to find anything," Amy said. She tried again to smile.

She put her hat down on the end table. Her mother was looking at the suitcase again. "Where is Burt?"

Amy walked to the window, pinched back the curtain, stared down at the sunlit street, afraid inside that Burt had followed her here. She spoke to the sunshine, and the fresh air and the freedom outside the window.

"I've left Burt, mother."

"What!" The word was thrown at her. "Why do you want to leave Burt?"

Amy turned slowly. Her mother was chewing at her fingernail.

"So that I can stay alive."

"Oh, for God's sake, Amy. Stop being so melodramatic. That sounds like something you got out of a movie."

"Maybe it does, but it isn't. I can't stand him. Mom, I can't live with him any more."

"Does he know you're here?"

"Not yet."

"Then we're going to call him."

"It won't do you any good."

"We'll see about that. Burt and I can handle you. Between us. You're going back to him. And you're going to behave."

"I'm not going back."

"Oh, stop talking like a fool. I tried hard enough to keep you from marrying. But you had to marry. You knew all the answers. You knew everything—"

"I didn't know anything—"

"You don't know anything now. Has ten months of marriage made you so wise? Has it taught you everything that I couldn't tell you?"

Amy gave a brief, sharp laugh. "No. It's taught me something else. All the things you didn't even try to tell me."

Her mother flushed. "I'm calling Burt. You can make up your mind. Marriage isn't easy—"

"Is that why you quit—both times?"

"It won't help you any to throw my mistakes up to me, Amy. I know how wrong I was. I know now how wrong and selfish and self-centered I was from the very first. You can't make me feel any worse than I already feel. As long as I've any breath, I'll try to keep you from making the mistakes I made."

She went to the telephone, picked it up.

Amy ran to her. She caught her mother's hand, pressing it down on the receiver.

"You can't call him."

"I'm going to call him. He's not going to like you running away.... I won't have him blaming me."

They stared into each other's faces, eyes clashing. Amy laughed at her. "You're afraid of him. You know—as well as I do—what he really is."

"Burt is a gentleman. I never met anyone any lovelier than Burt."

"You tried to keep me from marrying him. Why—if he was so lovely?"

"Oh, no, Amy. I gave my consent—reluctantly, and finally, only because it was Burt. I tried to keep you from marrying—not Burt—anyone. At fifteen, you were a baby. You still are. You were so smart and knew all the answers. But now you are going to listen to me."

"Mom. I won't go back to him. I'm afraid to."

"Why? What kind of nonsense are you talking?"

"It's not nonsense. I'm afraid of him when he drinks. I'm afraid of him—the things he says to me, the things he accuses me of. I'm afraid of him when he—goes to bed with me."

"What silly childish nonsense."

"Is it?"

"Of course a man likes to go to bed with his wife. If you don't like it, you have to endure it. It's a part of marriage—a part that will hold it together."

"Do you even know what I'm talking about?"

"Oh, yes. I know. The marriage didn't turn out to be like something in the movies and now you're running home to mama. Your husband wants you to assume your wifely duties and you can't bear it. He drinks? A lot of men drink."

"I don't have to like it when he accuses me of having men in the house because I don't want him—when he smells like a gutter. When—when—" she shook her head, did not continue.

"It's all a part of getting adjusted to each other, Amy. We'll call Burt and when he gets over here, we'll talk it all out."

"No."

Stella's jaw tightened. "Stop being a fool, Amy."

"I have stopped."

"Amy, you're not thinking. If you'd stop to think you'd know Burt is only like other men. Maybe he is a little insecure, a little jealous."

"A little jealous?" Amy shook her head, quivering. "Mother, he's not jealous. He's insane. He begins to accuse me of things and suddenly he's shaking—shaking all over."

"Amy, don't say such things."

"I don't want to say them. I've got to. They're true."

"I'm calling Burt," her mother said.

"You can't. He's not home."

"I'll call his shop."

"It won't do you any good, mother. He's not there. Do you think I would have stayed with him this long if there had been any way to escape him? I got away from him because he's gone. They—" she began to laugh and cry at once— "they drafted him." She could not speak for the laughter and sobbing. Then she whispered, "I prayed and prayed to be free of him—and they drafted him. Lord, how I pity them! But he wouldn't even go—up to that camp unless I went up there, too. So I went.... But as soon as they marched him inside that fence where he couldn't get away from them, I ran away. I came back home."

Chapter 2

Amy closed her bedroom door behind her. She leaned against it and looked about, feeling suddenly safe and secure. It was as if she were a little girl again.

She bit at her lip. That's what I really want, she thought. I want to run back away from all the ugliness I have gotten into with Burt. I want to have a good time again. I want to be young again.

She moved across to the bed. It was as her mother left it when she moved out with Burt. The old rag doll that she'd had since before her memory began was sprawled across a pillow.

Amy sat down on the bed and gathered up the doll. She let her gaze move across the high school annuals, the movie magazines. Her eyes brimmed with tears and her mouth trembled. Why had she run away from this? Why had she believed herself so grown up? How could she have been such a fool?

She let the rag doll topple from her hands. She touched the pillows piled across the spread. Her hand brushed a small lace pillow, and she stopped. Burt's mother had given her this small pillow when Amy had mentioned that she collected pillows to stack on her bed.

Burt's mother had died just after Burt and Amy married. Amy talked with her only once. But what a one time that had been. It had been a real scene—straight from queersville.

Amy had been going steady with Burt at the time. He'd taken Amy home to meet his mother.

The house was lovely, with aged but expensive furniture. It had the look of permanence, furniture tastefully chosen and kept because it was comfortable. But without being able to explain why, Amy got a shivery feeling along her spine the first time she walked into Burt's home.

There was the way the curtains were drawn at the windows, as if they'd yellowed and crisped with age, untouched because the windows were never opened to the sun.

The house was shadowy, and silent with the shadows.

And though Burt had prepared Amy for the fact that his mother was an invalid, she was not prepared to see the thin woman propped among pillows in the shadowed bedroom.

Burt's mother was in her forties but she appeared to be at least sixty. Her flesh was as yellowed and age-crisped as the window curtains, and as dry. Her eyes glowed with fever.

She tried to smile at them when they stood beside the bed but her smile was as dry as her flesh. She stared at them a long time, and Amy wondered if her lipstick were on straight, and if maybe she should have worn another dress.

Amy was suddenly aware that she, in her heels, was two inches taller than Burt. People often noticed this, but it did not matter to her. Now she was afraid this would be another reason for his mother to feel they were not right for each other.

"You're so young," Mrs. Reader said.

"But I know what I'm doing," replied Amy. She wondered how many times she'd said those words in the past few months to her mother alone.

The dry lips cracked into a smile, feverish eyes moved to Burt. "She's very lovely."

"Sure, she is," Burt said.

"Burt is lovely, too," Amy said, keeping her voice light, trying to say something that would please Burt's mother—to remind her of Burt's curly black hair and deep-set eyes under long dark lashes.

"Burt looks like his father," Mrs. Reader said—and the way she said it, it could mean anything.

Amy frowned, faintly puzzled.

Burt said, "Don't start that, Ma." He tightened his hand on Amy's arm. "Pa was a stampeder, Amy. He lived 'way out there' all the time. He was a real do-er. Ma has always been a real square."

"Why don't you go down to the corner and get us some ice cream, Burt?" his mother asked.

"Ma. You can't eat ice cream. What's the matter with you?"

"I'm sure Amy would like some. Burt, do as I ask. Please."

Amy felt Burt stiffen. She saw their gazes clashing.

After a moment, Burt said, "All right." He patted Amy's arm as he left the room. "Won't be but a few minutes."

Amy hoped not.

"That picture over there," Mrs. Reader said. "Burt's father painted it."

Amy stared at the picture. She wondered if this picture and others like it through the house had caused her feeling of apprehension. The picture made no sense to her. It was a violent splash of clashing and contrasting colors hurled upon the canvas in some kind of wild anger.

"There are more like it through the house," Mrs. Reader went on, "and there are many in the attic that I could never bring myself to display. You see, when Burt's father painted, he would paint dozens of canvases, dozens, day after day without stopping even to eat. Suddenly he would tire of painting, he would loathe the sight of canvas, the smell of oil and paint. Then he would compose music, sitting for days in the study, beating the piano in fury, until he would stride away from it in a rage. It was like that with sculpturing, weaving, writing. They were phases, in between his drinking, and sometimes a part of it." She tried to smile. "I've heard Burt explain his father to his friends. He called him a real-gone character. I'm afraid I must agree."

Amy sat beside the bed, unable to speak, unable to think what she should say. Her own muddled childhood seemed suddenly wholesome and normal in comparison to this madhouse.

"I tell you this," Mrs. Reader said after a moment, "because I believe you should know about us, about Burt's family, if you're going to marry Burt. His father left him the photography studio. Burt is quite good at his work, and he works steadily. All this is very commendable and hopeful. Perhaps he only looks like his father—perhaps he inherited his character traits from me. I hope so."

Her voice droned on, telling Amy that her ancestors belonged to New England, that they were New Englanders in the coldest, most repressed sense. She and her husband were not good for each other. She believed this after all these years. She'd often been tormented by the truth that her strict puritanical outlook had conflicted too terribly with Martin Reader's Bohemian view of life.

"You see, Amy, it's just that—well, I've been on a month-to-month existence for a good many years now. It cannot last much longer." Her voice tightened in rage against all the gods who kept her alive and suffering. "It cannot!"

"I'm sorry you're so ill," Amy said because this seemed the thing to say.

She sat tensely, wondering why Burt was gone so long.

"Yes. I'm sure you are." The woman's parchment face relaxed now, seemed almost serene. "The reason I am telling you this is because I may die at any moment—"

"Oh, I hope not—"

"We all hope not, but there it is. I may not be here to help you, to suggest to you, or even to shield you. Burt is a lovely boy, as you said. He is my only child. Maybe I've been too loving, too possessive, too protective. As a child, he had a violent temper. He could not tolerate to be crossed in any way.

"For a long time, we lived in a very bad phase. At school, when he raged against other boys, he was often beaten in fights on the grounds and after school. But he was never truly vanquished. Don't think I enjoy telling you this. It is something you must know. Every boy for a few years there who overcame Burt in a fight lost to him in some other way. Burt struck back and sometimes in cruel ways."

"Why, I'm sure he was just a boy," Amy said.

"Yes. Sometimes the lies he told about the other boys were shocking. And sometimes he could make them stick. As a child he was hated, Amy. He was shunned. And he grew up alone, and moody, and without a friend."

"Oh, I'm so sorry for him."

"Yes."

She heard Mrs. Reader exhale. She could not think why a mother would talk this way about her son to the girl he wanted to marry. Her mind swam. She felt confused. The only possible reason she could give herself was that this was another attempt by the grown-ups to keep her from marrying Burt.

She frowned, wondering if Mrs. Reader's mind were clear. It was certainly true that Burt had plenty of friends now. At twenty-one he owned his own photography studio. He belonged to luncheon clubs. Why, Mr. Troxler at the drugstore where Amy's mother was a clerk had introduced Burt to her. Perhaps in Mrs. Reader's fevered mind, the long ago childhood was all mixed up with Burt's present.

She felt very sorry for her.

But she felt something else, too. Her own resolve was hardened. They were trying to keep her from marrying Burt.

Amy had never had a happy home. Her mother divorced her father when Amy was only seven. They had raged and screamed at each other for as long as Amy could remember. Her mother's second husband was an

Air Force major. They lived outside air bases, and in married officer's quarters, and in all parts of the country. Only she never liked her stepfather, and if he and her mother couldn't find anything else to fight about, they fought about Amy.

She wanted a happy home, and she was sure she could have one with Burt....

"What did she say?" This was the first thing Burt said to Amy when they were in his car outside his mother's house. He then raved, "I'm going to sell that damned house the minute she dies!"

Amy sat in the convertible, and stared at Burt.

"What did she say?" Burt demanded.

"Why nothing, Burt." Amy frowned, wondering why she was evasive with him.

"Don't lie to me!"

"Why, I'm not lying."

"Oh, cut it out, Amy. You think I don't know why the old woman sent me out for ice cream? She wanted to yak at you. The old man was a drinker. A real rigger. She never understood him. She drove him to drink. And now she's sure I'm just like he was. Isn't that what she said?"

"Not exactly."

"What *did* she say?"

"Nothing, Burt. Nothing bad. About when you were a boy—"

"Oh—great. That's her all right. Why doesn't she go on and die? You tell me what she's got to live for. Will you just tell me?" He beat his hands against the steering wheel.

"She's got you, Burt—she's crazy about you."

"Sure. She's got one hell of a way of showing it. I ought to stay out of that house. I ought to stay away from her. That would show her how I thank her for talking about me."

The next time they went together to the old Reader house, it was to Burt's mother's funeral. The week after his mother died, Burt put the old house up for sale.

He thought it was a big joke that the real estate people insisted he remove all his father's old canvasses before they would even show the property.

Now, Amy wandered about the apartment, trying to escape her thoughts. But her mind was too filled with Burt. She remembered the way her mother had finally agreed to her marrying Burt. Burt talked with Stella alone for five hours one night after she got home from the drugstore.

That next morning Stella had told Amy she thought the marriage would be a good idea. She still believed Amy was a baby, immature, not old enough to understand love, or what she was getting into, but Burt was a lovely boy, and at twenty-one, he might have sense enough for both of them.

Amy's own doubts had been born that morning. She went to the high school for the last time that day. The other girls in the tenth grade were almost ill with envy. It was the way it had been the time she got Jimmy Dean's autograph a year before he was killed. She'd been only a child then, but Jimmy Dean had been her idol.

She walked slowly home alone from school, troubled for the first time about something that suddenly assumed frightening importance. She was suddenly sure Burt had lied to her about a matter that worried her now when she realized she was almost married to him. Her mind snagged on the thought when she thought about the dates the other girls her age could accept and that she was through with dating. As a matter of fact, she'd dated only one other boy since she'd met Burt. Her mind wheeled back, sick, to that date.

She hadn't really wanted to go with Tom—she was in love with Burt, didn't care about being with anyone else. It was a school dance though and Burt told her, "Sure, go ahead."

Tom had wanted to leave the dance early. He'd been drinking from a fifth hidden under a table. She decided it would be better to get home before he made trouble. He was staggering as they went down the steps from the auditorium. A car had raced away from the shadows. Amy's head had jerked up. It had looked like Burt's car.

Tom headed for the woods as soon as they were in his car. He didn't care what she said. He didn't even seem to hear her.

He slammed the car down an unpaved road to a bluff overlooking a dark lake. He cut off the ignition and pulled her against him.

"Tom—don't."

He laughed, pressing her against him, breathing through his opened mouth. He began to talk, telling her things, naming girls who were her friends, telling what they had done with him, or with other boys when they double dated. She tried not to listen, and yet she could not stop listening. "And Mavis wasn't even going steady." Tom was laughing, his hands thrusting. "It was just a date for her, baby. A date just like this one."

She heard an unmistakable sound, then he clutched her hand. She jerked herself away, slapped at the door handle. She jumped out of the car.

In the darkness, she looked around wildly. At first she was afraid she and Tom were the only people out here tonight. Then far across the darkness near the road she saw the dim outline of a car.

"Mister," Amy cried out. "Mister. Help me!"

Tom was laughing. He struggled out of the car, and lunged for her. She cried out and ran toward the parked car.

Then she saw there was a man standing outside the car in the deeper shadows of the overhanging tree. The man did not move. In a kind of sick horror Amy saw the man was leaning forward as though peering through the darkness—*watching* them.

Tom's arms caught her about the waist and he dragged her down into the grass with him.

Amy beat at Tom's face, scratching. The more she hit at him, the more he laughed. "Relax, baby. You ask Mary Ann, you ask Leah. They'll tell you about old Tom...."

With all her strength she pushed upward, driving Tom back from her. She came up on her knees. She started across the darkness toward the parked car. The man was standing there now, and he had moved forward, his whole body tense, watching them.

She cried out as Tom grabbed at her, trying to wrestle her into the grass again. Holding her fingers stiff, she struck at his face. He laughed and jerked his head back, but her slashing hand caught him in the Adam's apple. Tom fell back gasping, unable to speak, both hands catching at his throat.

Amy did not wait. She jumped and ran. She did not look back. The man at the road jumped into his car, started it, and raced away in the night.

He did not turn on his lights....

Burt was parked outside her mother's apartment when she got there. She was tired and miserable. He called to her and she got in his car, trembling.

"I thought I saw you," she said.

He gathered her in his arms, pressed against her. He held her tightly. She was too ill to pull away.

His voice sounded odd. "Where did you think you saw me?"

"When I was leaving the auditorium—it looked like your car."

He laughed, but his shaking hands did not stop moving. "It couldn't have been. I was playing poker with some fellows from the Exchange Club."

"And then Tom—took me out to park. There was a man out there—Burt, he was *watching* Tom attacking me!"

"Yeah?" Burt's voice was thick.

"Like—he got excitement—from watching."

He buried his face against her neck. "I guess there are men like that—"

"It—it wasn't you—Burt?" She did not know where she got the insane idea, but she could not shake it.

"You nuts?" He dragged her down on the seat. "You think I'm *that* kind? I'd of killed that Tom if I'd been there."

She nodded numbly. She felt ill, not even Burt's wild excitement could stir her. She felt as though she were ice inside.

A week later, she shivered every time she thought about that man in the shadows. She tried to tell herself there was no sense thinking about it. She had been all mixed up that night. When she and Burt were married, everything would be all right.... The first few weeks had been fine. Their apartment was brightly new, paint new. She was free with Burt's charge accounts to furnish it anyway that pleased her.

Then there was that night after the boy at the supermarket had asked her for a date.

And on the following night Burt had been wild again—wild with jealousy, but even more aroused by something else, something she couldn't understand.

She'd tried to make him stop talking about the boy at the supermarket. She pressed her mouth against his to silence him. She was wild with need for him, aroused by his feverish, exciting dalliance. For a wild insane time they forgot the supermarket, and the whole world was a supermarket of whirling insanity where the only way they could pay off the terrible need for each other was in anger and cruelty.

She fell away from Burt, covered her face, feeling somehow shamed and unclean. She could not say why. Burt was her husband. She pressed her eyes tightly shut. There was nothing good and uplifting in what they had done; there was no love in it; they had hated each other. Burt was enraged, wild with jealousy. She thought, *what is the matter with me?* I respond to his cruelty—the more he hurts me, the wilder I become.

He put his hands on her but she recoiled, withdrawing. She would not let him get her excited in that unholy manner. They would love each other as other people did, or they would not at all.

Then she heard his voice, cajoling, whispering, promising. His tone was low but insistent.

She tried to close her ears against him, but he kept after her. He started talking about Al—the boy at the supermarket again. What did lover boy look like? How big was he? Was he tall? How tall was he, Amy? A lot taller than your husband? Was he tall enough in bed?

She gasped, but did not speak. She remembered the way Tom had roused her against her will by the obscene things he kept mouthing about her girl friends, horrible and exciting things she listened to whether she wanted to or not. And now Burt was doing that to her.

He pulled her against him. She tried to pull away from him and she could not. She felt her throat grow taut. She felt the inescapable whirling and whirling, setting her whole body afire.

They did not sleep all night....

She felt odd returning to the supermarket at the end of the week. She thought the poor innocent clerk would somehow realize what had happened, because of him, between her and Burt.

Her face burned at the thought of meeting Al's gaze. He must know. He had to know. Yet that was silly. How could he know? He had caused some fearful thing between her and Burt, made them like two animals trying to destroy each other, and it was almost impossible to believe he didn't even know anything about it.

She went slowly through the supermarket aisles, delaying the moment when she would see Al again. But it didn't matter. She needn't have felt odd. The young clerk wasn't at the supermarket.

She never saw him again.

Once, a few months later, talking about something else, Burt happened to mention that the manager of the supermarket was a drinking pal of his. She tried to thrust this ugly thought from her mind. Burt wouldn't have the boy fired. She stopped thinking about it because she could not stand facing what she knew was the truth....

Chapter 3

The phone rang. Amy came running in from her mother's kitchen and picked up the receiver. Without stopping to think she said, "Hello."

Too late, she knew she'd made a mistake.

It was Burt.

She knew that even before he spoke. She recognized the incensed way he caught his breath. She looked about the room as if trapped. She wanted to laugh and cry at once. Her legs went weak suddenly as if they could no longer support the weight of her body.

She looked about her mother's apartment. She had dreamed that this would be—freedom. That was for laughs. She should have known better.

She felt suddenly ill, and her mother's apartment was a gloomy dungeon like all the other rooms in her life had become gloomy cells in the past ten months. She had awakened this morning with a sense of freedom for the first time in a year. Her mother had gone off to work, grumbling about young kids nowadays who married and divorced before people of her generation even finished high school.

And then the phone rang.

"Burt." Her voice was desolated.

"Yeah."

"Where are you, Burt?"

"Why didn't you stay here like I told you?"

"Burt—"

"Well. This time you stay where you are. Don't give me any more trouble, Amy. I'm telling you."

"Aren't you in camp?"

"I'll be at your old lady's place in a little while. I want you to be there."

"How did you get away, Burt?"

His laugh was cold. "I'll see you."

He slapped the receiver back in the cradle. The popping sound reverberated inside Amy's head like a Berber torture bell. She replaced the phone and stood there a long time.

The phone rang again almost at once and she stared at it, afraid to pick it up. It rang again, the sound insistent in the hum of early morning silence. She lifted it, pushed her hair back from her ear with the receiver. "Hello."

"Amy?"

"Yes."

"This is Irene, honey. Irene Haver. I was just talking to your mom here at Troxler's. She says you're back home for a visit."

"Yes."

"I'm off today. Thought maybe I'd drop by. We could have a real gab fest."

"Oh, no."

"What?"

"I mean—not this morning, Irene. Why don't you let me call you?"

Irene's voice was chilled. "Because I work. This is my day off. Sorry, kid."

"Oh, Irene. You know I don't mean to sound rude."

"It's all right. You don't want to see me—that's fine."

"Oh, stop it. It's—just that I've a headache this morning." She could not have Irene here when Burt came. She did not know what Burt might say or do. "I'm sure I'll feel better this afternoon. I—"

She stopped talking. She had to get accustomed to the idea that she was through with Burt Reader, she was leaving him, she had left him. She was going to divorce him. She didn't have to be afraid of him any more. She didn't have to obey his unreasonable commands. And if Irene Haver would come over, she didn't even have to be alone with him.

"Look, Irene. I'm sorry. I do feel down in the mouth. But seeing you might be just what I need. Why don't you come on over?"

"That's better. That sounds a lot more like you, doll."

"I'll make coffee."

She replaced the receiver and went into the kitchen. Her hands were numb. She almost dropped the coffee tin. She dreaded the moment when Burt would arrive and find Irene here. Irene was one of her oldest friends, the first girl she knew who quit school and got married. They had been in the ninth grade when Irene quit. Irene was older, fully developed, and she was boy crazy. Everybody, even Amy's mother, said marriage was the safest policy for Irene. Irene had stayed married for a year and a half; she had gotten a divorce and now worked in the electrical appliance plant.

Irene was wearing coveralls when she arrived. They were tan, had "Irene" lettered over her left breast pocket. Irene was heavier than Amy remembered her. Her breasts looked fuller under the coveralls and her hips sagged slightly.

Two years was a long time. A lot had happened to Irene.

She slumped into the couch, took her coffee black.

She stared at Amy with narrowed blue eyes. "How are you and Burt getting along?"

Irene was a divorcee and the first reaction she felt toward any man was doubt; she was elderly—nineteen—and there was nothing she didn't know. You couldn't deceive her about how a marriage was going.

Amy didn't try. "Not so good."

Irene wasn't astonished. She would have been surprised to hear a marriage was succeeding. "It isn't that men are bad," she said. "They're just such jerks. That's what's wrong."

"It's my fault," Amy said. "As much as Burt's."

"Why?"

"I guess I expected too much."

"You really believe that?"

"No. I thought we would have a good time when we got married—"

"A good time!"

"No, really. If he wasn't working, he never wanted to go anywhere. He got mad if a man so much as looked at me."

Irene shook her head. "From where I sit none of that sounds so bad."

"What are you talking about? You would think I was—old. He wanted me to sit around and never have any fun.... His idea of fun was drinking and he never paid any attention to me—unless he wanted something... you know."

Irene laughed. "Men want a lot of that, all right."

Amy looked at her hands. "I wouldn't mind that so much. I liked it too but I wanted to be loved. Not treated like—a—"

Irene smiled. "A married prosty?"

Amy nodded, then asked, "What did I do wrong?"

"You got married. Boy, I wish somebody had used a strap on me when I wanted to marry Roger.... You got anything to drink around here? I'm used to lacing my coffee this time of the morning."

"I think so."

Amy got up to find the bottle of whisky her mother kept for her guests. She had the sudden memory of her mother's coming in with some new boyfriend late at night and pouring one for the road. Many nights she had lain awake in bed listening to the mysterious giggling, the click of ice against the glasses.

Irene raised her voice, letting it trail after Amy into the kitchen. "I was such a damn fool. I thought anything in pants had to be wonderful. I got out in cars with them—and I couldn't get down to business fast enough. I just knew the next one I found was going to be as wonderful as I thought. Oh, brother. They're either stupid, or slow, or like rabbits. Pretty soon you get so you couldn't care about one of the jerks if he did turn out to be superman."

She laughed as she poured a long jigger into the half cup of black coffee. It brimmed the cup now, steaming. She lay back on the couch, watching the steam. "Take a bracer, kid," she told Amy. Amy shook her head. She didn't like the taste of whisky. "It takes your mind off your woes," Irene said. "Let me tell you. If I knew then what I know now, I'd marry Roger again, and stay married to him. He was a jerk, but I haven't met a man since Roger who wasn't a jerk in some way. Roger is as good as any. Only I didn't believe it, until it was too late."

Amy gasped. "You mean you're still in love with Roger?"

Irene laughed. "Don't bat it around, kid, but sometimes after dark, I walk past his house. I stand out in front for just a minute. Man, I'd die if anybody ever caught me there."

"What do you do that for?"

Irene sighed. "Because I get the urge for him. Just standing out there in front of his house in the dark. I don't have to see him through the window or anything. Just know he's in there, and I get a charge like crazy."

"Irene."

She shrugged. "Sure. It's the only buzz I get any more, too. Except with whisky. It's about the same."

"Why don't you tell Roger?"

"Why should I? He's married again. He's got a kid and another one on the way. When I see that stupid wife of his in the supermarket or somewhere, big as a barrel and wearing that stupid grin on her face, I could spit. Besides, why tell Roger? I wouldn't care that he's married. Hell, I know what marriage is. I know what it amounts to. If it would do me any good, I'd tell Roger how bad I want him all the time. But it wouldn't. You know what he thinks of me?" She took a long gulp of the hot coffee. "He thinks I'm just what I am—a fat bag."

Amy stirred uneasily in her chair. Was she seeing herself in another two years, bitter and alone and lonely, lacing coffee with whisky at ten in the morning?

There was a sharp knock at the door. Amy went tense and for a moment did not move. Irene stared at her over the top of her cup, questioningly.

"You want me to duck out, kid? If you got a john coming to see you. What the hell, you don't have to apologize to me. I see now why you tried to fake me off when I called. I'm sorry, kid. I'll butt out."

The sharp knock was repeated. With a twisted smile Amy got up and walked to the door. She moved woodenly. Her hand closed on the knob, but did not want to turn it. She opened the door.

Burt thrust it back and strode into the room. There was a narrowed look in his eyes, as if he expected to find some man with Amy, or hidden in a closet somewhere.

He was wearing a newly issued Army uniform. What made the uniform look so odd on Burt was that he wore only tailored suits and custom-made shirts. He was lost in the uniform. The collar was so loose around his throat that he looked emaciated.

Irene sat up on the couch and stared at Burt wordlessly.

It took even longer for Burt to realize that Amy's guest was a female. By the time this message had penetrated through his rage, he also remembered that he hated Irene Haver and always had.

"What are you doing here?" he said to Irene.

"She's visiting me." Amy's voice matched his.

"Cutting me to pieces, huh? Hacking me up?" Burt pulled off the cap, stood holding it in his tensed fingers.

"Hadn't got around to you, yet," Irene said in her breezy way. "You were next, Buster."

'Well, you can take a rain check," Burt said "I happen to want to talk to my wife. Alone. It happens I don't have too much time."

Irene did not move. She finished off her coffee.

Amy made an attempt. "Irene's spending the day with me, Burt."

He ignored her. His face was white, his hands holding his cap began to shake.

"I want to talk to my wife, Haver," he said. "You mind?"

Irene shrugged. "So talk."

Burt went around the couch, stood in front of it looking down at Irene. "You want to get out of here quiet? Or you want trouble?"

"Hell, Buster, I want trouble. You know Irene. I never did like it quiet."

Burt reached out, caught the front of Irene's coveralls.

Her voice was deadly cold. "Don't ever grab me like that, son, and leave your groin open like this. I can fix you quicker than—"

Amy said, "I'm sorry about this, Irene. Maybe you better call me—"

"Yeah." Burt's voice shook. "Call her, She won't be here. But you call her."

Burt stood at the window as the door closed behind Irene. Her last words to him were, "You do something to a uniform, Pretty Boy—and they ought to sue you for it."

He did not answer, did not turn from the window. He hunched his shoulders slightly as if shielding himself from the sound of her voice. He had dropped his hat on an end table and stood with his fists clenched.

When he heard the lock snick, he turned slowly, his face starkly white.

"What did you do it for, Amy?"

"What? Do what?"

"Calling Irene was a neat trick. Too bad it didn't work."

She shrugged. She did not answer him. She picked up Irene's empty coffee cup, moved toward the kitchen.

"Put that thing down." He strode around the couch, slapped the cup from her hand. They heard it smash on the floor. They did not look at it.

He searched her face. "I took you with me, Amy. I told you to stay up there."

"You knew I wouldn't."

"The hell I did. I didn't know anything of the kind. You think I'd have gone in the army if I'd known you were going to run out on me?"

"Stop talking like a fool. You had to go."

"I'm out now, ain't I? You ever hear of the Red Cross, Amy? You ever hear of emergency leaves? When a man's wife acts up, he can get the Red Cross to help him. That's what I did."

"I'm sorry, Burt. It won't do you any good."

"What are you talking about?"

"I'm through lying to you, Burt. I don't love you. I don't see how I ever loved you."

"Well, that just grabs me. Oh, that shakes me up. You're married to me and that's the way it's going to be."

"No, Burt. I'm getting a divorce."

"Don't say that." His hands shook wildly.

"It's the truth."

"You can't just get a divorce. I've got to let you get a divorce. And I won't do it. So you can get that out of your head. You can make your mind up you're going to settle down and behave."

"No. I'm leaving you."

"Going to cat around with Irene Haver, huh?"

"If I want to."

"Damn you!" He struck her suddenly in the mouth. She staggered back as if doing an intricate dance step. She hit the wall, stayed there, braced against it.

Blood showed at the corner of her mouth. She did not move to wipe it away. Burt groaned in his throat. "Don't make me do this, Amy. Don't make me do this."

"Nobody's making you do anything." Her voice was dead.

He walked toward her woodenly. His eyes glistened with tears. "You think I want to hit you?"

"Yes."

"You think you don't drive me until I can't help it?"

"You can get out, Burt. You can go back to camp and leave me alone. I'm divorcing you. I don't care what you do to me. You can kill me. But I've already told mom. I'm divorcing you."

He laughed suddenly, the sobbing laughter caught in his throat. "Sure. Tell your old lady. Bring everybody into it."

"She had to know."

"Did she? Did you tell her all of it? Did you tell her I can't have kids? Is that what you ran to tell her?"

"Oh, Burt. No."

"Sure you did. I can even hear you say you can't stay married to me, 'He can't even give me a baby.'"

"Please, Burt. Don't torture yourself and me."

"Isn't that what you told her?"

"I wouldn't, Burt."

"Why not? You think that's all it would take to turn her against me?"

"Burt. We don't even know it for true—"

"We know. That doctor told you, didn't he?"

"He could be wrong. They're wrong all the time."

He laughed, a sound bitter and anguished in his throat. "Oh, yes. That's been what you've been telling me from the first. He could be wrong. They are wrong all the time. You had to convince me of that, so if you brought home somebody else's brat—"

"Get out, Burt."

"I know when you're lying. I'll make your old lady tell me."

"Get out, Burt. It's no good. It's no use. You make me feel sorry for you—and then you knock all that down, too. Please just let me alone."

"Sure. I'll get out. When you get your suitcase and come back up there with me. You're going to stay up there until I can get out of this army."

"Get out?"

"Listen. You know the right people, you can do anything. When I tell them about you, how I'm married to a kid too young to know anything, even her own mind, running around on me, two-timing me with men she picks up—I'll get out, don't you worry about that."

"You can't, Burt. And it's no use even if you could."

He walked away from her, then turned suddenly on his heel and strode back to her.

"All right. Who is it?"

"What are you talking about now?"

"It's some other man. You're not fooling me. You haven't fooled me from the start. You couldn't wait to run back here and get shacked up with him when you thought I was in army camp and couldn't get out. I want his name."

"Don't be a fool. There's nobody."

"You can make it a lot easier on yourself, Amy, and on him, by telling me now."

She spread her hands, wanting to laugh helplessly because there was no sense talking to him. "There's nobody. The way I feel now I never want to see another man. But that doesn't change it. I don't want you, either."

"I'm running out of patience, Amy." His hands were shaking and he knotted them into fists. "What's his name?"

"Get out, Burt."

He backhanded her across the face. "His name. I want to know his name."

She staggered slightly, sliding along the wall. He stalked her. She stayed there, her face as white as his but marked by the imprint of his fingers. Her eyes clashed against his defiantly.

"I hate you," she whispered it.

"Answer me. I don't give a damn whether you hate me or not. I came here to get lover boy's name, and that's what I'm going to get."

She laughed at him suddenly with the tears streaming down her face.

He smashed his fist into her face. She toppled forward. Sobbing in his throat, he hit at her again. His fist caught her on the side of the head and she fell against him. He twisted his hand in her hair, shaking her.

He was sobbing. "You make me hurt you, Amy. You drive me until I don't know what I'm doing, You don't have to do it. Tell me. Tell me. Tell me!"

She shook her head.

He brought his left fist upward into her face again. She cried out and covered her face with both her hands, sagging to her knees.

"I want his name," he yelled at her.

There was blood on her mouth. On her knees she stared up at him. "Go to hell," she whispered. "You go to hell."

He reached down, caught the front of her dress and ripped it off. "You're my wife," he said. "You're going to stay my wife."

He thrust her back on the floor. She tried to fight away from him, clawing at him. He caught her arm and twisted it under her back. She lay there and stared at him, her eyes distended.

She heard the sobbing way he caught his breath. She heard the unsteady drip of a kitchen faucet. As if they were miles away, she heard the sound of cars in

the street below. She tried to fight free. He held her down with the weight of his body. He pulled at his own clothes, ripping the buttons, tearing them to get out of them. It was as if he vented his rage even on the clothing that stood between them. He ripped off her clothing. She felt hot tears spring into her burning eyes, and yet she felt herself go hotly liquid when he roughly caressed

her. Would he always have this terrible and cruel power over her? She felt her body relax, felt her legs become weak and lifeless—she was without will to resist. She felt the insane churning of her heart, the unspeakably hot way her body responded to the cruelty in him. She felt his mouth, his tongue, moving over her face, along her throat. She wanted to scream her hatred at him,

but her throat had gone dry, swollen so she could not speak aloud. She could only moan. She let her head writhe back and forth, but she was not fighting him any more. Her fingers, digging into his shoulders, became frantic. Suddenly he put his mouth over her mouth and she tasted her own blood, hot and salty, but it did not matter; not any more.

Chapter 4

"What in Heaven's name happened to you?"

The lawyer stared at Amy's puffed and swollen face. She had pushed the half-veil back above her eyes when she entered his office.

"I want a divorce," she said.

"Well. I should think you do." He motioned her toward a chair, a heavy-set man in his early forties, balding with the thin strands of hair combed across his crown. He shook his head. "Your face looks like something my wife might have done to me."

Amy sat down in the chair. Irene had said that this lawyer was the best in divorce cases. "I can't live with my husband any more. I want a divorce."

"Did he do that to your face?"

"Yes."

"Well, we can get you a divorce, on this," he said. "You won't need anything else." He pressed a button and almost at once his secretary appeared in the doorway carrying pad and pencils. She was a tall, slender woman wearing heavy-rimmed black glasses.

"Yes, Mr. Wallin?" she said.

Amy began to feel better at once. Robert Wallin's professional manner was reassuring. It was something like a doctor's confidence at a bedside. When he walked in you began to believe everything was going to be all right.

"Get a photographer," Wallin told his secretary. "Right away. We want to make some glamor shots of this."

He nodded toward Amy and she heard the secretary's sharp inhalation. "Yes, Mr. Wallin." She closed the door.

Amy pulled her gaze back to the lawyer. He was a stout man, of medium height. He weighed nearly two hundred. He looked as if he ate a lot of steak with mashed potatoes and gravy.

"You're practically free," he told her.

"It's not that simple," Amy said.

He shrugged and leaned back in his judge's chair behind his gleaming desk.

"It never is," he said. "You set up the obstacles. I'll try to bowl them over."

"My husband—he's in the army."

"Well. We can handle that. We can serve the papers on him there."

"Yes. But that's it. He'll fight the divorce if he finds out about it."

"Let him. That's his privilege." Wallin smiled. "I'd like to have him there in the court when I show the pictures we'll take."

"I'm afraid of him."

"I don't blame you. But we can get restraining orders that will handle him. Young lady, you're practically a free woman."

"I don't know what he might do if he found out." She remembered suddenly, flushing hotly, what had happened in the apartment. Burt had stayed with her until her mother came. Then he had wept, begging Stella to believe he never wanted to hurt Amy, that she had driven him insane, he didn't know what he was doing. He was trying to hold his little home together, he told Stella, and she began to weep with him.

Finally, he'd had to go back to the camp. He was on only a twelve-hour emergency pass and was going to be overdue before he could make it back. But he would not go until Amy promised she would not consider a divorce until he could get back to talk with her again. Stella had insisted that this was the least she could do. It was not as though Burt were on a pleasure trip up there, he was doing his duty to his country. Amy must promise to respect his wishes in this matter. It would give her time to think and she needed plenty of that. Although Amy's face was already swollen and bloated, Stella was convinced she was in the wrong and Burt was the injured party. Stella sent Burt away promising she would make Amy come to her senses and wait until he could get another pass.

She shivered, thinking that Burt could lie so brilliantly. He could tie Stella in knots, he could make her believe the baldest lies. She was afraid when he got in a divorce court. He could be so wounded, so completely right in the face of damaging evidence to the contrary.

"Why can't I get a divorce," she said, "and then let him be notified?"

"It can be handled. But what kind of settlement do you want?"

"I don't want any. I just want to be free."

"If he has any means, you're foolish not to get the best possible settlement."

"I don't care." Her voice quavered. "I just want to be free."

"How old are you?"

"Seventeen."

"Good lord. My own daughter is older than you and just this morning I told her she was just a baby."

Amy didn't speak.

He drew some lines on a pad. "Well, that's all beside the point, isn't it? You made a mistake, and you want out of it. I don't believe in these teen-age marriages. I sure oppose teen-age divorces—"

"I'll go to someone else."

"Wait a minute, child. Is this the way you have reacted to all attempts at counseling?" His voice was cold.

She flushed, remembering that a child guidance doctor had attempted to dissuade her from marriage at the high school. She had not listened to him, any more than she had listened to her mother. She did not believe then that these people who could not orderly control their own lives could know what was best for her.

She locked her hands in her lap, deciding to go along with this man. There was something about him that made you trust him. Irene had said that no one in the state could handle legal matters slicker than Robert Wallin.

"I'd hate very much to help you out of this marriage, and see you repeat the mistake in thirty days," Wallin said. "I believe you should have a divorce. I'll help you get one. But there's just one little concession you'll have to make to me. I expect to tell you how wrong you are, have been, and will be. I expect to do what's best for you and not always just what you want—"

"But if you tell Burt about the divorce, he'll get out of the army. I know he will."

"That's not easy," Wallin said.

"But Burt can do it. He's already trying. I just want to be free before I have to see him again."

"It's going to take six months at best."

"I don't care. Just so long as we get started."

"Well. We're already started. If you'll feel better, there's this I can do. In this state, we can publish the notice of divorcement—"

"He might read it."

Wallin laughed. "But we can publish it in the smallest and most obscure county weekly. He won't read it. Don't worry. I'll do that for you. In return, I expect you to hear me well, go along with what I tell you. I'm an overweight fool where my own life is concerned, but like everybody else I know what's best for the next fellow. My Grandma always used to say that everybody knows what to do with the devil except him that's got him. Well, that's me. I know what to do with your devil. I'll tell you."

She managed to pull her swollen mouth into the semblance of a smile. "All right," she said. "I'll be glad to have somebody else do my worrying for me for a while."

"That's the attitude. Everybody feels that way once in a while. Now you just relax and trust me. You're going to be all right."

She found herself pouring out her story to him. He was the easiest man she had ever found to talk to. Maybe her father would have been like him if she could have stayed with him. Wallin's gray eyes were kindly, and nothing she said shocked him or disturbed him, and not once did he look even mildly critical of her. There was nothing holier-than-thou in his attitude. She found herself telling him more than she'd intended, more than was necessary, but she had lied so long, had pretended for so many months that now when she could tell the truth, it was as if she were on a truth-kick, she could not get enough of it....

She had no idea she would stay in the lawyer's office as long as she had. She walked out, pulling the veil down over her discolored eyes, feeling clean and refreshed as though she'd been cleansed by her confession. It was as if her soul had been under a cold, cleansing and invigorating shower.

She walked slowly along the street, conscious mostly of an emptiness in her stomach. There was so much to think about, and she didn't want to think about any of it.

She glanced involuntarily over her shoulder. Burt wasn't back there, but she forever had the sense that he might be. She needed to talk to somebody, about Burt, about the big step of the divorce, what Burt might do to her if he found out before she was free. Would she ever be free of him?

She shivered in the bright sunlight.

She looked around, needing something, wanting something without knowing what it was. Across the street was a juke joint, the loud hard beat of the music reaching at her through the morning traffic sounds.

She walked toward the place, remembering when she had gone into it after school with the kids. A cold drink would make her feel better.

Amy crossed the street when the light changed, feeling an odd tightness about her heart as she came near the shop. The music was louder, pulling at her, pulling her back toward something forever lost to her.

She pushed open the door, went in. The place was crowded with kids, some were dancing on the postage-stamp area near the jukebox. Watching them, she sat in a booth, ordered a cherry-coke.

It all whirled in her head, the chattering, the music, the laughter, even the whispers. A girl and a boy were loving each other in a rear booth. Amy watched them, breathless, without meaning to stare.

She pulled her gaze away, emptier than ever.

At a table near her three girls had their heads pushed together, their curls bobbling as they laughed and whispered. They were smiling about something, and without even knowing why, Amy felt her face pull into a smile, smiling with them.

She shook her head. Why had she come in here? The sense of loneliness and loss was worse than ever. She watched the dancers another moment, let her gaze brush fleetingly across the lovers, then she got up, left money on the booth table and hurried out.

She walked into her mother's apartment. She stared at the place on the floor where Burt had dragged her down with him. Her face burned. Then she told herself she was going to be free of him. Her head tilted for the first time in weeks. And the sickening memory of the animal way he had treated her on the floor no longer made her feel ashamed and dirty. Anyhow, she reasoned, Burt was her husband, no matter what he did to her, no matter how much she despised what he did, she shouldn't feel unclean afterwards.

She was going to be free of it.

Her mother walked into the front room from the kitchen.

Stella's face looked haggard and she was nervously chewing at a hangnail.

Amy was startled. She did not expect her mother to be home at this hour. She was afraid her mother would see the change in her, the change that had begun in that lawyer's office.

Stella stared at her. "Where you been, Amy?"

"I was downtown."

"What were you doing?"

"Nothing. I—was just shopping."

"You didn't buy anything."

"Oh, mother. Do I have to buy something? I just went out."

"With your face like that?"

"Well, if you insist on my staying with Burt, you'll have to get used to my face like this."

"Amy, stop accusing Burt this way."

Amy shrugged. "All right. It was my fault. All my fault. Believe what you like."

She moved past her mother, going toward the bedroom.

Stella's voice stopped her. "Amy."

"Yes, mother?" Amy glanced over her shoulder.

"Amy—did you go see a lawyer?"

Amy felt the quick abrupt constriction around her heart. "Why no, mother. I did some window shopping."

Chapter 5

Amy stared at herself in the women's restroom mirror. It seemed odd to see herself in the tan coveralls with her name lettered over her left breast pocket. She had thought Irene Haver looked so odd wearing the coveralls that made her look overstuffed; it had seemed strange that Irene who'd always appeared made for loving and romance should be doing manual labor in an electrical appliance plant. And here I am now, Amy told her reflection, working along with Irene—and with all the other rows of women who looked like overstuffed men.

Drawing a deep breath, she tried to smile at her stout reflection. She was doing what she wanted to do.

There had been a hellish scene with Stella about what she should do while awaiting Burt's return from the army. It was clear enough what Burt wanted her to do. His daily letters read almost the same. He wanted her to stay in her mother's apartment, get no job, see no men, and wait for him.

She had not yet told her mother she was divorcing Burt. The weeks crawled stickily by and she wanted to tell her; she had lived so long with lies that she hated one more lie. She wanted to tell her mother the truth, but was afraid to. Her mother would tell Burt, and she didn't know what Burt could do to spoil it now, but he would think of something.

"I think I'll take a job at the appliance plant," Amy told her mother one night.

Her mother looked up from the stack of bills on the kitchen table. She chewed at her pencil.

"I don't think that's a good idea, Amy."

"You could use the help, couldn't you?"

"Burt sends you money. You have his allotment. I don't think you should go to work. I know Burt won't like it."

Amy felt herself growing warm. She wanted to cry out she no longer cared what Burt liked. Instead, she spoke quietly. "Irene says they need women in the small appliance division. It's easy and she's sure I could do it. I'm going to apply for the job. I should start doing something to support myself."

"Why?" Stella was edgy on this subject. She dropped her pencil and half turned in her chair to stare at Amy who was washing the dishes at the sink.

Amy shrugged. "We don't know what might happen."

"You're still thinking of leaving Burt, aren't you? Why don't you get that foolish idea out of your head? Burt loves you devotedly. I never saw a man love anyone so devotedly. A little drinking and a little jealousy—you should be able to tolerate that."

Amy ran the water hard in the sink, listening to its roar.

Her mother waited until it was silent in the room. "You drive poor Burt, Amy. If you'd meet him halfway, he wouldn't be violent. I saw that poor boy. It tore my heart out to see how he suffered because he had hit you. Yet, as he said, you are so obstinate that finally he gets wild and feels there is no way he can reach you except through physical violence. I don't approve of Burt's hitting you—but then, Burt hates it, too."

"Sure he does."

"He wants you to be his wife, Amy. He thinks you want to leave him."

"He knows I want to leave him. He has no right to try to hold me."

"How can you say that? He's your husband. He has a right to try to save his home."

"What kind of home? A place to stagger in drunk? A place where I am some kind of slave? I want to be a little bit happy. I'm too young to live like this—and I won't do it."

Stella looked ill. "I've got to work on these bills, Amy. I—I want you to stop talking this way. It frightens me."

Amy walked over to her mother's chair.

Her voice was a tense whisper. "What you are afraid of, is facing Burt and telling him that I am through—and there is nothing you can do about it. But if you would do that, just once, and then step out of it, tell him the rest of it is between him and me—you wouldn't have to be afraid of him any more."

Irene touched Amy's shoulder in the women's room at the appliance plant.

Amy started guiltily, completely lost in the memory of her scene with her mother. Well, she could not hide this truth from her any more. Tonight she would have to tell her she had taken a job at the appliance plant. Stella would be ill again.

"Ready to go?" Irene asked. "I want you to meet our foreman. He's the nicest of the brass—maybe because he's only small brass."

Amy walked with Irene out into the huge fluorescent-lighted room where women were already lined, chattering like magpies though talking was forbidden on every sign hung above the aisles. "They don't try to enforce that rule," Irene nodded toward the no talking signs. "They've learned they can't hire silent women. There just ain't any."

There were a few men working on this floor, but they were almost lost among the rows and rows of women. Amy tried to tell herself Burt would be glad she had a job in a department so predominantly female, but she could not get much of a lift from this thought. Burt would see those few men, that would be all he saw. She had lived with Burt over a year. She knew by now there was no way to please him. She remembered the things Burt's mother had told her that day in her sickroom. She'd been a little shocked that a mother would talk about her son in such a way. Now, she knew that Mrs. Reader had wanted to say a great deal more—and had not dared.

"Looks like a fine place," Amy said to Irene as they moved between two lines of women. She was aware the women glanced across their coveralled shoulders at the new employee.

"Here's our stand," Irene said. "You work here with me. Pretty soon one of the straw bosses will come looking for you. He might leave you here, or he might find some other place for you. Don't worry, you're going to be fine."

"All right." Amy sighed. She was glad she was here. The important thing was that she move toward becoming independent. All she was living for was the moment when her divorce became final.

"We're wrapping toasters today," Irene said. "They come down on this conveyor belt from upstairs. All we do is wrap them in insulating paper and put them in one of these cartons. Then we set the carton back on the conveyor belt and pick up the next one."

"What if we miss one?"

"Honey, don't be real square. That's what all these other dames are here for. You find out that most of them stop as few appliances as they can get away with. It's a racket. Most of them just try to look busy enough so the bosses won't interfere with their conversations."

"It doesn't seem honest," Amy said.

"It will after you've been here awhile. Goofing off along here is only one of the minor crimes. The company has come to expect it. Every hurry-up attempt has failed, so they just figure it as part of the day."

She lifted a toaster, wrapped it in insulating paper, making a neat and professional looking fold, but allowing almost a dozen toasters to move past on the conveyor belt while she accomplished it. Then she picked up a cardboard carton with its lids standing straight so the package could be slipped neatly and swiftly into it. But Irene set the carton on the ledge before her, folded back each lid of the carton and then set the toaster inside it. Then she straightened the lids again, but did not close them—this was someone else's job—and replaced the toaster on the belt.

Twenty minutes passed.

"Amy, this is Terry Collier," Irene said.

Amy turned from the conveyor belt and looked at the young foreman. He appeared to be in his middle twenties, tall and slender. He was not handsome—not in the masculine beauty pattern of Burt. His mouth was large and his gray eyes were large, too, vulnerable.

His tawny hair was mussed over his forehead and looked as if it would tumble back there no matter how often he combed it.

"Hello," she said.

She sensed that he was staring at her with just that faint interest that was too personal for the place and the situation. Instantly those gray eyes went blank and he studied the clipboard he carried.

"You Reader?" he said, not looking at her.

"That's right. Amy."

"Reader will do fine," he said. His voice sounded gruff.

Amy frowned faintly, wondering why her own heart should increase its tempo. She wanted nothing to do with a man, any man. She'd heard Irene and the other women near her talking about Terry Collier. There was a goodness about him that always showed through. He was so fair as a boss it was a wonder he hadn't been fired. If he thought the company was wrong and an employee right, he stood up for the employee until something gave. They smiled when they said that. They even smiled when they said he would even it out when he thought an employee was wrong and the company right. Everybody in here, Irene told her, tried to be right. Or if they couldn't be right, they tried to convince Terry Collier that they were.

She tried to ignore the uneven throbbing of her pulses. If she were attracted to Terry Collier because of his simple goodness, she would have none of it—that would be certain rebounding from Burt's self-centered manner and violent temper that struck out because nobody else was ever right, and he was never wrong. This was just a job. She wasn't going to fall for a man just because all the women thought he was perfect—and he had a wry, twisted smile.

She wanted nothing to do with love. She'd been there. She'd had it. Her mother said love never flourished on barren soil. If she treated Collier coldly maybe he would let her alone and she wouldn't even get to know him at all.

"First thing I'm supposed to tell you," Terry was saying, "is that if you goof off along here, it won't get you in any trouble. It gets me in trouble.

We got a quota. I got one job, seeing we keep to our quota. They don't even ask me to exceed it, just meet it." He had a low baritone voice, and a tired way of speaking, as if he had said this so often he no longer had any faith in it. "I know it won't do any good to tell you this. I've told all these other women—at least once, and they don't care. So why should you care? Still, the only thought on the matter is, I may not be the worst boss in the world. If I'm fired, the next one you get may be."

"I'll do the best I can." Amy said it sincerely.

"Sure you will." The tone of his voice was sardonic.

Amy flared. "I want this job. I'm not trying to cheat anybody."

He shrugged. "Fine."

Irene said quickly, "Amy, you can call him Terry. Everybody else does."

Terry's head came up. Those gray eyes struck against Amy's. She saw him stiffen, setting himself against her, and she could not think why.

"Mr. Collier is my name," he said. "And that will do nicely."

"Yes, sir, Mr. Collier," Amy said.

He flushed, straightened, tall, lean, gray eyes troubled. He shrugged and turned away. He stopped. "You'll get along fine here, Reader, if you can do the work."

Irene was stunned. "Why, Terry. That isn't fair. A two-year-old baby could do this work."

His smile was chilled. "That's right," he said. "But what I said still goes." He marked something on his clipboard and walked away. Amy watched him a moment, the way he walked, the way he held his head. She was thinking about the gentle tone of his voice. He couldn't really be tough, not even when he made the effort.

Irene turned back to the conveyor belt. Amy sensed that some of the other women near were watching her covertly.

Irene said, "He likes you."

"Sure he does," Amy said.

"No. Really. You're the first woman around here he's given this much attention to, I can tell you. Terry Collier believes in job before pleasure. He's never even dated women out of this department—and don't think they haven't tried."

"You mean he isn't married?"

"Not yet. But they're working on it."

"Maybe he thought I would try to flirt with him and he was putting me in my place," Amy said.

"Maybe." Irene laughed. "You do have that yummy fresh look—and most of the rest of us old bags around here are old bags. Because I can tell you, Terry Collier is the best foreman in this plant. It's not like this in all departments. Upstairs in Fred Hankins' line there's gossip and politics all the time. He dates his women, and turns them in—anything to polish up with the brass. We got it made down here and everybody in the place wants to work for Terry. They're always trying to get away from Fred before he dates them or fires them."

Amy glanced over her shoulder. Terry was far down the line but was staring at her. For a second their gazes clashed and then both looked away, quickly.

"Amy, would you get us a box hook, please?"

Amy turned from her place in line to the two coveralled women who had moved into Irene's station. Irene was off somewhere—Amy had already learned that Irene spent forty minutes of every hour on coffee breaks, or visiting, or in the women's lounge, smoking.

"Sure. Where do I get one?"

"In the stockroom," one of the women said. "You ask in there. They'll tell you."

The two women stood and waited with arms folded while Amy walked across the wide floor, following the arrows to the stockroom. Here were narrow dark aisles, stacked high with cartons and supplies. A boy was sprawled out on a mailing table.

"A box hook," Amy said, "where do I find them, please?"

The youth swung around, sitting up. He stared at her a moment, then jerked his head along the aisles.

She moved through one of the aisles, conscious of the breathless warmth of the place, the heated darkness. It was as if she were walking down a dark humid tunnel. She stepped out of the aisle and stopped.

She stared.

Her mouth was open, and her eyes were distended.

At first she didn't even believe what she saw. First there were the three men in coveralls, standing with their backs to her, then there was the other man and the girl on the table. They were all silent, the watching men as though they were spectators at some stag party.

Amy felt herself go weak. She stared at the girl, unable to pull her gaze away. They had peeled down her coveralls and removed her underthings. The man with her had forced her back against the table, half lifted her upon it.

It was the girl's face that Amy could not stop looking at. The girl was wild with excitement, her eyes were glazed and her mouth was parted. She had reached the state in which she was like some wild little animal in ecstasy of heat and passion. She no longer knew where she was, no longer cared what was happening to her. She was mewling, making noises in her throat.

Shaking her head, Amy stepped back, trying to turn around. She knocked over a stack of boxes. The three men turning, stared at her, their faces flushed.

"Well. Look who's here."

"Stand in line, baby."

"Sure, now honey, you're next."

She stumbled around, ran. Then she saw the youth from the mailing table and two other stock room men coming toward her. She looked around wildly. She was trapped in the narrow aisle. It was as if it were suddenly a nightmare.

The three men were laughing and moving after her.

"Come back, any time, baby," one of them yelled.

"We'll see you in the stock room, honey." The men from the front of the stock room were crowded beside her and they caught her, caressing her as she fought her way past them. "We got your new stock ready for you, baby."

"Come on back, honey. What's your rush?"

She wrenched herself free from the last one. Her body felt as though it was afire. She couldn't get those men from her mind, or the look on that girl's face. Their laughter grabbed after her.

"Got your new stock for you, honey."

"You got a standing invitation, honey—"

"Yeah. Standing."

She would not look back. It was as if their laughter struck against her as she ran.

Suddenly a man stepped around one of the aisle corners. He caught both her arms in his hands. His face was cold. His fingers tightened. He stared down into her eyes.

"I don't know what you were looking for, kid—"

Amy shook her head. She knew now why the two women had sent her back there. It was part of the initiation of a new employee. She could not go back now and face them. Would she ever be able to walk past this stockroom without remembering hotly, wildly what she had seen back in that breathless dark?

"Nothing. I—"

"Well. Get this straight. You keep your mouth shut. You understand."

Amy licked her lips. "Yes."

"You know what's good for you. You keep your mouth shut. We don't make nobody come back here. They come back here. It's up to them. You understand?"

She nodded again, and he released her suddenly. She turned and fled. She didn't stop running until she was inside the women's lounge.

Chapter 6

Amy saw Irene going through the outgoing line at the time clock ahead of her. She called out to her and Irene turned, a look of impatience on her face.

Irene was standing beyond the clock near the double doors of the exit when Amy rang out her card, replaced it in the racks and hurried to her.

"Irene. What was the hurry? Why didn't you wait for me?"

Irene shook her head. People passed them, streaming outward into the five p.m. sunshine, going toward the parking lots and the bus stops.

"Look, kid, will you go on in town without me tonight, huh?"

"Sure. What's up?"

Irene shrugged. "Nothing. Just some overtime work."

Amy stared at her. She'd been at the plant long enough now to know how little overtime there was for the conveyor lines. "You're kidding."

"Well, I'm not getting paid for it, if that's what you mean." Irene's voice remained sharp and impatient, as if she were full of anger. "But it is overtime and it is work."

"Irene, what's the matter? You act as if you're mad with me."

"Well, I'm not."

"What is wrong?"

"Nothing, kid. If I'm mad at anybody, it's myself." She was staring across Amy's shoulder, watching the stairway.

"Why don't you tell me about it?"

"Why don't you go on home? Haven't you got woes enough?"

"Something is wrong with you, Irene, and I just want to know what it is."

"Nothing is wrong." Irene made her voice a mockery of patience. "Look, kid. I got a date with Fred Hankins."

"The boss from upstairs?"

"Only Fred Hankins I know."

"But, Irene. You said he was a creep."

Irene shrugged. "Go on home, kid."

"Irene. Forget it. You don't want to date Fred Hankins. He's a creep—and he's married."

Irene laughed. "Married? What difference does that make? Look, Amy, get this. You got to stop caring if a man is married or not. That's for wives to worry about. If a woman is married, let her worry. We're not wives—not you and me. We're divorced dolls. That's what we are. We do what we can do—and the hell with any other women, because, baby, that's the way they feel about you."

"But—Fred Hankins."

"Look, Amy. Fred Hankins is a boss. He is the favorite boss of the company brass. It doesn't hurt to stay in good with him. They make changes around here all the time. One thing you can figure is that no matter what the changes are, they will do Fred Hankins no harm—and it don't hurt to be in good with him."

The next afternoon Amy wondered if Irene mentioned her name to Fred Hankins, because he was downstairs at her place in line. Maybe Irene had mentioned her, or maybe Fred Hankins could smell out the new girls.

The first thing he said to her was, "Hello there, Amy. I've had my eye on you for some time." The way he said it, it was as though this were the greatest single favor he could bestow upon her.

She smiled, and thanked him. He was not a bad looking man. In a way, he was good looking, and no one knew it better than he. He was in his early thirties. His dark hair was wavy.

She could feel the gazes of the other women on her. She tried to go on working.

He stepped closer. "You happy down here in this department, Amy?"

"Why sure." Her answer was immediate and honest. "Why not?"

He smiled at her. "Forty-eight bucks a week. That's not top pay around here. This department—" he let his mouth twist with contempt— "it's the lowest level. You could move up."

"I can do this work," she said with a self-deprecating smile. "Maybe I couldn't do any of the skilled—"

"Honey. Don't talk like that. We can always find something that's right—for the right person."

He waited to let her be properly impressed at this news.

"Tell you what," he said as if the thought had just occured to him. "Why don't you let me drive you home this afternoon after work? We could talk it over. I'm sure we could find a spot for you."

She glanced at him. He was looking her over. He didn't lick his lips, but he looked as if he might.

"Well, gee," she said. "I'd like to, Mr. Hankins. But this afternoon, I just can't—"

"If it's not important to you, that's all right with me." His voice was cold. He turned on his heel. She shivered, because there had been a threat implied in his tone. He did not waste time with her, the plant was swarming with quail. And the threat was that she could be replaced, even if she were not directly under his supervision.

She was nervous. When he was gone, she turned back to the conveyor belt, reached for a toaster.

She got her hands on it, lifted it and dropped it.

"All right, Reader. What the devil are you trying to do?"

Amy did not even pick up the toaster though she had knelt down to do it. She straightened up, staring at Terry Collier. Her eyes were brimmed with tears.

"I couldn't help it."

"Those things cost money, Reader. All you got to do is pick them up without dropping them, wrap them and put them in a box. You think that's too much for you?"

The other women had ceased working and were staring. They'd never heard Terry Collier talk to any of them like this.

"I don't think so."

He bent down, picked up the toaster. He checked it over carefully.

"You act like this is the first time—it ever happened," she said, her voice miserable.

"It's happened before. It doesn't have to happen."

She could not see that the toaster was damaged but Terry strode away from her, carrying the toaster. He put a damaged label on it and placed it on a conveyor that returned it upstairs.

He didn't come near her again, but he made up her mind for her. Weeks had passed since she had begun her divorce action against Burt. She had not dated once, she had not wanted to. Suddenly she did want a date and when she saw Fred Hankins walking toward the stairway later, she left the line and ran to meet him.

She intercepted him at the foot of the wide stairs. He glanced at her in a chilled way as if he'd never seen her before.

"I—broke that engagement," she said to him.

"What are you talking about?"

Puzzled she looked around to see if they were being overheard. Then she studied Fred's face to see if he were kidding her. He seemed quite serious. She forced herself to go on smiling.

"I mean—I'd like to ride home with you this afternoon."

"Oh? That?" He shrugged, giving her an odd smile. "I'm afraid not this afternoon. I'll be busy this afternoon. Maybe some other time, Reader."

He gave her a faint and twisted smile and went up the stairs. She stared at his back, hating him. He was the lord of this place. He could choose from dozens of women.

But the odd part of it was she returned to work, seeing that Terry Collier was watching her from the far end of the line. Her anger wasn't really directed at Fred Hankins at all.

It was Terry Collier she hated.

A week later, Amy walked with Fred Hankins across the parking lot to his car. Today he'd stopped by her place in line and told her that he could drive her home at five if she wanted him to. He did not mention the promotion.

"This is it," he said.

She did not know how she'd been sure he would own a red and white convertible. There was one thing certain. He may be married but he was not working at it. A man could not sneak around in a red and white convertible.

The first thing he did was to put the top down. They drove out of the parking lot and he turned the car away from town. Amy did not say anything.

"I hear you're divorced, Amy," he said. The wind rifled his hair on his forehead. His eyes narrowed and stroked her.

"I'm getting a divorce."

"Must be kind of lonely, huh?"

"I get along all right."

"Sure you do. A good-looking girl like you. But after you've been married—there must be a lot about marriage that you miss, eh?"

She did not answer. He drove less than two miles into the woods. He turned the convertible into a secluded road and drove along it to a place where a giant tree made a shadowed spot. He rolled into the shaded place and killed the engine. Wadded kleenex littered the stones of the street and winked white in the weeds.

She felt her heart pounding. She was angered at being treated this way, brought directly here as he must bring dozens of other women, making no pretense of anything except that they were tramps and he was taking advantage of the fact.

He turned on the seat and grinned at her. "You must be stuffy in those coveralls," he said. "Why don't you take them off."

"I'm all right."

"All right? You're better than that, honey. You're a little dream. But I get sick of looking at those coveralls. I want to see you without them. It's been a long time since I saw anyone as young and as pretty as you are."

He caught the zipper on the front of her coveralls and pulled it down deftly, expertly. He was familiar with these coveralls.

She caught his hand as he slipped it inside her coverall.

"Don't," she said.

His hand closed on her, tightly, hurting.

He leaned forward, spoke against her throat. "Honey, don't be a fool. A pretty little widow like you, and a man like me. We can make beautiful rock-and-roll together."

"No."

"You need a man, that's all that's wrong with you."

"I don't need you."

"How do you know? Baby, I'm something special. You ask the girls. Plenty of them would like to be where you are."

"Then you better get them."

"I don't think so. I think we're going to get along fine, you and me." His hand clutched at her again.

"Oh, no. Please. I want to go." She pushed his hand away.

"Don't make me mad, baby."

"I'm sorry. I want to go."

"You haven't started to be sorry."

She pushed away from him. "I didn't know men were so—so brutal about women as you."

"Pretty little widow," he said. He laughed and started the car. "You got a lot to learn, baby. Sorry I don't have the time to teach you." He wheeled the car around, sped back toward town. "But now you know where I am and what I want. When you get wise—let me know. I got no time for fooling around."

Chapter 7

She had only been at work about an hour one morning when one of the men in charge of personnel tapped her on the shoulder. When she turned she caught her breath as she recognized him. The first thing she thought was that Fred Hankins had had her fired for some reason. She could not think what she had done. Maybe when a foreman like Fred stood in with the bosses he did not have to give a reason for the things he did. Damn him! She looked about wildly for Terry Collier. She was going to tell him the truth about what had happened before she let them summarily fire her for not undressing on a back road for Fred Hankins.

She did not see Terry anywhere.

The personnel man said, "You Mrs. Burt Reader?"

She nodded, drawn taut, still looking for Terry.

"There's a telephone call for you."

Relief flooded through her. She was silent a moment feeling weak all over.

"Thank you." She moved away from him and started toward the glass partitioned office where the telephones were.

"Reader."

His voice stopped her. She paused, looking over her shoulder, frowning.

"Yes?"

"Is this a personal call? You know company rules about personal calls during business hours."

"How would I know?"

"There's the rule."

"I don't know anyone who would call me on personal business," she said.

He nodded. "All right. He says his name is Robert Wallin, an attorney."

She hurried toward the office, shaking her head. She felt helpless. Before they would even call her to the phone they found out who the caller was and what was the purpose of his call. Then they double-checked before they would let her accept it. But this was not important beside the fact that Wallin had called.

"Hello," she said.

"Amy? We have a hearing this morning at eleven in the judge's chambers. Now, this is the final moment—the hearing is a matter of form. Do you think you could get down here and go to his offices with me at eleven?"

"Yes, I'm sure I could."

"That's fine, Amy. You're almost a free woman."

She replaced the receiver. The people in the small office were busy at work. She spoke to the clerk in charge. "I'd like the rest of the day off," she said.

He glanced up at her. "See your foreman."

She nodded and walked out into the work room. The chattering of the women was deafening, louder than the machines.

She found Terry near the end of her line.

"I'd like the day off," she said.

He stared at her. "What?"

"I'd like the rest of the day off. They said to see you. Is it all right?"

He appeared exasperated. "Why, sure," he said in a mocking way. "Of course it's all right. Why, we run this place just for your convenience."

"You don't need to make a big thing out of it."

"The only payment we make for time off is sick leave. Are you sick?"

"No. I don't want to be paid." She wanted to laugh, despite the high anger she felt against Terry Collier.

"All right. I had to tell you. Go ahead."

"Thank you." She started away, but could not resist attempting to have the last word. "I hope you won't be unable to get work done without me."

"I'll get along," he replied.

A free woman, Amy walked out of the county building into the sunshine with Robert Wallin. She looked at the people hurrying along the street, at the cars parked at curbs, the buildings and the sky. It all looked different, better, and fresher and clean.

"Well. How do you feel? You are free. And you had no trouble."

Some of the good went out of the morning.

"What about Burt? What do you do now?"

"We'll send him a copy of the final decree. Since we testified in court we didn't know his whereabouts, we'll mail it to your last address and let it be forwarded to him at the training camp. Don't spend any more time worrying about him, Amy. He was a mistake, a bad mistake you made. Don't be in a hurry to make another one. Spend a little time being young." He glanced along the street, stared at a woman selling flowers near a hotel entrance. "I think most of the trouble in cases like yours is that children believe they're mature when they start paying adult prices at the movies. And then they see what fools the adults themselves are around them, and they feel—with some justification—that they are as smart as people two and three times their age.

"In many cases this is true—but this doesn't mean the child is mature, only that the adult is immature. They don't want to listen to adults they can neither trust nor respect. Now, Amy, you're a giant step ahead of other girls your age—or you can be if you will profit by what has happened to you. From now on, Amy, listen to the counseling of your own mind. Remember that you were a fool, deceiving yourself that such things as masculine prettiness are important. You can make a good life for yourself,

Amy, if you're smart enough to have profited by your mistakes."

She nodded. "I'm not going to rush back into marriage, if that's what you mean."

"That's part of what I mean. The rest of it is to listen to your reason more and your emotions less from now on. This isn't nearly as simple as it sounds, and I don't pretend it is. It's just something for you to think about. Good luck, Amy—and if you need me, let me hear from you."

She stood there in the center of the walk and watched him go away from her, a man of medium build, overweight, and overburdened with other people's woes and sordid errors. But there was about him that sense of self confidence and strength that always gave her a lift. She smiled thinking it would be easy to be strong if she could keep him near to reassure her. She did not know if he believed in the goodness of man, or only in his own power to repair wrongs, but whatever it was, he gave the people who needed him confidence.

You believed him when he told you that things were going to be all right. But the sad part of it was that when he walked away from her now, she knew it was final. There would be no need to see him again in his gleaming office smelling of leather and expensive cigar smoke, lined with thick books and carpeted with thick rugs. He had brought her this far, and now he had cut her free. She was a divorcee now.

She looked about again trying to find that sense of elation she'd had when she walked out into the sunshine. It was gone. In its place there was a winter-like chill. She looked about, frightened and young, and more frightened because she was so young—suddenly a divorcee, and suddenly so alone....

She wanted to tell her mother about the final decree, and a dozen times that night it was on the tip of her tongue to do it. But she did not feel equal to the scene that must follow. Her mother had a date that night.

Her date arrived about a quarter to eight and Stella was still dressing. Amy was sitting in the front room too excited even to see the magazine opened on her lap. She wished she had money enough to afford champagne. She would call Irene and they would have champagne to celebrate her freedom. The doorbell rang and she went to answer it.

The man who came in was a drug salesman. He did not have to tell her. She had met too many of them since her mother had been a clerk at Troxler's big drugstore downtown. Some of them her mother dated regularly when they hit town on their rounds. Amy could never say why, but this seemed a horrible idea. It was as if these men, always a little drunk, had a string of women, one for each town in his territory.

This man was a stranger, but not for more than half a minute. His blue eyes were watery with all he'd had to drink. His hair was thin across the top. He swiped the palm of his hand across it when he saw Amy. He looked her over laughing.

He called out, "Stella. You ready to go?"

Stella's laughter reached out from the bedroom. Amy shivered slightly. The sound of Stella's laughter was as abandoned as the salesman's; it was as though her laughter promised him she was as silly and giddy as his drinking had made him. And Amy knew better. Stella was a solemn and frightened woman; this was one reason she tried so hard to be a party-type girl for the salesmen she dated: she was afraid they wouldn't like her. She was more afraid of loneliness than anything.

"I'll be there in a shake, Jed." Her mother said.

"You better." Jed's eyes had not stopped crawling across Amy. "I don't know who this is out here, but she gets my blood pressure up. Who is this here gal, Stel?"

"That's my daughter Amy, Jed," Stella said from the bedroom. "Amy, why don't you pour Jed a drink while he's waiting."

"Yeah." Jed's gaze stroked her. "Why don't you?"

Jed trailed her, laughing and talking, into the kitchen. She heard him catch his breath when she stretched tall to get him a glass from the cabinet.

"What a body," he said. There was awe in his tone, awe at the way her ankles were stretched trim, her legs tautened, her hips pulled up, and her breasts lifted tight against the fabric of her frock. "What a body!"

She tried to ignore him. She moved to the sink and he stalked her. She heard the irregular sound of his breathing.

"What a body. What a mother. But—what a daughter."

"Say when." She still tried to ignore him.

He said in that awed voice, "There oughta be a law. There probably is a law."

She smiled faintly, despite herself. He was a lonely man, and there was such a deep, even if comic sincerity in his tone.

She felt his breath against her neck.

"Say, honey. Why don't we—get a friend for your ma—and make this thing a foursome?"

She forced herself to smile. "You don't really mean that, Jed."

"Don't I?" he said in that awed tone. "Don't I?"

"Of course not." She found some ice, dropped it in a glass. She didn't want to anger him; the only time her mother appeared really happy any more was on these infrequent dates.

"You're Mom's date, Jed." She kept her voice low.

"I know. I know."

She lifted the whisky, poured him a short drink. He laughed. "More than that. You drive me crazier than that."

He was breathless. She added another jigger.

He said, "I'm a big boy, honey. Takes a big drink for a big boy. A big drink—and a big girl."

She felt his admiring eyes on her, on the fresh rise of her breasts, the smooth slope of her stomach, and she caught her breath at the unwilling response of her own body. She tried to shut it from her mind. But it was there—her frustrated needs, the remembered thrills of nights with Burt. She couldn't forget just because she was no longer his wife.

She turned her face away, afraid that Jed would see into her eyes. She was sure they were vulnerable, revealing her frightened thoughts. She was divorced now—as Stella was, as Irene was. Both Stella and Irene ran from loneliness as though it were the worst evil on earth.

How long before she was like that?

She reached for a glass with trembling fingers, her back to Jed. He moved close and pressed against her and she bit her lip with a sense of shock.

He laughed, keeping it joking, but both of them knew it was no joke. His arms slipped around her, under her arms and he closed them across the upthrust of her breasts. He moved as if dancing to unheard music, raking her body with the pressure of his.

For a moment she responded to him, feeling his hands close on her, feeling him moving her body in that strange muted rhythm that neither of them heard but which was louder than any other sounds in the world. His right hand, spread wide, moved over her.

She pulled away. What was she doing? What was happening to her? He stood there, staring at her, eyes owlish, mouth parted slightly. He shook his head when she backed away from him, but he did not move after her.

She turned then, hurrying from the room, sorry for Jed, hating herself, running away from herself, and knowing she could never really do that.

Chapter 8

Burt was hitting her every time she lied to him. Mr. Wallin was standing to one side counting her lies by marking them on a blackboard. Her mother ran after her weeping about her lying, and yet she knew if she told the truth, it would be worse than her lying.

She woke up, bathed in sweat. The sheet was twisted around her. She sat up and snapped on the light. It was after one a.m. Her mother still wasn't home. Well, Stella was a big girl. Or she thought she was. She could take care of herself. Or she thought she could. Anyway, you couldn't tell her anything.

Amy got up, went into the kitchen and drank some heated milk. She returned to the bed and she prayed. It was a simple prayer.

She prayed that she would fall quickly to sleep.

She had to tell Stella about the divorce. Stella might rage, might even be ill, but sooner or later she was going to find out anyhow. For one thing, the final decree notice would be published in the local paper and like all divorcees, Stella was morbidly interested in the divorce notices. Every new marriage that failed seemed to reaffirm something she believed.

Amy was still nervous and taut-drawn when she went to work the next day.

"I got my decree," she told Irene.

Irene cheered aloud. But even seeing Irene smile didn't make Amy feel any better. Didn't misery want all the company it could get? She had been intimate enough with Irene Haver in these past six months to know how bitterly unhappy and mixed-up Irene was.

Irene went from work to the nearest bar. But when a man was pleasant to her, she withdrew, chilled because she knew precisely what he wanted, and when they let her alone she was more miserable than ever. All she talked about was finding a man who would marry her, but the way she expressed herself about marriage precluded any man's having such ideas about her. Immediately they began thinking along other lines—her body lines and the straight line that was the shortest distance between the bar and her bed.

She woke up every morning with a hangover and a resolution to stop toppling backwards for every man she met. Then she would abstain from sin and pleasure as she called it, and suddenly she'd find herself walking back and forth in the night darkness outside the house where Roger lived with his new wife, crazy with insatiable desire that was like something hot and crawling inside her, and she hurried away to the nearest bar knowing all the cold beer in the world couldn't put out that fire.

"Welcome to the club." Irene cried out loudly.

Terry Collier pushed his way through the women who'd stopped working to stare.

"All right, Reader," he said. "Cut out the noise."

She caught her breath, angered that he must blame her. He never spoke with angered voice to anyone of this department except her.

She did not say anything. She turned away quickly and went back to work.

Irene said, "It was my fault, boss. You see, Amy just got her divorce final papers. I was cheering."

Terry's voice was odd. "Why don't you let Reader's husband do the cheering?"

Amy caught her breath again, even more sharply and heeled around with fire in her eyes. But Terry was already walking away from them. She stared after, hating him.

Her hands were trembling when she went to order a new supply of cartons wheeled in from the stock room. She saw Terry coming toward her and she turned quickly away, bumping a stack of cartons and sending them tumbling and bumping across the tile floor.

He strode toward her and she stood tall, her fists clenched waiting for him.

It was an accident, even a fool could see it was an accident. She hoped he would say something about it. She could look for a new job tomorrow, but this day would end in satisfaction when she told him what she thought of him.

His voice was level. "Still celebrating?"

"I couldn't help it. It was an accident."

"Is that all you would say if those cartons had contained packaged appliances?"

She tilted her head, staring into his gray eyes, ready to tell him all the things she wanted to say, in all the words that Irene Haver might fluently use.

But she saw his vulnerable eyes waver, saw the color move slowly upward in his face, and what she read there was not smugness or persecution or petty boorishness.

She laughed suddenly.

More disconcerted, his face colored more deeply. His hand tightened on his clipboard. "Now it's something to laugh about—"

"No, Mr. Collier. It's you I'm laughing at."

He inhaled deeply, but before he spoke, he dampened his lips. "You can restack those cartons and return to work, Reader."

"Just a minute."

"Yes?"

She was still smiling, still staring into his face. "I just want to tell you something."

"Well, make it quick."

"Oh. It won't take me long. I want to tell you, I'm on to you. You're not fooling me, Terry Collier. You're no petty top boss. You're not even tough. All this lecturing and tough stuff with me doesn't fool me one bit—not any more, I can tell you."

For a moment he stood there, shoulders slack, staring at her. He gaped at her, then turned suddenly on his heel and knocked over another stack of cartons.

For another moment they stood staring at each other. Amy was laughing. Suddenly he shook his head and laughed with her.

He set aside his clipboard and knelt down to pick up cartons. She bent over helping him, still laughing. They did not say anything else.

At four-thirty that afternoon, Amy was humming as she wrapped appliances. Her touch was deft, professional and quick. She slipped them into cartons and reached for the next one. Her worry about telling her mother the truth of her divorce was out of her mind, and Burt was out of it, and she was living in a simple state of happiness.

"Reader—Amy."

Terry Collier was standing beside her. She felt her heart quicken. Immediately she frowned, mistrusting her emotions. Her heart had flipped when she was near Burt, too—two years ago.

His face was pale and he looked unsure of himself.

She couldn't help smiling. "Yes?"

"I wondered—if I could drive you home after work."

She was startled, and she didn't want to admit she was excited and pleased. She felt her own face growing warm. To cover her confusion, she pretended to stare at him in mock puzzlement as if she'd never seen him before.

"Now what's the matter?" he said.

"Oh—excuse me," she said, teasing him. "I thought you were Fred Hankins."

"Cut it out."

"Well, I know Terry Collier never dates the girls in his department. He doesn't believe in mixing business and pleasure. Why, everybody knows that."

"Stop making an issue out of it. I didn't—ask for a date. I just wanted to drive you home."

"Oh, but that's the way it starts," she went on teasing him, feeling elated, feeling the excited throb of her heart. "First, you'll take me home, and then you'll want a date. Soon you'll want to kiss me."

He smiled at her. Suddenly he was not shy, and his vulnerable eyes lightened. "Why do you think I treated you tough? That was the first thing I wanted to do—kiss you—months ago."

Terry drove into town slowly. His car was a year or two old, but it gleamed. You could see he spent a lot of time working on it and keeping it looking smart.

"This could be habit forming," he said. "I mean riding with you like this."

"I don't think so." There was a slight chill in her voice, even when she did not intend it to be.

He frowned. "Why not? Good Lord, Amy, I knew you were married when you came to work out here. I had to stay away from you because you were married. Well, damn it, you looked like what I've—been looking for. And I didn't want to make a fool out of myself. But, of course, I did anyhow."

"You've been sweet."

"Sweet. Oh, brother, what a horrible thing to say about any guy. I never wanted to be sweet. I kept my distance because you were married. You're not married now, Amy. Good Lord, I can still make a fool of myself, but in a lot of different ways."

"I don't want you to."

"Now what are you talking about?"

"I'll tell you. I like you. Maybe too much. I've liked you since that first day, too. And if I hadn't liked you, and if I didn't feel this way about you, I might say sure, I'd date you, all the time."

"I better turn up my hearing aid. That doesn't make pretty good sense."

"It makes sense, and you know it. You may not want to admit it, but you know it. Being with you is very pleasant. It would be great if that's what I wanted. Only it isn't."

He slowed the car even more. "All right. Give. What do you want?"

"I don't want anything. I don't want to get mixed up with you—or with anybody. It would be worse with you, because it would be easier to get all snarled up."

"What are you talking about?"

"I've been snarled up. I've been married, and I've been unhappy—and I don't want any more of it, thanks. I just want you to let me alone."

She looked forward to going to work in the morning, dreaded ringing out and returning home at five p.m. For a week Terry did not come near her unless he had to, and then he was very business-like. He did not lecture her any more, nor raise his voice. It was easy for her to tell him to stay away from her, but it was a kind of anxious agony when he did it. Still, because she was near him all day, she lived in a kind of spun-out happiness that lifted in the morning and sagged in the evening.

One afternoon at five he was outside the double glass exit doors when she came through them with Irene.

"Amy," he said.

She stopped, gave him a wan smile. Her heart slugged. Wasn't this just the sort of emotional tangle Robert Wallin had warned her to avoid?

Irene patted her arm and hurried away toward the bus stop.

"Couldn't I drive you home?" he said. "Small talk. Nothing of consequence. No entanglements."

She met his gaze. She wanted to say yes. She had been waiting for him to ask her again. But it was not going to be the way he promised. It couldn't go on being that, no matter how hard they tried. In fact, the harder they tried, the worse it would be for them.

He sighed and shrugged. "If the idea is that terrible, forget it." He tried to smile. "It's just that I live in the opposite direction from you, so of course it wouldn't be out of my way to take you home."

"All right," she said. "This time."

He grinned suddenly and exhaled. They walked together across the parking lot. She felt good with the late afternoon sunlight on her, and she was hardly aware of the streams of people hurrying around them, the rise of exhaust fumes from the cars speeding from the lot.

His shoulder touched hers as they walked, and both of them tensed. She knew she had to end this. She decided in that moment to quit her job at the appliance plant. Maybe she could get them to transfer her to another department. But this would not be very honest with herself. As long as she was out here she would see Terry Collier frequently, and that wasn't going to help get him out of her mind.

They reached Terry's car. He opened the door for her, closed it and went around to the other side. Her gaze moved across the lot, struck the red and white convertible owned by Fred Hankins. Fred and some woman in tan coveralls were just backing out of the parking space, and they were laughing.

Her heart sank. She could easily get herself transferred from Terry's department. Fred Hankins would take her in a minute. Well—first there would be that date with him, and that quick, sordid drive to the woods with him. That didn't matter. She could go to the woods and it would never touch her, would never matter as much as accidentally bumping Terry's arm as they walked, or feeling his hand suddenly covering hers.

"There's a party at the church my folks go to," Terry was saying. "I never go much any more. But they go—and I had to buy a couple tickets, I mean. You might like it. And Lord knows, you ought to feel safe enough from me at a church party."

She sank back against the seat, wanting to go with Terry. A church party. What a simple and uncomplicated thing. She closed her eyes for a moment, feeling them burn.

"Okay," he said. She heard the disappointment in Terry's tone. She'd hesitated so long that he'd taken her silence for refusal. "Lord, I don't blame you. A church party. I don't know. Thought you might have fun—and you could meet my folks."

She reached out, touched his hand on the steering wheel. She felt the roughness of it.

"I'd like to go, Terry."

"It's all right. Forget it. It was a square idea in the first place. A church party—"

"Terry, it would be fun."

"Oh, boy. I ought to have my head examined."

"I want to go—"

"Maybe I will have my head examined." He paused, stared at her. "What?"

"I want to go."

"Will you say that again?"

Amy laughed. "I'd love to go to the party with you."

He exhaled in a wild, exaggerated way. "What time shall I pick you up? Or maybe I better just stay with you until party time so you can't change your mind."

"I won't change my mind, Terry. When I say no to you—it isn't because I don't like you or—"

"Or what?" he said when she paused. "I learned a long time ago not to try to understand women. But you're even worse than any of the others. I don't even know what you mean when you say it right out loud."

Amy stared down at the seat between them. Their hands were locked tightly on the seat cover. Her fingers were entwined in his. This was crazy. She'd just gotten out of one emotional involvement. She certainly didn't trust her own judgment yet.

She withdrew her hand, moved over against the door and watched the town move by slowly.

She saw that Terry winced slightly when she moved away from him but he did not remark on it. Some of the pleasure of their first date was already dissipated. She frowned. She could not help it. In these past weeks a hurting kind of ache spread inside her whenever she thought of Terry. It was as bad with him; she would have to be blind to miss it. There was just one thing for her to do. She would have to quit her job at the plant. If she didn't see him any more she would forget him.

As soon as she made this decision she felt better, as if a heavy pall had been lifted from her mind. Robert Wallin would be proud of her. She was listening to her reason, and not her emotions. She would leave the plant and she would get Terry Collier out of her mind. With this firmly decided, she could relax. She could look forward to the party tonight. She could have fun. For the first time in over a year she could have a good time and be herself.

"Will you let me out downtown?" she said abruptly.

Terry nodded. "Sure. Whatever you want."

"Oh, cheer up," she said, as though he had followed the complex processes of her thinking and should realize that tonight was to be a time of fun for them.

"Sure. Cheer. Ha. Ha," he said, his voice flat.

She laughed at him "I only want to buy a dress. I want something very feminine and silly—you know? You must be sick of seeing women in these coveralls."

She remembered Fred Hankins suddenly. He was the man who hated seeing women in tan coveralls, but he saw a great many more of them out of their coveralls than Terry did. Fred was a boy who would help you out of your coveralls any time.

"Don't you want me to wait for you?" Terry asked.

"You must have a lot to do."

"Sure. I want to wait for you. Let me find a parking place."

Amy spent thirty minutes finding just the dress she wanted. Finally she passed up all the filmy party dresses and decided on a knit of nylon ribbon. It would not be too daring for a church social, but she could be aware of her good lines in it, and Terry would be aware of them, and so would everyone who looked at her. Suddenly this was the most important consideration, that she look young and beautifully put together.

As she waited for the clerk to fold the dress and put it in a flat box, she thought ahead to what her mother would say when she saw the dress. Stella would know she was coming alive: this would be the first time she had shown an interest in clothes in the past six months.

Terry grinned at her and pretended to brush away imaginary cobwebs that had been spun around him while he waited. She laughed, "I told you not to wait."

"May I say something?"

"Sure." She got into the car beside him, holding the box on her lap.

"You sure you won't pull your chill act on me?"

"Say it and see."

"I'd rather sit around and wait for you than be with anybody else I know."

There was simple honesty in his simple statement of fact. She glanced at him suddenly, pleased that he was not handsome, that there were the faint memories of boyhood freckles across his nose, that his wide eyes showed their thoughts too easily, that his mouth was large and his chin square and tilted slightly. And he was too slender, far too thin. She liked him exactly as he was.

"Thank you," she said.

He moved the car out into the traffic. "Shall I pick you up about seven?" he said. "I know that doesn't give you a lot of time, but church parties begin early. You mind?"

Now her mind was moving again, troubled. She did not answer him for a moment. If Terry came to the apartment, it would start Stella asking questions, and she wanted no trouble. She would give up her job at the plant and she wouldn't see Terry again. Meantime, as long as things were running almost smoothly at the apartment, why not leave them that way?

"Look," she said, "I know how we can save time. I'll meet you downtown here in the lobby of the Congress Hotel. At seven."

But he was not fooled; she didn't want him coming to her apartment, and this was obvious. Meeting her in the hotel lobby wasn't what he wanted.

"You won't have to come across town," she said.

"Sure."

He was silent the rest of the way to the apartment. He stopped at the curb outside, and gave her a twisted smile. "See you," he said.

She bent down, smiling at him from the curb. "We'll have fun," she told him. "You'll see."

"I know I will."

"See you at seven—Fred."

He leaned across the car seat and said, "Boy, that's one thing I wish you wouldn't call me—even when you're teasing."

"Oh, you're pretty much like him," she said with tongue in cheek. "Just your approach is different."

She turned on her heel and crossed the walk before he could say anything. She went smiling up the stairs, seeking her key in her purse as she went. She didn't have much time and so many things to do before seven.

The door was opened before she reached it and Amy stopped in the corridor, not breathing, feeling sick.

Burt was standing in the doorway.

Chapter 9

"Come on in," Burt said.

There was a faint smile on his face that pulled contempt lines in arcs from his nostrils. His forehead, splotched with drops of sweat, glistened in the light. His shirt was sweated around his armpits. He kept clenching and flexing his fingers, but his voice was very casual.

The next thing Amy saw was that Burt was not wearing his ill-fitting army uniform. She'd heard that army men no longer were required to wear uniforms when on leave—but there was something about Burt tonight. He had been in the army about seven months. He was no longer in it. He did not have to tell her this, her own slugging heart assured her it was the worst thing that could happen to her—and so quite naturally it had happened.

Burt was out of the army.

This was evident in the way he wore his tailored slacks, expensive slip-on shoes, and custom-tailored shirt that tapered from his thick chest to his lean hips. Once she had thought him beautiful in a masculine way.

He was still pretty.

She looked about wildly, wanting a place to run, some way out of here.

She bit her lip. There was no escape. All she could do was to plod forward as if she were wading through deep sand. Her legs trembling, she was afraid she would fall.

Her quivering fingers tightened on the dress box. She wished she could hide that box.

"Come on in," Burt said again in that flat and overly casual manner.

She nodded and walked near to him, aware of the toilet water he used, the after-shave lotion, the body powder.

She turned slightly to sidle past him into the apartment. She saw Stella sitting on the couch. Stella looked white and shaken. Burt had put her mother through purgatory, this was certain.

Burt caught her arm, his fingers digging into her flesh, bruising her. Her head tilted and her gaze struck against his, hating him.

He laughed at her and new perspiration popped out across his forehead, but he kept his voice coldly under control.

"Why, Amy, aren't you going to give your husband a kiss?"

"What's the matter with you, Amy?" her mother said in a shaken way from the couch. "Is this any way to behave? You haven't seen darling Burt in months."

But Amy was not thinking about her mother's opinion of her behavior, or of Burt's demand that she kiss her husband. She was free. She was thinking about Robert Wallin promising her she was all right now. Burt was no longer her husband.

She didn't owe him anything. She wrenched free of his hand, moved into the living room.

"I don't want you to touch me," she said.

Her mother gasped, but Amy did not look at her.

"Well, now, that's just too bad, because I'm going to touch you. It's a husband's privilege."

He stalked after her. She placed the dress box on a table. He glanced at it, and his mouth tightened.

"What's wrong, Amy?" His voice mocked her. "Why, your mother was much more pleased to see me than you are."

"I'm not pleased to see you at all."

"You haven't even said anything about my civilian uniform," he said, ignoring her sharp answer. "That's right, baby, I'm a civilian. Back getting basic training in being a husband and building a little home."

She whispered it. "How did you get out? How *could* you get out?"

He laughed at her, and only the way he clenched his hands told of his struggle to keep his temper leashed. "You can do anything, baby, if you try hard enough, and know the right people. I've always done everything I wanted to do. And I always will. Marriage hardship, that's my case. My little home is breaking up. I got a right to keep my little home together. I don't know where I went wrong before, but I got out of the army so I could patch up my troubles."

Her voice sounded odd in her own ears. "You're too late, Burt."

He laughed. "Oh, no. Mom and I been talking about it. It's never too late if two people are willing to work at marriage—"

"Oh, stop it, Burt. Didn't you get the divorce papers?"

"You're not going to divorce me."

"I'm not going to? I have done it. You must have gotten a notice of the final decree."

His mouth twisted into a laugh, but his eyes were brimmed with tears of rage.

"Oh, you mean this?" From his rear pocket he took a folded envelope and shook the decree from it. He stared at it a moment, laughter a choked sound in his throat. "You mean this paper? Why, Amy, I would have torn it up when I got it, but I wanted you to see me do it. I want you to see what I think of this paper."

He ripped it across, and ripped it again, the sound of tearing paper loud in the room. Then he crushed it in his fist and threw it into her face.

Stella caught her breath, but that was the only sound in the room. The bits of paper showered about Amy's feet.

"Quite a gesture," she said coldly. "But it doesn't mean a thing. It's still legal—still final."

His voice was lower than ever, charged with the tension that shook him, but barely above a hoarse whisper.

"You don't understand, Amy. That's just paper to me. Just paper. I married you in a church, and it was for all time—till death do us part. That was what the minister said. I heard him say it. That's the way I want it, and that's the way it's going to be."

"Yes. That's all that ever matters to you. The way you want it."

He paced the room, walking back and forth in front of her.

"I found out, Amy, that's all that matters in this world. Everybody is selfish. Everybody takes what he wants and the hell with anybody else. I found that out when I was a kid. I tried to be a nice guy. I wanted to get along with the other kids. All I asked was that they let me have what was mine. But I found out they wouldn't let me do that. When I tried to take what I wanted and what was mine, kids that were bigger than I was—wouldn't let me." Perspiration stood along his hairline, glistening at the carefully brushed widow's peak. "I took plenty of beatings. But I always got what I wanted. I always got back at them, maybe I didn't have any friends, but those bastards learned to think twice before they jumped me. There are plenty of ways of getting what you want, and keeping what you want. I keep what's mine, Amy. And you're mine."

She stared at him helplessly. Time was slipping past, and she didn't even know how to get rid of him.

He turned and glanced at Stella. "Mom, maybe you can see how it is with me. I was a lonely kid. I grew up in a house as crazy as any you ever heard of. My old man was a wild Indian—a stampeder who couldn't stand to be tied down—and all my mother wanted in this world was to tie him down. I guess she did. I guess he finally was tied down—and it killed him. If he had had what he wanted, he might be alive right now."

He heeled around and faced Amy, his deep eyes tortured. "I never wanted any other girl but you, Amy. All the others I knew were dirty and used and pawed-over. Running around with every man that asked them. Oh, I knew about them. But then you came along—young and fresh, not used. I knew I could have what I wanted—a girl no other guy ever had. You were young and I'd make you what I wanted you to be."

He laughed, a hurting sound in his throat. "I never forced you to marry me, Amy. You used to come to the studio to see me. Even when I told you I was too old for you, you came anyway. You were crazy about me. You wouldn't stay away from me, and you were what I wanted. We were married—and I'm going to keep you."

"I was a kid," Amy said, shaking her head. "I made a mistake. I—didn't love you. I knew right away I didn't. I tried to make a go of it.... You were selfish, and selfcentered, and you drank all the time."

"Why wouldn't I drink?" His voice rose slightly now, in his own defense. "A wife who didn't want me—the only girl I could love, and she didn't want me to touch her."

"All right, Burt. It's over. It was all a mistake and it's over, and let's forget it."

He shook his head. "It's not over, Amy. It never will be over. Maybe I made some mistakes. But I'm willing to try again."

"But I'm not." She spoke each word separately and coldly.

"Then, that's too bad, because you are going to."

"Burt, I've got a divorce. I'm free of you, and you can't make me do anything."

He laughed suddenly and dragged his hand across his mouth. "Oh, but baby, I can make you wish you had."

She stared at him a moment, then she turned on her heel and strode toward the bedroom.

He ran after her, caught her arm and spun her around. She stared down into his eyes, more conscious than ever that she was taller than he and that he resented it.

"I know what's the matter, Amy. You got some new man. That's been the trouble right from the first. It's like I told Mom here, I have to forgive you—you're just a kid. You don't know any better."

"There's nobody else, Burt."

"There's another guy."

"Don't start this, Burt."

"Who is he, Amy?" His voice was deadly, cold.

She shook her head, refusing to answer. Her eyes filled with tears. Her gaze struck against the dress box. She felt more helpless than ever.

"Burt, darling," Stella said. "It's like I told you—Amy hasn't had a date. She hasn't had one date, not the whole time."

His voice was savage. He spoke across his shoulder. "You stay out of this. How could you know what she's done? You told me you didn't even know she was getting a divorce! She doesn't even get home here until six o'clock. How do you know what she's been doing?"

"Maybe—maybe she's had to work late." Stella's voice was lame.

"I stopped to buy me a new dress." Amy spoke slowly and deliberately.

"Sure you did," Burt said. "Nothing like a new dress to please a new man, is there, Amy?"

He strode across to the table, ripped open the package, shook the dress out of it. He held it up. The knit dress looked sizes too small for Amy held up like that.

He made a moaning sound in his throat. "Why wear this, Amy? Why not go naked? That's what you want, isn't it? Show yourself off. Give men the hots."

"It's a pretty dress and I like it."

"Sure. A pretty dress to show what you've got—and a lot easier to get into than coveralls."

"Oh, Burt, love," Stella said. "I'm sure Amy doesn't feel that way."

"You don't know anything about her." Burt hurled the dress to the floor. He walked across it and caught Amy's arm. "Who brought you home, Amy?"

"Nobody."

"You lying slut. I stood at that window and saw his car. Saw you simpering at him like a two-bit tramp."

"All right. It was a boy who works at the plant. It's nobody important."

"Is that who you bought the dress to show off for, Amy? What's his name? You might as well tell me because I'll find out anyhow."

"Why don't you just find out then?"

She saw the vein throbbing in his temple, saw him clench his fist. His eyes were murderous. Only at the last minute was he able to keep from hitting her in the face.

"Who brought you home?" he said again.

"Why don't you tell him, Amy?" Stella said. "You're only upsetting him—"

"She's only driving me nuts."

"Burt has a right to know, dear," Stella's voice quavered.

Amy looked helplessly at her mother, wondering how she could believe this. She massaged her aching throat, pulled away from Burt and went toward the bedroom again.

"Where are you going?" Burt said.

"I'm going to wash my hands. You mind?"

Stella stood up. "Amy, you must make an effort to get along with Burt. He's been so upset that the army gave him a discharge. No wonder he's been out of his mind the way you treat him. Now, I'm sure if you just make an effort, you and Burt can patch up your differences and get along just fine."

Amy walked woodenly across the bedroom. Behind her, she could hear her mother's frightened voice speaking soothingly to Burt. Burt did not say anything to Stella.

Amy went into the bathroom and locked the door behind her. She sank to the floor and laid her head against the cool side of the tub. She felt the tears welling into her eyes, spilling. She did not touch her face.

She did not make any effort to prepare for her date with Terry. What was the sense in it? If she tried to leave, Burt might get violent, or if he let her go, he would follow her. Why get Terry mixed up in this ugly business?

At last she heard her mother knocking on the door. "Amy. Dinner is getting cold. Come on, dear. You'll feel better after you eat."

Amy went listlessly into the front room after she had washed and dried the dinner dishes. She sat on the divan.

Stella had her hat on. "I'll just run out and leave you two children alone," she said. She practically ran to the front door as though afraid they might stop her. She could not wait to escape them. Amy's mouth twisted bitterly. Who could blame her?

Burt came to the divan. Neither of them had eaten anything. His hands were shaking. He sat down beside her, and pushed his hand under her dress, caressing her leg. She felt her flesh quiver but she did not draw away. It did not matter what he did to her.

The kitchen clock struck softly, but the sound was loud in the apartment. It was seven o'clock. When Burt's hand moved, she pressed her legs tightly together, staring in front of her.

"Stop playing hard to keep, Amy. You know it tears me up."

"It's no act. I don't want to fight with you any more, Burt. But it's all over."

He tightened his fingers on the warm flesh of her leg. He closed his fingers until he forced her to cry out.

"You're wrong, baby. It's not ever going to be over. Not between us."

The long minutes ticked away. Burt tried to thrust his hand higher. She held herself rigidly. She kept her face straight, staring with wide dry eyes at the walls.

He said, "I missed you when I was in that army, baby. Sometimes I felt like I couldn't stand it."

She did not say anything.

"Is this the way you treat lover-boy, Amy?"

She held her breath, but did not speak. Her eyes brimmed with tears. Terry was downtown at the Congress Hotel, striding around in the lobby, looking for her.

"What's his name, Amy?"

In her imagination she could see Terry, dressed for the party, slicked up, his cowlick already toppling his tawny hair over his forehead. His eyes would be puzzled now, and showing his hurt.

"You wouldn't fight lover boy like this, would you, Amy?"

Suppose he called here, worried about her? Burt was waiting for something like that. He wouldn't allow her to answer the phone. Her heart pounded. Her gaze moved, touched the telephone.

"It's been a long time, Amy. I'm nuts wanting you."

She scarcely heard him.

"Of course, if you been loving on the back roads with lover boy— Is that why you don't want me to touch you, Amy?"

She closed her eyes tightly. After a moment, he laughed at her. He got up and went into the kitchen. Amy sat tensely, waiting to hear that telephone ring. If Terry called, her hell hadn't even begun. Burt would never stop until he learned the name of the man who called. She sat there, straining against the sound that would rip the silence of the room.

Burt returned with two cans of Stella's beer. He went over, snapped on the TV, and tuned in a boxing match. He held out a can of beer to Amy. When she didn't take it, he cursed her and pressed the chilled can into her hand.

"What's wrong, baby? We got all the comforts of home here. Stop fighting it, Amy. Stop fighting it and relax."

Why not? she thought suddenly. If she got drunk enough she could escape him. Stella could leave, but the only way Amy could escape was to drink so much she would not even know he was in the house. She turned up the beer can, drinking deeply. She was thinking, how does it work, Irene? How much must I drink before I don't care any more? How much will I need before Burt isn't Burt at all but just a nameless, faceless blob on this couch beside me?

That's how much I've got to have....

She lay sleepless most of the night. She could not get Terry out of her mind.

Sometime before dawn she swung out of bed. She found the knit dress wadded on the floor where Burt had hurled it last night.

Burt was sprawled out asleep on the divan. She moved stealthily. He did not waken.

She put the dress in the box, took her coveralls to the bathroom. In twenty minutes she let herself out of the apartment, carrying the dress box.

She ate breakfast downtown, sitting over a third cup of coffee until it was time to catch a bus to the plant.

She had been working an hour before she saw Terry. She stopped working, turned to face him, smiling. He tried to pull his wide mouth into the semblance of a smile but he did not come near her.

Her hands trembled and she dropped an appliance. She waited for him to come striding to her.

He let someone else pick it up, tag it "damaged" and return it upstairs. He pretended he didn't even see it.

She worked, watching for him. But he did not come near her all day.

At five she ran along the check-out line, pushing her way through the crowd, not hearing their protests. They didn't really care that she shoved in ahead of them. Women were often in a rush they didn't care to stop to explain. Today it was Reader, tomorrow it might be one of them. They were very tolerant.

She rang out, replaced her card, her hand trembling. Carrying her dress box, she ran through the double doors and went across the parking lot to Terry's car.

She was standing beside it when he got there.

"Terry."

"Hello."

"Terry, I'm so sorry I couldn't get there last night."

His mouth pulled. His eyes showed the pain, but he kept his voice level. "It's all right, Amy. I should have had better sense than to ask you in the first place."

Chapter 10

Terry gave her a curt nod, went around his car and got in. Amy was aware of people streaming past her to the other cars. She heard their laughter and calling to each other as though they were from another planet. They lived in a happy, untroubled world, and she was sealed away from them in time and space.

She moved her hand uncertainly and touched the door handle, opening the door beside her.

She lifted her head, meeting Terry's eyes in a half-frightened, questioning way.

"Will you take me home, Terry? Please?"

She saw the hurt darken his gray eyes. And she saw a lot of other things, too; the long empty time he had prowled the lobby of the Congress Hotel waiting for her; the time at last when he'd had to admit she wasn't coming but he had gone on waiting anyhow. She saw the lies he'd had to tell his parents when he met them finally at the church social.

She saw the way he had lain in his bed, sprawled on his back, staring at the darkened ceiling, thinking of all the neat and cutting things he would say to her the next time he saw her, and finally the decision that to say anything at all was prolonging the clown act. He had made his pitch, and this gal had fed him curves all the way. Well, he had to see her at work. This couldn't be avoided. There was one thing to do, keep out of her way, the way you'd jump aside for speeding trucks on the streets.

"Please, Terry?"

"Sure," he said. His voice was flat.

"I want to talk to you."

"Sure you do."

She perched on the edge of the seat, watching him. "Will you wait for me to get my things?"

"Haven't you got them?"

"I'm sorry, Terry. I ran out here to stop you before you got away. I was afraid to take time to stop at my locker."

He exhaled. Here was another slow-breaking curve, but he wasn't even going to offer at it.

"I'll wait."

"Are you in a hurry?"

"I said I'd wait."

She hurried across the parking lot toward the building employee's entrance. She opened her locker feverishly, got her purse and the dress box. She went running out to him.

She was breathless when she got in the car. Her face was flushed. He looked at her a moment, his eyes going over her flushed face in a soft way—but when their gazes crossed, his eyes went flat.

She put the box on the outside of the seat. She exhaled and took his hand in both of hers. He tried to move away, but she smiled and would not release him. He'd create a scene trying to pull his hand away. She knew him well enough by now. Terry Collier hated scenes.

"Terry."

"Okay, Amy. Okay. So your grandma died last night. You just couldn't make it."

She pressed his hand, smiling. "Something like that. I'm here now."

"That s nice."

"You aren't glad?"

"Sure, I'm pleased. You didn't stand me up last night after all. You're just a little late. About twenty-three hours late. Why wouldn't I be pleased?"

"Yes," Amy said. "It could have been much worse."

"There are only twenty-four hours in a day."

"Aren't you glad you waited?" She felt good being with him, a sense of unexplained elation, of well-being. It made her want to laugh, to make Terry laugh.

His face was bleak. "All right, Amy. I give up. What's the point? What you trying to do to me? You want me to yell uncle? Uncle! You want me to admit I been crazy about you since you walked into this place? I admit it. Now, you can go away and leave me alone."

"Why would I want to do that?"

"I don't know. But I sure don't know why not, either. I'm beat, Amy. If you get a strong charge from having guys all mixed-up about you, you've made your point here. Let up. I'm bleeding."

She had not released his hand.

Now she released her hold with her right hand, keeping her fingers locked in his, feeling the warmth, the strength of his hand. He did not pull away from her now.

She opened the box, thinking with a quick, sharp hurt of the way Burt had hurled the dress on the floor last night and walked on it. She shook the scene from her mind. She wouldn't think about it, and she wouldn't think about Burt, either.

She showed him the dress. "You like it?"

He looked it over. "Sure. What part of squaresville you think I come from? It's one of those dresses that cling to you like syrup, isn't it?"

"It's supposed to."

"Then why wouldn't I like it?"

"I look pretty in it. It's the one I bought last night."

"Yes." He exhaled. "After I got home, I sat around until midnight. I kept telling myself you'd call and say your grandma died or something."

"Oh, Terry, I'm sorry. But I am here now. And I brought along my new dress."

"It looks fine—even in the box."

"Terry. Will you take me somewhere tonight—if I wear it?"

He was silent, staring through the windshield.

"I never wore it for anybody else, Terry. I thought about you when I bought it. How it wouldn't look anything like tan coveralls."

Silence was between them for long moments, and then Terry exhaled. "Where do you want to go?"

"I don't care. Only, let's don't go home. Take me to a filling station and I'll put this dress on and comb my hair."

"What about me? I'm in my work clothes," he said.

"You look beautiful."

They ate supper in a lodge fifty miles from the city. The dining room was built on the banks of a swift-flowing creek. The waters of the creek had been walled in and flowed through the room which was lush with luxuriant lillies and waterflowers. Small bridges had been built across the creek linking the two sides of the dining area. The room was lighted with indirect tubes and wall candles. It glowed yellowly and they could see their reflections in the ceiling to floor glass walls.

"Why don't you tell me what it is that you've got against me?" Terry said. "I'm a pretty nice character. Dogs wag their tails. Children kick me—but they always smile when they kick me."

"You're a wonderful character."

"Yeah. Is that why you've fought me like virus pneumonia?"

She shook her head. She crumbled a roll in her plate, watching the way his reflection held its head in the glass.

"It isn't you I've fought, Terry. It's myself and what I know could happen to us if I let it. We could get very serious about each other."

"This is evil?"

"Yes."

"Boy. I been reading the wrong books."

"Terry. I've been married. I've been there. I've had it. I know what marriage is."

"Yeah? That sounds real interesting. Like out of the mouths of babes."

"You ever been married?"

"No."

"Then let me knock it. I feel about marriage the way Irene Haver does. Nobody cares about whether a man is married or not—except his own wife. Or if the man cares, the wife doesn't. Two people who care about each other can't seem to get together. They think they're going to be fine—and in a few years, the husband is Fred Hankins, dating every woman he can get his hands on."

His mouth pulled into a crooked smile. "You must be silly if you think I'm going to defend marriage."

"Oh?" She looked up, wise and young, and suspicious. "You got a better idea?"

He shook his head. "There isn't any better idea. Marriage doesn't need any defense. I mean, it isn't something that works automatically, like pushing a button. But if two people really want each other, and try—God never invented anything any better."

Her mouth pulled. "You've never been married. How do you know?"

"I've never had a barracuda bite my leg off, either, but I'm sure they could do it. Look, Amy, I've lived in the same house with my mother and father for all the years of my life—except when I was in the navy. I grant you, they're squares, old fashioned. But they love each other. Right now, today. Maybe it hasn't been easy. My old man never was a professional man, or a skilled laborer. He was a guy who went out and got a job and worked hard, and kept it as long as he could.

"And Ma? Hell, she saved money, just a little bit—even though there were six of us kids. Six of us, with oatmeal and eggs and milk for breakfast. But when Pa was out of work, she had a little bit of money put aside, and nobody helped them and they never asked for help. And they were too busy raising us kids to fight about other men, or other women, or crazy incompatibility because Pa was tired when he got home from work and didn't notice the way Ma fixed her hair, or didn't take her to dances, or maybe some other guy was better looking."

Amy looked at him, her gaze soft and warm. "That's fine for them, Terry. But it wasn't that way for my Ma. Or Irene. Or me."

"All right. So marriage is a jungle. I know Irene believes it's a jungle—she has to. If she didn't believe that, she'd be more lost than she is."

She started to speak but he cut her off. "Maybe it didn't work for you—or your mother. I'm not finding any fault. I'm not blaming you or your mother—or your husbands. Just ask yourself one thing, what did you want? Did you want that marriage to work—or did you want some magic time that would make everything easier for you?"

She bit her lip. "I wanted it to work—at first."

"And then?"

She shook her head, her eyes bright with tears. "He was insanely jealous, and he drank, and he was selfish. He wanted a brand new car whether we owed everybody or not. He had his clubs, and the dues, and the bills for buying drinks for everybody he thought could do him some favors."

"Boy. When you hate, you really hate, don't you?"

"I never wanted to."

"Maybe sometime I'll take you to meet my folks." He smiled at her.

"All right."

"They're squares. Might give you some laughs. But they'll love you—and that's what I really want."

"Stop it, Terry. Please."

"Okay. Then let's stop hating people and dance a little, shall we?"

Later, Terry parked his car outside the apartment where Amy lived with her mother. The street was a long dark tunnel with the wind tossing scraps of papers along the pavement. Trees rustled in the parkways. Most of the houses were dark. Even sitting close against Terry where she'd been all the way home, Amy was chilled. She shivered.

"What's the matter?" Terry said.

She did not answer. She was thinking that tonight made her more understanding of Irene Haver and the complex existence Irene found herself in. Irene had been married and had grown accustomed to going home to bed after an evening out. A kiss was not enough, a kiss left you dissatisfied and empty-stomached. All the juices that stirred in you were stirring and you were left incomplete and it drew your nerves taut, and you went wild, wondering what to do with yourself.

This was true of Irene and it was just as true of her. She was a divorcee, and this was one of the agonies a divorcee had to live with—unless she solved her problem the way Irene did, with faceless, nameless men from nameless bars, and enough to drink so their names and their faces didn't matter.

"Goodnight," she said. Her voice quavered. If she'd never been married at seventeen she would never have suspected the way an evening could end.

She moved away from him, but his hand on her shoulder pressed her back and she turned her face toward him, her eyes closing heavily. She felt suddenly drugged, with an ache across the bridge of her nose and an emptiness like a void around her heart.

His hand slipped under her upper arm, closed on her and she gasped a little at his touch. She felt the insides of her legs burn as if she were feverish. She twisted a little on the car seat trying to press her fevered body against him.

She stopped, was able to stop only when she struck the steering wheel and realized where she was. She was a divorcee. She did not belong to this man, and if she were abandoned with him, he would believe like every man had since Adam that she was like this with all men.

Right now she thought she was crazy about Terry. She had thought she was crazy about Burt, too, a long time ago in this same wild way. Maybe this was what was wrong. Maybe Burt was right about her, maybe she was no good, maybe any man could push her over, and she had to justify it within herself by thinking she was in love with him.

Maybe it had been like this with Irene at first.

"Oh," she moaned in her throat.

She pulled away from the heat of his mouth, slid across the seat.

She felt cold this far from his arms. "Goodnight," she said.

"Will I see you again?" His voice had the faint touch of panic in it.

"Yes—of course."

She slammed the door and ran across the walk, her heels clicking on the pavement. She heard Terry start his car and move away.

Burt grabbed her from the darkness of the foyer. He clapped his hand over her mouth to keep her from screaming. She held herself tense, staring at him, eyes distended.

His voice quavered with rage. "Boy! You really had to work late tonight."

She made a sound against the palm of his hand.

"Got on your slut's dress, I see." His voice shook. He snagged her dress front in his trembling fist and ripped it. "But you're not going to wear it any more. I told you. I told you last night."

He was shaking all over and his voice was quavering so badly he could hardly speak.

He thrust her back against the wall, held her there with her head pinned against it. His eyes were tormented. "The guy. The guy, Amy. Who is he? What's his name?"

She shook her head. His left hand slipped down from her mouth, closed on her throat. He clenched his shaking fist and poised it before her eyes.

She spoke through her choked throat. "If you hit me, I'll scream, Burt. I'll never stop screaming."

He banged her head against the wall, his fingers closed on her throat.

"You'll regret this, Amy," he said. His body shook, wracked with his dry, helpless sobbing. "You're going to regret it almost as much as lover boy."

They stayed there for a timeless eternity staring into each other's eyes. His fist tightened on her throat so she gulped loudly for air and then he released her. She wavered a moment, but supported herself against the wall.

He stared at her torn dress and exposed breast. Woodenly she lifted her arm and held the torn dress against her shoulder.

He heeled about suddenly and strode down the steps. She did not know how long she stayed there. At last, when she could no longer hear his footsteps on the pavement she moved away from the wall and tiredly climbed the stairs.

Chapter 11

Terry was waiting for Amy outside the plant exit the next afternoon at five. She came through the doors with Irene. When she saw Terry, her heart sank.

Irene smiled. "See you, kid."

She moved away to walk alone to the bus stop. But Amy caught her arm. "Wait a minute."

Irene stared at her. "You nuts?"

"Please. Just wait." She had to whisper this, Terry was coming toward them smiling.

"Hi," Terry said.

"Who's this character?" Irene said.

"Could I drive you home, Amy?" Terry said.

Amy's mouth was dry. She hated the puzzled hurt that she would see in Terry's gray eyes. But since last night she could not get Burt's threat out of her mind. She did not want to get Terry involved in something that would get him hurt. There was no way to know what Burt would do. And certainly Burt would be watching to see who brought her home from work.

“Not tonight,” Amy said, trying to smile. “I promised I’d stop off with Irene.”

“Fine,” he said. “I’ll take both of you.”

Amy chewed her lip. “Not this time, Terry. You mind?”

He winced. She saw the way he shivered slightly. He tried to smile. “Sure,” he said.

They watched him walk away to his car. Amy moved toward the bus stop. Irene was regarding her as if she didn’t know how to get off a psychiatrist’s couch.

“What’s happened to you?”

“I don’t want to—” Amy stopped. “I don’t want to get too serious with Terry, that’s all.”

“Oh, fine. You got so many boy friends? Maybe you’ll toss me your rejects.” Irene glanced over her shoulder. “You can start with Collier.”

“Let’s hurry,” Amy said. “We’ll miss the bus.”

Irene shook her head, still puzzled. “We sure will,” she said in a hollow voice.

Stella was preparing dinner when Amy got home.

Amy dropped her purse on the living-room couch. She stood in the kitchen doorway. Stella’s eyes were swollen. She had been crying.

“Mom. What’s the matter?”

Stella sniffled, went on punching a fork at the three pork chops in the electric fry pan. Wisps of steam flowed upward past her cheeks.

“What is it, Mom? What you doing home so early?”

“Why not?” Stella said. “I lost my job.”

“You’re joking.” Amy remembered she had been afraid this had happened the day she arrived here from the army base town after she’d left Burt. But she hadn’t truly believed it then. Mom was a fixture at Troxler’s. Down there people said Stella had been at Troxler’s longer than the marble-topped soda bar. Troxler was an old-time druggist who puttered among his mortars, pestles and powders. Stella ran the place.

“No. I’m not joking. He just fired me. Just told me to go home. Oh, he gave me two weeks pay. But he said I wouldn’t need to work any more.”

“Why?”

“He didn’t say why. He wouldn’t even talk about it.”

“Mom. There’s some mistake. There’s got to be.”

“Sure. After all the years I’ve been there.”

“Why don’t you call him? Make him tell you why.”

“I did call him. After I got home. He wouldn’t talk to me.”

Amy shook her head. “This doesn’t sound like Doc at all.”

Stella made a sniffling sound, but did not answer. Her voice sounded full of tears when she finally spoke. "Dinner is almost ready. You better get washed up."

The doorbell rang and Amy's heart sank. She did not doubt who was there. She glanced at her mother, but Stella sniffled and jerked her head toward the living room.

"You better answer it, Amy."

Amy opened the door only enough to see that it was Burt standing there. He wore a cold and twisted smile.

"What do you want?"

He laughed. "Can't I come in?"

"Mom doesn't feel well."

"She won't mind if I come in. I came over to dinner. It's all right. She asked me to." His mouth pulled again, and Amy stared at him, feeling intuitively that something was very wrong. Burt seemed entirely too pleased with himself.

She tried to tell herself perhaps it was only that Burt had been out at the plant parking lot and seen that she rode the bus home. Perhaps he was certain his threat had frightened her. This was true. She was more afraid for Terry than for herself.

She stepped aside and Burt entered the living room. Stella put the pork chops on the table along with mashed potatoes, an apple salad and green peas. She gave Burt a wry smile. "Hello, Burt dear, won't you sit down?"

Burt sat down at the dining table as though he belonged there, as if he intended being here as long as Amy insisted upon staying in her mother's apartment.

As soon as Stella sat down at the table, she looked at Burt, trying to smile. "I wanted to talk to you, Burt. You're such a good friend of Doc Troxler's. Maybe you could do something."

Burt glanced at Amy, and there was a faint smile about his eyes. He pursed his mouth, waiting, listening.

"Why? What's up, Mom?" he said.

"Troxler fired me today."

Burt's gaze raked Amy's again, and he pulled his mouth into a grimace of pained surprise. "Gosh, I'm sorry to hear that. I never thought he'd fire you. After all these years."

"Yes," Stella said, "after all these years."

"What could you have done to make Doc mad?"

"I didn't do anything. I know I didn't. That's why I want you to talk to him."

Burt pursed his lips again. "I'm certainly sorry to hear you had trouble."

Amy flared. "She didn't have any trouble. She just got fired. Without explanation."

"Now, Amy." Burt looked as if he would laugh. He kept his face averted from Stella. He was staring into Amy's eyes. "It must be something. Doc Troxler wouldn't fire someone like your mother just for no reason at all."

"Well, maybe he wouldn't. But he did," Amy said. "If he'll listen to you, you could talk to him. At least, you could find out for Mom why she was fired."

"Well, I don't know," Burt said.

"Please, Burt," Stella said. "Something is wrong. Why, you should have seen Doc's face. It was deadly white. He hardly wanted to talk to me." She faced Burt again. "Couldn't you just talk to him, Burt?"

Burt spoke to Stella, but his gaze was fixed intently upon Amy. "Maybe I could fix it up for you, Mom," he said. "That is—if Amy wants me to—if Amy thinks I ought to interfere—if Amy wants me to speak to your boss, I mean."

Amy's heart was slugging. Her throat grew tight and she felt ill with her unfounded suspicions.

"What have I got to do with it?" she whispered.

Stella spoke emptily, "Why, of course Amy wants you to do whatever you can for us, Burt."

He hadn't moved his gaze from Amy's face. "Do you, Amy?"

She could not fathom what kind of blackmail this was. "Of course I want you to help her get her job back."

Burt sighed expansively as though something between them were all settled. He helped himself to potatoes, a pork chop and peas. He ate hungrily.

Amy, staring at him, was unable to eat at all.

"You'll call him?" Stella said.

Burt patted her hand. "Eat your supper, Mom. You got nothing to worry about. You know there's nothing I wouldn't do for Amy. Amy wants me to help you. I'll help you, because I can't fail Amy. You got your job back."

Amy demanded, "What have I got to do with it?"

Stella shook her head at Amy warningly, silently pleading with her to go along with Burt. Burt's smile was pulling at his mouth again. There was a streak of grease on his pretty chin. Amy wanted to spit at him. She lowered her gaze and did not speak.

Burt said, "I'm sure the old man was hasty today, Mom. He couldn't do without you. Go back to work tomorrow."

Amy swallowed the lump in her throat. The way Burt said this, it was as though it were all in his hands, rather than a decision Doc Troxler should make.

"I couldn't do that," Stella said. "You don't know how he acted. Won't you call him tonight?"

Burt shrugged. "Sure. If that's what you and Amy want."

He pushed away from the table, went to the telephone. He dialed the drugstore number without even looking it up.

When Troxler finally came to the phone, Burt said, "Hey, Doc. That little matter we were talking about. Looks like it was all a mistake. Yeah, just talk." He listened for a long time, finally he said, his voice sharp, "Well, it was all just talk, and she's coming back to work in the morning."

He replaced the receiver. He had not taken his gaze off Amy's face all during his conversation. Stella looked on the brink of hysterical tears. "What was it, Burt? He told you about it?"

Burt thrust his tongue in his cheek. "Oh, he mentioned it to me this afternoon. But the whole thing was just talk. Just some drug salesman got drunk and—"

Stella was standing up. She had knocked over her chair. "Burt, you've got to tell me what it is that man said. Who was it? What salesman? What was his name?"

"Mom. I'm telling you. You're making a big thing out of it. It's nothing. Now forget it and go back to work in the morning."

Burt wanted Amy to go for a drive after she'd finished the dishes. She agreed. She waited only until they were in the car. Her voice was choked. "Burt, you got my mother fired."

He shrugged, not even bothering to deny it. "What the hell? I got it back for her, didn't I?"

"You blackened her reputation, Burt. You told some horrible lies about her. So terrible that old man Troxler believed them."

Smiling, Burt drove along the street. He seemed more pleased than ever with himself. "Only that some drug salesman was bragging in a bar that he had Stella on one of the tables in back of the drugstore after closing hours—that they went back there every time he was in town."

She wanted to hit him. Her arm trembled. She knotted her hands in her lap.

"Burt, you can't lie about people like that. Ruin their lives."

"Can't I?"

"And then come and eat her supper as though nothing is wrong."

"Nothing is wrong now, Amy."

"Nothing except that you've lied about my mother. Dirty, awful lies, that turned Doc Troxler against her after all these years."

"I had to do it, Amy."

"How can you say such a thing?"

He slowed the car. His voice was chilled. "I had to show you, Amy."

"Show me what?" Her voice was hollow.

"What could happen—what will happen if you don't stay away from lover boy."

She shook her head. She whispered. "You're crazy, Burt—insane."

"If I am, Amy, you drove me that way. It's your fault. No matter what happens. It's your fault. Don't forget it."

Chapter 12

On Friday, Terry was waiting for Amy outside the plant exit.

"Amy." His voice was chilled. She shook her head, wanting to run. But this time Irene said nothing, only walked rapidly away. It was as though she and Terry had agreed upon this strategy between them.

She tried to smile at him. Terry was hurt, and she didn't want him hurt. The harder she tried to stay away from him, the more he was in her mind. She dreamed about him, and when she was away from Burt, she began to plan how she might see Terry after all. She needed to see him. She needed the warmth she felt when he was near.

"I've asked you five times this week to let me take you home," Terry said. "Once more can't hurt. Only this time, if you say no, I'm going to carry you out to the car. So why don't you smile and say yes real sweetly?"

She smiled, but it was empty. She said yes, but her gaze searched the huge parking lot, looking for Burt's convertible.

"I want you to meet my folks," Terry said.

"Oh, Terry, why?" She was miserable, watching the cars behind them while she pretended not to.

His voice remained level. He let the other speeding cars race past them. "Because I think they ought to meet the girl I'm going to marry."

"Oh, Terry." She cried this out, feeling the prickling of perspiration about her face and throat.

"It's true," his voice remained matter of fact. "I might not have known so soon, but all this week, without you—after I kissed you that night—I haven't got you out of my mind. I'll make you happy, Amy."

"Terry. You've got to let me go."

His voice lowered. "I'm listening, Amy. Tell me why."

The sounds of the cars and trucks speeding past were loud. Exhaust fumes made the late afternoon gray. She heard sudden bursts of laughter from cars passing, sounds abruptly loud, and abruptly gone. She did not answer at once. How could she tell him about Burt? How could she make him understand the fear she felt? If she told him about Burt he might try to do something about him—and she shivered with this thought.

"I don't love you, Terry," she said at last.

"You'll have to do better than that. A lot better. I know better than that. And you know better."

"I don't want to love you."

He smiled, his voice tender. "Maybe I didn't want to love you at first, either. But there it is—only it isn't anything you can talk about, Amy. Not like this. Not casually. I love you like people are supposed to love. I love you like nobody else loves, because nobody else is me."

Tears brimmed her eyes, spilled along her cheeks.

"Oh, Terry. No."

"Look. You got married once. You made a mistake. Maybe I been wrong once or twice, but that doesn't mean I've got to give up trying. We'll do everything right—only, for God's sake, try."

"Oh, Terry."

"You're repeating yourself."

"I—don't know what else to say. I can't marry you, Terry. I can't see you any more."

His voice chilled. "Are you—giving me the business about something, Amy? You are divorced. I know that. Just as I know there's nobody else. Just as I know you do love me. Something is wrong. Tell me about it."

"I can't, Terry. Not now, I can't."

"Then I'm not going to let you go until you agree to come meet my folks."

Finally, Amy spread her hands. "All right, Terry. I will. Tomorrow night."

He didn't bother talking with her all the rest of the way to her apartment. He was still singing when she told him good-bye.

She had crossed the walk and was almost at the building entrance when she heard a car careen into the curb behind her, brakes screeching.

Burt stared up at her a moment then slammed the car into drive, going in pursuit of Terry's car. Frantically Amy searched the street ahead of Burt's convertible. Terry lived the opposite way across town. He had already turned off the street and was doubling back. She stood rigid, listening to Burt's engine race, the squeal of his tires as he went around the corner.

She did not move. She remained there at the side of the door. In less than three minutes Burt returned, brakes screeching again when he stopped at the curb. The convertible rocked for a moment after he killed the engine.

Burt leaped out of the car and ran across the walk. He strode up the steps to her.

"All right, Amy. The guy. Who is he?"

She met his gaze levelly, didn't answer.

"The guy's name, Amy. Tell me his name. This is my wife he's crossing me with. He's busted up my little family and I want to talk to him about it."

"I'm not your wife, Burt."

He caught Amy's arm and twisted it, thrusting her into the apartment foyer ahead of him. Some children were standing watching them from the walk. The whole street was suddenly quiet, the way it is at dinner time. He was hurting her. She did not protest. She tried to keep the pain out of her face. She walked ahead of him up the stairs.

Going up the steps, his voice was low and sounded labored as though he were out of breath. "You can make it a lot easier on yourself, Amy. You can tell me his name. Because I got the word for you. You're quitting that job out there. I already called them and told them you were. I told them I was your husband and you asked me to call."

She caught her breath but did not say anything. They crossed the corridor and he motioned her to unlock the door. She unlocked it, pushed it open and stepped inside. He struck her suddenly on the side of the head and she staggered, moaning, and fell on the couch. She did not move. Burt growled something and strode toward her. Then he looked up and saw Stella in the kitchen doorway.

Burt stood there motionless. His fists unclenched and he dropped his hands to his sides. His face was white.

Amy watched him from the couch. She did not bother to look at Stella. Her mother had seen the way Burt hit her. Burt did not care what he did, but he must be justified, he must justify himself with any witnesses.

"I begged her, Mom," he cried out. "But she goes out with these men. Men she picks up, Mom. I can't stand it. You don't think I want to hit her, do you?"

Stella looked at him for a long time. "I don't know, Burt," she said at last. "All I know is that Mr. Troxler admitted to me today who told him what that drug salesman was supposed to have said."

Burt paced to the window. He stood there with his head cocked, staring into the street. He would move his head back and forth every few minutes as if talking silently to himself, justifying himself, telling himself that he was right and the rest of them were wrong.

"Mom, he must have been joking," he said finally. He turned from the window with a sick grin on his face.

"He wasn't joking, Burt. You lied to him about me."

"You crazy, Mom? Why would I do a thing like that? A drug salesman did tell me that. In—a bar. He did—"

"What was his name, Burt?" Stella said.

"Oh—I don't know. Some guy. Told me. I happened to mention it to old Troxler. Yeah. I mentioned it to him. As a joke. As a joke, for hell's sake. But Old Troxler took me serious."

"Why don't you get out of here?" Amy said to him.

His white face went taut. He spun on his heel. "That's got nothing to do with us, Amy. Nothing. This salesman told me and—"

"Stop lying, Burt," Amy said.

"That don't change that you're two-timing me with some guy at the plant. I want his name."

"There's nobody, Burt. And if there were, I wouldn't have anything to say to you."

Burt flopped into a reading chair. "What the hell then?" he said. "We might as well get comfortable. We're going to be here a long time."

They ate supper in silence. Afterwards, Stella got dressed. "Doc wants me to work tonight," she said. She looked at Amy. "Will you be all right?"

Amy spread her hands. "Why not? What can he do to me he hasn't already done?"

Burt jumped up. "You can stop blaming me. Why you blaming me? Whatever happens, it's your fault. You're my wife. If you want to settle down and act like a wife and stop cheating on me, we don't have to have any trouble."

Amy stared at him and did not speak. After a moment, Stella exhaled. She touched Amy's shoulder. "I won't be late," she said.

When the door closed behind her, Burt sat on the couch beside Amy. She tried to get up but he caught her arms, pressed her back. "Stop treating me like this, Amy. I'm going nuts."

"Burt, let me alone."

His hands tore at her clothing. His breath was hot against her face. "What's the matter? You wish I was lover boy?"

"Let me alone."

"You know what I'd do if he walked in here right now, don't you? I'd break him apart. You know that."

"Stop talking like this, Burt. Just stop coming here."

"Why? What will you do? Tell lover-boy?"

Amy looked around, feeling trapped. There was nothing she could do against him, and yet she would not be treated like this the rest of her life.

Her head tilted. She glanced at the telephone. "I'll tell the police. I swear it. You've no right to come here like this."

His mouth twisted. He got up, walked to the telephone. He checked a number on the inside cover of the phone book and dialed, watching Amy. After a moment, he said, "Police department? Just a moment."

He held out the receiver.

She stared at it, thinking that if she told the police there would be trouble, notoriety, but maybe she could keep Burt away. Amy took the telephone.

Burt stood with his body pressed close against hers, his hands kneading her body as she tried to talk. "Hello, police department?" A man said yes. "A man is here and refuses to leave." She gave her address.

She replaced the receiver.

Burt caught a handful of her hair, bent her face back, talked against her cheek, his breath hot and sharp. "That's fine. Now shall we get real comfortable till they get here?"

He smashed his mouth over hers. She fought, feeling the revulsion making her ill. Burt laughed at her. "Got to give you something to tell the cops."

Abruptly she knew she'd been wrong even to accept his dare and talk to the police. She could not say why but she knew Burt had trapped her, though she could not think how. He had been too anxious to have her call police. She was breathless with fear. He ran his hands over her, mussed her dress as her hair was mussed.

The knock at the door came more quickly than she had believed it could. The police must have been cruising in the neighborhood.

Amy tried to straighten her clothes but Burt caught her arm, dragged her after him across the room. He opened the door.

The detective came in, looking the apartment over. He knew Burt and nodded to him. He showed his badge. "Where is he? The guy that forced his way in here."

Burt said, "What is this, Officer Blakeney?"

The detective hesitated. "We got a complaint. A man forced his way into this apartment, wouldn't leave."

Burt laughed. He glanced at Amy, his mouth twisting in contempt. "I'll be damned. So that's your cheap racket, is it?"

"What's this?" the detective said.

Burt handed him his business card. "She invited me up here, Officer Blakeney. We were married—she, well, she stepped out on me. Men. I hate to talk about it. We had to get a divorce. I wanted to give her alimony. But the courts didn't award her any. I guess she's had it tough. I didn't think she'd try to force money out of me this way. I'm sorry, Officer, but this looks like a shakedown."

"That's not true," Amy cried. But she could not look at the officer's face. He was solidly aligned behind Burt. Burt was a business man. She knew how she looked after Burt had worked her over. She knew how the apartment looked, and what the detective thought, what Burt wanted him to think.

"I want you to arrest us, Blakeney," Burt's voice was very sorrowful.

"Now wait a minute," the detective said.

"No. If she thinks I'll pay her to avoid notoriety that might harm my business, well she's wrong.... She asked me up here.... That makes her guilty of something. Doesn't it, Blakeney?"

"Plenty." The detective touched Amy's arm. "Let's go, sister."

Amy shook her head. "It's not what you think. It's all a mistake."

"A mistake can't be settled so easily," the cop said. "Procuring is a crime—"

"I wasn't. I wasn't!"

"We'll let the judge decide that."

Burt's voice was shocked and low-keyed. "She was—well, she was like this with men—before the divorce. But I never thought she'd get so—"

Tears streamed down Amy's face. "Please listen to me."

The detective said, "You dames always scream when you get yourselves in a mess."

Burt removed a fifty dollar bill from his wallet, creased it, put it with his card. His voice sounded injured. "I can't drag her any lower, Blakeney. Here. You know me. You know my business. You know where you can find me. You know I'm too intelligent to offer you this as a bribe. This is for your trouble. After all, she—well, she was my wife. And, well, you wouldn't have a case unless I signed a complaint, would you?"

Blakeney considered for half a minute. He took the money and the card, pocketed them. "No, Mr. Reader. I guess not." His gaze moved over Amy, remembering her, already seeing her as a name in the vice card files. "Watch your step in this town, sister. You owe Mr. Reader plenty. Next time—I'll really fix you."

He walked out, closed the door behind him. Amy turned and walked woodenly back to the divan. She sank down upon it, pressing her head against it, burying her fevered face. Her lips felt numb and her arms were leaden.

Burt stood over her. "Any smarter now, Amy? You learned your lesson yet?"

She barely moved her head. God help her, she'd learned. She was helpless against him. She was too tired to fight him any more.

Chapter 13

That night Amy slept only fitfully. She was out of bed, haggard and bone-weary before six the next morning. She had breakfast prepared when Stella came out of the bedroom.

Stella looked at her, worried. "Amy, you—you look older than I am this morning."

Amy shook her head. "I am older."

"There must be something you can do, Amy."

Amy's laugh was flat. "Oh, so now you admit that maybe—just maybe I was right."

Stella sighed. "I was thinking, Amy. Maybe you could go away. Somewhere. It doesn't matter where. For a while."

Amy spoke to the tabletop, her voice flat and without hope. "Where would I go that he wouldn't follow me?"

"There must be something you can do, Amy."

"Sure. There is. I can marry him again. I can be Mrs. Burt Reader again." She stared at the ceiling, eyes brimmed with tears. "Why not? What difference does it make?"

"Amy. There must be something."

But her voice was weak. Her mother was as helpless as she was. They did not speak again. Stella piled the breakfast dishes in the sink and had to have another cup of black coffee before she could go to work at all.

Irene rang the doorbell and Amy went with her down the steps. They went along the walk toward the bus stop. Amy saw Burt's car parked at the curb, awaiting them. She looked around for somewhere to run. There was no place to hide.

Burt leaned across the seat. "Where you going, Amy?"

"We're going to work," Irene told him when Amy did not answer.

"I thought I told you, Amy. I called those people yesterday. I told them my wife was quitting."

"That's fine," Amy said. "And I'll just tell them I don't have any husband."

"You don't know when you're well off, do you, Amy?"

He swung his door open. "Get in. I'll drive you to work."

Irene moved to get in the car. Amy caught her arm.

"Get in," Burt said.

Amy bit her lip. She shrugged. She got into the car, and Irene sat beside her. Irene was puzzled but she said nothing, watching the buildings flow past.

Burt said, "You like your job, Irene?"

"Oh, sure. It's a job."

"But you're not crazy about it, like Amy? I mean, she's got this guy out there she's nuts about. She has to go to work there. You know, what's his name—?"

Amy caught her breath, squeezed Irene's arm. But she was too late. Irene laughed. "You mean Terry?"

"Terry?" Burt savored the name on his lips. "A boss, eh?"

"Terry Collier," Amy said, her voice cold. "He's our boss. All the women are crazy about him. Aren't they, Irene?"

"Oh, sure," Irene said.

Burt parked near the employee's entrance. He said, voice meaningful, "So long, Irene. Amy'll be in soon."

"I'll wait," Irene said.

"So long, Irene." Burt's voice was cold. "Beat it." When she was gone he said, "Terry Collier. Funny how long it took me to latch on to that name. He must be a real stampeder, huh? How old is he? What does he look like? Where does he take you to bed down?"

"I've got to go, Burt. I'll be late."

"Got to hurry to lover boy?"

She couldn't take it any more. She slapped down on the door handle. She moved to get out. Burt caught her arm. "In a hurry to get to Terry-boy—the lover-boy?"

"Let me alone, Burt. Let him alone."

"Worried about lover boy?"

He reached past her, snapped open the glove compartment. She saw the black-gleaming automatic before he pulled it from the compartment and held it in his fist.

"Why have you got that thing?" she said.

"A man needs a gun, that's all. A man has to protect his wife from men that won't leave her alone."

"Not even you would use that thing."

"No. Not if you behave yourself. It's no crime to use it, Amy, if a man is protecting his little home—if that's the only way he can protect it."

She stared into his face. He laughed suddenly. She wrenched free.

"You think about it, Amy." His voice taunted her.

Her throat felt dry and taut and she could not swallow. She slammed the door behind her and ran from him across the parking lot....

Burt was waiting for her at five that afternoon, sitting in his convertible in the parking lot. His car was the first thing Amy saw when she came out of the building walking with Terry.

The breathless heat struck her in the face after leaving the air-conditioned building. The brilliance of the sun made her squint her eyes, its whiteness was a sharp pain.

She pretended not to see Burt or his car. He blew his horn once but she did not turn her head.

She got in Terry's car, holding her breath. She knew Burt had started his car and was sitting there, waiting for them. Terry got under the wheel, started the car and backed around, moving in the sluggish traffic toward the lot exit and the highway into town.

She saw Burt try to bull his convertible into the line behind her, but the car back of Terry's wouldn't give way. Drivers out here were too accustomed to this attempt to give way when they had a place in the crowded exit lanes.

"Terry." She was astonished at the odd quality of her own voice. "I've got to talk to you. I've got to tell you something I should have told you a long time ago."

"You love me?" He smiled. "I been waiting a long time to hear that, all right."

"Terry. I'm in trouble. If I keep seeing you, I may get you in trouble."

"Okay, honey. Tell me about it. I've known all along something was from left field. Tell me about it."

She glanced out the rear window of the car wondering what she could tell Terry that would make sense. How could she tell him that Burt would not recognize the divorce, would not let her alone? How could she tell him that she was mortally afraid of Burt—as much for Terry as for herself?

"My ex-husband, Terry. He won't let me alone. He wants me to remarry him."

"Do you want to?"

"I want to marry you," she cried out. "But I'm afraid, Terry. I don't know what he might do. Couldn't we run away? Couldn't we go away together—where he couldn't find us?"

Terry put his arm around her, pulled her against him. "Why should we run, Amy? We haven't done anything."

She cried out suddenly. Burt's convertible was a blur moving past them. Abruptly Burt jerked his convertible to the right trying to force them off the road.

Terry slammed on brakes, pulling his car just enough to the right to avoid being sideswiped.

"It's Burt," she whispered. "He's—trying to run us off the road."

"Let him. I used to drive drag races—a long time ago when I didn't have any more sense than he just showed."

"He hasn't any sense. He'll do anything to hurt us."

A car ahead had forced Burt into the outer lane again. He was slowing, trying to wait for them. Car horns set up a caterwauling behind him because both lanes were crowded to capacity in the five o'clock rush.

The inside lane moved forward suddenly and Terry stepped on the gas. As he drew near the rear of Burt's convertible, Burt began weaving it toward them. Terry slowed and then stepped hard on the gas, gliding past Burt who was caught between two cars in his lane. Burt pulled suddenly into the right lane and car horns wailed in protest two blocks back of them.

Behind them, Terry and Amy suddenly heard the scream of a police siren. They waited, watching the highway, but they did not see Burt again.

"Cops got him," Terry said.

"That—won't help any. It will only make him madder than ever."

"You got to stop being scared of him, Amy."

"How can I?"

"Marry me—and I'll take care of you."

"If I married you, I'd only get you hurt."

"Let me worry about that. You can't go on like this, Amy. You look ill. Now, listen to me. I told Mom I was bringing you home tonight. I'll pick you up at eight. Mom has got all the family coming. It's a real party. I haven't talked about anything but you for the past eight months. They're all crazy to meet you. We'll tell them we're going to be married. Right away. Only you got to mean it, Amy. You can't go on like this—and you got to let me take care of you."

"Can't we—go away somewhere?"

"We don't have to run away, Amy. All you got to do is start trusting me. Just a little bit."

She nodded, her face streaked with tears. "What a crazy proposal," she said. "What a crazy way to get married."

"I don't care how I get you. Just so I get you."

She nodded again. "All right, Terry. I will marry you. I don't care what happens. I'm so tired. You got to fight for me now."

"It's a pleasure," he said.

Terry parked outside the apartment house. He held her tear-stained face in his hands and kissed. "Stop worrying, baby. You're going to be all right." His voice was soft and gentle, and reassuring.

There was the screech of tires, the scream of brakes. Burt pulled so sharply in front of Terry's car that he dented Terry's front fender, crumpling it in.

He jumped out of his car, ran around on the side walk lunging toward Terry who was getting out of his car.

"There you are!" Burt's voice was raging. "Why don't you let her alone? This is my wife. You're breaking up my little home, you son of a bitch."

He caught at Terry's shirt, twisting it, sobbing and hitting at him.

Terry caught Burt's wrists, twisted them, until Burt stopped struggling and stood with his wrists held upward and parted, staring up at Terry.

Watching them, Amy felt her heart sink. She remembered what Burt's mother had told her. The boys who overcame Burt physically suffered cruelly, and suddenly remembering that, seeing the way Burt stopped fighting, Amy was more afraid than she had ever been in her life. She had never even known before what fear could be.

She backed away unable to speak.

Terry kept his voice low. It was almost gentle. "I don't want any trouble with you, fellow. All Amy's got to do is tell me she doesn't want to see me, that will stop me. But nothing you can say will stop me. It's real simple. Amy and I are going to be married. Now, I don't want any trouble with you, but I won't run from it. So, if I see you again—or if Amy says you've been bothering her. Well, look, fellow, just get smart and let Amy alone. Just do that. Just let her alone."

Burt whimpered, that agonized voice justifying himself, putting himself in the right, everybody else in the wrong. "I love her. She's my wife. You don't know what she's done to me—"

"I don't want to know."

"She'll tell you I drink. I don't want to drink. But she—I can't help it, what she does to me. I can't live if I don't drink."

"We all got it tough."

"Maybe she tells you I hit her. Wait until she steps out on you. Wait until she's done to you what she's done to me—you'll know I'm in hell."

Terry released Burt's wrists and stepped back away from him.

"You got it real tough, fellow. So maybe you better go somewhere and get yourself a drink. I'm going to stand right here until you're gone. I'm not even going to say anything about that fender. You have a drink, you'll feel better. But you make any more trouble, I'm going to take out the cost of that fender—from your face. Do you understand me?"

Burt backed away. He tossed one quick glance at Amy and then he was in his car. He roared away, weaving down the street.

Amy walked woodenly to Terry. "I'm afraid," she said. "You don't know him, Terry."

"He's not my type. I don't want to know him."

"He's dangerous."

"Amy, he's just a pretty boy who isn't used to people not doing everything he tells them to do. Get him out of your mind. I'll be back at eight. I love you, Amy. You got nothing to worry about."

She stood there, chilled in the dying sunlight. Terry had to straighten the fender off his front tire enough so it would turn. Amy shook her head. This wasn't the end of anything, only Terry believed people were civilized. Terry just didn't know.

Chapter 14

For a long time Amy sat on the living-room divan and stared at the telephone. Terry would be home by now. She had to call him and tell him she was not coming to the party, not going to see him any more.

Her eyes blurred with tears. She loved Terry, and she had a right to be happy. If she let Terry go, she was throwing away her chance to be happy, and she knew this for sure now. If she were ever going to be sure she loved anyone—she knew that Terry was made for her.

The telephone rang beside her and she trembled. For a moment she could not even reach over and lift the receiver. It rang again, and finally the sound was no longer frightening.

It was Stella. "Amy, I'm working late tonight. I won't be home to dinner. Will you be all right?"

"Yes. Fine." It was on the tip of Amy's tongue to tell Stella she wouldn't be home, either, she was invited to meet Terry's parents. But she did not say it. She was afraid that Stella might tell Burt.

She got up tiredly, undressing as she went through the bedroom. She stepped out of her clothes and took a warm shower. The room grew steamy, and she felt more tired than ever. She turned the water on full cold, feeling the stinging spray against her bare flesh.

She turned off the shower, stepped out on the bath mat. She stared at her reflection in the full length door mirror. For a long time she did not move. She was still young, her flesh pink and fresh and firm. Her breasts stood round and did not sag. She tried to tell herself she was new, but it was not true. She was used—Burt had used her, and Terry deserved better. She was bringing him trouble, too.

Her eyes stung with tears. She went into the bedroom and dressed slowly. It occurred to her she should eat something but she was not hungry. As she made up her face, she paused, meeting her own gaze.

"Stop being afraid, Amy," she told herself. Her voice was savage. "You've a right to be happy. Only, you've got to do what you want to do."

Her smile was faint, and it pulled at her newly made-up mouth. That was simple enough. She knew what she wanted to do all right. She wanted to marry Terry. She wanted to make Terry happy.

For a moment longer she did not move, thinking about this. When she'd married Burt she hadn't known what she wanted, except the excitement of being married. What had Terry asked her? Had she really wanted her marriage to succeed? She hadn't wanted it to work because she hadn't even stopped to think what she wanted. And now, with a feeling of warmth she said it again inside her mind, she knew what she wanted—she wanted to marry Terry and make him happy.

She dressed quickly now with more care than she ever had before. The pale blue linen frock she chose wasn't new, but she liked it and Stella always said it did something for her eyes. Your eyes are so important, she thought, people look at them and judge you by your eyes—and I want these people to love me.

It was only a little after seven and she was all dressed, ready to go to Terry's party. She laughed. It didn't matter. She wanted to be ready when Terry got there.

She snapped off the bedroom light and went into the living room. She heard a rustling sound, caught her breath, standing perfectly still.

Burt was staring at her from the divan.

He let his eyes go over her slowly. "All dressed up," he said. "Where you think you're going?"

She couldn't answer. Standing rigid, she watched him get up and walk toward her.

"How—did you get in here?" she managed to whisper.

"Hell, Amy. Let's talk about the important matters. Stella gave me a key when I first got home. But you know me. I do what I want to do. I do everything I want to do."

"You got to let me alone, Burt."

"No. You're coming back home with me. To our own little apartment. You're not breaking up our little home, Amy."

"You're crazy, Burt."

He nodded, grabbing her arms, tightening his hands on them, looking slightly upward into her eyes because she was wearing high heels.

"You don't know how crazy. Either you're staying away from Terry Collier, or I'm going to kill him. It's that simple."

He pulled that automatic from his pocket and hefted it in his right hand, staring at it, forcing her to stare at it.

"He's not going to have you, Amy. I'll kill him before I'll let him have you."

He stepped closer, speaking against her face. She could smell the whisky strong on his breath.

"Burt. You're sick."

"Stop saying that."

"You can't just kill somebody and get away with it."

"Don't worry. I got that angle covered, too. He'll be standing somewhere alone some night—I can wait. And I'll keep watching until I got him like I want him. I'll press this trigger and then I'll drive away."

She tried to laugh at him. "You won't get away with it. They'll find the gun. They'll get you."

He had the answer for that, too. "Will that bring lover-boy back to life? Is that the way you want him—dead? Then you just stay with him and that's the way you'll have him—nice and dead."

She pushed by him. She went to the telephone. He ran after her, grabbed her hand. "What you think you're going to do?"

"I'm going to call Terry."

"Oh, fine. You call Lover Boy. Get him over here. Think I'll let him get near me again?"

He caught her arm and hurled her away from the phone. She toppled, losing her balance, and fell against the wall.

Burt ran after her. Rage made his eyes wild and pulled ridges in his face. She tried to get up and he knocked her down. Her face bled. Burt cursed her. When she stayed there against the wall and would not move he screamed at her, bent over, grabbed the front of her dress and jerked her to her feet.

The dress ripped and her breast burned, showing in bloody lines where his fingernails raked her flesh. Holding her by the front of her dress, he slapped her back and forth across the face. Her cheeks became inflamed and blue, bruised.

He pressed the cold gun against her face. "I'll kill you."

"Yes." Amy nodded. "Go ahead. Please."

His hand on the gun trembled. "Step out on me, will you? Run to that no good."

Her mouth was torn, his ring had ripped a gash in her cheek.

"I won't go, Burt. I won't go. I'll call him. If you'll—just let him alone."

"That's better. Where was he taking you?"

"It doesn't matter, Burt."

"It matters. Answer me."

"I told you I'd call him."

"Sure. You'd like that. You think he could tell by your voice. He'd come running over here looking for me, wouldn't he?"

"No. Burt, I'll tell him not to."

"Where's he taking you?"

"Nowhere. It was a party, Burt. For me. At his home."

"They didn't invite your husband, though."

"Burt—you're sick—mad."

He jabbed the gun harder against the side of her head. "Sure you'll go. You'll go to that party. Just like you are. Maybe when Lover Boy sees what trouble he makes for us—maybe he'll let you alone."

She shook her head, pleading. But Burt thrust the gun in his pocket. His face was pulled into a pleased smile now. He was thinking ahead to what would happen when they saw Amy like this and knew their meddling and breaking up his home had caused it.

He thrust her toward the door. Amy could taste the blood in her mouth, feel the sting of it on her breast. Her face was swollen and bruised. "Burt, I can't go like this."

"You're on your way, baby." He found the Collier address in the phone book, grabbed up her light wrap. He tossed it over her shoulder and forced her ahead of him out of the apartment.

At the head of the stairs, she caught his arm. "Anything, Burt—don't make me go to that party."

He lashed out, struck her with the back of his hand. She would have fallen but he grabbed her. She pressed herself against the wall.

"You wanted to go to that party, baby. You're going. You can shut up talking about it."

He led her across the walk, shoved her into his car, slammed the door. She pressed her hands over her face, He got in under the wheel, drove swiftly, recklessly. She hoped he would kill them before he got across town.

He slammed on the brakes and stopped in front of the house. Other cars were parked along the quiet street. She saw Terry's family through the lighted windows. Happy people, laughing and talking, who wouldn't even understand the kind of hell she lived in.

"Get out," Burt said.

She pressed against the car seat. "I can't, Burt."

He slapped open the door beside her. "Get in there. They're waiting for you. You wanted this party. Okay, I brought you. I'll sit right here until you get in there. You don't get in there, I'll drag you in. They wouldn't like that. I'm not invited."

She could not move. He thrust her out of the car. "Go on. Don't push me any further, Amy."

She got out of the car. Her legs were rubbery. She tried to stop crying but tears welled and spilled anyway. Her stomach was tied in knots. But somehow, those lights looked like an escape. She walked slowly toward them.

She went up the steps. The front door opened and Terry came through it, on his way to pick her up.

She heard Burt's convertible motor roar as he gunned it away from the front of the house.

Terry said, "Amy. My God, Amy." He ran to her and caught her in his arms. She pressed herself against him, sobbing.

His family pushed through the door, stood staring at her. She didn't have to see their faces. She heard the way they caught their breath. She knew what they thought of her—and the hell she brought to their home with her.

Chapter 15

"Terry. What's the matter?" There was numbed horror in his mother's voice. Things like this didn't happen in her life. There was a buzz of shocked, horrified talk and then they were silent staring at the way Amy sobbed, clinging to Terry.

Terry lifted her up in his arms and carried her through the brightly lighted front room to a bedroom. Gently he placed her on the bed.

He spoke over his shoulder. "Sis. Get some water and cool cloths."

The rest of his family, his parents, his five brothers and sisters, their families knotted outside the bedroom door.

Terry's sister was a slender, dark-haired girl a few years older than Terry. She sat beside Amy on the bed and bathed her face. Terry sat on the other side of her. She clung to his arm, trying to stop crying.

"You're all right," he kept telling her.

"Sure," his sister said. "But I'll bet the truck that hit you is a wreck."

Amy cried again and pressed her face against Terry's arm.

She could hear the whispers from the door. These were good and gentle people, but something like this was out of their reach. Their shocked whispers washed over Amy. She has made Terry so unhappy all these months. Now this!

Terry spoke over his shoulder. "Can't you people go watch television, or something?"

The whispers stopped. Amy did not stir, but knew his family had moved away from the bedroom door.

Terry asked, "Did—Burt do this, Amy?"

She nodded. "It doesn't matter, Terry. I can't drag you into this."

"She's right, Terry," his sister said. Her voice was very soft and very unhappy.

"You stay out of this, or I won't let you bathe her face."

"She's unhappy and it looks like trying to see you is prolonging it." His sister's voice remained soft but was firm.

Amy shivered.

Terry said, "Well, I'll be damned. I never thought you'd have such little understanding."

"It's no use, Terry," Amy said. "None of your people could understand. I can't blame them. I don't want to turn them against you."

"Listen. If these people will turn against me after all these years over a little thing like you, I'm lucky without them."

His sister spoke again. "She's telling you the truth, Terry. You're only asking to get your heart broken."

"That does it," Terry said. "You're excommunicated, Connie. Get out. Maybe I'll let you come to the wedding. I don't know."

"We don't want you hurt any more, Terry. Any of us."

"Out."

Amy caught his arm. "Please, Terry, she's right."

Connie was standing up beside the bed. She caught her breath, stared down at Amy. Suddenly she said, "No. I see I was wrong." She sat down again. "Amy, I'm sorry. You do love him, don't you? Well, we're all fools here. We're crazy about Terry. We don't want his heart broken."

Terry said, "The trouble with you people is you've overlooked the fact that Terry is a big boy now. He can have his heart broken if he wants to."

But Amy shook her head. All this that she was in was too foreign to their lives, too ugly and too evil.

"Call the police," Connie said. "Get them after this screwball. He's psycho. He's dangerous."

"He'll lie," Amy said. "They'll believe him."

Connie said, "He can't deny what he's done to you now. That's enough to put him away for a while."

"A while?" Amy's voice rose. "And he'll be planning what he'll do when he's free."

She sat up and Terry pulled her into his arms. His voice was soft. "We'll get your things. You can stay here with mom and dad until we are married. He won't try anything else."

"But, Terry, they'll never understand anyone like me."

"If they don't, that's too bad for them. If you were hurt in a car accident, they'd understand that."

"Terry. I'd only get you hurt."

His voice rasped. "That's nuts. We'll get married and we'll live like normal people. Do you feel all right? We'll go get you some clothes, and bring you back here. You don't have to worry about that guy any more."

Amy nodded. He helped her up from the bed. He glanced at Connie. "It's up to you, sis. You brief the family while I'm gone. Anybody says one word that hurts this kid's feelings, we'll both walk out of here and you'll never see us again."

Connie smiled. "I think I can get that across."

"All right, Amy," Terry said. "Let's go."

He held her close at his side. They went through the front room. It was suddenly silent when they entered, and no one breathed until they went through the front door.

Terry's voice was soft. "They'll read Connie. By the time you get back, they'll be waiting with their arms out."

Amy didn't believe it, but she didn't say anything. She was too tired, and she didn't believe in anything any more.

They went down the steps and along the walk to his car.

Burt roared by in his convertible. There was the sound of his engine like malicious laughter, the plume of exhaust smoke in the dark night, the screech of his tires when he slammed on his brakes to make the turn at the end of the block.

Amy was trembling all over. Terry's arm tightened on her.

"It's him, Terry. He's still riding around. Waiting."

"You got to forget that guy, Amy. You got to start forgetting him. Now. Tonight."

He opened the door of his car, helped her in. Amy slid far across the seat so that she was close against Terry when he got in under the wheel. He started the engine.

She pressed close against him, holding her breath, listening for the terrible speeding roar of Burt's car from the darkness behind them.

Terry drove steadily. She looked up at him to see if he were afraid. His face showed nothing. She bit her swollen lip. He still thought Burt was a civilized being. He still didn't know. She held herself tense, waiting for the impact when Burt slammed his car into Terry's.

They did not see Burt's convertible on the long drive across town. But she knew it was back there. It was worse not seeing it.

Terry parked his car out front of the apartment house. Amy glanced up at the living room windows. The lights glowed. This didn't mean Stella was home. She remembered that Burt had left them burning when they walked out.

"You're coming with me," she said.

"Sure."

"I'll hurry."

"I told you. Take your time. You're through being afraid of this character."

She tried to laugh as they crossed the walk. "All right. I'll try. It might take a little time."

He put his arm around her. "You'll make it."

Her head spun when they went up the steps. She was afraid to look toward the shadowed places, afraid she would see Burt's savage face, waiting for them in the dark. She moved faster. "I won't leave Mom a note," she said. "We can call her, from your house."

"Anything you want," Terry said.

They came off the stairs and went along the corridor. Amy's hands trembled on her key. She was afraid to open that door.

Chapter 16

Working frantically, Amy packed a bag yet she felt she was moving with a dragging slowness. Terry sat on the side of her bed flicking through a magazine. He looked at ease though Amy was sure he was drawn as taut inside as she. He kept telling her to relax.

"You got a new kind of life now, Amy. You don't have to run from anything."

She nodded, but she barely heard him. She felt like a child, frightened and alone. She had run back home hoping to escape Burt, hoping she would be protected and safe. What a childish thing, she told herself now. When you began to grow up the first thing you truly learned was that you can't run away from your fears—they race after you and they grow as they race. And she hadn't wanted to face her troubles at all. She had wanted someone else to face all her woes for her.

"Be ready," she said, "in a minute."

He glanced up from the magazine, gave her his twisted smile.

She moved about the room, her mind whirling with her thoughts. She was starting a new kind of life. She looked at this room, at this apartment, thinking how she had run back here like a child, thinking she could put all her hurts behind her because she was displeased with the life she'd made with Burt. She had been so sure she was soured on marriage when she returned here from the army town.

She tossed some underthings into the bag, then had to stop and fold them, her hands trembling. What a wild, crazy thing she'd done, marrying Burt. She wouldn't listen to anybody and she'd had over a year of heartache—and now she lived in terror.

"I'm afraid," she said aloud, mostly to herself.

"It's all over, honey," Terry said.

She gave him a wan smile, trying to believe him. But all the time she was listening for Burt's wild raging. She waited, tense. Burt would burst into the apartment, his gun in his hand, his eyes wild.

She looked at Terry. He was so at ease, so good he had no understanding of a man like Burt. She couldn't let anything happen to Terry. What happened to her didn't matter—not any more.

She got her nightgown, some underthings, her tooth brush and cosmetics. Her mind was filled with fear. She could not think what she would need. She threw a couple dresses into the bag. Actually, she could not look beyond this apartment. She could not believe they would get away from it.

"This will do," she said. Her voice sounded odd in her own ears. She closed the suitcase, snapped it. "I'll tell Mom to pack my things."

She heard him get up from the bed, tossing the magazine aside. She turned to face him and caught a glimpse of herself in a mirror.

She stood rigid, staring. She'd carefully avoided looking at herself.

She cried out, a whimpering hurt sound. She looked as if she were made-up for a part in a horror movie. I Was A Teen-Age Witch. I said No to Burt Reader.

She covered her face with her hands and turned away.

Terry came to her and his arms went around her.

"You're all right," he said.

"How can you love me, the way I look?"

He kissed her gently. "I don't know. It beats me."

"I'll—change my dress."

"I think that would be fine."

She pulled the torn dress away, went to the closet, found a simple print frock. It did not matter what she wore, only that she got out of here.

She pulled it down over her head, wriggling into it.

"Think," Terry said. "I'm the guy going to have you like this all the rest of my life."

She pulled down at the frock, straightening and smoothing it. She glanced at her bruised face in the mirror. Her eyes brimmed with tears.

"I'm not good enough for you, Terry."

"Did I ever say you were?"

She turned and caught him in her arms. "Don't let anything happen to you," she whispered. "Please don't ever change."

He caught her head in his palms, and kissed her mouth. She felt her heart throb swiftly. Her hands closed on his arm, this was the lasting and deep kind of devotion that made life a good thing for people who were right for each other.

She pulled away from him, anxious. "Come on, Terry. We got to get out of here. Hurry."

He got her bag, glanced around. "Sure you haven't forgotten anything?"

"I've forgotten everything. But it doesn't matter. Come on. Let's get out of here."

She walked close beside Terry. They crossed the front room. She did not look around. She was not going to look back. All she wanted right now was to get Terry out of this.

He opened the front door. She stood just ahead of him a moment, forcing him to pause in the doorway. She listened, holding her breath, searching the corridor, the darkened stairs. She didn't see Burt.

Terry snapped off the lights behind them, closed the apartment door.

Terry said, "Funny. First time I ever saw you, I knew I was going to have you. You know—this was made for me. But sometimes then, I got kind of beat. I didn't see how I would accomplish it. And now—here we are."

She pressed close against him, taking his arm, hurrying him.

They went down the stairs and Amy felt as though she could not breathe. The tension had drawn her so taut that her heart seemed barely beating at all.

She clung to Terry's arm, afraid to look behind them, afraid of the dark places. She was afraid of the silence.

Terry reached to open the front door.

Amy stopped him, pressing down on his hand.

"Wait a minute, Terry."

"I told you, Amy. Forget him."

She nodded.

"All right, Terry. I will. After tonight. I just—want to be sure." She moved past him, cracked the door, glanced through to the walk. The street was dark and loud with a rising wind, and she watched shadows of trees tremble on the pavement. She looked both ways along the curb. There was no sign of Burt's car out there.

"Come on," she said. Her voice quavered. "Let's hurry."

Terry walked beside her down the steps. She watched their shadows on the walk, elongated in the light from the apartment foyer behind them.

They moved toward Terry's car.

Amy sucked in her breath, feeling suddenly weak and as if paralyzed with fear.

She didn't really hear Burt behind them, she just knew intuitively that he was there, that he had been waiting and he had stepped out of the dark places and that death had come with him.

She wanted to scream. She opened her mouth to scream but her vocal chords were paralyzed.

She tried to speak Terry's name, but she could not make a sound.

She managed to turn around. All she could think was no matter what happened to her, Terry must not be hurt.

Her eyes distended, she stared at the movement in the darkness.

Burt was coming toward them, stalking them almost like a cat, a wild insane animal without reasoning powers.

When she stopped walking, Terry paused. He turned to speak to her. That was when Terry saw Burt.

Terry dropped the suitcase, set himself for Burt. Wildly, Amy saw that still Terry underestimated Burt—Terry did not see the gun Burt carried.

Amy screamed at last.

The sound of her scream ripped at the night, beat against the walls of the buildings along the street, at all the windows.

Terry saw the gun in Burt's hand. For an instant he hesitated, still unable to believe Burt was so insane. Then he reacted, grabbing Amy's arm. He dragged her away from Burt, pulling her around behind him.

Burt waved the gun, sobbing something at them. It was unintelligible. His words no longer made sense. He was crying, raging, but his voice was lost in the rising wind.

Burt yelled something. Amy did not take her gaze from his stark, rigid face. She still could not tell what he was saying, but his meaning was terribly clear to her. He jerked up the gun and as Terry took a step forward, Amy saw Burt was going to shoot him, almost point-blank.

She caught the suitcase up in both her hands, threw it toward the gun in Burt's hand She watched it lurch across the walk between them, striking Burt at the instant the gun fired.

She was blinded by the fire from the gun, deafened by the sound of it. The sharp sound battered at her mind, got inside and whirled and never stopped whirling. She screamed again, running forward trying to put herself between Burt and Terry.

The sound of Burt's gun drowned everything else. In that moment there was a complete and breathless silence. Still moving toward Burt, Amy turned and looked across her shoulder at Terry.

Terry was still going toward Burt, his arms extended. The impact of the bullet had driven him back so he stumbled before he could catch his balance.

She saw him take two long steps forward and then he crumpled as though he had tripped over something. He fell to the walk and did not speak.

She opened her mouth wide, screams pouring out.

She heard Burt's voice, savage and raging. He was yelling at her to stop screaming. He had jerked the gun up again, holding it on Terry. He was shouting at her to get out of his way.

She was hardly aware of his raging. She was not afraid of him any more. He had shot Terry. He had done everything to her now that he could ever do.

She was filled with the rage to kill, to destroy Burt. She saw that he was going to shoot Terry again.

When his gun came up, Amy lunged forward, scratching at Burt's face, her hands like claws. He had made her as wild as he was now. She could think nothing except he had shot Terry and she had to destroy him. She was clawing at him, hitting at him and without even realizing it she was kicking at him.

He threw up his arm to backhand her away and suddenly she brought her leg upward with all her strength.

Burt seemed to fall away from her, gagging and moaning. He doubled up, suddenly in terrible agony.

Behind her, Amy heard the screech of brakes, a man yelled something. Burt was doubled up, but when he saw the men in the car, he twisted around, still holding his groin, and ran in the darkness.

His heels were loud against the walk.

"Halt!"

She heard the man yelling at Burt from behind her.

She heard the sharp report of a gun, and then she heard it again.

Distantly, as if in incalculable space removed from her, she saw Burt far down the walk, still crouched over in agony, still running toward the place where he'd left his convertible concealed in the shadows.

She saw him stumble, throwing his arms out before him and then he sprawled out on the walk.

A policeman with drawn gun ran up to Burt, turned him over, then called to his companion. "This one's dead."

Amy turned dazedly toward Terry. He did not move. She crumpled to the walk beside him. She buried her face against him, whispering his name. Then they were helping her up and she was begging them not to take her away from Terry.

She heard the wail of the ambulance, and then they carried Terry into it, and she was in the ambulance with him but they would not let her near Terry sprawled white and silent on the stretcher. An interne was working over him.

None of it was real, nothing was real. Amy went with the nurses and internes into the hospital Out Ward. They led her to a white chair and told her to wait there. An interne came and gave her a sedative. She had no recollection of how long she waited.

At last she was aware of Terry's family, tight-lipped and grim, coming along the corridor where she was sitting.

Amy looked up but they did not speak to her, or if they did, she didn't hear them. She knew what they thought of her, they didn't understand the evil she lived in but she had brought it to them with her, and she had dragged Terry into it.

Then after a long time she was aware that Connie had pulled up a chair close to hers.

Connie talked for a long time before Amy understood a word of what she was saying. Connie kept talking. Finally the words, "He's going to be all right," were repeated often enough that they got through the incredible space to Amy, and then when she understood this, she became aware of other words.

Connie was saying, "I got worried about you and Terry. I was afraid something would happen. I called the police. They got there as quickly as they could—not quickly enough."

Amy looked up. She saw Terry's family then through the gray mist of her tears. They were not scowling after all. They did not hate her. They were smiling.

Terry's mother whispered, reassuring her. "Terry's all right. He's going to be all right."

Then the door to Terry's room opened and a doctor stepped out into the corridor.

The doctor said, "Is there someone named Amy out here? Terry is all right, but he won't rest until he's talked to someone named Amy. He keeps calling Amy—I don't know, maybe she's got some medicine I don't know about."

Connie laughed suddenly, her eyes bright with tears. She helped Amy up from the chair. "That's you, honey. Terry wants you."

Amy nodded, tears streaming down her cheeks now. She looked once at his family, and she saw their faces were kindly, and then she was anxious to see Terry, because only Terry mattered.

And she straightened at her hair with the backs of her fingers, dabbed at her tears, wiping them away, and she went through the door to him, hurrying in to start her new life.

THE END

HARRY WHITTINGTON BIBLIOGRAPHY

Vengeance Valley (1946)
Her Sin (1946)
Slay Ride for a Lady (1950)
The Brass Monkey (1951)
Call Me Killer (1951)
Fires That Destroy (1951)
The Lady Was a Tramp (1951)
Satan's Widow (1951)
Forever Evil (1952)
Married to Murder (1951; reprinted 1959)
Murder is My Mistress (1951)
Drawn to Evil (1952)
Mourn the Hangman (1952)
Prime Sucker (1952)
Cracker Girl (1953)
So Dead My Love! (1953)
Vengeful Sinner (1953; reprinted as Nightclub Sinner, 1954; abridged as Die, Lover, 1960)
Saddle the Storm (1954)
Wild Oats (1954)
The Woman is Mine (1954)
You'll Die Next! (1954)
The Naked Jungle (1955)
One Got Away (1955)
Across That River (1956)
Desire in the Dust (1956)
Brute in Brass (1956; reprinted as Forgive Me, Killer, 1987)
The Humming Box (1956)
Saturday Night Town (1956)
Sinner's Club (1956; reprinted as Teenage Jungle, 1958)
A Woman on the Place (1956)
Man in the Shadow (1957) [screenplay novelization]
T'as des Visions! (1957, France)
One Deadly Dawn (1957)
Play for Keeps (1957)
Temptations of Valerie (1957) [screenplay novelization]
Trouble Rides Tall (1958)
Web of Murder (1958)
Backwoods Tramp (1959; reprinted as A Moment to Prey, 1987)
Halfway to Hell (1959)
Lust for Love (1959)
Strictly for the Boys (1959)
Strange Bargain (1959)
Strangers on Friday (1959)
A Ticket to Hell (1959)
Connolly's Woman (1960)
The Devil Wears Wings (1960)
Heat of Night (1960)
Hell Can Wait (1960)
A Night for Screaming (1960)
Nita's Place (1960)
Rebel Woman (1960)
Trouble Rides Tall (1960)
Vengeance is the Spur (1960)
Desert Stake-Out (1961)
God's Back Was Turned (1961)
Guerilla Girls (1961)
Journey Into Violence (1961)
The Searching Rider (1961)
A Trap for Sam Dodge (1961)
The Young Nurses (1961)
A Haven for the Damned (1962)
Hot as Fire Cold as Ice (1962)
69 Babylon Park (1962)
Wild Sky (1962)
Cora is a Nympho (1963)
Don't Speak to Strange Girls (1963)
Drygulch Town (1963)
Prairie Raiders (1963; reprinted as by Hondo Wells, 1977)
Cross the Red Creek (1964)
Fall of the Roman Empire (1964) [screenplay novelization]
High Fury (1964)
Hangrope Town (1964)

The Man from U.N.C.L.E #2: The Doomsday Affair (1965)
Valley of Savage Men (1965)
Wild Lonesome (1965)
Doomsday Mission (1967)
Bonanza: Treachery Trail (1968; pub in Germany as Ponderosa in Gefahr)
Burden's Mission (1968)
Charro! (1969)
Rampage (1978)
Sicilian Woman (1979)

As Ashley Carter

Master of Blackoaks (1976)
Sword of the Golden Stud (1977)
Panama (1978)
Secret of Blackoaks (1978)
Taproots of Falconhurst (1978)
Scandal of Falconhurst (1980)
Heritage of Blackoaks (1981)
Rogue of Falconhurst (1983)
Against All Gods (1983, UK)
A Darkling Moon (1985, UK)
Embrace the Wind (1985, UK; pub in the US as by Blaine Stevens)
A Farewell to Blackoaks (1986, UK)
Miz Lucretia of Falconhurst (1986)
Mandingo Mansa (1986, UK; pub in the US as Mandingo Master)
Strange Harvest (1986, UK)
Falconhurst Fugitive (1988)

As Curt Colman

Flesh Mother (1965)
Flamingo Terrace (1965)
Hell Bait (1966)
Sinsurance (1966)
The Taste of Desire (1966)
Sin Deep (1966)
Latent Lovers (1966)
Sinners After Six (1966)
Balcony of Shame (1967)
Mask of Lust (1967)
The Grim Peeper (1967)

As John Dexter:

Saddle Sinners (1964)
Lust Dupe (1964)
Pushover (1964)
Sin Psycho (1964)
Flesh Curse (1964)
Sharing Sharon (1965)
Shame Union (1965)
The Wedding Affair (1965)
Baptism in Shame (1965)
Sin Fishers (1966)
Passion Burned (1966)
Remembered Sin (1966)
The Sinning Room (1966)
Blood Lust Orgy (1966)
The Abortionists (1966)

As Tabor Evans

Longarm on the Humboldt (1981)
Longarm and the Golden Lady (1981)
Longarm and the Blue Norther (1981)
Longarm in Silver City (1982)
Longarm in Boulder Canyon (1982)
Longarm in the Big Thicket (1982)

As Whit Harrison

Body and Passion (1952)
Girl on Parole (1952; reprinted as Man Crazy, 1960)
Sailor's Weekend (1952)
Savage Love (1952; reprinted as by Harry Whittington as Native Girl, 1959)
Swamp Kill (1952)
Violent Night (1952)
Army Girl (1953)
Rapture Alley (1953)
Strip the Town Naked (1960)
Any Woman He Wanted (1961)
A Woman Possessed (1961)

As Kel Holland

Strange Young Wife (1963)
The Tempted (1964)

As Lance Horner

Golden Stud (1975)

As Harriet Kathryn Meyers

Small Town Nurse (1962)
Prodigal Nurse (1963)

As Blaine Stevens

The Outlanders (1979)
Embrace the Wind (1982)
Island of Kings (1989)

As Clay Stuart

His Brother's Wife (1964)

As Harry White

Shadow at Noon (1955; reprinted as by Hondo Wells, 1977)

As Hallam Whitney

Backwoods Hussy (1952; reprinted as Lisa, 1965)
Shack Road (1953)
Backwoods Shack (1954)
City Girl (1954)
Shanty Road (1954; reprinted as by Whit Harrison, 1956)
The Wild Seed (1956)

As Henry Whittier/ Henri Whittier

Nightmare Alibi (1972)
Another Man's Claim (1973)

As J. X. Williams

Lust Farm (1964)
Flesh Avenger (1964)
The Shame Hiders (1964)
Lust Buyer (1965)
Passion Flayed (1965)
Man Hater (1965)
Passion Hangover (1965)
Passion Cache (1966)
Baby Face (1966)
Flesh Snare (1966)

As Howard Winslow

The Mexican Connection (1972)

Classic hardboiled fiction from the King of the Paperbacks...

Harry Whittington

A Night for Screaming / Any Woman He Wanted

$19.95 978-1-933586-08-3

"[*A Night for Screaming*] is pure Harry. The damned thing is almost on fire, it reads so fast." – Ed Gorman, *Gormania*

To Find Cora / Like Mink Like Murder / Body and Passion

$21.95 978-1-933586-25-0

"Harry Whittington was the king of plot and pace, and he could write anything well. He's 100 percent perfect entertainment." – Joe R. Lansdale

Rapture Alley / Winter Girl / Strictly for the Boys

$21.95 978-1-933586-36-6

"Whittington was an innovator, often turning archetypical characters and plots on their head, and finding wild new ways to tell stories from unusual angles."
– Cullen Gallagher, *Pulp Serenade*

A Haven for the Damned

$9.99 978-1-933586-75-5

Black Gat #1. "A wild, savage romp and pure Whittington: raw noir that has the feel of a Jim Thompson novel crossed with a Russ Meyer film."
– Brian Greene, *The Life Sentence.*

Trouble Rides Tall / Cross the Red Creek / Desert Stake-Out

$21.95 978-1-944520-11-3

"If these three Whittington novels are the only westerns crime fiction fans ever read, they will have experienced some of the best the genre has to offer."
– Alan Cranis, *Bookgasm*

"Harry Whittington delivers every time." – Bill Crider

Stark House Press, 1315 H Street, Eureka, CA 95501
griffinskye3@sbcglobal.net / www.StarkHousePress.com
Available from your local bookstore, or order direct or via our website.

Printed in Great Britain
by Amazon

27022494R00190